Nobleman Zavalnia

OR

BELARUS IN FANTASTICAL TALES

Nobleman Zavalnia

OR

BELARUS IN FANTASTICAL TALES

Written by Jan Barszczewski
Translated by Olya Ianovskaia
Illustrated by Nasta Lee

Nobleman Zavalnia or Belarus in Fantastical Tales (1846)

The Wooden Old Man and the Insect Woman (1847)

The Soul Not in Its Own Body (1849)

by Jan Barszczewski

First Grunwald edition

ISBN 978-1-7383142-9-4 (illustrated premium softcover)
ISBN 978-1-7383142-2-5 (trade paperback)
ISBN 978-1-7383142-3-2 (e-book)

Library and Archives Canada Cataloguing in Publication

Title: Nobleman Zavalnia, or, Belarus in fantastical tales / written by Jan Barszczewski
translated by Olya Ianovskaia ; illustrated by Nasta Lee.

Other titles: Szlachcic Zawalnia czyli Białoruś w fantastycznych opowiadaniach
English Names: Barshchèŭski, I͡An, author. | Ianovskaia, Olya, 1983- translator.
Description: Translation of: Szlachcic Zawalnia czyli Białoruś w fantastycznych
opowiadaniach. | In English, translated from the Polish.
Identifiers: Canadiana (print) 20250275554 | Canadiana (ebook) 20250279517 | ISBN
9781738314294 (hardcover) | ISBN 9781738314225 (softcover) | ISBN 9781738314232
(EPUB)
Subjects: LCGFT: Short stories.
Classification: LCC PG7158.B27 S9513 2025 | DDC 891.8/536—dc23

Published by:

Grunwald Publishing Inc.
P.O. Box 405
Minden Hills, ON
Canada, K0M 2K0
grunwald.ca

CONTENTS

PREFACE

Nearly two centuries have passed since Jan Barszczewski (ca. 1790s–1851) published *Nobleman Zavalnia or Belarus in Fantastical Tales* in Polish in 1846. Until now, English readers have never had the chance to read the book in full. This translation finally opens the door to a work that sits at the intersection of folklore, folk horror, political allegory, and national myth-making. It is a text that captures both the warm cadence of oral storytelling and the chill of supernatural dread, while at the same time speaking in code about the historical trauma of a nation partitioned, annexed, and silenced.

Barszczewski frames his collection as stories told to nobleman Zavalnia, a gregarious landowner who gathers guests at his hearth. The stories – thirty-eight in the original edition – span ghost tales, moral parables, supernatural encounters, and lyrical sketches of nature. Through Zavalnia's voice and the voices of his guests, Barszczewski offers a panorama of Belarusian life, one in which history, politics, and folklore intertwine.

Mikola Khaustovich, who translated *Zavalnia* into Belarusian three decades ago, rightly described it as an encrypted allegory: history disguised as folk tale, a national epic under the veil of parable. For him, the figure of the Weeping Woman who wanders battlefields in Barszczewski's imagination is Belarus itself – defeated, silenced, but alive.

It is impossible to separate *Zavalnia* from its political context. Originally written in Polish, the language of the educated elite of the time, the book appeared after the Russian Empire had already partitioned the Grand Duchy of Lithuania and the Kingdom of Poland, annexing much of what makes up Belarus today. Belarusian language was forbidden in print, and to write of Belarus in Belarusian was to risk suppression. So Barszczewski did what others of his generation did: he wrote in Polish, embedding the memory of his homeland in allegory. To read *Zavalnia* is to witness literature functioning as both folklore and resistance.

The allegorical layer of *Zavalnia* cannot be overstated. Barszczewski wrote in a time when censorship was severe. Open political critique was impossible. Instead, he encrypted his message: sorcerers and dark guests stand in for imperial agents; traitors meet tragic fates; communities survive through memory, storytelling, and the endurance of custom. For readers attuned to the context, the allegory is clear. *Zavalnia* is not only myth and horror; it is also manifesto, testimony, and code.

The stories are set in 1816-1817. Following the eruption of Mount Tambora in 1815, the global climate was thrown into chaos. In Europe, this produced the infamous "year without a summer" in 1816. In Belarus, 1817 became legend: a year of strange warmth, disrupted harvests, and social unease. By anchoring his tales in that year, Barszczewski fused local memory with universal upheaval. Nature itself seemed to testify that the world had slipped off its axis, just as the political world of the former Grand Duchy had collapsed after the partitions.

One of the silences in *Zavalnia* is equally revealing: the unquestioned presence of serfdom. In the 1840s, when Barszczewski published much of his work, Belarusian peasants were still bound to the land, obligated to perform *corvée* labor – unpaid, compulsory work for landlords. It was only in 1861, less than two decades later, that serfdom was abolished across the Russian Empire. Yet in *Zavalnia* this system is treated as natural and eternal. It structures every relationship between noble and peasant, and it is never questioned. To modern readers, this silence is startling. It shows how deeply normalized serfdom was in Barszczewski's world, and how even literature of the uncanny could not imagine life beyond it.

The texture of Barszczewski's storytelling comes from its mix of parable and folklore. Witches, restless spirits, enchanted forests, and moral betrayals sit side by side with peasant songs, religious customs, and descriptions of *corvée* labor. For this reason, some have described *Zavalnia* as a kind of "European voodoo" – a body of folk horror that emerges not from imported Gothic conventions but from local mythology. What distinguishes it is its rootedness: these are stories of a particular landscape, the northern Belarusian forests and fields, filled with placenames that resist neat translation. In this edition, we have chosen to anglicize and transliterate from Belarusian, but consistency across all names – personal, geographic, or cultural – is nearly impossible. Multiple variants exist in Belarusian, Polish, and russified English spellings. The inconsistency itself is part of the cultural history of the region.

For cultural flavor, we also preserve forms of address that have no exact English equivalent: Pan, Pani, and Panna, corresponding roughly to Mr., Mrs., and Miss. These words situate characters in the social world of nineteenth-century Belarus, marking respect, class, and gender in ways that "Mr." and "Mrs." cannot fully capture.

Barszczewski also embeds himself into the fiction. The character of Janka, Zavalnia's nephew, is more than a device. He is the stand-in for Jan himself – the listener, the apprentice, the inheritor of memory. Through Janka, Barszczewski inscribes his younger self into the narrative, a witness to the stories that shaped him. The book becomes at once a collection of folk tales and a memoir of listening, a portrait of how one becomes an author through inheritance.

The text has its own afterlife. *The Wooden Old Man and the Insect Woman* (1847) was written after the original stories and depicts the narrator's return to Belarus following eighteen years of absence, a natural continuation of the *Zavalnia* tales. By contrast, *The Soul Not in Its Own Body* reflects Barszczewski's later years, when he had settled in and explored Ukraine not long before his death from tuberculosis in 1851. Together, these pieces are often published with *Zavalnia* as companion works, extending the allegorical arc into themes of exile, return, and the final journeys of the author's life.

Barszczewski's prose differs from German Romanticism or French realism. It is neither imitation nor derivation. Instead, it is mythological historicism: history retold as folklore, political trauma encrypted as supernatural fable. It is not Gothic imported from abroad but Gothic grown in Belarusian soil. This difference matters. It explains why Maksim Haretski, one of the leading Belarusian prose writers of the early twentieth century and author of *Two Souls* (which we have also translated into English), turned to Barszczewski. Haretski translated several of the *Zavalnia* tales into Belarusian and urged that more follow. To honor that connection, our translation of *Zavalnia* deliberately mirrors the translation of Haretski's phrasing when identical expressions appear in both books. In this way, the continuity of Belarusian literature carries across languages and centuries.

Why bring this book to English readers today? Because its concerns are not merely historical. Folklore and literature remain tools of resistance, just as they were in

Barszczewski's day. To read *Zavalnia* now is to hear a voice from 1846 speaking directly to the present: a reminder that storytelling can be a weapon, and that memory itself resists empire.

It is also to acknowledge a unique contribution to European literature: a work that predates modern folk horror, that sits uneasily between Romantic tale and political allegory, that captures a region often absent from the European canon. *Zavalnia* is almost 200 years old, and yet this is its first complete translation into English. Its arrival expands the literary map, and allows Belarus to speak in its own mythic register to readers far beyond its borders.

Barszczewski's *Zavalnia* is a strange and powerful book. It is a collection of tales, a national allegory, a folk horror cycle, a memoir, and a political manifesto all at once. To enter its world is to sit by nobleman Zavalnia's hearth, listen to stories that slip between history and myth, and hear the encrypted memory of a land that refused to disappear.

The Publisher

2025

Nobleman Zavalnia

OR

BELARUS IN FANTASTICAL TALES

VOLUME ONE

A FEW WORDS FROM THE AUTHOR

Among the Belarusian people, certain ancient legends still endure today. Passed from mouth to mouth, they have grown as obscure as the myths of antiquity. The people of this land – especially in the districts of Polatsk, Nievel, and Siebezh – have, since time immemorial, borne such hardship that their very nature has changed. Sorrow and solemn reflection are etched onto their faces. In their imagination, malevolent spirits drift endlessly – servants of wicked lords, sorcerers, and their enemies alike.

I was born and raised among them. Their laments and sorrowful tales, like the rustling of wild forests, led me into somber contemplation, and from childhood, they became my only dream.

I recalled fragments of these ancestral memories in ballads – my solitary refrain. These songs marked the beginning of what I now set out to recount more fully. It is human nature to move from singing to storytelling, especially of those things that weigh most on our hearts. Six volumes of such tales will follow, one after another, painting above all the northern reaches of Belarus, for this corner of the earth is the dearest to my memory.

I do not imitate the forms beloved by the novelists of England, Germany, or France. I believe that foreign attire does not suit the face of the Belarusian people, for the loquacity of other nations is alien to them. I took my form from nature itself. Each day, the orphan laments her misfortune, recounting all she has suffered in this world – and all her lifelong sorrow gathers into one tale, though she gives no thought to what she might say tomorrow.

Jan Barszczewski
Petersburg, September 8, 1844

SKETCH OF NORTHERN BELARUS

Travelers approaching Belarus from the north see large villages that sprawl like towns, gleaming whitewashed churches and stone manor houses – called *dvarý* by the local people – amid broad cultivated fields, scattered pine woods, and birch groves. They often hear the prolonged singing of a peasant, echoing far into the distance, or the notes of a shepherd's horn drifting over hills and valleys. On Sundays, as the sun nears the horizon, one may meet village girls in festive percale or silk dresses, surrounded by courting youths. They dance in circles, singing folk songs, while the elders sit on porches, reflecting on times past and present.

But as one nears the borders of the Siebezh and Nievel districts, the land darkens. Vast forests rise on the horizon like clouds. Scattered amid these woods are the thatched huts of the poor. Occasionally, a traveler may glimpse a moss-covered chapel, an iron cross peeking through the pines. Two or three bells hang from pine posts at the gate. Gravestones and crosses lie around it. Rarely does one see a well-built manor house there. Few churches capture the vision of an architect or show off the grandeur of a wealthy patron. From the River Lovats to the Dzvina, where the Palata and Drysa rivers meet it, this somber and wild landscape stretches forth.

Narrow rocky roads wind through the hills, skirting wild lake shores and vanishing into the forest. In the impoverished villages, a gloomy silence reigns, on holidays and workdays alike. Occasionally, the voice of a reaper or ploughman breaks through, betraying his troubled thoughts; crop failures often shatter the hopes of those who labor the land.

It was in this land that I spent my childhood years. After leaving my companions at the Polatsk Academy, with no books save a few in Latin and Greek, I wandered alone in a pleasant reverie through shadowed forests and along deserted lake shores. I loved to read the book of nature, opening each evening to a sky full of millions of stars shining above, spelling out God's omnipotence. On the earth below, teeming with multitudes of plants and animals, I read the mercy and will of the Creator. That book taught me poetry and emotion more truthfully than the verbose modern critics, who seek to tailor God-given gifts of talent and emotion like frock coats to their own crooked cut.

The stories told by the elders – folk tales recalling events, passed down from person to person since ancient times – were, to me, the true history of this land, the character and the feeling of the Belarusian soul.

Though fate carried me far away, how often my solitary thoughts return from the banks of the Neva to this land where I spent the best years of my life, where memory paints so many dear recollections vividly in my imagination! I remember the area around Nievel, not far from Rabschyzna, where nature has raised tall hills like the stories of immense buildings. Centuries have hidden them under the shades of forests. Still others gleam with golden sand under the bright sunlight. What a variety of landscapes, what marvelous views!

Should a visitor climb to the top of Pachanouskaya Hill and look out over the wild surroundings, they would see the lakes scattered here and there, reflecting the daylight like mirrors; above their shores, dark forests lie asleep, and peasant huts dot and darken the hillsides. But one sees no city walls, no towers of an old castle. A person forgets the world there. There are no debates about Egypt and Turkey in the French Chamber there, nor any talk of the English Parliament, the war with the Chinese, or of railways, or of Daguerre's astonishing invention. Only the whistle of a shepherd, the crack of a hunter's gun in the forest, or the wind rushing through the treetops momentarily breaks the silence...

Closer to Polatsk, Lake Nieszczarda stretches out for miles, eroding the sandy hills along its banks. To the south lie flood meadows, scattered with clumps of willow. Here and there, streams from afar snake through the reeds, vanishing into the overflowing waters of the lake. In spring, this land is paradise. Birds of all kinds seem to gather from every corner of the world. Thousands of different voices – melodious, wild, and tender – echo above the waters, meadows and forests: the call of the cuckoo, the trill of the nightingale, the cry of the bittern in the reeds, the sharp squawks of ducks... This wondrous harmony and this symphony of nature transported my imagination into a kind of enchanted realm.

Even now these places, where in my childhood I witnessed so many wonders of nature, these groves, these green shores of Nieszczarda, memory paints them for me like a dreamt-of garden. I recall the folk tales tied to this land, to the hills, trees, and Nieszczarda itself – they are still told among the people. And though it is hard to find literal truth in their stories, they preserve traces of the region's past, for even now, in certain places, one can observe earthworks raised by human hands. These are undoubtedly the remnants of wars that no historian has mentioned. Sometimes one encounters mounds covered with forests. Perhaps, under the shade of the whispering pines lies a warrior, long forgotten by name. I have heard many stories from ordinary people about ancient battles, though so much has been mixed in with fables and marvels that what remains is but a faint trace of the past, without the names of those involved. I will recount one folk tale from this area.

On the southern side of Lake Nieszczarda stands a hill, washed by water on three sides. On that hill is a small wooden chapel and a few pine trees. There, in the sand, people often find old silver coins weathered by centuries, glass trinkets once used as ornaments, and rusted fragments of ancient weapons. They say there was once a town on this peninsula. But whose town it was and who ruled it, no one knows. The local people, who lived in remote forest villages, were long spared the raids of the roving tribes that passed through these lands in search of plunder. But one day, a fearsome giant named *Kniazha*,[1] lured to the shores of Nieszczarda by the hope of rich spoils, besieged the town with a horde of bandits. He overcame its weak defenses, plundered the homes, killed the inhabitants, stripped the churches of icons, looted the sacred vessels, destroyed the chapel, and threw its bells into the lake. Then, he and his band settled in the ruined town. But God, in a wondrous way, sent punishment upon the blasphemers. The bells that lay in the dark depths of the lake rang out each day at sunrise and sunset, breaking the silence of Nieszczarda's wild shores. Terrified by the sound, the birds flew off into the skies. Trembling with fear, deer and elk fled into the deepest forests. At midnight, a plague resembling a black orb would float through the night air, and wherever it touched a house, no one within would survive. In this way, *Kniazha*'s entire band perished. Seized with panic, he fled with a few companions, leaving behind his treasure buried in the hill.

But he didn't get far beyond the lake before he met his death. To this day, locals point to a massive mound called *Kniazha*'s Grave.

Many other tales still circulate among the simple folk of this land. Some contain echoes of historical events, while others spring more from fantasy and the melancholic spirit of forest-dwelling people, whose nature inclines them to vivid imagination and striking images. I have retold some of these folk legends in ballads published in three volumes of the almanac *Niezabudka*: "The Maiden's Spring," which lies north of Polatsk, hidden in ancient forest; "The Two Birches," which locals still point out near the shores of Lake Shevina; "The Barrows"; and "The Rusalka,"[2] taken from the song of a sorceress who, mourning her beloved, sings:

> *'Little geese, little swans,*
> *Drop a feather down to me,*
> *So I might fly away with thee.'*

On Sundays, village markets are sometimes held nearby. People come from neighboring hamlets to attend Mass. In the cemetery, one can witness scenes that bring sorrow to the soul: a widow with her small children kneels by a wooden cross on her husband's grave, while a young orphan grieves by the resting place of her parents with a voice that pierces the heart. If you came close and listened to their words, you'd hear them envying the dead – their tearful laments could move even the heart of stone.

After Mass, the people gather near the tavern. There, several Jews appear selling ribbons, needles, and shiny adornments for clothing. A Belarusian bagpipe calls out, and the music begins under the open sky. Warmed by *harelka*, young lads and old men alike dance until they're dripping with sweat; their joy often spills over into wild abandon. And the mournful women, who were weeping over the graves of their husbands and fathers a short time ago, soon whirl to the sound of the bagpipe, singing:

> *'Praise to You, Christ the King,*
> *My husband lies in the cemetery,*
> *Now I'm rid of trouble,*
> *And I've had my* harelka *too.'*

Or :

> *'That Wednesday has passed,*
> *I went to corvée[3] without a bite to eat,*
> *I reaped all day without complaint,*
> *And bowed to the wicked bailiff.*
> *Now there's no cause for sorrow –*
> *The bailiff's drunk and passed out in the tavern.'*

There is something deeply melancholic in many of the songs sung by this simple folk, whether in the lyrics or the melodies. Even wedding songs, which bless the couple with joy and happiness, carry a touch of sadness, as if the singers do not quite trust in what fate has in store. But the wedding rituals themselves are full of chivalrous fire. Before the groom arrives at the bride's home, he trains his horse to leap through fire. Then, as he and his retinue ride off to fetch the bride, they don red caps, drape red kerchiefs across their chests, and gallop across the hills. At the gate they pause: straw is set alight, and they leap over the flames on horseback. Even here, flaming sheaves are tossed in the horses' faces, blocking the open gate. Still, they push through. The groom enters the house with his head bowed and takes his seat at the table. The wedding hymn *'Bless, O Lord, the Wedding Celebration'* resounds, and the wedding feast begins. But in the course of such feasts, strange things may occur.

Belarus, like other nations, still remembers some of its old gods. When the rye blooms in the field, *rusalkas* swing on birch trees, their long hair flowing in the wind as they sing. Their laughter echoes in the depths of the forests and startles those who gather mushrooms or berries. The forest god – the lord of wilderness – avoids human eyes, he conceals himself in his domains, taking many forms: crossing a meadow, he shrinks so small that he vanishes into thick grass; wandering through the woods, he stands as tall as the tallest pines. He is the guardian of forest beasts and birds. They say that people have seen great flocks of squirrels being moved by him from one forest to another – he was saving them from fire, having foreseen where the blaze would break out.

The celebration of *Kupalle* is known to almost all Slavic peoples. In Belarus, on June 23rd, after sunset, the *Festival of Kupala*, or *Kupalle Night*, takes place. That night, people search for hidden treasures. Fortunate is the one who finds the fern blossom, for they gain the ability to perceive treasure buried deep in the earth and can take as much gold as they desire. Women, together with young men and girls, wait for sunrise beside pitch-burning bonfires, singing:

> *'Ivan and Marya,*
> *On the hill is the bathhouse.*
> *Where Ivan bathed,*
> *The shore swayed;*
> *Where Marya bathed,*
> *The grass spread out.'*

Other similar songs echo through the fields until the sun brightens the sky.

In this part of Belarus, *Kupalle* is full of extraordinary events. According to the local people, all of nature rejoices on this night. Fishermen see the lake surface covered with a white, moonlike glow. Though the sky is clear and the air still, sparkling waves strike the shores and scatter into droplets that shimmer in the air like stars. This wondrous scene stirs the reeds, awakens the wild ducks and other waterfowl, which, drawn by the magical glow, rise and circle above the lake.

Trees in the forest are said to move from place to place, their rustling branches murmuring to one another. They whisper of someone who, wandering in the woods that night, found the fern blossom and beheld not only the treasures hidden in the earth, but also strange marvels of nature. This person understood the speech of every creature and heard how oaks from distant groves gathered together, forming a circle, and whispered to one another like old warriors, recalling heroic deeds and ancient glories. Lindens and birches boasted of their beauty. Trimmed and straightened in classical fashion, some guests from nearby gardens chattered about the flirtations of manor girls and the mischief of young gentrymen, of which they had often been silent witnesses. These frivolous tales were listened to with disdain by the solemn spruces and pines. Willows stood by the riverbank, gazing into the watery mirror, asking one another which reflection suited whom, and all of these marvels continued until sunrise.

The sunrise that follows this sleepless, festive night is also something special. The crowd in the field finishes its dancing and singing and turns silently toward the sky, as if expecting something wondrous to appear above the blazing edge of the horizon. The sun rises, climbs above the hills and forests, and before everyone's eyes, breaks into tiny sparkling stars, then gathers itself once more into a single fiery orb. It is encircled by countless rainbow halos, and it flickers as it spins on its axis. This phenomenon repeats several times – thus the sun "plays" each year on June 24th.

In addition to the above-mentioned wonders, the people of this region believe in magical herbs. *Razryu-trava* – the "breaking herb" – is said to work marvels on iron, breaking locks and chains to free prisoners. If a scythe strikes it during haymaking, the blade will shatter into pieces. *Peralyot-trava* – the "flying herb" – is said to move from place to place. Its rainbow-colored blossom shimmers like a star as it travels. Fortunate is the one who finds it: no obstacle in life will stop them, and their every wish will come true. This is the herb of happiness.

Dreaming of happiness on this earth, people have imagined it in many forms. The Greeks and Romans believed in blind Fortuna, who, by spinning her eternal wheel, raises people to the clouds only to cast them into the abyss. The Belarusian people imagined a kind of flying herb, in pursuing of which many have lost their way, never returning to their native homes. And I, seeking it far away, left behind the land where the happiest days of my life had passed. Now, in the northern capital,[4] gazing upon the theater of the great world, I read a book that sometimes makes me laugh, and sometimes draws tears. That book is the book of human characters and hearts.

My native land – your highlands rise in pride,
Your meadows and your waters, reed-banked wide,
Your forests where the sunlight never gleams –
You live in me, a vision born of dreams,
In spring's green shade, in golden morning's hue –
An enchanted painting, ever fresh and true.
I hear the reaper's mournful evening call,
The herdsman's tune in dusky forest hall,
Or, when the peasant – home from toil released –
Gathers beneath his roof for twilight's feast,
He listens to the elder's quiet tone,
Telling of deeds by long-lost heroes known –
Their battles, wonders, glories dimly cast,
Tales handed down from ages in the past.

NOBLEMAN ZAVALNIA

My uncle, Pan Zavalnia, a rather wealthy nobleman with a modest estate, lived in the northern and remote part of Belarus. His estate was situated in a charming location. North of the residence stretched Nieszczarda, a vast lake resembling a sea bay. When the wind rose, a steady noise would roll off the lake, and through the window one could see how foam-covered waves lifted and dropped the fishing boats. South of the manor, the lowlands greened with willow thickets, and occasional mounds were overgrown with birches and lindens. To the west stretched expansive meadows. From the east, a river flowed through the land and emptied into Nieszczarda. Spring here was extraordinarily beautiful, when the meadows flooded, and the voices of birds returning from warmer lands rang out over the forests and the lake.

Pan Zavalnia loved nature. His greatest pleasure was planting trees, and although his house stood on a hill, it couldn't be seen from half a mile away – it was surrounded on all sides by forest. Only fishermen out on the lake could glimpse the whole building. He was born with the soul of a poet. Though he never wrote in verse or prose, he was deeply moved by stories of robbers, heroes, miracles, and magic. Each night, he would only fall asleep after hearing a fantastical tale. It became customary that a servant tell him a simple folk story before bed and he would always listen patiently, even if the same story was repeated dozens of times. Whenever he had a visitor – a traveler, a poor wanderer, or a questor in need – he received them warmly: fed them, gave them shelter, and fulfilled their wishes. But in return, he always asked for a story. This was especially true in autumn, when the nights were long. The guest he valued most was the one who could recount the most tales and had all kinds of stories and wonders to share.

When I arrived at his home, he was very glad to see me. He asked after the esteemed people in whose service I had spent many years, and spoke at length about his household – about the birches, lindens, and maples that spread their branches wide over the roof. He praised some neighbors while criticizing others for caring only about dogs and hunting. Finally, after a long conversation about this and that, he said to me:

"You are an educated man – you went to a Jesuit school, read many books, and spoke with learned people. You must know all kinds of tales. Tell me something interesting this evening."

So I tried to recall something worth retelling. I had read nothing besides the works of historians and classical writers. The history of nations is not the most engaging subject for someone uninterested in the theater of the world and the cast of characters performing its scenes. For my uncle, the Bible was the only true history – but from secular books, he had learned that Alexander the Great, eager to discover the height of the sky and the depth of the sea, once flew on griffins and descended to the ocean floor. Such courage astonished and delighted him. I needed to tell him something just as marvelous, so I decided to begin with Homer's *Odyssey*, which is full of wonders and magic, just like our own folk tales.

Around ten o'clock in the evening, once the villagers had finished their work and my uncle had said his prayers, the household gathered, as usual, to hear new tales. But this time, he said:

"Well, Janka, tell us something interesting. I'll listen carefully, as I don't think I'll fall asleep quickly tonight."

To make the story more accessible for the listeners, I briefly recounted the main Greek gods, goddesses, and heroes, then the golden apple, the judgment of Paris, and the siege of Troy. Everyone listened with interest and amazement. I heard some of the servants say:

"This story is impossible to remember, it is too complicated."

After a long silence, my uncle asked:

"Was any of this ever true?"

"The pagans once believed it," I replied. "It was before the birth of Christ. History tells us about those people and also about their religion."

"And this is what the Jesuits teach you in school? What for?"

"Those who study must learn a bit of everything," I said.

"Well then, go on."

And so I continued without pause. It was already past midnight when the listeners finally dispersed. I heard the servants quietly repeating among themselves:

"We can't learn this tale, it's all too foreign. I couldn't remember a thing."

After a while, I heard my uncle snoring loudly. Pleased with this, I made the sign of the cross and fell asleep, content with my success.

The next morning, as master of the manor, my uncle rose early, inspected every corner of his small estate, and returned to the house. Approaching me while I was still dozing, he called out:

"Ah, I see you like to sleep like a lord! Get up, that's a sin for simple folk. They'll say you're lazy! But your story yesterday was too learned, I can't remember a single one of those pagan gods. Still, there will be more. You'll stay here until spring, and you'll tell me many more stories about this and that on these long winter nights.”

During my nearly five-week stay at my uncle's house, I had to lull him to sleep each night with retellings from famous poems by Greek and Latin authors. From *The Odyssey*, he liked best the wisdom of Ulysses on the shores of Circe and the island of the Cyclopes. He said to me over and over:

“Maybe, long ago, there really were such enormous giants, but it's strange that they had just one eye on their foreheads. And what a trickster that Ulysses was – got him drunk, gouged out his eye, and escaped on a ram.”

He also couldn't forget the sixth book of Virgil, when Aeneas descends into the Underworld. He often said:

“Though he was a pagan, what noble feeling and love for his father, to go to such a dangerous place for him! But what a strange faith they had. Our souls go to Heaven, but they invented a heavenly kingdom deep underground. Strange!”

One day, while talking to me, he asked whether I had been to Polatsk recently.

“I haven't had a chance to go in nearly a year,” I replied.

“If you do go,” he said, “ask the Jesuit fathers how my Stas and Yuzik are doing in their studies. Oh, there's nothing wrong with being educated! Like those stories you tell from all those books – an unlearned man couldn't even dream up such things. It's good to know everything. When I was in Polatsk, my late wife, God rest her soul, and I asked the prefect not to spare the rod.”

“The Holy Spirit counsels with the rod. The rod offends no child of God.”

“Ah, those are wonderful verses, the rod teaches both wisdom and faith. Some of our young lords, spoiled by their parents, do nothing but play with horses and dogs. They don't even make the sign of a cross when they enter a church. What joy for the parents – God's punishment, that's all!"

It was already the first days of November. Sitting alone by the window, I listened to the howling of the autumn wind and the rustling of the birches and maples that rose densely above the roof. The whirlwind swept yellow leaves through the yard, tossing them into the air. Everything was still. Now and then a dog would bark when a passerby went by, or some animal appeared out of the woods. My mind drifted into a melancholy reverie.

The woman who ran my uncle's household came in. She was the sister of his late wife, already in her mature years. Seeing that I was deep in thought, she said:

"You must be lonely here, Pan Janka. You're a young man, and you have no one to talk to. Perhaps these nightly stories have worn you out. Just wait, once Nieszczarda freezes, a great road will stretch across the lake, right to the manor. Oh! Then Pan Zavalnia will invite many guests, each with stories of their own to tell."

Many days passed. The frost sparkled under calm and clear skies. The lake fell asleep beneath a thick slab of ice. Snow spilled down from the clouds.

Winter had arrived.

A wide road formed across Nieszczarda. Travelers passed through, carts loaded with flax and hemp headed toward Riga. A band of fishermen moved across the ice.

My uncle and I often visited their fishing spots to admire the catch. The added benefit was that, after a full day out in the cold, my uncle would fall asleep quickly, and I had the evenings to myself. We had more visitors too, and in their presence, my uncle praised both me and Jesuit schooling, saying he'd heard many new stories from me, tales so clever that they were too difficult to remember. I welcomed the visitors as well, as some of them took my place as storyteller, and I found it more pleasant to listen than to speak.

One evening was especially dark. The sky was thick with clouds, not a single star in sight. Snow fell heavily. Suddenly, a northern wind began to blow, and a terrible storm and blizzard set in. The windows were buried in snow, and the wind howled mournfully outside, as if over the grave of nature itself. You couldn't see your hand in front of you. The dogs barked in the yard, as though chasing a wild animal.

I stepped outside, listening carefully to see whether a pack of wolves had approached, for such predators often hunt during blizzards, prowling near villages in search of prey. I took a loaded gun in case I caught sight of their glittering eyes. Then I heard cries from the direction of the lake – many desperate voices calling out, as if overwhelmed by danger and unable to find their way. I returned to the house and told my uncle.

"Travelers," he said. "The snowstorm has buried the road, they've strayed onto the lake and don't know where to go."

With that, he lit a candle and placed it on the windowsill.

Pan Zavalnia had made it his habit on stormy nights. His Christian heart was filled with love for his neighbor, and he was always glad to have guests, to talk with them and to listen to their tales. When lost travelers saw the light in the window, they rejoiced like sailors weary from stormy seas, spotting a harbor lantern far off in the dark. They would gather at my uncle's manor as though at a roadside tavern to warm themselves and rest their horses.

The wind did not let up. The house stood ringed by snowdrifts like high white embankments. Amid the roar of the storm, one could hear the crunch of snow beneath heavy wheels. Then came a knock on the gate, and a voice shouted:

"Randar! Randar![5] Open the gate! Oh, what a blizzard, we are freezing, and the horses can barely go on! Randar! Randar! Open up!"

A farmhand trudged out through the snow, grumbling about falling into a drift.

"Hold your horses, I'm coming. Why all the shouting? This isn't Randar's house – this is Pan Zavalnia's."

"Oh, sir!" they cried, mistaking him for the master. "Let us stay the night! The road is buried in snow, we can't see a thing."

"Do you know any tales or stories?" he asked.

"We'll come up with something, if it pleases the good sir."

The gates opened. Several carts rolled into the courtyard. My uncle came out to meet them and said:

"Well then, you'll have supper and hay for your horses, but only on one condition: one of you must tell me an interesting tale."

"Gladly, sir," the peasants replied, taking off their hats and bowing.

They unhitched the horses and tied them to the carts, fed them hay, and went into the servants' room, shaking snow from their coats. Supper was brought to them. Afterwards, some of the travelers came into my uncle's room. He gave them each a glass of *harelka*, seated them, then lay down in bed, ready to listen. The whole household gathered, and I sat nearby, eager to hear new folk tales I hadn't heard before.

A Sorcerer and the Dragon Hatched from a Rooster's Egg

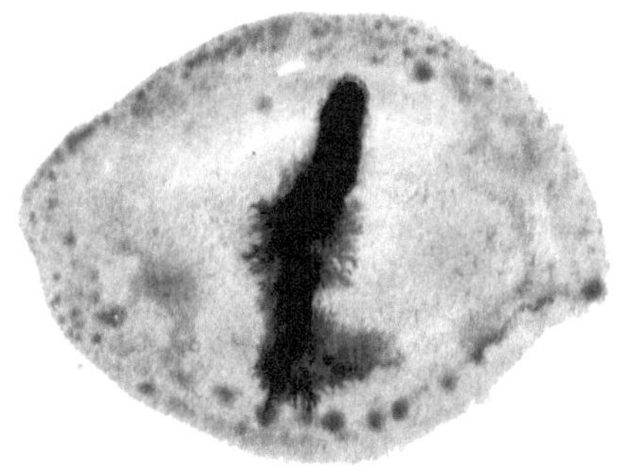

Not every reader will understand the Belarusian language, so I have decided to write these folk tales, which I heard from the mouths of simple folk, in a literal translation into Polish as much as I can.

The traveler was not a young man, his hair was already gray, but he was still healthy and strong. When he spoke about his past, he seemed to grow younger. After pondering for a moment, he began:

"I won't tell you a tale, sir, but a true account of what actually happened to me. Life can be bitter, but if one has faith in God, He will show mercy and set things right. Woe to those who, in their lust for wealth, sell their souls to the devil.

When I was young, we had a master, K.G. he was called. A cruel man, and I shudder to recall his deeds. He would marry off boys and girls without the slightest regard for their wishes or happiness. Neither pleas nor tears moved him. He did whatever pleased him, tormenting people without a drop of pity. A horse or a dog mattered more to him than a Christian soul. He had a servant, Karpa, an evil man as well. Both of them, first the master and then the servant, sold their souls to the devil. And here's how it happened.

One day, a strange man appeared at our estate, no one knew where he came from. I still remember his face and clothing clearly: short and thin, always pale, with a huge nose resembling the beak of a predatory bird, furry eyebrows, and a gaze like that of a madman or a desperate soul. He wore black garments that were odd, nothing like what our gentry or priests wear. No one could say whether he was a civilian or some kind of monk. When he spoke to the master, it was in an incomprehensible language. Only later did we learn that he was a sorcerer, and he had taught the master how to make gold and other devilish tricks.

At that time, I was still very young, but I had to take night shifts as a watchman. I would walk around the master's buildings, striking a hammer against an iron plate. I often saw a light burning in the master's room at midnight, and he was always busy with the sorcerer. Everyone else was asleep that night. Silence ruled the courtyard, while bats and black birds darted through the air above the master's roof. An owl perched on the rooftop laughed, or sometimes cried like an infant. I was seized by fear. But after making the sign of a cross and whispering a prayer, I felt a little better. Gaining courage, I quietly crept up to the master's window and peeked inside to see what they were doing.

Suddenly, I saw a horrifying creature by the wall – God, it's frightening to even recall. A gigantic toad! It turned its fiery eyes on me. I jumped back and ran like a madman, not stopping until I'd put two hundred paces between us. I was trembling all over. It seemed to me that this was Satan himself, guarding the master's windows in that monstrous form so that no one would spy on their rituals. I recited the '*Angel of God*' prayer. Though it was a clear, warm summer night, I shook as if chilled to the bone. Thank God, the rooster soon crowed. The light in the room went out, and, somewhat calmed, I waited for sunrise.

The second incident was just as strange. I was chopping wood in the forest at sunset when I saw the master and the sorcerer walking down the road. They turned into a dense spruce thicket. Curious, I followed them and hid behind a tree, certain that something magical was about to happen. The forest was quiet, only a woodpecker tapped on a distant rotting trunk. I saw the master sit down on an old uprooted tree, while the sorcerer stood beside him, holding by the head a huge snake, which was coiled around his right arm like a black ribbon. I don't know what happened next, as I ran away in terror.

The third incident was even more terrifying. I didn't see it with my own eyes, but I heard about it from trustworthy people, and the entire region was talking about it. At midnight, the master, his devilish guest, and the servant Karpa led a black goat out of the barn and took it to the cemetery. People say they dug up a corpse from its grave, the sorcerer donned the dead man's coat, and they sacrificed the goat, using its blood and flesh in horrifying rituals. It's dreadful even to recall what happened that night. People say monstrous beasts filled the sky, creatures shaped like bears, boars, and wolves roamed the cemetery, shrieking so loudly that the master and Karpa fainted in terror. I don't know who revived them, but the next morning the sorcerer was gone, and no one ever saw him again. The master became gloomy. Though he had gold and everything he desired, he grew more savage, and no one could please him. He even expelled Karpa from the estate."

As the traveler told his tale, the listeners whispered among themselves, *"So frightening – it makes your skin crawl."*

My uncle remarked:

"He must have been a Freemason at some point, or kept company with unbelievers, because a man without faith is capable of anything. But what happened next?"

The traveler continued:

"After he was expelled from the estate, Karpa was taken in as a laborer by a wealthy farmer. But he was more of a burden than a help. Having lived at the manor since childhood, he had grown lazy, stubborn, and disobedient. The steward received constant complaints, moving him from one household to another, but he couldn't stay anywhere long.

At last, Karpa pleaded with the steward to speak to the master on his behalf, asking for his own house and a few acres of land. He promised he would work harder if he had his own place and responsibilities. The master agreed. A new house was built for him, a choice plot of land was parceled out, and he was given a couple of horses, several cows, and other livestock to breed.

Eventually, he decided to marry. But no peasant's daughter wanted him – no one trusted Karpa or his household. Everyone knew he lacked faith and had no God in his heart.

My parents once lived in that village, and we had a neighbor named Harasim. He was a hard-working man, content with what he had. He served the master faithfully and paid his dues on time. Harasim had only one daughter,

Agapka. She was beautiful: healthy and rosy, like a ripe berry. When she dressed for the fair – with a ribbon in her braid and a red corset – she gleamed like a poppy in bloom. No one could take their eyes off her. Everyone wanted to dance with her, and the bagpiper always played his finest tunes when she was near. Ah! I'll admit it – I loved her deeply back then. And even now, I sigh whenever I think of her.

Karpa liked her too. He decided to pursue her, but he knew the girl didn't love him, and that her parents didn't want him for a son-in-law. They rejected the matchmakers he had sent. To get his way, Karpa went to the master and asked him to command Agapka to marry him. When her parents heard about this, they pleaded with the steward and the entire community to intervene. Agapka, they said, was still too young and wouldn't be able to manage a household on her own. Karpa's farm was visibly falling into ruin, and nothing good could come of it. At the request of the steward and the villagers, the master postponed the wedding by a year and ordered Karpa to prove himself by then, to show what improvements he had made, and how much money he had earned.

I also loved Agapka, but I didn't dare even dream of marrying her. I feared the master's wrath, and I couldn't compete with Karpa, for he was a manor man, with friendships among sorcerers. If he had discovered my feelings for Agapka, he surely would have destroyed me. So I suffered in silence, praying to God that this innocent lamb wouldn't fall into the claws of a mad wolf. But things turned out differently than I feared.

A dishonest and lazy man, Karpa sought counsel from Paramon, the most feared sorcerer in the region. Karpa told him everything: about his love for Agapka and the conditions the master had imposed on him for the year. He begged Paramon to reveal a way to get rich quickly, swearing he would give anything – even sell his soul to the devil – if only he could reach his goal.

From a wooden box, Paramon took out a packet of seeds wrapped in paper, handed them to Karpa, and said:

'If you don't already have a black rooster, find one. Feed it these seeds. In a few days, it will lay an egg no larger than a pigeon's. Carry this egg under your left armpit for one full month. When it hatches, a small lizard will emerge. Keep it with you and feed it milk from the palm of your hand every day. It will grow quickly, and before long, wings will sprout from its sides. In a month's time, the lizard will become a winged dragon. It will fulfill your every command. If it comes in its black form, it will bring you rye, wheat, and other grains. If it arrives wreathed in flame, it will deliver gold and silver. If you want to be rich, live in harmony with it, but beware: if you anger it, it will burn your house to the ground, along with everything in it.'

Karpa eagerly followed this godless advice. He raised the dreadful dragon. But the magic didn't stay hidden for long. His monster began to appear just after sunset, in plain sight of villagers returning home late in the evening.

One night, while I was grazing horses, I saw that creature flying. Sparks scattered from it like glowing iron beneath a blacksmith's hammer. Right above Karpa's house, it broke into tiny pieces and vanished. The sky was clear, there wasn't a single cloud, and the stars shimmered in the vault of heaven.

'Oh God,' I thought, 'nothing is hidden from You. You are the judge of human affairs, yet people forget this.'

Within just a few months, Karpa became a wealthy man. Whenever he came to a fair or a holiday celebration, he would swagger into the tavern with his hands on his hips, red cap askew, chin held high as if nothing in the world could touch him. He threw coins onto the table by the handful, ordering whatever he pleased and treating everyone to a drink. Karpa boasted loudly that the master was like a brother to him and would never refuse him anything, that he could do as he pleased, and that Agapka ought to be glad to marry him, because he had the money to buy any bride he wanted.

Hearing this, Agapka wept bitterly. She knew that both her wishes and her parents' will meant nothing. Everything was in the hands of the master, and he had neither compassion nor mercy. She knew Karpa's character all too well, both his soul and his habits. And sometimes, she overheard neighbors whispering that he was in league with Paramon, that demons served him, and had brought him heaps of gold. But that gold brought her no joy. Agapka dreamed of a husband who was hardworking, pious, and kind.

The year passed. Karpa bought fancy gifts for the master, and arrived on a fine steed to remind him of the promise. They sent for Agapka's father and ordered him to prepare for the wedding. Poor Harasim and his wife wept over their child's fate and prayed that God would be her protector. Agapka hid her sorrow, not wanting to grieve her parents even more. She took her beloved silk ribbons and a few pieces of linen she had woven herself, and went to the church. There, she hung them before the icon of the Holy Mother and fell prostrate, weeping and sobbing. Those who witnessed it couldn't hold back their own tears. After the service, she dried her eyes and returned home with a face that was calm and composed, as if at peace.

My love and compassion for Agapka were stronger than my fear. I went to Harasim's house. New thoughts and bold intentions stirred inside me, and I resolved to hide her from tyranny and grief in some faraway place.

On my way to the village, I saw Agapka alone in the fields, wandering and crying. In a mournful voice, she sang a song of gratitude to her parents for their care. I approached and took her hand. Wanting to ease her suffering, I offered my help.

'Agapka! I know the reason for your tears. I know the suffering of your father and mother. Karpa is a godless man, he bribed the master and ignored your wishes, and your parents' will. Listen to my words, if you feel even a sliver of the affection for me that I feel for you and for your family. There are high mountains covered in dense forest, and near our villages lie deep, dark woods. No human eye has ever seen their depths – they stretch endlessly. Let's leave these lands. Let's hide from everyone we know in that wilderness. I will be your guardian and your guide. The world is wide, and we will find a place in it for ourselves. Somewhere, kind-hearted people will give refuge to those fleeing injustice. You and I are innocent in the eyes of both God and man. We will earn our bread through hard work. God will grant us health and strength. He will care for us, even in those dark forests.'

My eyes blurred with tears as I spoke. Agapka looked at me and replied:

'I love you, but I cannot go with you. It would only bring more suffering to my parents. It is better that I am the one sacrificed to this misfortune, and they be left in peace.'

Having said this, she hurried home.

I stood there for a long time, not knowing what to do. Despairing, I turned to go home, but, as if in a trance, I ran back into the fields, and wandered through the woods. Crushed by loneliness, I didn't know where to go or what to do.

Then the decree came. Karpa and Agapka were to be married at church on Sunday. Karpa, cheerful and boastful, stood upright at the altar, his hair trimmed in lordly fashion, a silk scarf around his neck, shiny boots on his feet, and an overcoat sewn from fine cloth, the kind the master sometimes wore. Anyone who didn't know that Karpa was once one of us would have taken off their hat and bowed to him from half a mile away. Agapka, by contrast, looked sorrowful and pale. She seemed completely changed, like someone consumed by illness. The sparkle in her eyes had been extinguished by tears. People said that the wedding candles burned very dimly, and they whispered to one another: *'There will be no happiness here, their life will be overshadowed by sorrow.'*

From the church, Karpa, his young wife and his wedding party went to pay respects to the master. From there, they made their way to Agapka's parents' house. The wedding was strange, to say the least. Having grown up as a servant at the manor, Karpa scoffed at our village customs. He didn't ride his horse through burning straw. The guests gave no traditional speeches. No wedding songs were sung. They didn't even invite the bagpiper, and the youth didn't dance. The celebration at Harasim's house felt more like a funeral. Before long, the newlyweds and their guests departed for their new home, where Karpa boasted of his wealth and lordly status at every step, seeking praise from everyone around.

He summoned the bagpiper, tossed him a few silver coins like a clerk paying a day's wage, and ordered him to play. He also generously paid some women to sing. With forced politeness, he invited the boys and girls to dance. There was no sincerity in it, just as there was no lack of food and drink. Glasses of *harelka* passed from hand to hand without pause. The house rang with music, the youth danced, Karpa boasted of his years in manor service and the favor he had earned from the master. Only Agapka stood still like a shadow. It hurt even to look at her.

Outside, the courtyard was dark but quiet. It was midnight. The sky was clear. The stars had shifted across the heavens. Inside, the guests were already well drunk and still making merry. Suddenly, a blinding flash of light lit up the house, and a strange rumbling thundered just beyond the wall. The candle flames dimmed. Everyone fell silent and stared at one another.

Pale and visibly shaken, Karpa muttered: 'My guest has arrived.'

Then, as if nothing had happened, he changed the subject and spoke to his guests about something else. But at that moment, something eerie descended over house. An unease spread among the guests. Some began to see frightening and inexplicable things, both outside and in the dark corners of the room. One swore he saw a hairy monster peering in through the window. Another claimed a coal-black dwarf with a massive head was sitting on the stove. Yet another believed he saw the very sorcerer who had once taught the master to make gold and practice devilry. Sensing their fear, Karpa laughed and said it was just strong *harelka* playing tricks on them. Then he ordered the bagpiper to keep playing and singing. Amid the noise and confusion, the incident was soon half-forgotten.

Then the door swung open and in walked the sorcerer Paramon. He cast a slow, burning gaze across the guests. His fiery eyes glowed from beneath thick, bushy brows. Still standing in the doorway, he said:

'Greetings, good company! May joy never leave such a cheerful gathering. I wish the newlyweds harmony, love, and riches. May they always host and entertain their neighbors and good friends with such joy.'

Karpa stepped forward to greet him and offered him the place of honor. The guests made room. Paramon sat at the table, leaned against the wall, and surveyed everyone before him with careful attention. Karpa served him *harelka* and snacks.

'So, where's your little Agapka, the young mistress of the house? Is she so busy? Or has she forgotten about me? I've aged, of course... but she's young still, and has much to learn about how to live in this world.'

Karpa brought Agapka forward. Paramon looked at her sorrowful face and said:

'Do not grieve. In time, you'll learn to love. Everything will turn out just fine.'

Among the guests was Akim, a peasant from the same district and a subject of Pan K.G., who had once been on bitter terms with Paramon. He was in high spirits, and never one to turn down a drink. Emboldened by alcohol and memories of past disagreements, he planted his hands on his hips, thrust out his right leg, stood squarely before Paramon, looked him in the eye, and said:

'Ah! Greetings! The cat licked its tail, expecting you as a guest.'

Everyone turned to look at Akim, displeased that, drunk on *harelka*, he dared to mock Paramon so openly. They feared a misfortune might follow, after all, everyone believed in Paramon's magical powers. People said he could bring madness and disease upon a person or turn an entire wedding party into wolves, if he so wished.

Paramon looked at him with a scornful smile:

'And you,' he said mockingly, 'sometimes sneak into the master's or the neighbors' pantries, or into the yard where linens are drying, and you do it so quietly that not even the dog or the night watchman notices.'

'Ha! I remember well how they once accused me of

stealing linen,' Akim replied. 'You did your divination with a sieve, calling out the names of every peasant in the area. The sieve turned when my name came up... and Gryshka the Bagpiper's too. The steward's wife believed your sorcery, and we were beaten half to death. And later, it turned out we were innocent, punished for nothing. Your deeds are vile, and there is no justice in your magic.'

Then Gryshka the Bagpiper joined in:

'Ha! Yes, I remember that, too. You know, it would be fair to thank you for that 'magic' with a good solid beating, one so thorough that you wouldn't be able to stand back up again.'

Paramon could not endure having his sorcery dismissed as fraud. His eyes flashed, his face turned crimson, and he leapt up from the bench, frightening everyone. Karpa rushed over, grabbing him by the shoulders, pleading with him to forgive the peasants, insisting they were drunk and did not know what they were saying. Seeing the commotion, Agapka ran over as well. She took Paramon's hand and apologized for the offense he had suffered, pleading for his forgiveness. Then she turned to Akim and Gryshka and asked them to forget the past and make peace with Paramon. Karpa poured more *harelka,* and urged everyone to drink and let bygones be bygones.

The sorcerer calmed down.

'Alright,' he said. 'Don't worry, I'll reconcile. I've no desire to ruin your celebration. In fact, I want the evening to become even more cheerful. Let Gryshka play the bagpipes, and let Akim dance.'

Then, with a cunning smile, he added, 'Well, go on, then. The host and young hostess are inviting us to share a drink of *harelka.* The roosters haven't crowed yet, now's the perfect time to have some fun.'

Karpa, Agapka, and the guests all urged Akim and Gryshka to sit at the table with Paramon. Akim didn't refuse the *harelka*. Gryshka followed suit, accepting a drink straight from Paramon's hand. Then came another round.

'Peace! Peace and reconciliation among us!' the guests cried. 'The tables are heavy with food and drink, let's toast, let's celebrate, and wish the newlyweds wealth, health, and long life!'

Gryshka began to play a wild *kazachok*. The guests shouted, calling for the *tsiareshka*, singing:

> *'Tsiareshka got into trouble,*
> *His wife went off with another.'*

But Gryshka paid no attention. He ignored every request, playing and playing his own strange, feverish tune. Then Akim sprang into the center of the room and began to dance like a madman.

Everyone stared in shock, no one could understand what had come over him. Akim's eyes bulged, his face twisted unnaturally. People begged one to stop playing and the other to stop dancing. But nothing helped. They heard no one. They were beyond reason. Both had gone mad.

The guests tried to hold them back, but they mumbled unintelligibly, broke free, and danced even harder. Gryshka's fingers flew over the pipes. Paramon stood to the side, watching, and laughed.

'Don't touch them,' he said. 'Let them have their fun. Next time, they won't be so eager to pick a fight.'

Karpa begged him to forgive the offenders and make it stop.

'Let them go on a little longer,' Paramon replied. 'This will teach them to respect and honor people who are wiser than them.'

The torment went on for some time. Midnight passed. The rooster crowed a second time. At last, Gryshka's strength gave out, he dropped the bagpipes and collapsed unconscious onto the floor. Akim staggered, blackened in the face, as if dying. Satisfied with his revenge, Paramon whispered something under his breath, gave them each a bit of water, and, once they came to, took his hat, bowed to the hosts, and went home.

The incident cast a shadow over the entire celebration. One by one, the guests rose, thanked the hosts for their hospitality, offered their wishes for happiness and prosperity, and quietly took their leave."

At this point, Pan Zavalnia interrupted:

"They say that in the old days, when people cared more about God's glory, sorcerers like that were burned at the stake or thrown into rivers. Do you hear that, Janka? That's what happens to people who make pacts with the devil. One must be cautious in this world. I've heard of many wicked sorcerers like Paramon in my lifetime."

"Uncle, maybe he used some herbs," I replied. "Maybe he spiked the *harelka* with henbane or some other poison that drives people mad."

"It's not herbs that cause this – it's the devil," he insisted. "It's a shame that educated people don't believe in such things anymore. I once knew a young noble who talked the way you do, like he'd never studied the catechism or the Ten Commandments. But go on, what happened next?"

"After the wedding," the traveler continued, "Karpa began living very differently. He quickly built a second house with large windows, and planted a garden with blooming cherries and apples. He made his homestead resemble a noble estate more than a peasant's hut. Karpa grew so arrogant that he even planted the same flowers under his windows as those in the master's garden, useless flowers that served no purpose. He forbade Agapka to wear her bodice or headscarf and ordered her to dress in the same chintz dresses that noblewomen wore. She resisted. She knew that if anyone saw her in such fine clothes, they'd call her lazy. But she had to obey. So she watered the flowers dressed like a lady, while Karpa's many hired hands worked the fields and brought in the harvest. The master began visiting often. Karpa had money and status, but is that happiness?

He found no peace of mind. He never spoke a kind word to any of his workers. And Agapka could never please him. Her rare smile seemed mocking to him. He took her quiet obedience for stupidity. The modesty and prayers her mother had taught her were an annoyance to him. One day, he forbade her to speak to any of the workers. He became angry that she was too slow. God alone knew what he even wanted.

Sometimes, he scolded her for being lazy, even though she went to bed well after sunset. He did not want her praying or doing any work in the evening. From time to time, he would rise at midnight and whisper to someone through the door or the window, then run off into the night and not return until the rooster crowed.

He had friends to whom he gave money and with whom he drowned his restlessness in *harelka*. Sometimes he disappeared for days at a time, and no one saw him at all.

One evening, while the servants rested after the day's work, Agapka sat alone in the house, waiting for her husband. Suddenly, a flash of light, sharp as lightning, lit up the walls. Then darkness returned. A strange unease gripped her heart. She glanced into the corners of the room, as if sensing something lurking there. The cat hissed, jumped down from the doorframe, and froze in the middle of the room, bristling, its eyes gleaming restlessly. Then, a stranger entered. He was a young man, handsomely dressed, with golden rings on every finger and a wide red sash around his waist. Agapka stared at the unfamiliar face. It was attractive, but his gaze was sharp and penetrating. It frightened her.

'Greetings, young mistress,' the stranger said. 'Why do you sit here so lonely, like an orphan? You look into my eyes, but you do not recognize me. I, however, have seen you many times and know you well. Where is your husband, Karpa?'

'I don't know,' she replied. 'I haven't seen him in three days. He is probably with some acquaintances... or maybe he went to town. I heard him say something about that.'

'What business would he have in town? He's off enjoying himself, yet he doesn't even know how to savour his good fortune. He has plenty of gold and silver, but what good is that? He could work wonders. He could build a house more splendid than this one – like the ones in fairy tales: its walls gleaming with silver and gold, gilded in pure gold. He could plant an orchard where golden and silver apples grow, where birds of paradise sing. The flowers beneath your windows would shine brighter than the stars in the sky. Even this very cat would sit on your lap and purr stories from ancient times. Nobles would flock to see such marvels. He could live better than a king. You are young, noble-hearted, and wiser than he is. Take charge of the estate. I will help you, and together, we will amaze the world.'

Saying this, he sat down on the bench beside her.

Looking into his eyes, Agapka asked softly:

'Have you known my husband long?'

'I've known him since childhood,' the stranger replied. 'I wander the world, and I serve those whom fortune favors. You are more fortunate than most – and I sincerely wish to serve you.'

'Who are you? What is your name?'

'Why do you need to know my name?' he said. 'I am your friend. Just accept my offer, agree to what I ask, and you will know everything in due time.'

As he spoke, the stranger sprinkled gold onto the floor. Then, meeting her gaze, he added:

'Look, this is what I can do.'

'I do not seek wealth,' Agapka replied. 'I only want peace of mind. And may the Blessed Virgin Mary protect me.'

The moment she uttered the name of the Blessed Virgin, he burst into flames and vanished on the spot. With a piercing scream, Agapka ran out the door and collapsed, unconscious. Her cry woke the household. The servants rushed to help and found her lying motionless in the hallway, though lifeless. They barely revived her. No one slept that night. Agapka remained awake, while the servants sat around her, worried.

Karpa returned the following morning. When he was told what had happened, his expression changed. He began pacing the room, troubled and deep in thought. At last, he approached his wife and said:

'What have you done? If the seeds are sown, the harvest must come. Otherwise, there will be ridicule and misfortune.'

'I didn't sow those evil seeds,' she replied through tears. 'I would rather die than reap from such a harvest.'

At this, he lunged at her in fury, fists clenched, but she slipped out the door and hid until his anger passed.

From that point on, Karpa completely neglected the farm. He rarely sent his servants to carry out the duties owed to his master. But the steward turned a blind eye and forgave everything, because Karpa had told the master he intended to buy his freedom and the land he lived on, promising a great sum of money in exchange.

One evening, Karpa stood up, walked to the window, and sat there, brooding, as he often did. It was clear that he was talking to himself. His wife begged him to stop.

'I'll return tomorrow,' Karpa replied. Then he slammed the door behind him and disappeared. No one knew where he went.

Afraid to sleep alone, Agapka called a servant girl to stay with her. But as soon as she dozed off, she felt a searing touch on her hand, hot as fire. She opened her eyes and saw the man who had frightened her earlier. He was standing there, strangely dressed, his eyes burning like two candles. The hat and sash he wore glowed red like embers or molten iron. Agapka froze in fear, barely able to lift her hand to cross herself. As soon as she did, the figure vanished.

Agapka woke the servant girl and told her everything. They spoke for a while, trying to calm their nerves, but no sooner had they begun to feel at ease than the figure reappeared. And once again, he vanished when they invoked the names of Jesus and Mary. They jumped out of bed, lit a candle, and prayed until the rooster crowed.

The next day, Agapka sent the servant girl to her parents with a message about the apparitions, asking them to visit and advise her on what to do in these circumstances.

Word soon spread throughout the district that a dragon had appeared to Agapka several times, frightening her in various ways. Karpa, however, denied everything. He claimed the rumors were false, that his wife had gone mad, or that the devil was tormenting her because of her sins.

One evening, as the sun was setting and the day's work in the fields was finished, Harasim and his wife came to visit their daughter. When Agapka saw them through the window, she ran out to greet them, brought them into the house, and, with eyes full of tears, told them about her suffering, the strange changes in her husband, and the appearances of a monstrous being that served him, disguised in human form.

'Well,' said Harasim, 'I told the steward and the others on the estate before the wedding that Karpa had raised a dragon to gain his wealth. But they just laughed: *'Stupid peasant, you're talking nonsense,'* they said. When word got to the master, he flew into a rage: *'Listen, peasant,'* he said, *'if you keep babbling this rubbish, you'll get five hundred lashes and your head shaved like a lunatic.'* What will they say now?'

Crying, Harasim's wife turned to Agapka.

'Once we finish the harvest,' she said, 'we'll go together to the Blessed Virgin of Orphans to try to convince Karpa to come with us and confess. God will have mercy. Here, take these blessed herbs and some incense from the church. Burn them in the house every evening, and, God willing, things will get better.'

Karpa was not at home. Dusk had fallen, and the room was growing darker. The night was warm, the sky was clear, and the air so still that even a hair wouldn't stir on one's head. The weather was beautiful. After supper, the farmhands went off to sleep in the fields with the horses, while the others bedded down in the barn on fresh hay. But Agapka carried on talking with her parents – she still had much weighing on her heart. The house was quiet, save for the faint crackle of a candlewick burning low. Agapka leaned over the coals and sprinkled some of the blessed herbs onto the glowing embers. Instantly, there came a sound from behind the wall, like a sudden gust of wind. A flash of light shot through the house. Everyone froze.

'He's here,' Agapka whispered, distressed. They all fell silent, muttering prayers under their breath, waiting to see what would happen next. Pots near the stove began to rattle. One flew into the air, then crashed to the floor, shattering into pieces. A jug of *kvass* that sat on the bench leapt onto the table, then hurled itself to the ground, smashing to bits. The cat, eyes glowing with fear, bolted under the bench and hid. Household items began to fly from corner to corner.

Harasim's wife took off her copper cross, the one that had been blessed during confession in Yukhavichy, at the Jubilee.

'May it protect you,' she said, and placed the cross around her daughter's neck.

No sooner had the devout woman spoken those words than pebbles, small as hail, began flying from the dark corners of the house, ricocheting off the walls. Then, from behind the stove, heavy stones, some weighing several pounds, were hurled through the air. But invoking the protection of the Blessed Mother, everyone escaped the house unharmed.

All the estate serfs gathered outside, drawn by the noise and confusion. Stones of all sizes hurled out from windows and slammed into walls. No one dared approach the building. Everyone stood at a distance, their eyes locked on the strange phenomenon, unsure of what to do.

Midnight passed, the rooster crowed. The storm of stones slowly ceased. But no one dared go inside. The serfs waited in the courtyard until sunrise, while Agapka left with her parents and returned to their home.

By the time the sun had risen high, the livestock had

been taken to pasture, and the laborers had gone out with their scythes and plows. That's when Karpa returned. The house stood empty. He encountered only the sole servant woman, who had come back from the field upon seeing her master arrive.

'What is going on here?' Karpa asked. 'Where is my wife?'

The woman told him everything. Karpa turned pale. His face twisted in horror.

'She's ruined me!' he cried and ran off at once to find the sorcerer Paramon.

News of the event spread quickly throughout the district. At the manor, some claimed it was the work of the devil. Others scoffed, saying it was all mischief and pranks. Harasim went to the local priest and begged him to come to Karpa's estate that very day and bless the house that had clearly fallen under demonic power.

By evening, a crowd of curious onlookers from all over the region had gathered to witness the marvel for themselves. The steward arrived with a band of strong, brave young men from the estate. They didn't believe in demons and hoped to catch the trickster red-handed. Ignoring all warnings, a few of them opened the front door and attempted to enter the house, but the moment they stepped across the threshold, they turned and fled, screaming. A stone had struck one of them so hard that it nearly knocked him unconscious.

The crowd kept its distance from the house, watching in fear and amazement as the stones continued to pour out.

Despair had completely changed Karpa. Pale as a ghost, he cursed his wife, the neighbors, and the servants. He tried to break into the house himself but had to be restrained. Paramon stood nearby, muttering something under his breath, but his magic had no effect. Even Pan K.G. came in person, unable to suppress his curiosity. But he too did not dare approach the house. Instead, he ordered it to be surrounded and waited to see how this horror would end.

At last, the priest arrived, clad in his chaplain's vestments. He began the holy rite, and as soon as he approached the house with holy water, the entire building erupted in flames. Within moments, it collapsed into a heap of blazing ruin.

Witnessing the devil's revenge, the crowd stood stunned, shaking their heads in disbelief. And everyone who was there saw it with their own eyes: the very spot where the house had stood was now nothing but scorched earth and smoking embers. The priest returned home shaken, lamenting the foolishness of his flock. As Paramon departed, he shook his head and cursed the wretched Karpa:

'What a fool – you sowed, now you reap.'

Across the district, from humble huts to manor halls, people spoke of the event for a long time.

Karpa disappeared after the fire. He vanished without a trace, never returning to his friends, his father-in-law, or his wife. Rumors spread. Some said he had joined a band of horse thieves, smuggling stolen livestock from Belarus to Pskou or Vialikiya Luki. The master even sent the innkeeper Chaim to investigate. Others claimed to have seen Karpa, wild-eyed and broken, roaming the forests like a madman, fleeing at the sound of human voices.

Weeks passed. One day, a hunter was walking along the lake, searching for ducks. The sky was overcast. The waves lapped angrily at the shore. From afar, he spotted several crows gathered by the water. He fired his gun, the birds scattered and vanished into the forest. As he approached, he saw a body washed up on the sand, foam still clinging to it. He ran to report it to the manor. The authorities were notified. The body was difficult to identify, but the clothes and a ring on the hand confirmed it was Karpa.

Thus ended the life of the unfortunate man. They buried him right there on the shore, without prayer or priest."

The traveler fell silent.

"Tell me," asked Pan Zavalnia, "what became of Agapka?"

"Agapka lived with her parents for several more years, always sick from grief and fear. After her parents passed, she wasted away like a candle. May she reign in heaven. In her virtuous and chaste life, she was an example to all the women of our district. Though these events took place long ago, even now, in the spot where she once watered flowers with her tears, cherries and apples grow, and each spring, the most beautiful flowers bloom. The village girls gather them into wreaths and place them before the image of the Blessed Virgin Mary."

"Why didn't you marry her once she became a widow?" asked Pan Zavalnia. "You loved her once, didn't you? She would have made the best wife. A good wife is the greatest treasure, because where there is love and harmony in the home, there is God's blessing. Even I live as well as I do, thanks be to God, and maintain the order in this household because my late wife and I built it together."

"After that sorrowful wedding," I replied, "I asked the master to let me leave for foreign lands, somewhere, where it would be easier to earn money, build a home, and pay my dues. I also hoped that distance would help me forget what I had seen and what had caused me such pain. I wandered for many years across Russia, near Novgorod,

Staraya Russa, even close to St. Petersburg, doing the hardest work. I helped build roads through swamps and wilderness, dug deep ditches, sometimes standing in water from dawn till dusk. Praise God, I endured it all without ruining my health. I came back with money, and that's when I heard about what had happened to Karpa... and about the death of poor Agapka."

"And Paramon? Is he still alive?"

"He died without the last rites. His grave lies in a field without a cross."

"Well, Janka," said Pan Zavalnia, "do you like our simple stories? They are true and easier to follow than those tales you told me about pagan gods and goddesses. No one remembers such stories anymore, except bookish men."

"I love stories like these," I said. "There is God's truth in the imagination of simple folk."

As Pan Zavalnia spoke to me, the servants whispered among themselves: "Such a good story... I could listen all night without falling asleep."

"Well then," said Zavalnia, "let's hear what your companion will tell us next. These stories from your life, they're both frightening and fascinating."

Daring Deeds

"I too once knew a man like Karpa, and he paid dearly for it. The world today is corrupt. There are many brazen and idle people, ready to commit all sorts of evil, deaf to any word of kindness."

"I also remember better times," said Pan Zavalnia. "In those days, there were many good nobles in our lands! The peace and humility that reigned in this sanctuary of the Lord were a joy to behold: everyone held a rosary and a prayer book in hand, respected their elders, and loved their neighbors. But now, at church, all you hear is whispering and laughter – people come only to flaunt their fancy clothes. Fashion and Freemasonry have ruined them, and others suffer for it."

"It seems to me, Uncle, that people have always been the same, then as now: some were good, some bad, some happy, some wretched."

"Oh no, Janka! You haven't seen what the elders have seen. Those old days are gone and may never return, it may only get worse. Well then, tell us your story," he said, turning to the traveler.

"When I was still very young, there lived a peasant named Anton in our village. He had a fine farm and never knew poverty. Since he had no children, he took in an orphaned boy of unknown parentage, christened him, and named him Vasyl. Anton raised the boy as his own. When Vasyl came of age, he began to herd cattle, but he was lazy and mischievous. Complaints poured in: he'd let cows trample the sown fields, hurl insults at others, or throw stones. People came to Anton with grievances, but he loved the boy and turned a deaf ear to their words. He indulged Vasyl in everything. And as Vasyl grew, he only became worse, quarrelsome and unruly.

One time, we were gathered for *corvée* labor. It was after St. Peter's Day, and Vasyl had also been sent to work. As usual, he quarreled with everyone, unable to utter a kind word to save his life. It was a scorching day. The warden ordered us to lay down our scythes and take a break. It was time to eat and rest. Sitting in a circle on the meadow, we chatted about this and that.

Suddenly, we noticed a peasant who had wandered off toward the edge of the grove. He began waving and shouting:

'Hurry, hurry! Come here – I'll show you something incredible!'

We all ran over. He pointed toward the woods:

'Look what's happening.'

What we saw was beyond belief. A *liasun*,[6] a forest spirit, was walking through the trees, its head towering above the pines. Ahead of it, vast packs of squirrels, hares, and other animals poured into the fields; above them, black grouse, partridges, and other birds scattered into the sky. The *liasun* emerged from the forest, then suddenly shrank into the shape of a dwarf. Instantly, butterflies and other insects rose from the grasses and meadows, swarming the landscape like a dark cloud.

Brazen Vasyl picked up a stone, marched over to where the *liasun* stood among the tall grass, and hurled the rock at it, shouting:

'Get out! Be gone!'

The *liasun* let out a terrible cry, so loud and strange that the leaves fell from the trees. Then it rose from the grass like a giant black bird, flapped its wings loudly, and vanished behind the forest. We were paralyzed with fear. We turned to Vasyl, stunned by what he'd done. Proud of himself, he just laughed and laughed.

There was an older man among us who said gravely:

'I've heard from the elders that such recklessness brings misfortune. The forests will burn, disease will strike the livestock... and you, Vasyl, will not escape punishment.'

'What do I care?' Vasyl scoffed. 'I'm glad I hit that demon squarely with a stone. That'll teach him not to drive *our* birds and beasts from *our* woods.'

Word of this spread quickly. Boys like Vasyl praised his courage, and he bragged about his deed wherever he went. But those who knew better listened to him with disdain. Even Anton, a quiet man, was saddened when he heard the tale.

The second incident was even more frightening, it still makes my hair stand on end just thinking about it. One day, again during *corvée* labor, we were stacking hay. The weather was clear and calm. Then, from the east, a dark cloud appeared. Thunder rumbled low, as though deep underground. Suddenly, we saw a whirlwind whip across the field near our haystacks, spinning sand and debris high into the air as it advanced. We stood in awe, watching. But Vasyl, he threw down his rake, ran into the open, and stood directly in its path. Stretching out his hand, he shouted:

'How are you, brother?'

And from within the swirling dust, a hand reached out, black as coal. The whirlwind spun on, drifting across the field. We were frozen with fear. Vasyl returned to us, but no one dared speak a word. We all understood then: he had made a pact with the accursed spirit.

After that, no one wanted to talk to him. Even those who once counted him a friend began to avoid him. Everyone was afraid.

Word spread quickly through the district, until even the master and the steward heard of it. They didn't believe the stories. But one day, the master asked Vasyl directly if what people were saying was true. Vasyl cursed everyone and spat back:

'Those fools will believe anything they just want something to gossip about.'

The master let it go.

Anton, a good man, tried to awaken Vasyl's fear of God, to correct his ways. He begged him to go to church, to say his prayers. But Vasyl mocked it all. He scorned everyone, and instead of attending Mass, he headed straight to the tavern.

Eventually, Vasyl decided to marry. Anton hoped that a good wife might change him for the better. He sent matchmakers not only to families in his own village but also to neighboring ones. But every offer was refused. The tales of Vasyl's wickedness had traveled far and wide.

Vasyl scoffed at them all. He mocked everything, claiming he'd already chosen the perfect bride. At first, he kept her identity secret, but then announced that he was in love with Aliuta, daughter of Aryna, that he had declared his love to her, and she had accepted.

Anton was devastated. He pleaded with Vasyl to reconsider. People said that Aryna was a wicked woman and a witch, and the apple doesn't fall far from the tree. Her daughter might be the same. But all his advice was in vain. Vasyl began to visit Aryna's house more and more.

Some neighbors laughed, saying, '*Like meets like – a perfect match.*'

Others said Aliuta might be a good wife, that she wouldn't follow her mother's path. Still others claimed Vasyl had been bewitched, that this wasn't love at all, but a spell cast by a woman more powerful than even the spirits he consorted with.

Anton did everything he could to stop him. Finally, he threatened to disown Vasyl, said that he would never welcome such a bride into his home, and that he would not help the young couple establish a household.

'I don't ask anything from anyone,' Vasyl replied. 'I'll find the means myself, and I will get money too. And one day even a guardian like you might come begging me for help.'

Anton turned to his godfather Martin for help. Martin was a respected and well-liked man – talkative, kind, always ready with advice. People trusted him. He promised Anton that he would look into the matter and do everything he could to steer the young man away from his dangerous path. He even vowed to stay close to Vasyl and dissuade him from the relationship whenever possible.

But once Vasyl learned that his guardian would no longer support him, he made up his mind to seek treasures, even if they were enchanted and belonged to the devil himself. Two *versts*[7] from our village, by the roadside, there was a mound flanked on both sides by dark fir forest. At its summit lay a massive stone the locals called the Serpent's Stone.

This is what the elders said:

'One calm, clear summer night, a blazing serpent flew across the sky, from the north to the south. Fire clung to its body, and it glittered as if carrying gold and silver for some sinner who had sold his soul. Many travelers returning from *corvée* labor saw it. Suddenly, the heavens split open, and a radiant beam of divine light pierced the sky. People fell to their knees in prayer. Struck by the light, the serpent froze in midair, crashed onto the mound, and turned to stone. The treasure it carried – gold and silver – sank into the earth at that very spot. Since then, strange visions had been seen on the hill. Some saw a woman in flames, weeping atop the stone, drying her tears with a handkerchief that blazed like fire. Others, walking past late at night, encountered stout black dwarfs, prancing like barrels across the hill. Still others saw black goats leaping from the ground up onto the stone, then vanishing into the ground again.'

As the rumor went, whoever dared to spend the night on that stone would possess the treasure.

Vasyl was brave. He feared no phantoms. He had already greeted the devil once, calling him "brother" as he rode the whirlwind.

At sunset, twilight stretched across the fields. Vasyl climbed the mound and sat atop the stone. The sky clouded over. Darkness spread across the land. Silence enveloped everything. An owl cried from deep in the forest. And then the visions began. He saw snakes slithering from under the stone, hissing as they danced in wide, twisted circles around a horned creature with a dog's head and a goat's legs. But Vasyl did not flinch. He waited, certain that the treasure would reveal itself soon.

Suddenly, he noticed someone approaching, veering off the road.

It was Martin.

'What are you doing here?' he asked with a smile. 'Looking for treasures?'

'Yes, I am, but why are you here? You stopped me at the threshold, snatched happiness from my hands, and deserve to have your head smashed with a rock.'

'Don't be angry. Let me tell you about a better treasure.'

He sat down beside Vasyl on the stone.

'Listen, Vasyl, go home. Health and honest work are the greatest treasures a man can have. Seeking help from unclean spirits is a sin. You're still young. If you work hard, God will help you. Anton is childless. If you do right by him, everything he owns will be yours one day.'

Vasyl spat in anger and walked away, muttering curses under his breath.

He did not return home after that. Seeing Vasyl's resistance, Anton gave up trying and waited to see how it would end. Acquaintances brought back rumours. Some said Vasyl had joined a gang, made his money through theft and drank it all away at the tavern. Others claimed he was living with Aryna, learning witchcraft, and had been spotted with her and Aliuta wandering the swamps and forest by the lake, gathering herbs said to never dry of dew.[8] Still others swore they had hidden behind a shrub and overheard Aryna explaining the terrifying power of a plant she had pulled from the earth.

Determined to help, Martin repeatedly tried to meet with him, but to no avail. He did not dare to visit Aryna's house, fearing the witch and whatever hospitality she might offer.

One Sunday evening, villagers gathered at the tavern with their friends and kin to drink, talk over troubles, seek advice, and pass the time. Hoping to run into Vasyl, Martin went too.

They sat at the table. Yosel the Jew, the tavernkeeper, was only glad to pour *harelka* for the guests. He set glasses on the table, and tallied debts with chalk on the wall. They agreed he'd visit in the fall, when the new bread came in. He would treat the guests to *harelka*, and they would return the favor with their grain.

Martin entered. Some were glad to see him and invited him over to the table, offering him a drink. The conversation soon turned to Vasyl and his beloved. Some praised Aliuta, saying she was a fine girl and would have made a good wife, if only she had chosen a good man and not Vasyl, who had sold his soul to the devil. There were a few drunks who even praised Vasyl. Still others cursed him, and cursed Aliuta and Aryna too, calling them the most disgraceful people in the district.

As the noise and bickering went on, Yosel, who stood near the end of the table, raised his voice:

'Listen, you speak unfairly about Vasyl. Vasyl is good and exact, and always proper. When he comes here with his friends, he always pays in cash. He always has money. And Aliuta, oh she is a good girl, she knows how to dress! Like a young noblewoman. I see nothing wrong with Aryna either. So what if she casts spells? She does it to make a living. We all need money, so she helps out by healing people with her herbs.'

As he spoke, the doors burst open with a loud thud.

Vasyl strode in, head held high, hat tilted at an angle. He had several companions by his side. He glanced around, spotted Martin, and frowned.

'How are you, Vasyl?' said Yosel. 'I haven't seen you in three days. My Sora and I were wondering where you'd gone. We were just talking about you now.'

'I know what they say about me,' Vasyl replied. 'Dogs bark, and the wind carries it. I don't care.' He sat heavy on a bench, leaned across the table, and barked, 'Bring us *harelka* – the good kind.'

'Maybe Vasyl wants to order some sweet *harelka*?' Yosel said. 'I brought it from the city – though it is expensive.'

'Bring me the expensive one,' said Vasyl and tossed several silver coins on the table.

In the blink of an eye, Yosel brought out a glass and a bottle of *harelka*.

At the other table, people watched in surprise. Some gave sideways glances, whispering and smirking. Maksim, already well into his drink, laughed aloud and shouted:

'Oh! I see you, brother Vasyl! You must be wealthier than the rest of us, already drinking the noblemen's *harelka*. What happened? You must have spent the night by the Serpent's Stone and found a pile of silver? Or maybe Aryna, your soon-to-be mother-in-law, stuffed your pockets full of coins with one of her spells. Now that's a man!'

Vasyl glared at him.

'No one from our table talked to you or asked for your opinion. Keep out of it, or I'll sew your mouth shut so tight, you'll never run it again.'

'Sew my mouth shut? Oh, oh! Hear that, everyone? He must have already learned to cast spells from Aryna, knows how to stitch lips shut! Oh, oh! Better be careful not to end up a cripple like your future mother-in-law. Do you know why she limps on that left leg of hers?'

'Be silent. No one wants to talk to you.'

'No one wants to talk? Fine, but they will listen. And I'll tell everyone – listen up! – I'll tell all of you why Aryna limps. It was Gryshka's doing, he played a trick on her. He told me himself in secret.

One evening, after sundown, he was coming back from the fields with his scythe. Suddenly, he heard a witch's voice calling the cows, naming each one by its color. And sure enough, in the stillness of the evening, he could hear the cows lowing back from the village. His own cows began to moo right there in the barn. He got scared, thinking he'd lose all his milk, so he rushed off toward the voice to catch the witch red-handed. He crept through the alley, and what did he see? Aryna, sitting on the fence, hair wild and tangled, casting spells, singing like a madwoman.

'*This is bad*,' he thought. '*I need to stop her somehow*.' So he ran home and put consecrated herbs and a wax candle above the barn door. But he'd barely taken a few steps when a magpie swooped in, scattered the herbs, pecked at the candle. Gryshka rushed into the house, grabbed his gun, loaded it with small shot, and fired. Feathers scattered, but the magpie escaped.

The next day, Gryshka heard that Aryna had injured her left leg and was bedridden. He understood at once and thought to himself: '*She got her warning*.' But he feared her revenge.

Soon after, she cast a *zalom* – a crop curse – in his rye field. But he burned the cursed object over aspen wood, and, people said, the witch herself barely escaped with her life.'

Enraged, Vasyl grabbed a bottle and hurled it at Maksim, striking him squarely in the chest. They lunged at each other, and a brawl broke out in the tavern.

Fortunately, the steward from the nearby manor happened to be riding past on horseback.

He heard the piercing screams of the tavern keeper and turned toward the noise. Yosel ran to meet him, arms flailing.

'Oh, benefactor! There's been a killing in the tavern – violence! These drunkards have turned everything upside down!'

The steward leapt from his horse and forced his way between the fighters. He shouted that everyone involved would be severely punished for disorderly drinking and would pay for the damage. The threat sobered them in an instant.

The steward drove everyone out and ordered them to go home. They scattered in different directions, hurling threats and curses at one another.

Yosel stayed behind and explained the situation to the steward and what had started the fight. But he didn't blame Vasyl.

'This needs to be reported to the lords. Fools talk nonsense, they spread lies about a poor widow and the girl who has done nothing wrong. They go on about Aryna and witchcraft. I've never seen any of that. I know that she helps a great many people with her herbs. Only recently, I saw her cure Miss Taresa's face rash at the manor. She dropped a few pebbles into a bowl of cold water, whispered something, and the cold water started boiling as if it were over fire. She told Taresa to wash her face with it, and the rash cleared right up. These spells don't harm people – they help. I hope Pan Steward will relay this to the master and mistress, because it's painful to listen to such slander. Oh, and I had such fine sweet *harelka*, but those drunkards smashed the bottle and spilled it. Sora!' Yosel called. 'I have a little more sweet *harelka* left. Bring some for Pan Steward and fetch some pickles. I have excellent pickled pike.'

The steward drank the *harelka*, had a bite of pickle, and reassured the tavern keeper that he would be compensated for his losses. Then he rode off.

The following day, Aryna herself came to the manor in tears. She pleaded before the master and the mistress, saying that ill-wishers were slandering her, accusing her of witchcraft, of breaks in the rye, and of stealing milk from cows. She swore she had never harmed anyone. Yes, she tried to help people, curing illnesses and various ailments with herbs, but the power of these herbs, she said, was known only to her. And yet, she lamented, this hostility towards her spread through the entire district.

'They also say Vasyl, raised by Anton, has made a pact with the devil, but that's pure invention. It's true Vasyl is a young man, he is rash because he hasn't yet known real hardship. But with time, he will change and become wiser and more sensible. He courted my daughter, and people slander her too, the poor orphan girl, saying awful things.'

'I've heard', replied the master, 'that Vasyl has been disobedient toward his guardian, and that he once faced a whirlwind and greeted it as if it were his own brother. That's no small thing. He should stop such foolishness. It's better to live righteously before God. Tell him to come to his senses, to go to church, to work hard. Now, go home and rest. We'll host your daughter's wedding here at the manor. The housekeeper spoke highly of your daughter, and I've also heard from others that she is a good, hardworking girl.'

That very day, the master summoned Anton and ordered Vasyl to apologize to his guardian. He also commanded Anton not to prevent Vasyl's marriage to Aliuta, but to aid them instead, as they were both orphans.

The master promised to grant them the best land and provide cattle to help start their household.

'But surely, sir,' Anton protested, 'you've heard what people say? That Aryna is a witch? Some claim she steals milk from cows, causes mischief, even turns into a magpie and flies about...they say there are witnesses.'

'Don't listen to gossip. Aryna is a good woman, and Aliuta, her daughter, will be a good wife and a capable housekeeper. Let none of that trouble you. I assure you – you'll be satisfied.'

'As you will, sir,' said Anton. He furrowed his brow, scratched his head, and went home.

A few days later, the priest announced the banns. Soon after, the wedding was held. People from across the district came to the manor – not out of love for the newlyweds, but because they knew there'd be a lavish feast and plenty of *harelka*. There were no traditional village rites. But before the ceremony, the young couple knelt before the master and mistress of the manor, then before Anton and Aryna, asking for their blessing. They did the same again after the wedding ceremony. Aliuta was dressed beautifully. The lady of the manor had given her a pair of earrings that sparkled like firelight. She wore a red corset with golden clasps, and red ribbons in her hair. When she sat at the table and they undid her long braid, tears streamed from her black eyes down her pale cheeks. Everyone looked at her with affection. Then the women sang a wedding song, one traditionally sung to orphan girls on their wedding day. Everyone wept, even those who had once spoken ill of her. I loved that song so much... I still know it by heart.

WEDDING SONG FOR AN ORPHAN

Oh, you can tell by the wedding day,
That it's not the father giving her away,
The yard is grand, but few have gathered:
I have no kin,
Oh, I shall send the gray cuckoo
To find my kinfolk.
The cuckoo flies,
And kinfolk arrive.
Oh, I would have sent a nightingale,
But the nightingale refuses.
Oh, I would send a cuckoo
To summon my father dear:
But to my dear father,
The gray cuckoo won't fly back,
And my father replies: "Gladly would I rise,
To go to my child,
To give my blessing;
But the oaken boards
Have bound my feet,
I cannot rise."
The damp earth
Has sealed the door
And veiled the window;
My dear father
Was not allowed to come to my wedding.

I must admit that I too could not hold back tears, seeing Aliuta before me and listening to this song. She truly was an orphan, having no one but her old mother. The master had brought her family from far away. They used to live beyond the Dzvina River, and Aliuta's father died shortly after they arrived in our land.

The guests celebrated, drank with one another, and enjoyed themselves. The bagpipes played, and dancing continued all night. But there was no disorder and no brawling because the master and the steward checked in often to ensure things stayed in good order.

After the festivities, the master and Anton both helped the newlyweds generously. From the very first day, Vasyl had several horses, cows, and other livestock, new buildings and several *dzesiacinas*[9] of fertile land."

"But I'm curious," said Pan Zavalnia. "Did Aliuta manage to reform him? You know the saying: he who marries, changes."

"No, sir. People also say: if a foal is born bald, the wolves will devour it with that very baldness."

"What a strange world! Tell me more."

"Vasyl was terribly unlucky on his farm. For a while, it seemed that he had truly changed for the better. But misfortunes began to hound him one after another. If the village herd was driven to pasture, a wolf would come from the forest and snatch a ram – and always, without fail, it was his ram that got taken. This happened several times, as if the wolf knew which animals were his. If geese wandered into the field, a fox would sneak in and kill them – and, again, it was always his geese. Once, one of his cows strayed toward the lake, wandered into a swamp, and by the time help arrived, it had drowned. These endless losses nearly drove him to poverty.

Then came the fire. A forest blaze broke out. Folk from the entire district gathered to help, but could not contain it. Like waves moving across a lake, the flames engulfed the entire forest. The thick branches of fir and pine ignited in a flash, and the smoke rose so dark and dense that you couldn't see or breathe. It blanketed the entire land and sky. We burned our clothes running through the forest, throwing water, beating at the flames – but there was no salvation. Vasyl's house was nearby. A spark landed on the granary, and the grain burned down.

Villagers said it was the revenge of that first spirit, *liasun*, whom Vasyl had struck with a stone long ago, when it was moving animals and birds from one forest to another. An old man had warned him: '*There will be fires and cattle plague in your destiny.*'

Torn by grief, Vasyl began frequenting the tavern. His wife and mother-in-law toiled day and night, hoping to change him. But he returned to his reckless, godless ways.

One evening, Anton, Martin, and others who truly cared for Vasyl came to speak with him. They urged him to bear misfortune with dignity, to have patience, and to trust that God would one day set things right.

A storm rolled in. Vasyl sat by the window, deep in thought. The wind howled outside the wall, and Vasyl murmured, as if in a trance:

'My brother, howling, flew past my house – to roam the wide fields and deep forests. Soon I will follow him there.'

His words chilled the room. Aliuta broke into tears. When Anton warned him he was slipping back into godlessness, Vasyl slammed the door and stormed out.

One late evening, Vasyl ran into his old drinking companions at the tavern. Already quite drunk, he declared:

'I'm broke – but soon I'll be rich. I've got a plan. I'll spend the night at the Serpent's Stone. I'll bow to the demons – and maybe they'll throw some money my way.'

Everyone laughed, mocking him, saying that he didn't have the courage. Vasyl stood up, grabbed his hat, and said:

'I'll prove that I'm not afraid of any ghosts!'

He left the tavern, and walked into the night toward the Serpent's Stone.

He never came back.

Days passed. Then weeks. Then months. Vasyl was gone. Old acquaintances pitied him. His wife and mother-in-law wept for him. No word ever came. No one knew if he was alive or dead.

Rumors swirled. Some claimed he had joined a gang of robbers in the forests near Vialikiya Luki and Pskou. Others said *liasun* had lured him deep into the woods. Still others swore they had heard Vasyl's voice and *liasun's* laughter while out foraging mushrooms.

Many things were said. But one thing was certain: Vasyl disappeared forever.

Old Aryna, watching her daughter cry day after day, wasted away and was buried in the ground. Aliuta remains to this day in the manor – neither wife, nor widow.

"This is what comes of drunkenness and reckless pride," said Pan Zavalnia. "He had a good guardian. He had kind benefactors. He could have lived a peaceful life. But instead he quarreled with *liasun*, chased accursed treasure, shook hands with the whirlwind in the fields and called it brother. You see, Janka, a young man must be cautious in this world. You must think before you act."

"I don't know, Uncle." I replied. "What's the sin in calling the whirlwind a brother? Even now, on a stormy night, as snow beats the windows, if I were to say: '*Fly, brother, to the north – maybe I'll follow you soon*' – what is the harm in that?"

"Call someone a brother only if they are truly like you. As for the whirlwind, the common folk say it's the devil racing through the fields, bringing harm."

As Pan Zavalnia spoke, the traveler looked at me and nodded: "You don't believe because you haven't seen it yourself."

"Well then," said Zavalnia, "let the third man tell us a tale, something else about what once happened in the world. Let us listen."

The Serpent's Crown

"My masters had a huntsman named Siamion. His house stood not far from the estate. Siamion was not bound to perform *corvée* labor, and his sole responsibility was to guard the forest, accompany the master on hunts, and deliver wild game whenever ordered from the manor, especially when guests were expected or before a grand celebration.

One day, the steward came banging on his window and shouting:

'Siamion, the master says you must bring a couple of black grouse, two pairs of capercaillie, and some partridges by Sunday, no matter what. So don't be lazy, take your gun and my pointer, and go hunting.'

Siamion hurried – it was already Wednesday. He grabbed his gun, stopped by the manor, and went deep into the woods with the pointer. But he had picked a poor time for hunting: all day he wandered and saw nothing but woodpeckers tapping away at dry pines. That night, he slept in the forest and nearly froze – it was already autumn. The next morning, before sunrise, he resumed his search, but it was all in vain. Not a single game bird appeared. Only the wind whispered through the trees. Driven by hunger, the dog abandoned him and ran home. Exhausted, sullen, and at a loss of what to do, Siamion headed back.

He sat on a log and thought to himself: *'It will end badly. The master won't believe that I did my best, he will think I'm lazy. I'd kneel before the devil himself if only he'd help me today.'*

No sooner had he thought this than a huge black dog appeared out of nowhere. It sat before him and stared with terrifying eyes. Siamion called to it, but it did not move – only stared. A cold unease crept over him, and chills ran down his spine.

Then, an elderly man emerged from the depths of the forest. His hair was tangled, brows thick, his face weathered by sun and wind. He wore a long robe that reached his feet. He sat down on a stump beside Siamion and said:

'I see your bag is empty, and your face is grim. It looks like the hunt didn't go well.'

'I've wandered the forest for two days,' Siamion replied. 'I'm exhausted, and my dog ran off from hunger. I haven't fired a single shot. Where have all the birds gone? I was ordered to bring game by Sunday, but where will I find it? Things are looking bad.'

'Don't worry,' said the old man. 'Listen carefully. I'll

help you. Tomorrow is September 14. In the evening, head to Elk Mountain. You'll walk through the night – it's far, surrounded by dark forests. You'll reach it at dawn. You'll see the slopes covered with snakes. Don't be afraid, they won't harm you. You'll find the Serpent King among them. Lay a white handkerchief before him, kneel, and bow. He'll toss his golden crown onto the handkerchief and then retreat into his winter shelter with the rest. But mark my words: as you travel to Elk Mountain through the night, fear nothing, marvel at nothing, or all your effort will be in vain.'

Once you get the Serpent's crown, this black dog, which now sits before you, will always meet you and lead you through forest paths whenever you go hunting, and each time you will shoot as much game as you desire. But fear nothing, marvel at nothing, because faltering in heart or spirit will bring you bad luck. Do not let such feelings into your soul.

Saying this, the old man disappeared into the depths of the woods, and the black dog silently followed him.

Siamion stood watching for a long time, then slowly turned homeward. There, he retrieved a white handkerchief, slung his gun over his shoulder, and set out for Elk Mountain. Dusk fell as he entered the forest. Darkness settled among the dense pines and firs. He walked deeper and deeper into the heart of the woods. Night fell. Only a few stars pierced the thick canopy above. He was the only human soul in that vast wilderness, surrounded by the calls of owls and the rustle of startled animals. Yet he was no stranger to the forest at night, so this journey did not frighten him.

But as midnight struck, terrifying creatures appeared on his path. A monstrous bear rose on its hind legs, roaring and ready to charge. A pack of wolves, bristling, with eyes like coals and jaws flecked with blood, encircled him. Yet Siamion walked on fearlessly. Then a giant, taller than the trees, blocked his way. He uprooted a pine tree and brandished it like a bolt of lightning. Still, the huntsman pressed forward, undeterred.

The crescent moon broke through the clouds. In the distance, Siamion saw a palace shimmering with gold and silver. He walked toward it through an enchanted garden where spring and summer coexisted: brilliant flowers bloomed and luscious fruits ripened on the boughs. A cuckoo called mournfully from a tree, a nightingale sang from the bushes, and the thrushes and starlings raised a chorus so clear that he seemed to understand their joyful songs. Girls wearing wreaths of flowers approached him, dancing and beckoning him closer.

But Siamion paid no attention. He did not marvel and did not pause.

The illusion faded. The autumn wind returned. The eastern sky was turning red with dawn. He quickened his pace toward the Elk Mountain.

At last, he reached the designated place. The slope before him writhed with snakes. They hissed but parted to make way for him. The sun was rising. Then he saw it: the largest serpent he had ever laid his eyes on. It moved boldly, and gold gleamed upon its head. Siamion laid the white handkerchief before the great serpent and knelt. The serpent dropped its crown onto the cloth and slithered away, the rest of the serpents following behind, vanishing over the crest of the mountain. Overjoyed, Siamion picked up the golden crown – two glowing leaves fused at the tips – and made his way down.

As he descended, the huge black dog appeared and locked eyes with him, as if beckoning him to follow. Siamion obeyed. The dog would stop now and then, fixing its gaze on a tree. There, hidden among the branches, sat a grouse or capercaillie. Siamion fired a few shots, and soon he had all the birds he needed: black grouse, capercaillie, partridges. As he neared home, the dog halted in the field, watched him for a moment, then disappeared from sight.

The masters praised Siamion for his hunting skills, while the steward and the serfs marveled at his luck. No one could understand how he had managed to return with so much game – and all without a dog.

From that day on, Siamion's reputation grew. He became the most renowned hunter in the district. Each time he went into the woods, the black dog appeared, guiding him. Siamion would return with so much game that there was enough not only for the manor's kitchen, but also for the peasants to sell at the market.

Soon, rumors began to spread. Some said that Siamion was a sorcerer. A few servants claimed they had seen him in the woods, accompanied by a black dog that would linger there after Siamion departed. Akim, who had once been the hunter's friend, decided to find out for himself. One evening, he quietly crept up to Siamion's window. He heard the hunter speaking to someone. When Akim peeked in, he saw Siamion petting the very same black dog that always met him in the forest. At that moment, the dog turned its bloodshot eyes toward Akim and glared. Akim stumbled backward and fled into the night.

For years afterward, the district buzzed with talk. Many speculated that Siamion had taken the devil as his servant. But the gentry only laughed at such tales and believed none of it. Though once, during a hunt, the master noticed that birds seemed to fly directly toward Siamion, and that he never missed a shot.

In a nearby village lived a young woman named Marysia. She was beautiful and pious, the daughter of devout parents. Many young men admired her, and Siamion was no exception. Relying on his reputation and the master's favor, he hoped that she would become his wife.

One day, while out hunting, he saw Marysia walking along the edge of her field, gathering wild strawberries. She wore a flower wreath on her head, and the blossoms suited her so perfectly that she looked like a vision from a dream. Siamion approached and asked for some berries. The girl did not refuse him. The hunter asked if she liked him.

'I've heard people say you use sorcery,' she replied. 'And I fear sorcerers.'

'Oh, no, Marysia, I have never practiced sorcery and do not know anything of such disgraceful things.'

'I wear a cross around my neck that was consecrated during the Jubilee. It can absolve your sins. If what you say is true – kiss my cross.'

'Gladly,' Siamion replied.

No sooner had his lips touched the cross than a huge serpent rose from the grass beside them, lifting its head as if to strike Marysia. She let out a terrified scream. Instinctively, Siamion grabbed a stone and hurled it at the serpent. It hissed, writhed, and vanished into the grass. At that moment, the black dog appeared, barked once, and vanished just as suddenly.

Marysia trembled with fear, pale as a ghost. Siamion gently took her arm and led her home. Afterward, he returned to the forest to hunt, but the black dog was nowhere to be found.

He saw a capercaillie and fired, but instead of a bird, a rotten stump crashed to the ground. Alarmed, Siamion turned back. Things were no better at home. A swarm of snakes slithered out from beneath the hearth and the bench, hissing all the while. In a panic, he opened a chest and took out the Serpent's crown, but it was no longer golden. All that remained were two withered birch leaves. He stood there, stunned, not knowing what to do.

The snakes tormented poor Siamion for a long time. They gave him no peace: not at home, nor anywhere else. When he visited neighbors, a snake would often appear before him, unafraid of anyone around."

At that moment, someone knocked at the gate, and the dogs barked. A servant ran out, then returned and announced that Pan Maragowski had arrived. Pan Zavalnia leapt out of bed, quickly dressed, and went out to greet the guest.

"Will you allow me to stay overnight, Pan Zavalnia," said Maragowski. "In a storm like this one, your house is the only refuge. And these fellows," he glanced at the travellers, "have also taken shelter here and are probably keeping the host well entertained with stories."

One by one, the peasants and servants withdrew to the servants' quarters.

"Forgive the intrusion," Maragowski continued, "but I have someone who can replace any storyteller. My coachman Jakush could go all night telling of his adventures. Just let him unharness the horses first. I'm frozen to the bone!"

Pan Zavalnia immediately ordered his kinswoman to prepare supper.

"Well then, Pan Assessor, perhaps a drop of *harelka*? It will warm you up. I take it you're headed to Polatsk to collect your son for Christmas? That's good, let the lad rest from his studies and return to the family."

"And will you be bringing your children, Stas and Yuzik, home too?"

"I must, I must. I plan to send someone for them the day after tomorrow."

"Let me fetch them for you," said Maragowski.

"I'd be very grateful for your kindness."

Then, turning to me, Pan Maragowski asked if I would come and stay at his house for a few days over Christmas. He said he had invited many young guests and assured me that I would find their company enjoyable.

Supper was served shortly afterward. While speaking with the guest, my uncle kept praising me:

"My dear Janka – he hasn't wasted his years with the Jesuits. He knows a great deal from all kinds of books."

"And does he care for our Belarusian tales?" Maragowski asked.

"When some traveling peasants recently came by and recounted what they'd seen and heard in their lives, I noticed that Janka was hanging onto their every word. He loves such stories. And in truth, the tales were remarkable – about sorcery, and people who made pacts with evil spirits."

"Well, my coachman Jakush has seen and heard a great deal too. Once he starts telling his stories – God only knows where he gets it all. And when it comes to werewolves – he can spot one at a glance. Just before the storm broke, we encountered two wolves standing at the edge of the road. I raised my gun to shoot, but Jakush shouted, 'Don't shoot, sir! They have human souls. If you kill one, his soul will descend into hell without atonement for his sins, and you'll answer for it before God!' He hadn't even finished when the wolves vanished into the woods."

Jakush was called in after supper.

"Well then, Jakush," said Maragowski. "To thank the host for his kindness on this stormy night, tell us something about werewolves, but be sure to tell the truth."

The Werewolf

"Not everything that happens in life is meant for our eyes, but I will tell you a tale that I once heard from a neighbor. It's about a poor soul turned into a wolf by a sorcerer, a soul that suffered terribly, wandering the forests for many years.

Not far from the town of Nievel, there lived a peasant named Marka. People knew him well, some remember him even now. His life was unusual. No one had ever seen him joyful, he was always sullen, restless, as if he had lost something dear. He avoided gatherings. When others went to the fair to enjoy themselves, to dance or meet at the tavern on a day off, Marka remained alone, either at home or wandering out in the fields, sorrowful and withdrawn.

Sometimes people would ask him why he lived like this, and Marka would only say:

'I've endured too much. Nothing in this world interests me anymore. I am dead to the world.'

My neighbor had been close to him, and one day Marka told him the story of his life:

'There was a time when I was full of joy. No festival or celebration passed me by. I lived for music, dancing, and good cheer. But it didn't last long. I met Alena, a beautiful girl, the daughter of well-off parents. I liked her more than any other girl. I visited her parents' house often and did all I could to show her how much I cared.

She grew fond of me too. And that's where my misfortune began.

Many men courted Alena, including one named Ilya. He kept the master informed about everything and anything, always currying his favor. The master gave him special privileges: Ilya could fish in the estate's lakes anytime he pleased, buy livestock cheaply and sell it at a profit. He was often sent into town for errands and each time lined his pockets. Cheating and stealing from the master, he became a rich man. He had many friends and the master's favor. The master believed Ilya was his most loyal servant, and he loved and trusted him more than any of us.

So, this arrogant Ilya sent matchmakers to Alena's parents, but they were turned away. Alena had told her parents she didn't love him.

When he found out, Ilya said:

'It's not about what Alena wants — it's about what the master commands. If she won't agree willingly, she'll obey when ordered.'

He went to the manor and made his case. And just like that, Alena was ordered to marry him.

Knowing how I felt about Alena, the neighbors began to mock me. They laughed at my foolish love, saying I was too bold to hope that someone like me could win her hand. Their ridicule made my blood boil, and I'd reply that Ilya won't enjoy the master's favor for long, that his fortune, built on deceit and theft, will bring him nothing but sorrow, that Alena deserves better – a man who is honest, even if he's poor.

Ilya heard the rumors people were spreading about him and vowed to take his revenge the moment the opportunity presented itself.

The wedding day drew near. Alena's parents, well aware of my love for their daughter, came to speak with me. They told me that the master's will could not be undone, no matter how unjust or cruel it seemed. They begged me to accept my fate, to remain their friend, and to attend the wedding. Reluctantly, I agreed.

The celebration was grand, larger than most fairs. The bride and groom were both wealthy, and people gathered from far and wide. There were songs and dancing in every corner of the yard. Alena wore rich garments and was radiant. Guests surrounded her with congratulations and blessings. Even the master himself attended the festivities. Ilya welcomed him proudly. As the master and Ilya walked among the guests, Ilya caught sight of me. I stood in the background, silent and withdrawn. Nothing about this celebration brought me joy. On the contrary, all the merriment only deepened my sorrow. Ilya glanced at me with a smirk, and walked on with the master.

A while later, Artsiom the Bagpiper, an old man, came over and said:

'Why so sad? Drink some *harelka* with me. Let the sorrow pass, join in the joy like everyone else.'

He took my hand and led me to a table piled with bottles and food. I didn't resist. We each took two shots of *harelka*. Just then, a stranger sitting nearby gave me a sidelong glance, smiled, and said,

'Now he'll dance!'

Suddenly, Artsiom rose and picked up his bagpipes. He began to play, while my heart grew heavier.

Not long after, my neighbor approached. He looked me in the eyes and asked:

'What's the matter? Why is your gaze so terrifying, like that of a beast?'

Another voice followed:

'Look at his eyes – they shine like a wolf's.'

Others nearby eyed me with unease.

I didn't understand what was happening to me. My body trembled uncontrollably. It felt like everyone around meant me harm.

Alena stood nearby, speaking with her mother. When she saw me, her face went pale, and she cried out in fright:

'Ah, what is happening to him! Look, Mother, his eyes are terrifying. He must leave here at once!'

Alena's words struck me like a bolt of lightning. My vision blurred. I nearly fainted. I stumbled away from the feast and ran down the road, not knowing where I was going. On the path, I came upon a woman walking with a small child.

'Ah! Don't look at my child,' she cried. 'You will kill him with your terrifying gaze.'

I fled from the frightened woman and hurried home. When I reached my house, my own dog did not recognize me. I tried to calm it with my voice, but all in vain. I tried to speak, but no words came: a moan like a howl tore from my chest. A piercing dread overcame me. My neighbor's servant looked at me and recoiled in fear.

'Why are your face and hands covered in fur?' he gasped.

I looked down at myself, and, without thinking, fled the house and ran into the field. The grazing animals scattered. Dogs barked and chased me, so I darted into the forest for cover.

I pushed through thickets and stumbled into the

darkness beneath the fir trees. There, I looked again. My hands and my feet – they had become the paws of a wolf. I tried to cry out in anguish, but only another dreadful howl escaped me.

I wandered through mountains and forests in the form of a terrifying beast, but with the mind and heart of a man. I reflected on my past and on my current state, but only found deeper torment. I did not know whether this misery would ever end. I fed myself by finding bird nests in the brush, catching hares and small animals. This was my food. I never approached human dwellings, knowing that people were my enemy, and they would only be too glad to kill me. Still, I never wanted to harm them.

Sometimes on Sundays, I listened to the ringing of church bells and howled, praying to God to take pity on me. Time and again, I tried to sneak into a village at night and approach the church, but the village dogs drove me away. On occasion, I would hear human shouts and gunshots. I would flee back to the forest as fast as I could just to hide myself from the danger.

Each morning, I howled to greet the rising sun. I prayed to the heavens for the strength to survive the day.

In autumn and on long winter nights, I huddled under thick fir branches, trembling with cold. The howling wind would stir memories of my old life. In the dead of winter, I often wandered for days, starving, weak and searching the barren land for something to eat. My sleep was always short. My dreams were always of the past: my parents' home, friends of my youth, kind neighbors, the moment I fell in love with Alena, our conversations, her cheerful eyes, her graceful figure in a festive dress, with a flower wreath on her head. All this came to me in my dreams but seemed so real. Sometimes she appeared uneasy. She would chase me away, just as she had that day at the wedding, when Artsiom tricked me into drinking the enchanted *harelka*. I'd wake from these dreams trembling all over. I lived like this for years.

My hatred for people only deepened the more I thought about their deceit, their cruelty, and how readily they turn on their own kind. I decided to harm them in every way possible. I destroyed their livestock and poultry whenever I could, just as they destroy one another whenever an opportunity arises.

Once – and I remember it as clearly as if it happened today – it was springtime, the forest was turning green, the days were warm and bright. I crept through the edge of the woods toward the village where Artsiom lived. I saw shepherds on a hill tending cattle. Artsiom was plowing a field, and not far off, a young girl was guarding a flock of geese. He called her over by name – Hanka – and sent her home to fetch something. She returned quickly and resumed watching the geese.

I realized she was his daughter. As I watched them from the thicket, a burning rage surged within me. Artsiom, a vile man, had driven me to this state – an outcast, living as a terrifying beast, a wolf. So let him taste that grief himself, let him grieve over the loss of his own child!

I sprang out from the woods and snatched the girl. She screamed. Her father shouted and ran toward us, calling for help. The shepherds yelled. The dogs came after me, sinking their teeth into my flanks until I bled. But nothing could stop me. I held on to her and fled further and further into the depths of the forest. I carried her far, deep into wilderness, where no path could lead her back home.

I left her there.

She lay motionless for a long time. When she came to, she cried, wandering through the forest in desperation.

Her sobs echoed through the pines and fir trees. But I, drunk with vengeance, left her behind to the silence of the woods.

I moved away from the place where the victim of my rage wandered searching for a way out. But my revenge did not bring much satisfaction. Once the fury passed, it struck me that Hanka, an innocent child, was suffering without guilt. I returned to the place where I had left her, but she was nowhere to be found. The forest was silent, her voice no longer echoed through the trees.

An unbearable sorrow came over me. I understood then that revenge could not soothe my torment. Wherever I went, I was pursued by the father's despair, the cries of the child I had abandoned, and the relentless memory of the dogs' fangs tearing into my flesh. I moved from forest to forest, but nowhere did I find peace. Sleep fled from me, and even in the rare moments of rest, I heard again the weeping of the father, the sobbing of the girl, and felt the hounds maul my body.

One day, I came upon a group of peasants who looked vaguely familiar. They rested in the shade of a grove, hiding from the midday sun. Their horses grazed freely nearby, unhitched and unbothered. I crept close and listened from behind a thicket. One of them spoke about me:

'Where is Marka now, wandering in a wolf's skin? Poor soul. He's been suffering for years. If only he could find the witch Aksinia! They say she knows how to turn people into beasts and how to turn them back. No one knows exactly where she lives, but they say it's somewhere in these forests, among these hills.'

Those words brought me hope. I resolved then and there to search every hill and thicket, every shadowed path of this vast wilderness, until I found Aksinia's dwelling. For many days and nights I wandered without rest through the wild and tangled underbrush. From the highest ridges I surveyed the land below, hoping they might conceal her solitary hut.

I ran from the forest into a meadow. The morning was clear and still. I spotted a cat in the grass – white neck and paws, with a striped back of light and dark gray, and bright, lively eyes. It leapt and twisted among the flowers, chasing butterflies. Hidden in the bush, I watched its playful games for a long while. At last, I decided to catch it. I sprang, but it dodged like the wind and darted up the hill. I gave chase, and just as I was about to grasp it, it turned into a magpie and flew low over the grass.

Still in pursuit, I saw a lonely hut. The magpie landed on the roof and became a cat again. Around the house, there were cats everywhere – perched on the roof, sitting on window sills, sprawled in the yard. I realized that this was where the witch Aksinia lived.

I hesitated for a long time, wondering whether to go to her. I knew she would not welcome me in my wolf form. I needed to approach her somewhere on a walk, fall at her feet, and beg her to take pity on me. So I hid in the brush and waited for fate to grant me the right moment.

The sun slipped behind the forests and hills. Twilight crept over the treetops, but the lake nearby, girdled by willows, still glimmered with fading light. Then I saw all the cats – from the roof, yard, and window – run to the meadow, tear grass with their teeth, and in a blink, transform into young women. Some scattered through the bushes, sang songs, and danced in circles. Others gathered flowers and wove wreaths. I too ran into the meadow. I saw a plant with tiny blue blossoms. No sooner had I picked and swallowed it than I became a man once more. Unspeakable joy overwhelmed me as I joined the carefree *rusalkas*, danced with them, rejoicing, forgetting all about my curse.

The revelry lasted late into the night. The birds had gone silent, save for the occasional call of an owl. One large owl flew onto the witch's roof, its eyes glowing as it let out a laugh and wailed like a newborn child. The forest began to rustle. The lake water splashed against the shore.[10] The *rusalkas* screamed: '*Midnight! Midnight!*' – and in that instant, they all turned into cats and ran to Aksinia's yard. Some leapt to the roof, others slipped through the windows. A wolf once again, I ran to the forest, curled under a fir tree, and brooded. I mourned that my humanity had lasted only a moment. I resolved to return, if only to forget my fate for a little while longer.

I waited until the following evening. Again the cats transformed into girls, and I became human. I joined them once more, full of joy, and time passed unnoticed. But one of them eyed me with disdain and said:

'I don't like you.'

'Why don't you like me?' I asked, stepping closer.

'Because I saw you change into a wolf, and I hate wolves. It is because of a wolf that I am cursed.'

'How so?'

'I used to live with my parents and tend our geese in the fields. One day, a wolf snatched me and carried me off into the woods. He left me there and vanished. I wandered the forest, weeping and screaming, not knowing which way to go. Suddenly, at the sound of my voice, Aksinia appeared, first as a black bird, then as a woman. She took my hand and said: '*You will not leave these woods. Wild beasts will tear you apart. You might as well come live with me. Life is sweet here – songs and dancing every night. You are young, and probably love to dance.*' At first, I didn't want to listen to her. But I knew that no one would help me in that wilderness, so I gave in. I don't remember how I ended up in this house. Oh, cursed werewolf! Why didn't you tear me apart in the forest? Better that than to live as a beast by day and forget my suffering for only a few fleeting hours.'

As I listened to Hanka's lament, I trembled and turned into a wolf once more. And in my ears echoed the father's despair, the sobs of the poor girl, and the dogs tearing into my flesh. I dashed into the forest and ran all night without rest, unable to escape my memories and those dogs.

Life became unbearable. I could find no peace. I wandered in anguish through the forests and hills without hope of deliverance from my torment.

One day, I passed by a field where plowmen rested under a birch. A priest rode up the road, dismounted, and joined them. They talked for a long time about different spiritual matters. The priest spoke of peace and kindness, urged them to forgive, to never seek revenge, for vengeance offends God and lowers men to the level of beasts. But charity, he said, draws down divine mercy.

Hearing this, I vowed not only to cease harming humans, but to serve and protect them however I could. Perhaps, I thought, God would show me mercy too, for my soul remained immortal.

Days passed. I wandered, pondering: what good can I do in the form of this despised wolf? As soon as I approach a human dwelling, people shout and set their dogs on me, forcing me to escape to the forest as fast as possible.

Yet I did not give up. I drove away foxes that crept toward geese and turkeys that have been left carelessly in the field. When bears neared the cattle, I rushed ahead to scatter the herd to safety and alert the shepherds. A few times, I rescued a ram that had been snatched from the herd of some poor widow. Living this way, my thoughts grew calmer. I even slept a little better, though not by much. Pleasant dreams carried the visions of my former human life.

Then came August. The weather was fine. I roamed my native region when the rye stood golden in the fields. And there I saw Alena. She was reaping grain in her field. Beside her, a small boy lay asleep on the sheaves. I felt joy, watching her living a happy, peaceful life with her family. God had blessed their household, and the rye had yielded well.

Suddenly, a wolf burst from the forest and snatched the child. Alena ran after it.

'Save my child!' she screamed and fainted.

I leapt after the wolf, overtook it, and wrested the boy from its jaws. He was unharmed. I brought him back to his mother. Villagers rushed to help and marvelled at the sight. But I fled to the forest.

A deep calm came over me. I lay down beneath a tree and drifted off to sleep. In my dream, I returned to the days of my happy youth. I was light as a bird, soaring through gardens more beautiful than any I'd ever seen. Birds sang in radiant plumage more striking than our spring flowers. Clear spring waters sparkled. Trees were in fragrant bloom, and some bore ripe fruit. On a hilltop, great lily-cups opened wide, releasing their sweet scent. Just as I reached to pluck one, Hanka appeared before me, wearing a gown as white as the lily itself, and said:

'Do not pick them. I planted these lilies on my grave, and watered them with my tears'.

Saying this, she vanished.

I drifted from the garden into wild emptiness, wandered through ancient pines, and came to a tall mountain. I wanted to climb to the very top to survey the surroundings and see the village where my parents' house had once stood, but an abyss blocked my way.

Here, I met a *volat*.[11] He took me by the hand,

commanded me to follow him, and led me through the woods to a vast crossroads in the field, where many travelers rode and walked. We climbed a hill to a grave with a wooden cross and a spade stuck in the ground. The *volat* ordered me to dig up the grave and retrieve the corpse. Frightened, I obeyed, and dug up a huge skeleton.

'This will be your body,' he said to me. 'You will lie in it and weep, until you are called to a new life...'

I trembled with fear, begged him for mercy, but the *volat* pushed me. I fell into the grave, onto the chest of the corpse. Wrestling with death, I woke up.

I was a man. I was wearing the same clothes I had worn to Alena's wedding. It seemed unreal. I did not dare move, fearing the dream would dissolve. At last, I lifted my eyes to the sky and thanked God for having mercy on me.

I rose from the earth with joy beyond words. The trees, the birds – everything seemed to rejoice with me. How sweet is God's mercy! How wretched is the fate of a man when it becomes like that of a beast!'"

As Jakush finished speaking, the rooster crowed a second time. From his pocket, Pan Maragowski took out an old-fashioned watch that resembled a flattened globe.

"Oh," he said, "it's after one. Well, sir, it's time for rest. We can't listen to all of Jakush's tales in one night – he's got enough to last us a month. And he would gladly talk until dawn."

"Thank you very much, Master Assessor, for giving me the pleasure. I'll admit it: such tales give me real delight, especially when told so well. Jakush is a clever man with an extraordinary memory. He didn't miss a single detail of poor Marka's life. But Pan Assessor, don't leave early tomorrow. The wind is still howling outside, and there might well be another blizzard by morning."

"A storm's not so terrible by day," replied the guest. "We'll find our way. Good night, sir."

Jakush withdrew to the servants' quarters. Maragowski retired to his bed, which had long since been prepared for him. After wishing my uncle and the guest good night, I went to my room. The candles were extinguished. All was silent, save for the wind wailing at the walls, and the faint chirping of a cricket beneath the stove...

END OF VOLUME ONE

VOLUME TWO

MEMORIES OF VISITING MY HOMELAND

The land where one spent the joyful days of youth, where conversation and leisure were filled with sincere warmth and the trust of kind souls, mentors, and companions – that land glows brightest in memory when one lives far away in foreign places. It seems as though the golden age has never ended there, that wondrous time before misfortune and sorrow. In those memories, the rivers flow with milk and honey. Who does not yearn for home from afar? Home, the dwelling place of our thoughts and desires. Oh, if only I had wings!

Once, I too hurried from the North, toward the banks of the Dzvina, to see again the sights etched so vividly into my soul. As I approached my homeland, it seemed the oaks and pines bowed in greeting, welcoming back an old friend. The distant shimmer of hills and lakes stirred recollections of long ago. Here flows the swift Drysa River, hurrying to meet the Dzvina through dense forests and sandy groves, awakening memories and stirring thought. There once stood a village upon this bank, now long vanished, consumed by fire, overgrown with grass. Time has erased it from the earth, but not from my soul. It still bears witness to the year when locals fled into the forest to escape the storms of the great Napoleonic War.

The evening was calm, the clouds in the western sky tinged rose. Supper was cooking over a fire on the sandy bank of the Drysa. Pine logs blazed, their flame dancing in the mirror of still water. Gathered in a circle, neighbors and kin sat together, speaking of the French army's arrival in Polatsk and of battles fought across White Rus. There was sorrow, compassion, and trembling hope in their words. Meanwhile, I was absorbed in the silver flash of a fish leaping through the quiet water, the cries of birds from the forest, and a squirrel that, leaping from branch to branch, lured me deeper into the woods. As I chased it, a low rumble thundered from beyond the forest, where the pink clouds thickened in the west. It roared without pause, as though from beneath the earth. I ran back and asked:

"What is that? Surely a storm is coming?"

My father broke the silence and said:

"That is the storm in Kliastitsy, on St. Petersburg road. It has come here from distant lands, casting hailstorms of lead. It's headed north, but in vain – strong winds and frosts will meet it there."

Worry shadowed every face. Tears in their eyes, frightened women whispered prayers, certain that every blast took dozens of lives. They trembled as if Judgment Day had come. That night passed without sleep, full of conversation. The old men recalled days long past and speculated about what might lie ahead, their thoughts flickering with hope. I wished I had wings, so that I might glimpse the theater of war and the valour of our soldiers with my own eyes.

And nearby, ever vivid, lay the hills and meadows overgrown with memory, where silver streams ran bright and lakes mirrored the sky. Athos! Far away now in foreign lands, do you still think back to the beauty of your native land? Do memories of our adventures, dreams, and conversations come to mind? Every path here was sacred, every corner filled with gods of ancient Greece and Rome. Here, was our New Arcadia. Here, the naiads crowned their brows with lilies. Here, the nymphs danced in the meadows, and the goat-footed satyrs roamed the woods. Oh, blissful youth! To the young, the world is paradise, wonder abound. Ancient Greece and all of antiquity were reborn in our dreams and words. Do you remember? That mount was Olympus, abode of Apollo and the Muses. That flowering plain we named the Vale of Tempe. And yonder rise Thermopylae, where King Leonidas and his Spartans perished, facing down the vast Persian army.

We sought to bring the wonders of the whole world to this little corner of earth.

Do you remember that sunset we once witnessed together? What a sky it was! Thick clouds stretched across the horizon, their edges aglow with ruby light. Fire poured down like a waterfall. Golden rays shot upward between violet shadows. We stood spellbound as the clouds gathered. The sun vanished. Lightning flashed. Thunder growled across the west. Looking up, the shepherd said, "*A stormy night is coming*," and hurried back to the village with his herd. As for us, we sought shelter in a house known for the kindness and hospitality of its master.

Oh, what dread the Belarusian peasant feels during a stormy night! When the fields are ripening, it threatens to wipe away a year's labour in a single hour. The peasant greets it with prayers on his lips and tolling church bells, his eyes turned skyward.

Inside the peasant home, tension hangs in the air. Cats and dogs are driven out, for it is believed that the evil spirit flees thunder by hiding in their bodies. Consecrated herbs are thrown onto the coals. After every flash of lightning, a trembling prayer is whispered aloud.

All around is darkness. The sky and the earth are one. Like a fiery serpent, lightning streaks from cloud to cloud, thunder shakes the walls, hail and rain lash the windows, and the wind howls like a demon. Midnight passes. No one sleeps. The entire household prays. Alina stands at her mother's side, her face white as a lily. Like an angel of comfort, calm and full of faith, she speaks of God's will and mercy.

Otto! Do you remember that night? You heard neither thunder nor wind, your soul was full of sunlight, for the brightness of Alina's eyes met yours and pierced straight into your heart. That night was a bright dream. And now, far from your father's land, do those eyes still visit you in dream or sorrow? Truly, time destroys everything.

The stars returned to the heavens, and the wind chased the last clouds over the forested hills. Dawn reddened the sky, and the sun rose. Roofs had been torn from homes, ears of grain lay flattened in the fields, meadows were littered with sand washed down from the hills, as tall pines and elms lay fallen like Greek warriors after Thermopylae. The storm had left its terrifying footprint everywhere the eye could see.

I came upon an ancient oak, a hundred years old — still standing, unbowed by wind or rain. The storm had not felled this noble hero! It will spread its branches yet, offering rest and shade to the wanderer beneath the summer sun. That oak remembers our ancestors and will shelter our descendants.

On holidays, peasants gather here. I watched their merriment. They brought tables from their homes, and the elders sat with *harelka*, recalling their lives, their neighbors, their masters, and the land watered with their own sweat, which sparsely rewarded them for their toil. In the cool shade, a bagpiper inflated his goatskin bag, and the youth began to whirl in dance and courtship. Sometimes, a soldier passing through would join the feast, forget his distant homeland, eager to dance with a local beauty, and in that moment, he is the happiest man alive.

Not far from there, by the Drysa River, stands the Krasnapol[12] estate, surrounded by forests on all sides. Local tales say that long ago, in pagan times, a prince named Boy lived there, a mighty strongman, an *asilak,*[13] famed throughout White Rus. He ruled these wild territories from the Drysa's banks. His pastime was the hunt: bow in hand, he roamed the forest chasing moose and wild game. He had two loyal hounds: one named Staury, the other Haury. They were strong and clever – even the fiercest bear stood no chance, they would tear it apart like a hare.

If, during a hunt, the prince became lost or surrounded by enemies, he would release his dogs, and they would slay them and guide Boy safely home.

The dogs saved him many times and were his dearest companions. Boy ordered his subjects to honour them as the highest members of his retinue. And when they died of old age, holidays were proclaimed in their memory.

People gathered at the site of their burial, bringing food and drink. They feasted until late into the night. The scraps and bones were burned in the fire as they chanted the dogs' names: '*Staury! Haury!*' – calling their spirits from the netherworld.

Even now, some villagers secretly honour this rite each year, just before Pentecost. The head of the household bends under the table with a morsel of food in hand and calls out thrice: *'Staury, Haury, come, come to us!'*

They say that sometimes, huge black dogs appear at the call only to vanish at once. Perhaps it is an illusion. Perhaps it is devilry. Or perhaps it is merely the imagination of the Belarusian soul, which sees spirit and wonder in every shadow – a spirit in water,[14] in the land,[15] in the household,[16] in the forest,[17] and a spirit guarding ancient treasures.

POLATSK

I passed through several forests and saw the city of Polatsk spread across a broad, open plain. The towers of St. Stephen's Cathedral and St. Sophia Cathedral on Castle Hill rose high into the mist, their silhouettes seemingly reaching for the clouds, towering above the city and its surroundings. Reflecting on the past, I conjured their image in my mind – a heaviness settled over my heart, and with tearful eyes I greeted those ancient walls.

Immersed in sorrowful recollections, I approached the city. The gardens of Spas[18] reminded me of the spring promenades, a kind of theater among thick lindens and beneath the open sky. There, under the careful eye of our teachers, a youthful imagination first learned to recognize the Creator of this world, His providence over all living things, and to admire the beauty of heaven and earth.

Not far from the Palata River stands the brick church of St. Francis Xavier. There lie the graves of the virtuous Jesuit fathers, secular scholars, and elders with whom I was once acquainted – dear friends of my youth. An indescribable feeling overtook me. My soul looked upon them as though they were angels ascending to heaven. I offered up my prayers and stood for a long time in contemplation, absorbing the silence of that sacred place. The old times, old customs, and old rites stirred again in memory. O joy! Those better days sleep still in their native land. But I? To what shore shall I sail, where shall I find rest after this stormy voyage?

On a wide plain beyond the Palata there lies a small lake, its surface catching the sun like polished glass. This is Valovae Lake. It is said to have once lain within the very heart of the city. Before the baptism of the land, the sanctuaries of *Piarun*[19] and *Baba Yaga*[20] stood on its banks, but no trace of them remains.

In the vicinity of Polatsk, every corner has its place in the historical memory of the people. On the far side of the Dzvina, a few *versts* away, stands the modest church of St. Casimir. Local legend says that St. Casimir appeared here before the army of his countrymen and led them across the swift river. Even now, people point to the sandy underwater ridge at Struny, where the army is said to have crossed. There is also the Church of Barys and Hleb,[21] allegedly built by the saints themselves through miraculous means. And Ekimania, the estate of the Belikovich family, right on the steep banks of the Dzvina, reveals a view of Polatsk like something from a magical panorama. During the spring flood, one can hear songs and music rising from the boats sailing toward Riga. This land still guards a trove of ancient stories, passed down in local folk tales.

So much has changed in the city during my eighteen years away. Only the old ramparts still remain, thick with green grass, and the two rivers that converge here still flow in their same banks. Here and there stand scorched brick ruins and blackened hearths, stark reminders of the fires that have so often swept through this place. Lost in thought, I wandered the streets like a stranger. From the old Jesuit cathedral tower, the clock struck – and that sound gripped my heart like the voice of a dear old friend. I had known it since childhood: it had once marked our hours of study and rest, roused me for work at dawn. But now it seemed to echo only one message with its chime: *fugit irreparabile tempus.*[22]

The bells of the churches also stirred my soul, bringing the past to life once more. Athos, do you remember that great bell that summoned us to lessons in both sacred and secular studies, and to daily prayer in the chapel? That bell is silent now. It rings only in our hearts and memories.

The sweetest time in life is the spring of one's youth, when the blossoms of the mind first open, when imagination soars free, and the heart is filled with great hopes, still untroubled by the tempests that so often shatter human dreams. It is a time of sacred joy, when a youth returns home after study, filled with thoughts of teachers and friends.

Easter was near. Oh, how fervently we fulfilled our religious duties! Those days of recollection and preparation for Easter confession brought such peace to the soul. On Holy Thursday, each class, under the guidance of a teacher, visited the prisons and hospitals offering charity and alms to the poor. Anyone untouched by such acts of love for one's neighbor must have a heart of stone.

At Jesuit schools, holidays began on the first of August. After exams, the students were promoted to higher grades, and the names of the most distinguished pupils were published in little books to incentivize further learning.

On that day, Polatsk became like the capital of all White Rus. The clatter of carts rang through the streets. Guests arrived: some to attend the feast day of St. Ignatius Loyola,[23] others to thank the teachers who had educated their children, and others still for the theatrical performance that the Polatsk Academy[24] students would stage. Merchants from everywhere gathered to sell their wares at high profit.

Before Christmas, there were exams and competitions[25] for the youngest students. In front of parents, guardians, and teachers, they quizzed each other on Latin grammar. Rewards were laid out before them. The event always opened with these memorable words:

> "*Domini emule, a quo incipiemus?*"
> "*A signo Sancti Crucis.*"
> "*Quid est signum Sancti Crucis?*"
> "*Est munimentum corporis et animae.*"
> "*Faciamus signum Sancti Crucis.*"
> "*Faciamus.*"[26]

At that, everyone knelt. After the prayer, the debates and demonstrations of learning began.

Otto! Recall those happy days. Recall our friends, our companions, the teachers who spoke to us so often of faith, of God, of Christian duty and the sciences. Back then, the world seemed like paradise, for we saw only kindness, sincerity, and loyalty in those around us. But now... we have read the pages of misfortune. Autumn has come, and the bitter fruit has ripened. I often repeat this verse to myself:

> '*I recall when the bell would ring,*
> *Calling our friends to gather near;*
> *The heart knew neither pain nor sting,*
> *Nor fate, nor worldly fear.*
> *But alas, how time has flown –*
> *That true joy now a phantom seems.*
> *The bell has stilled its cheerful tone,*
> *It tolls now only in our dreams.*
> *I sailed the world's unsteady tide,*
> *Not seeking fame or golden prize –*
> *But because all men must ride*
> *The sea beneath these mortal skies.*'

When I was correcting the proofs of this very page, I was overcome with feeling. My thoughts, borne on the wind of memory, flew again to the clear waters of the Palata. I remembered the noble towers of my native city. I saw once more the modest roof of that beloved school, its long corridors, the flicker of candlelight in the cathedral, the hymns echoing beneath its ornamented ceiling, the organ's sacred swell stirring piety in the soul.

I remembered the town square filled with people, the solemn procession of the Holy Child, the familiar music rising from the church porch. I remembered our good teachers and loyal friends, the tall rampart and the bridge across the quiet river. I saw once again the lonely pillar amidst golden wheat, the sandy road to Spas, the innocent games on the green meadow, the warmth of the radiant sun, the cool hush of the pinewood, the open blue sky – and the soul, so pure, so cloudless, so untarnished. A happy soul! That, that was the cradle of my youth![27]

FISHERMAN RODZKA

In quiet swamps, devils are born.
- A Belarusian proverb

My uncle looked out the window at the lake and said to me:

"Why hasn't Rodzka brought the fish yet? It's nearly Christmas Eve. On his way back from Polatsk, Pan Maragowski might stop by for the holidays, and other neighbors might visit as well."

"He likely had no luck. I remember hearing fishermen complain that the catch has been poor lately, perhaps he got his hopes up for nothing."

"Oh no, Janka! You know him well – he's exceptional at his craft, and never comes home empty-handed. He knows all the underwater hideouts. It's as if he can see through the ice, knowing exactly where the bream, pike, and other fish lie in wait. In autumn, when the sky is black with clouds and the wind howls, I watch from the window as he casts his net into the lake. The storm tosses up foam-covered waves, and yet he, like a sea diver, reappears atop the water in his boat, vanishing again amid the roaring swells. Only white terns circle above him. Even in the worst of storms, he's brought me fish and returned home safely – and he lives on an island so far from here that you can barely make it out on the clearest day."

"He is certainly brave – but has he himself ever faced misfortune?"

"He himself has never faced trouble. But he has saved many inexperienced fishermen from perishing in storms. The stories people tell of him are so fantastical, they're hard to believe. Some say Rodzka, knowing which fish are best caught in stormy weather and which in calm, can summon wind to stir the lake when needed, or send it away to still the water, then sail home across the mirror-like surface, his boat full of fish, singing as he goes. For this, some say he is a sorcerer."

"Do evil spirits really serve him? After all, uncle, you yourself believe that sorcerers exist."

"I do. But Rodzka is a good man, so people say. Sorcerers are in league with evil and bring harm, but I've never heard of him harming anyone. He goes to church every Sunday and prays devoutly. He's a subject of the Jesuit fathers."

As we spoke, the dog barked in the yard. Zavalnia looked out the window.

"Well," he said, "speak of the devil, and he appears. At last, Rodzka is bringing the fish."

Rodzka entered the room holding a bag made of old fishing net, frozen stiff from the cold, as if woven from wire. The silver scales of freshly caught fish gleamed through the mesh.

Rodzka was short, with a pale, gaunt face, and damp, disheveled hair hanging over his shoulders. At that moment, he resembled Triton himself, risen from the depths, blowing his conch in the company of Neptune or Amphitrite. The fisherman bowed and poured the fish onto the floor.

"I've been waiting a long while," said Zavalnia. "Watching from the window, beginning to worry that some misfortune had befallen you."

"Thank God, my efforts have not been in vain today. It's a busy time – everyone wants fish, and I had deliveries to make to the good lords and neighbors."

"But in winter," I asked, "do you really summon the wind to help the catch? They say *vadzianik* obeys you, as do the wind and the waves."

He looked at me with a smile and replied:

"My messengers are the white terns who bring on the wind and the storm, but they are not here now. They have flown to warmer lands. No, sir, do not believe everything people say. The Jesuits do not teach us to summon evil spirits for help. God helps those who work hard, and I want to know no secrets that burden the soul."

My uncle interrupted:

"Janka is still young. He doesn't believe in magic, he was only teasing."

Zavalnia then ordered the fish gathered from the floor, paid Rodzka, seated him on the bench, and served him *harelka* and bread.

After eating and drinking, Rodzka glanced at me and said:

"Young people don't yet know what happens in the world, and so they don't believe. I could tell you much, but it's late. The sun is low. I must be off."

Sensing he might have a story to tell, my uncle poured him another glass and said:

"Tell us something interesting, something you've seen yourself, or heard from the old folks. The sky is clear now, and there's no wind – you won't lose your way. Even if a snowstorm rises, every clump of reeds will show you the way, for you've known every inch of this lake since childhood."

Rodzka was now a little drunk, his face had softened, his cheeks grown ruddy.

"All right. I'll tell you how evil spirits began to breed in these parts because of magic and malicious folk."

"Can evil spirits breed like animals?" I asked.

"They can. For human malice is their finest food. In

these parts, the old folks still remember better times, when there were many good, diligent, and honest people. Back then, every landowner had enough land, and the land gave forth an abundant yield. There was enough bread, and the livestock thrived. The lakes and rivers teemed with fish, and the youth, playing by the shore with nothing more than willow rods and twine, hauled in so many fish they could hardly carry them home.

There were few lords in those days, and they were pious men who lived far beyond the Dzvina. But now? Now every petty half-noble, master of a few crumbling huts, drives about in carriages, dresses in foreign finery, scheming to squeeze the last coin from his land, selling the livestock, the bread, and the very sweat of the peasants' brow. Come spring, the poor folk have nothing left but bitter lupines to eat.

And to wring even more profit from the lakes, these lords invite the Astashou fishermen each winter. People say those men send an evil spirit under the ice to herd fish into their nets. They've emptied the waters, corrupted the youth, teaching them wicked songs, godless ways, and witchery. The priests and elders warned us, but no one listened. And so, evil spirits multiplied, so many that they began to show themselves even in broad daylight before entire crowds of people, something unheard of before.

I'll tell you now of a marvel once seen on Lake Rasony, which lies not far from our own Nieszczarda, no more than thirty *versts*, as you know. I heard it from a fellow who, like me, serves the Jesuits.

One spring evening, a group of peasants was returning home from *corvée*. The sun had not yet set, but with Sunday drawing near, the steward had dismissed them early. The evening was calm, the sky clear. Cuckoos called mournfully from the tall birches. Larks trilled above. In the brush, nightingales sang. The young men rode on horseback, laughing and recounting their adventures. The elders talked of farms and fences. Then, suddenly, they heard music – beyond the woods, someone was playing the bagpipes and singing so loudly that the echo rolled across the fields. And they all knew the song:

I played the bagpipes, eh oh,
On the priest's meadow, eh oh,
But it wasn't a bagpipe, eh oh,
It was a gallows, eh oh,
It hanged me, eh oh,
In a foreign land, eh oh.

They came through the woods and stood upon the banks of Lake Rasony. The water was calm, still as glass. Trees reflected as if in a painting. But in the middle of the lake – may God save us! – a black demon sat upon the water, coal-black and terrible, with long arms and a massive head. He sat cross-legged, playing the bagpipes, and sang that dreadful tune in a voice that chilled the blood. Muttering prayers, the peasants fled along the shoreline. The sun had already dipped, but the sound of those bagpipes and infernal singing followed them for a long time.

There is also the story of the small lake near Halubova manor, surrounded by marsh on all sides. Many brave men have tried to reach it in summer, thinking they could walk across its mossy surface like canvas, only to vanish without a trace into the abyss beneath. Hunters look wistfully at the flocks of ducks that rest there, knowing they'll never reach them. There is a legend about that small lake.

Once upon a time, it had been a great lake, teeming with fish. On a nearby hill stood a village, and by the roadside, a tavern. Every winter, the Astashou fishermen came to fish the lake. But one year, the estate owner denied them permission and allowed only his own peasants to fish. Our fishermen toiled for days but wasted their efforts – every haul brought just a paltry few, barely worth the net. After much discussion, they agreed on a plan: they would try casting their net at midnight. Perhaps, under cover of darkness, fortune might favor them.

This happened during *Kalyady*, the midwinter festival, when peasants from nearby villages gathered at the tavern each evening to celebrate – revelry that continued until the Feast of the Three Kings.

Right at midnight, clouds overtook the sky, and the wind began to blow in from the fields. Inside the tavern, music played, the youth sang and danced, and the elders sat at the table swapping tales over a glass of *harelka*. Suddenly, a fisherman burst through the door, snow-covered from head to toe, his coat and sleeves frozen stiff.

'Brothers, stop your dancing and singing,' he cried. 'Hurry to the lake! So many bream have filled the net that we cannot pull it out. Come help us, and you'll be rewarded.'

No sooner had he said this than a dreadful moan echoed from the darkest corner behind the woodstove: '*Oh! Oh! What a pity!*'

And with that, a terrible monster flew out the door, sending the tavern into chaos. Some guests began to pray and hurried home together; others rushed out with the fisherman toward the lake.

But they arrived too late – the devil had already done his work. They hauled in the net, but it had been sliced clean through, as if by a blade, and not a single fish remained.

They stood in silence, the truth of it was clear to

everyone. Then someone spoke up:

'The evil spirit won't win. Listen to me: tomorrow we'll repair the net properly, ask the priest to bless both the water and the net, and the day after, with God's help, we'll cast again. The devil won't pull the same trick twice.'

Not far from the lake, atop a hill, stood a fisherman's hut with a thatched roof. That night, while his family slept, the fisherman sat repairing the net, brooding over the terrible events.

The forest nearby rustled in the storm. The wind howled against the walls, and soon a fierce blizzard rose, piling snowdrifts high around the hut, burying the windows. The black dog at the fisherman's feet growled low, as if sensing an evil presence, and the fisherman was seized by an inexplicable fear.

Then he heard someone knocking at the window and shouting:

'Neighbor! Neighbor! Have mercy! Lend me your cart, there is trouble in my house! I must bring my children to their grandparents, it's not far!'

'In such a storm?' the fisherman called back. 'I wouldn't send a dog out into this weather, and you mean to go with children? Come in and warm yourself, spend the night here. You can set out in the morning.'

'I cannot wait till morning, and the storm does not frighten me. Have pity, don't refuse me! I'll return the cart before sunrise, and repay you as best I can.'

'Well, if it's so urgent, then take it.'

The fisherman opened the window and looked out into the yard, but saw neither the neighbor nor the cart – only the wind was swirling the snowdrifts across the ground.

Startled by how swiftly the man had vanished – managing to harness the horse and depart faster than he himself had opened the window – he sat back down on the bench, wondering what misfortune had befallen the neighbor, what trouble could drive a man to travel with children in such a storm. Lost in his thoughts, he put out the fire, lay down on the bench, and soon fell into an uneasy sleep.

His sleep did not last long, for even in his dreams, he saw the great catch from the lake slip through the torn net and vanish into the depths. With a jolt, he awoke and roused his wife, asking her to warm his breakfast, for he needed to meet his friends and return to the lake.

When he stepped out into the yard, he found his cart covered in thick frost, and inside it lay a giant bream. He stood staring in disbelief. What kind of apparition was this? He called his wife and the rest of the family, and told them about the neighbor who had come at midnight to borrow the cart. They all listened, amazed, but no one could explain what had happened.

When the sun rose, the fishermen gathered. The parish priest arrived and blessed the lake and the net with holy water. Crowds from nearby villages gathered to watch. They stood off the ice as the net was cast, and when it was pulled from the depths there wasn't a single fish inside. A silence fell. Everyone stood baffled. Then one fisherman, troubled, recounted how the evil spirit had come at night and borrowed his cart, likely using it to carry away all the fish to some hidden place.

The men gathered their net, and, one by one, they slowly dispersed.

From that day onward, no one dared cast a net in that lake again. It was left abandoned, and over time it grew thick with algae, its surface smothered in green moss. Only a single patch of water remains visible, glimmering faintly from afar."

"Have you heard anything," said Zavalnia, "about Hluhoe Lake? It's surrounded on all sides by dense forest, not far from the river that flows from Nieszczarda into the Drysa. They say that even in the clearest weather, you won't see the reflection of sun, clouds, stars, or moon in that lake. Its waters are always murky, and at night, terrible apparitions appear.

One hunter told me that while pursuing capercaillies, he once spent the night near its shore. He claimed he saw monsters creeping along the bank, and bubbles on the water morphing into long, shadowy shapes like great arrows streaking across the surface on fiery wings. And when the rooster crowed from some distant village, the apparitions dissolved, vanishing into the mist."

"Oh! I know that lake well," said Rodzka, "and I've heard many tales of its strange wonders. It is an eerie place. When women go gathering mushrooms or berries near its shores, they always try to return home well before dusk, for something terrible laughs and groans there after sunset.

I will tell you of some unheard-of wonders, but mark my words, these things truly happened in this world.

Not far from here, on the western shore of Lake Nieszczarda, atop a hill where an estate still stands, there once lived a very wealthy nobleman, Pan Z. All the wild forests stretching up to the very banks of the Drysa belonged to him. That same lake, Hluhoe Lake, located in the dark woods, was already being overtaken by weeds. No boat had floated on it in living memory, and no fisherman dared cast a net there.

One winter, Pan Z. decided to try his luck. He summoned his senior fisherman and said:

'Tomorrow, gather the men, take the net to Hluhoe

Lake, and cast it. No one has fished there in years – it must be teeming with all kinds of fish.'

'We can't do that, sir,' said the fisherman. 'I've never fished there myself, but I've heard the bottom is tangled with roots. We risk destroying the net.'

'Where would the roots come from if there was never a forest in the lake? Don't believe such nonsense. You'll cast the net tomorrow.'

'Then let the master first ask the priest to bless the lake and the net,' said the fisherman. 'Because – and this is God's own truth – the devil has long made his home in that lake.'

'Have you seen him yourself, to speak such foolishness?'

'Sir, ask the people. Everyone knows of the strange happenings there: monsters slinking along the shores, moaning and laughter rising from beneath the water. Even the bravest souls flee that place come sunset.'

'I don't want to hear another word of your superstitions. You'll fish there tomorrow, no matter what.'

'Without the blessing of the water?' the fisherman asked.

'There is no need,' the nobleman replied.

The fisherman scratched his head and walked slowly back to the village. He gathered his companions and told them what had been ordered. The men discussed and argued long into the evening, fearful of bringing misfortune upon themselves. But the master's will had to be done.

The next morning, the fishermen arrived at Hluhoe Lake and stopped in the middle of a small, circular clearing. Around them, dark forest loomed – fir and pine, their snow-laden branches bent low, encircling the lake like white walls. In summer, no wind stirred waves here; in winter, not even the fiercest gusts could whirl the snow. The day was cloudy, and a heavy silence hung in the air. The fishermen removed their hats, murmured their prayers, chose a place to break the ice, and began their work.

They cast the net, and as they pulled it back, a strange rustling rose beneath the ice, a hissing, a wild squealing, as though thousands of creatures were locked in combat. The fishermen shivered with unease, their skin crawling with goosebumps. Still, they kept together, thinking perhaps they'd caught a tangled mass of eels.

But when they finally hauled the net to the surface – God save us from ever seeing such a thing! – it was crawling with tiny demons.

Some were shaped like crayfish, covered in coarse black fur; others looked like spiders the size of cats; still others resembled puppies, but with unnaturally long legs. Words fail to describe the horror. Rats, lizards, bats, moles – all horrid beasts – crawled across the ice and tumbled through the snow, shrieking and hissing and letting out blood-curdling cries.

The fishermen realized that they had stumbled upon a devil's nest.

Unable to bear the sight, they dropped the net and fled."

"Did the Astashou fishermen ever fish in that lake?"

"Even our great-grandfathers had no memories of anyone fishing there."

"Then who brought the evil spirits there?"

"You know the organist from Rasony, a good and learned man. He often spoke to us of miraculous things found in the holy books, of how God created this world. Once, on a market day, he invited us to his home. We sat around his table, each with a glass of *harelka*, and in the course of our conversation, he said something I've never forgotten.

'The great sin of Adam,' he told us, 'was that he listened to Eve and tasted the apple from the forbidden tree. For that, God cursed the earth. But even greater was the sin of Cain, who raised his hand against his brother.'

Oh! How many Cains there are now in this world, killing their brothers. Many sinners hid in those dark woods near Hluhoe Lake. Pan Z. brought them there, criminals from distant corners of the earth, where men ride dogs instead of horses and know neither God, nor faith, nor love for their fellow man. They took root near that lake, and in time, the devil himself settled among them.

But Pan Z. was a wicked man himself, a fool led astray by his own arrogance. He will answer to God for not believing. Had he summoned a priest to bless the lake and the net, there would have been no fear, and their labor would not have been in vain."

"The priests and good people still speak the truth, but their words bounce off men's hearts like peas off a wall. That is why God does not bless us. That is why life grows harder with each passing year."

I turned to the fisherman and asked:

"And what of our own Lake Nieszczarda? Do evil spirits dwell there too? Have you seen them?"

"What are you saying, sir?!" he cried. "May God forbid such a thing! Before I leave home, I always make the sign of the cross and recite a prayer – just as the Jesuits have taught us. And besides, although the Astashou fishermen once fished here and disturbed the waters, even they could not let the devil rule unchecked – there are churches on Nieszczarda's shores. In spring, when the lake is still and the morning air is calm, I've seen the reflection of those churches and their crosses gleam in the water like stars in the heavens. And on holy days, when the bells ring for Mass, their sound carries across the entire lake. People in boats cross themselves and whisper prayers. Thank God, we still revere the holy faith – and the devil flees from cross and prayer."

"That's true," my uncle added. "Our peasants are not like others. Many times, on my way to Polatsk, I've stopped the horses just to listen to their singing as they worked the fields:

> *'Oh! Our Savior Lord,*
> *The one beloved heart,*
> *We raise our hands and eyes to heaven,*
> *Asking for forgiveness of sins.'*

Such devotion moves a man to tears. But how long will it last? Evil spreads like a creeping shadow, and those who know the ways of the world predict nothing good."

Rodzka sighed, gazed out the window, then quietly picked up his hat and the bag in which he had delivered the fish.

"You're in a hurry to get home, but it's not late yet," said Zavalnia.

"I've set the net and the lines," replied Rodzka. "I ought to check whether God has granted anything, dusk is drawing near."

"If you catch something, bring me more. I live by the road, and people come to visit me, thank God."

"If God is kind to me," Rodzka said, bowing, "I won't forget you."

And with that, he took his bag and departed.

"I like that fisherman," my uncle said, watching him

go. "He is a decent and hardworking man. If you ever visit his island, you'll see right away what kind of person he is. His house – though modest, with a thatched roof, and not overly large – stands in a picturesque spot on a hill. A small orchard full of apple and cherry trees surrounds it. Everything is neat and well-tended. He keeps horses, cows, and sheep. His fields are as well cared for as his orchard. The grass in the meadows grows thick and green, and nearby there is a grove of tall birches. More than once, during calm summer weather, I've taken my boat out to his island. He always welcomed me with joy, and his wife, a truly hospitable woman, received me graciously, serving freshly caught bream, wonderfully prepared."

"He is a fortunate man," I said. "On his island, it seems the golden age has not yet passed. He has no neighbors to share the field with, and the wolves and bears do not trouble his livestock."

"There is only one drawback," my uncle replied. "On certain days, he must perform *corvée*, sending a worker by boat to transport horses across the lake, nearly a quarter of a *verst*."

AUHINIA, THE BLACKSMITH'S WIFE

As we talked, my uncle's kinwoman, Pani Malhreta, entered the room.

"Oh heavens!" she exclaimed. "What strange things are happening in the world!"

Zavalnia looked at her in surprise:

"Well, what's the matter with you?"

"The blacksmith's wife, Auhinia, came by. The things she told me, just thinking of them sends a chill down my spine."

"Then invite her in so she can tell us as well. I am curious to hear what wonders are stirring in the world."

Auhinia entered. She was a lively, talkative woman, and the godmother[28] of nearly everyone in the area.

"Well then, Auhinia," said my uncle, "what tale did you tell Pani Malhreta that left her moaning and exclaiming so?"

"Oh, sir! Such strange things, just to speak of them makes the heart tremble. Only today, no sooner had I finished cooking and covered the stove, than a beggar came into the house, pale as a dove. He sat on the bench, murmuring prayers. I set a bowl of cabbage soup before him. After he finished eating, I asked:

'From what lands has the Lord sent you, old man?'

'From afar,' he replied.

'And what news from the world?'

'The news is grim,' he said. 'Unheard-of marvels are taking place in the house of a wealthy man. The moment his son was born, he sat up and shouted aloud, '*Give me food!'* Everyone was stunned, but they gave him half a loaf of bread.[29] He devoured it in an instant, then jumped up and ran to the door. There, a full tub of water stood waiting. He leapt into it and vanished beneath the surface. They rushed to pull him out, but found only a fish. They laid it on the table, unsure what to do. At once they sent for the priest. He came and crossed the fish, and it turned back into a baby. So they baptized him right away.

That child is growing up, but is always cold like a fish. And the old folks say, when he cried out for food, they should've given him a stone instead of bread. They say it's an omen of poor harvests and famine. And worse, if he grows up cold like a fish, and – God forbid – if he grows up clever, he'll bring much trouble."

"And do you believe all that?" my uncle asked. "Somewhere, they must be casting bells just to ring louder and spread such tales across the land. A baby turning into a fish and growing up cold as ice – who ever heard of such a thing?"

"Sir, you say the bells are being cast, but in our churches, all the bells are still intact. Bronze doesn't shatter like pottery," said Auhinia.

"Janka," Zavalnia turned to me, "do you believe any of this?"

"Uncle," I replied, "I think such stories are born of people's sorrow and the burdens of daily toil."

"Perhaps you're right. Still, tell us more, Auhinia. What else have you heard?"

"Varka Plaksuniha has died."

"May she rest in peace. But that's no marvel: people are born and they die."

"But she died a Christian death. She confessed and received communion. She changed completely while in

Polatsk, thank God."

"Was she such a great sinner then?"

"Oh, I know everything! Her mother – what a scandalous life she led! And she herself – may God not recall her sins – had that birthmark on her lip. It brought her more grief than you can imagine."

"You must know all this for certain, since everyone bares their soul to you."

"Well, I baptize nearly every child in this entire area, they're all my godchildren. Everyone loves me. The women are always glad to sit down for a chat. So yes, I know everything: who does what and how they live. And as for Varka's mother, she was a famous witch. Didn't you know that, sir?"

"I know nothing of it. Tell me about the mother and the daughter."

The Birthmark on the Lip

"The name of Varka's mother was Prakseda. She lived in a tavern by the Drysa River, not far from the Krasnapol estate. Her husband worked as a steward on a small manor farm. Prakseda fared well. Though her tavern lay off the main road and was seldom visited, she managed to save money quickly. She never seemed troubled, often bought new dresses, and always wore the finest clothes.

The neighbors suspected her of stealing milk from the cows of nearby villages, for she kept barely any livestock of her own, yet sold plenty of butter and cheese in the city. And so, rumors spread far and wide: they said Prakseda would hang a white towel on the wall, place a bucket beneath it, and from either end of the towel, streams of milk would pour down into the pail. In no time at all, her jugs would be full.

Some locals resolved to catch her in the act and report her to the master. One evening, they harnessed a horse and rode toward her tavern, thinking to find her red-handed. It was only six *versts* from their village, a road they knew so well they could have found it blindfolded. Yet what happened? Though the path was familiar, they wandered all night, utterly lost, riding through the dark with no sense of where they were. When morning came, they discovered they had been going in circles all around the tavern itself and yet had not been able to find it. Exhausted and baffled, they returned home, having spent the whole night without sleep.

Refusing to give up, they decided to try again, but this time to arrive before sunset. They bought some *harelka* at the tavern, drank a glass each, and then, pretending to be very drunk, laid down on the benches as if to sleep. All the while, each one kept a careful watch from under half-closed lids, waiting to see what the tavern keeper would do at midnight.

Eventually, the light was extinguished, though the tavern wasn't entirely dark: the full moon shone straight through the window, bathing the room in pale light. Time passed. When they heard a rooster crow from the barn, they figured midnight must have long since passed and that they'd waited in vain.

Then one of the men rose, stepped out onto the porch and there he beheld a strange and fearful sight. A huge rooster, with crane-like legs, was perched on the ladder, dressed in German garb, and wearing a hat. It crowed loudly into the night. Horrified, the man rushed back inside and told the others what he had seen.

They lit the lamp at once, went outside crossing themselves, hurriedly harnessed the horses, and rode off toward home. Near their village, they came upon some farmhands returning from work. Having just finished supper, they were leading their horses home for the night. The men pointed to the western sky that was tinged with red, and said that midnight was still far off.

So for the second time, they had failed to catch Prakseda in the act of stealing milk. Nonetheless, they went to the master and told him everything they had witnessed, even about the demon in German clothes, crowing like a rooster atop the ladder. But neither the master, the steward, nor anyone else at the manor believed them. They only laughed. And so Prakseda lived on in peace, undisturbed, and continued to practice her witchcraft.

She gave birth to a daughter, who was baptized with the name Varka. People whispered that Prakseda never crossed her child, not when putting her to sleep, nor when lifting her from the cradle. Worse still – and this is too frightening to recall! – many night workers claimed that, while Prakseda slept peacefully, they saw a small black dwarf with a huge head sitting by the cradle, rocking little Varka and staring deeply into her eyes.

As the girl grew, she became more beautiful with each passing year. She bore a small birthmark upon her lip, but the young men insisted it did not mar her appearance. On the contrary, it only added to her allure. Yet the more people praised the mark, the faster it grew. Some began to warn Prakseda that it might one day spoil the girl's face. But she paid them no heed, until that very birthmark brought misfortune.

When Varka turned sixteen, a young nobleman passed through the area one night. No one knew who he was or where he had come from. They said his face was always pale, his nose sharp and long, his hair stiff and black as a raven's wing. He had a piercing gaze and it was hard to meet his eyes.

He became enamored with Varka and began frequenting the tavern, which greatly pleased Prakseda, as she dreamed of marrying her daughter into nobility.

Soon afterward, the birthmark on Varka's lip began to grow even faster. People whispered that the visiting nobleman must have kissed her.

By the time Varka turned eighteen, the birthmark on her lip had grown quite large, though it had not yet marred her beauty. It still charmed young men, and she relished the attention, surrounded by a crowd of admirers. Yet she rejected them all, for her mother had convinced her that she would marry better than any noble-born lady.

Now, sir, let me tell you what came of all this.

There was a young man named Mikhas, who served as a lackey and huntsman. He was in love with Varka. One day, he overheard the bagpiper Akhrem making fun of her, telling others that Varka had been kissed by an evil spirit because she never made the sign of the cross, and that was why the mark on her mouth had grown so large.

Offended, the huntsman vowed to take revenge on Akhrem for insulting his beloved's honor. He believed that in doing so, he might win the favor of both mother and daughter.

That Sunday, youth gathered at Prakseda's tavern. Among them were several lackeys, and Mikhas had also come down from the estate. Some cast admiring glances at the tavern keeper's daughter, marveling at her beauty. Others whispered among themselves, mockingly calling her the "little lady."

Akhrem the Bagpiper soon arrived. He was welcomed, seated on a bench, and offered *harelka*. Cheerful, he began to play and sing. There were several young girls from the neighboring village, and the lads invited them, and Varka, to dance.

Amidst the merry revelry, a clay pot suddenly tumbled from its place high atop the stove, crashing to the floor. Empty bottles on the table began to whistle eerily, as though someone were blowing into their necks, and small objects dropped from shelves and scattered across the floor in every corner of the room.

'You're shaking the whole tavern with your dancing!' grumbled Prakseda, bending down to collect the fallen trinkets.

At that moment, a huge cat leapt down from the stove to the floor. All dancing ceased as the guests watched it, but the cat vanished without a trace, as if it had never been there at all.

Breaking the heavy silence, Akhrem spoke:

'Don't be afraid, dance on! It's just the young nobleman playing tricks on us. You know, the one who's always visiting here.'

Prakseda glared at him, leaned toward the huntsman, and whispered something into his ear. Then she disappeared behind a curtain into a small room partitioned off from the main hall.

Unfazed, Akhrem took up his bagpipes again and resumed playing. But Mikhas strode forward and knocked the instrument from his hands.

'A true bagpiper,' he sneered, 'puffed-up lips and an empty head.'

The bagpiper gave him a scornful look and shot back:

'And you are a true lord's lackey: short and stout, with a greasy snout – fit only for licking plates.'

The huntsman raised his hand to strike, but Akhrem caught his arm before the blow landed. The other guests quickly stepped in, pulling Mikhas aside, urging him to let it go. They told him the bagpiper was drunk and would soon regret his loose tongue once the *harelka* wore off. But Prakseda was not so easily calmed. She declared that Akhrem would not get away with insulting her daughter and would pay dearly for it.

Fearing the quarrel might grow into something darker, the guests urged Akhrem to be silent and go home. Drawn-out grudges were dangerous, especially here.

Akhrem took their advice. He slung his bagpipes under his arm, tilted his hat askew, sang a tune to himself, and made his way out the door. The others lingered long into the evening, trying in vain to soothe Prakseda's anger and ease the sorrow that clouded Varka's face.

Around midnight, the guests began to leave the tavern one by one. As they walked home in silence, each of them heard it: the sound of bagpipes echoing deep within the forest. They wondered what it could mean, how Akhrem had ended up in the woods, and with whom.

The night was clear and calm. The music carried far across the countryside, ringing with eerie clarity. Dogs barked endlessly in the villages. Peasants stepped out of their huts, confused and weary. Some whispered that perhaps *liasun* had lured the bagpiper into the woods. Others guessed it was some drunkards who had wandered off and kept up the revelry, forgetting that Monday morning would demand an early rise.

At dawn, just as the eastern sky began to pale, a group of night workers, who had been nearby tending to their horses, realized the bagpipes had not stopped all night. They decided to follow the sound into the spruce forest. There, in the gloom beneath the trees, they found Akhrem seated on a rotting log, playing his bagpipes with glassy, vacant eyes, unaware of their presence. One of the workers stepped forward, laid a hand on his shoulder, and said:

'In the name of the Father and the Son – what has

come over you? For whom have you been playing all night, alone in this forest?'

No sooner had the words been spoken than the bagpipes slipped from Akhrem's hands. His whole body stiffened, his face darkened, and he could not speak.

The workers took him by the arms, helped him onto a horse, and brought him back to the village. Akhrem lay ill for a long time, and when he finally began to recover, he told them what little he remembered:

'As I left the tavern, still singing to myself and making my way home, I ran into someone I thought I knew. He looked and sounded like a distant cousin. He asked:

'Where are you coming from, and where are you going?'

'I was at Prakseda's tavern, and now I'm heading home.'

'So soon? Were you bored there? Do you no longer fancy Varka? Such a pretty girl – why, that birthmark suits her better than pearls suit a noble lady.'

'Ah, you're talking nonsense, brother,' I replied. 'Some young nobleman convinced himself the birthmark was lovely, and now everyone repeats it. But wait and see, it will grow so large that it'll ruin her face entirely. No one will even look at her then.'

'Oh, brother, you are strange. How can you know that the birthmark will ruin her face?'

'I would tell you,' I said, 'but I'm afraid. That huntsman Mikhas, who's in love with her, is mad. He nearly beat me for speaking the truth. And Prakseda herself chased me out of the tavern.'

'And what sort of truth did you dare speak?'

'Don't tell anyone, brother, but I said the devil had kissed her.'

'Ha-ha-ha! You fool!'

'Talking like that, we reached the village. His house

was brightly lit, bustling with guests. There were many young people inside, girls with colorful ribbons in their braids and silver or gold clasps on their bodices. Their round cheeks glowed with health, their dark brows framed fiery eyes. I stared in amazement. The host welcomed me, poured *harelka*, served fresh *bliny*. The girls crowded around, looking into my eyes, begging for a lively tune. I couldn't refuse. I played with all my heart, and they danced in a whirling circle. I played all night long, though it seemed only an hour had passed.

But when the night worker laid his hand on my shoulder and said, '*In the name of the Father and the Son,*' everything vanished in an instant – the house, the guests, even my cousin. I found myself sitting alone in the forest, on a rotting log, my hands still clutching the bagpipe, my body frozen in terror.'

Akhrem realized that this was all the doing of Mikhas the Huntsman, and resolved to take revenge. He sought out someone said to be just as skilled in witchcraft as Prakseda, and begged him to curse Mikhas's hunt. From that day on, Mikhas could not hit a single beast, not even from a few steps away. People mocked him openly, and he soon lost the master's favor."

"So how did it all end?" asked Zavalnia.

"Very badly. Mikhas was a vengeful man. One day, after another failed hunt, he crossed paths with Akhrem. An argument broke out. In a fit of rage, Mikhas shot him in the leg. Akhrem nearly died from the wound.

Soon after, Mikhas himself fell ill. His body weakened, his skin turned dark, like a corpse. The manor doctor visited him daily, but nothing helped. He died. Some said it was consumption that carried him off. Others whispered that something had been slipped into his drink. Let God be the judge."

"Ah," said my uncle with a sigh, "the gentry care little whether their people live in harmony like brothers or tear each other apart. They will answer for it before the Lord! How could they allow such hatred to fester between the huntsman and the bagpiper? But go on, Auhinia, tell us more about Varka."

"That young nobleman I spoke of – the one who used to visit Prakseda's tavern – he never returned. No one ever learned who he was or where he came from. As for the others, those who once sang praises of Varka's beauty and admired the mark on her lip, they stopped coming as well, fearing to be caught up in the feud between the bagpiper and the huntsman. Over the years, the birthmark grew larger, until at last it spoiled her face entirely.

The neighbors whispered among themselves: '*Well, now Varka won't be married. She'll grow old living with her mother. Who would want her now?*' She was no longer the beauty she once was, and bad rumors clung to her like shadow. In her presence, they mocked her: '*Just wait, young lady, your prince will arrive any day now, in a fancy carriage.*' Varka said nothing. She only lowered her head and wept in secret.

One winter, a wealthy merchant from Polatsk named Jakush Plaksun came to the area, perhaps the good sir knows the wooden house he owns near the Palata River, not far from the stone column topped with a statue of St. John. He was traveling through the villages, buying flax, and happened to stay several days at Prakseda's inn. There, he saw Varka and took a great liking to her. He proposed, and she did not refuse, after all, he was young, owned his own home, was kindhearted, and, most importantly, a free man.

After receiving Varka's consent, Plaksun went to the

manor to declare his intention and paid her dowry. The master was pleased and gave his blessing without hesitation. The servants, however, exchanged mocking glances and whispered among themselves: '*What a fitting surname, Plaksun!*[30] *He'll marry her, and he'll weep bitter tears, true to his name. What a strange man, to marry the daughter of a wicked woman, and a girl with an ugly birthmark on her mouth that no water can wash off, a stain that's ruined her face.*'

The news spread quickly. Neighbors marveled and gossiped. Some claimed that Prakseda had bewitched the merchant and fed him some sort of potion to ignite such passion for her daughter. Envious tongues wagged, warning Plaksun of impending misfortune. But he was so deeply in love with Varka that he dismissed all rumors.

He returned to Polatsk and went straight to the Jesuit monastery to speak with Father Buda, the priest he respected most, whose guidance he often sought and valued.

'How are you, Jakush?' the priest greeted him. 'I haven't seen you in some time. I suppose you've been traveling and trading?'

'Indeed, Father. Winter is the time to prepare for spring, to gather goods and fill the barges that will set out once the ice breaks on the Dzvina.'

'Quite so,' nodded Father Buda. 'So I take it you've bought flax that you take to Riga? I hear the harvest in Albrechtau and the other Polatsk estates was plentiful. The price may not be as high this year.'

'Thanks be to God,' said Plaksun. 'I expect a fair price. But I've also found something else – a wife. I've bought both: goods and a bride.'

'Congratulations! Have you married already?'

'Not yet, Father. Only engaged. She was a serf, and I paid her price to the estate. I truly love her, she has a calm and gentle heart.'

'Then you are blessed,' said Father Buda. 'A calm and gentle nature is a treasure. And being born a serf brings no shame, neither to you nor to her. It is not noble birth that gives worth to a soul, but an honest, chaste life.'

'But, Father,' Plaksun said, 'there's something troubling me. Many people speak ill of her. They claim her mother is a witch, and say the girl has been touched by the devil. Should I give any weight to such talk? I stayed at her mother's tavern a whole week and saw nothing suspicious.'

'It is true that people are eager to cast stones at sinners, forgetting that Christ said, '*Let he who is without sin cast the first stone.*' Still, one must not outright deny the existence of evil or sorcery. But I tell you this, Jakush: he who places his trust in God and prays with sincerity has nothing to fear. Before your wedding, pray together with your bride. Confess. I place you under God's protection. Here, take these two icons of the Virgin Mary. They are blessed and carry the power of absolution. One is for you, and one for your future wife. Live in God's grace, and He will not abandon you.'

With the priest's blessing, Plaksun ordered a silk dress for Varka, bought her fine scarves and jeweled combs, hired city musicians, and invited a host of friends and acquaintances. He returned to the village laden with gifts and accompanied by his retinue.

Varka, her parents, and the villagers – freed from their duties for the occasion – greeted him with unspeakable joy. Plaksun presented Varka with rich gifts and the consecrated icon from Father Buda. The girl accepted everything with quiet gratitude, and her heart filled with warmth at the depth of his affections for her.

The next day, before the wedding, the young couple followed the priest's instructions to the letter. And so the wedding began, boisterous and grand. Several landowners from neighboring villages arrived, the servants were excused from work, and curious folk from all around gathered at the tavern to join the feast. All eyes turned to Varka, now richly dressed and radiant. The birthmark on her lip had faded so much, it was scarcely visible.

Music played, the youth danced, and wine flowed. They drank to the health of the newlyweds, wishing them wealth, joy, and a long and happy life.

The merry celebrations continued late into the night. The sky was clear, calm, and full of stars. But as the clock struck midnight, the sharp crack of a whip rang out. The guests rushed to the windows. A black carriage had stopped outside the tavern. It was drawn by six black horses, with a coachman seated on the box and footmen in fine coats standing by. Plaksun and Prakseda, along with her husband, ran out into the yard to meet them, but at that very instant, the carriage, the horses and the footmen vanished before the eyes of the entire wedding party. Not a trace remained. Stunned, Plaksun and his father-in-law returned indoors, while Prakseda stood pale as a corpse, trembling with unease.

Then, someone saw a frightful face peering in through the window, and a wave of terror swept through the guests. Poor Varka trembled, pale and ready to faint.

'Do not be afraid,' her husband whispered, holding her. 'God watches over us.' He urged the guests to continue celebrating, to pay no heed to these strange happenings.

But outside, a sudden storm broke loose. The wind howled and shook the building. A great gust tore the roof clean off the tavern. Forgetting all about the celebration, the guests stood in silence, murmuring their prayers. And as soon as dawn broke, they quietly took their leave and returned to their homes.

Plaksun, with his wife, mother-in-law, and entire entourage, departed for Polatsk.

The roofless tavern still stands, abandoned. After receiving her freedom from the estate, Prakseda moved to live with her daughter. And, as people say, she changed completely. She became devout, went to Mass daily, observed the holy days, and fulfilled all the duties of a Christian. She died peacefully in Plaksun's house.

And now, I've heard that Varka has passed away as well. Ah! Everyone in Polatsk loved her. She was quiet, kind-hearted, and generous. Not a single beggar ever left her doorstep without comfort or alms. The mark on her lip had vanished completely, and they say she looked like an angel. But my dear sir," said Auhinia, rising, "I've spoken so much, I didn't notice the dark creeping in. It's late, I must return home."

"The evening is clear and calm," said Zavalnia. "There's nothing to fear. And it's not more than a *verst* to your home."

"I have a request," she said. "Sir, you are kind and generous. Perhaps you'll grant me this small favor."

"Helping one's kin is the duty of every Christian," he replied.

"*Kalyady* is nearly here," she said, "and it so happens we have no grain at all. Please, grant us a few measures of rye. In spring, my husband will forge plowshares and other tools for you in return. Or we'll repay you in whatever way we can."

"Gladly," said Zavalnia. "Your husband is a good, diligent man. Pani Malhreta, please see that Auhinia receives a quarter of rye, a gallon of barley groats, and a gallon of peas. Let this be for your holiday table."

The blacksmith's wife bowed low before my uncle and followed Pani Malhreta to the pantry.

THE BLIND FRANCISAK

It was dark in the yard. The sky was studded with stars, the trees stood still beneath a coat of hoarfrost, only the cold tapped against the wall from time to time. As if expecting someone, my uncle glanced out the window, then turned to me and said:

"The weather is fair. I don't think we'll be having any guests tonight. So, Janka, recall something from your store of learned tales. The nights are long now, and there's still plenty of time to sleep before the first stars of dawn."

Supper was served. Still at the table, I rummaged through my memory, sorting through events from ancient history, searching for a tale of strange happenings that might suit my uncle's tastes.

After supper, he paced the room in his usual manner, reciting his evening prayers. Then, slipping into bed, he asked:

"And what gods and goddesses will you be telling me about tonight?"

"I'll tell you, dear Uncle, about the founding of the city of Rome."

"Is that not the same Rome where His Holiness lives? Ah! This should be an interesting and beautiful tale."

"The very same," I replied.

"Well, go on then. I'm listening closely."

I began by explaining how the Romans descended from the Trojans, and told of Proca, King of the Albans, of Amulius and Numitor, and of Rhea Silvia, who, though a vestal virgin, bore twin sons, Romulus and Remus, to the god of war, Mars. I told how the infants were set adrift in a basket on the river Tiber, and how, when the waters cast them ashore, a she-wolf, hearing their cries, came and suckled them as though they were her own.

My uncle was astonished that a wild beast could show such mercy and love for children. He interrupted:

"There must have been werewolves in ancient times. Surely that she-wolf had once been a woman and kept a human soul, for how else could she feel such tenderness? Or perhaps God, in His mercy, worked a miracle for the sake of the innocent babes."

I continued, telling how the twins were found by Faustulus, how they were raised among shepherds, and how they later built Rome upon the very spot where the river had carried them ashore.

Just then, the dogs barked and someone knocked at the gate. A servant came running to report that the blind man, Francisak, had arrived.

My uncle quickly got out of bed, and as soon as he lit the lamp, Francisak stepped inside. With his right hand, he clung to his guide; with his left, he tapped the cane before him, feeling out any obstacles in his path.

"Praise be to Jesus Christ," said the blind man, stepping over the threshold. "Is Pan Zavalnia at home?"

"At home, at home," my uncle replied warmly, greeting him with joy. He helped him remove his heavy winter garments and invited him to sit. At once, he ordered that the horse be unharnessed and fed oats, and that the coachman be served *harelka* and a hot meal. Then he sent for Pani Malhreta to prepare a quick supper for the guest.

"Where have you been?" Zavalnia asked. "We haven't seen you in over half a year. Your friends have often spoken of you, saying: '*Where's our Francisak now? He must be far away. May kind souls meet him on the road, and may he never know misfortune on his long journey!*'"

"I've traveled all over Belarus," said Francisak, "and

even wandered through part of Livonia. I've known warmth and welcome, and I've met stone-hearted men who have never known mercy."

"Livonia must be a fortunate land. They say the soil yields better than ours. The nobles are wealthier, with fine palaces and grand titles – barons and counts."

"I am blind. I never saw their palaces. All I know is that those fine lords rarely speak to the poor. A cripple may wait a lifetime and never hear a word from them."

"Ah! It's a hard life, when a man must beg for compassion from those who don't believe sorrow exists."

"I won't be traveling far anymore," Francisak said. "Thanks be to God, I've found patrons in these parts. Pan B. has granted me an island on his estate at Lake Rablo. A little house, a garden, a small plot of land – just enough for me. There my bones will find their rest."

"Ah, I know that lake," said Zavalnia. "I've visited it many times, and that island too. I remember a little hut on the hill. Pines whispered overhead, waves rippled across the water. The view was somber, yes, but it pleased me greatly."

"People praise those places," said the blind man, "but to me, blind as I am, they bring no joy. The rustling of woods and waters only draws me into melancholy thoughts."

My uncle talked with Francisak for a long time.

At last, supper was served. My uncle gently led the blind man to the table and, sitting beside him, ensured he had everything he needed.

After the meal, he had a bed brought into the room and placed beside his own. Then he took me by the hand, led me to Francisak, and told him that I had finished school with the Jesuit priests. Zavalnia praised the stories I had relayed to him, noting that the difficult names of pagan gods were hard to remember. He then asked Francisak to tell us something he had heard on his travels.

"My tale is not long, but it is an interesting one. It's about a strange woman seen in various corners of Belarus. I'll tell you what I've heard from those who claim to have seen her with their own eyes."

The Weeping Woman

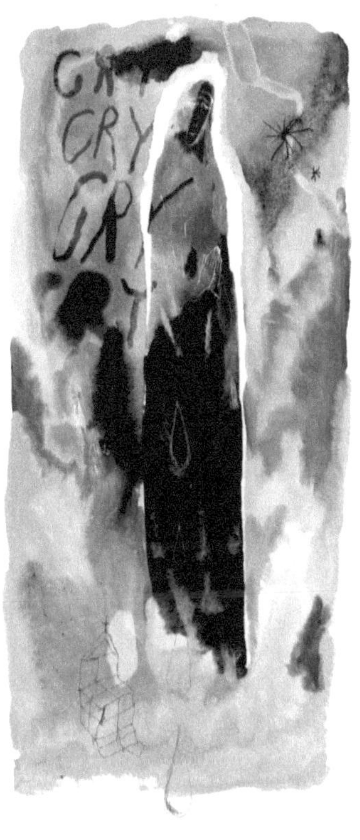

"This woman is of striking beauty. Her garments are white as snow, she wears a black headpiece and a shawl draped over her shoulders. Though her face is tanned by wind and sun, it is lovely and pleasant to look upon. Her eyes are full of feeling, always glistening with tears. She appears most often in abandoned homes, empty churches, and ruined chapels. She has also been seen under trees or out in the open field. After sunset, she sits on a stone, laments her fate with a sorrowful voice, and weeps bitterly. Those who have dared approach her say they heard her murmur, '*I have no one to confide the secret of my heart to!*'

Once, when I was returning from Polatsk, an innkeeper at a roadside tavern told me of an abandoned house near the road beyond a birch grove, with a small cherry orchard beside it. A peasant had once lived there, but he and his entire family were sent away by their masters to a distant place. Their cows and horses were taken as well.

A blind cripple passed by there one day, led by a small boy. Hearing a mournful song from the house, they thought someone might be living there, and approached to beg for alms. As they stepped inside, the blind man began his usual prayer-song: '*Oh, Savior, our Lord...*'

'But this house has no windows, no doors, and no one lives here,' the boy said. 'We've turned off the road for nothing.'

Just then, a woman appeared in the center of the room, her face sorrowful, she was dressed in mourning.

'Pray,' she said. 'God is everywhere, and He will help you.'

She threw a handful of silver coins into the blind man's hat and vanished.

The cripple later showed those coins to everyone. They bore the images of kings on one side and the *Pahonia*[31] on the other.

Not far from the road to Viciebsk, there is an abandoned chapel. After sunset, people saw the woman sitting on the steps, crying. Her lament echoed far into the fields.

People spoke of the Weeping Woman in hushed tones. Some feared she foretold misfortune, war, plague, or famine. The elders agreed that she heralded sorrow. But the younger folk thought differently. They whispered that wherever the Weeping Woman appeared, treasure must lie hidden in the earth. And that idea was to everyone's liking.

There was a crippled man living at the edge of the village who had once wandered the whole world. Now back with his family, he survived on alms and often repeated:

'Brothers! Her tears and lamentations do not promise gold or silver. She weeps for the *sviatynia* – the sacred that you have forgotten. You think only of wealth, but poverty and sorrow await you.'

The villagers mocked him. And one night, while everyone slept, a group of young men decided they would dig up the treasure themselves.

The chapel lay four *versts* from the village. Taking tools, young peasants hurried there in the dark, hoping to finish their search before the first rooster crowed.

The place was foreboding. A dense fir forest rustled nearby. An owl hooted mournfully. The moon barely peeked through ragged clouds. The chapel stood on a hill among birches, like a tombstone.

They worked through the night, digging deep pits, but found only rotten planks and skulls. It was once a cemetery, long overgrown. All that remained were faint, moss-covered stones.

Summer nights are short. Soon the sky blushed in the east. They gave up their search, filled in the pits, and started home.

The sun had risen, the lark was singing, and the morning mist had lifted when they saw her standing by the hazel bushes at the roadside, facing east. In her hands, she held a bright ribbon, fluttering like a lightning bolt in the breeze.

No sooner had one of them said, '*Let's go to her*' that the apparition vanished.

On the very spot where the Weeping Woman had stood, a large wasp nest hung from a branch. In the morning sunbeams, the wasps swarmed like golden sparks.

'Listen,' one of them said. 'Let's wrap the nest in a scarf, go to the old cripple, wake him up and say we found treasure near the chapel, and then throw the nest into his window. Let the old man go mad!'

The others agreed. They went to his house, woke him with shouts, tossed the wasp nest through the window, and ran off, laughing.

But a miracle happened. The old man saw gold scattered across the ground before him. And as he stood in stunned silence, it is said that the same woman who had wept on the threshold of the chapel appeared before him and spoke:

'Take half of this treasure for yourself, and give the other half to the poor and the crippled. God helps my suffering children.'

With that, she vanished.

In Livonia, there was another incident. On the estate of Pan M., the ruins of an ancient castle still stood. They say that long ago there was a city there, for now and then, the river floods and washes the earth away, revealing the stone foundations of vanished structures. Glass shards, rusted iron ornaments, fragments of weaponry, and even copper or silver coins blackened by time are often found in the sand.

Every evening at sunset, the Weeping Woman appeared there. She wove garlands of wildflowers and hung them on the ruins, then sat upon a stone and sobbed bitterly, throwing up her hands in anguish. Travelers returning home late would sometimes hear her sorrowful lament from afar. They went home with heavy hearts and told others what they had heard.

There were curious souls too. Hearing the cries of the strange woman, they crept closer in the twilight and, by the words she uttered, concluded that some bereft mother was mourning her children. But as soon as one dared to approach and ask who she was and what misfortune had befallen her, the woman would vanish. Her voice would not return until the following night.

No one knew what to make of it. Dark speculation spread. Some spoke of her as if she were a comet, a fiery broom sweeping across the sky. They tried to discover whence she came and where she went, but their efforts were in vain. Like a spirit, she seemed to descend from the air and vanish back into it.

It is said that even Pan M. did not dismiss these tales. Once, returning home late, he too had heard the weeping upon the ruins. Though he could not decipher the voice, he pondered and put his trust in the peasants who dreamed only of profit, hoping that the ghostly voice spoke of gold and silver buried deep in the ground. So Pan M. summoned his steward and commanded:

'Gather the men. Tomorrow they will begin to dig in the castle ruins. There must be gold in the ground, for how else can you explain that strange vision? Surely, the Weeping Woman wants to show us the treasure.'

'I heard the words of the Weeping Woman. She mourned the loss of her children. There was no mention of treasure buried in the ground. I think there is a warning hidden in her grief.'

'You sound like an owl spooking people with bad omens. I have no interest in your superstitions. I've been meaning to excavate that site for some time. If we find relics of the past, so much the better. And if someone expects the treasure to appear in the form of a weeping ghost – well, that wouldn't be such a terrible sight either. Let it be what it will. We start tomorrow.'

'But what if this treasure is cursed? What if it is guarded by spirits, and the deeper we dig, the deeper it sinks into the ground? Then we will only waste our time. And even if we manage to lay hands on it, what if it brings nothing but sorrow? I once heard that a man took a single coin from an enchanted hoard, and his hands withered as if gripped by some terrible disease.'

'It is shameful even to listen to such nonsense. You babble like a peasant with no sense. No coin can harm me.'

'Then why do the rich and powerful still suffer from melancholy and disease?'

'Enough. Gather the men tomorrow and bring them to the ruins. I will come myself and show you where to dig.'

The steward was a petty noble by birth but no different from the common folk in his beliefs. He only shrugged and went to do as he was told.

The sun had barely risen when a group of men stood at the ruins awaiting orders. When Pan M. arrived, he pointed to the very spot where the Weeping Woman was most often seen near a stone and commanded to dig there.

The layer of earth was shallow, scarcely more than a cubit and a half. They soon struck stone and cleared away the soil to uncover the buried walls of a vault. They labored for days, resting only at noon, when the sun was the hottest. At last, they exposed iron doors with small windows on either side, their rusted iron bars still holding firmly.

They broke down the doors and opened the crypt.

No sunlight had touched the air within for centuries. It was as cold and still as a grave. Torch in hand, they entered. Fear clutched their hearts, for all around, strewn on the floor and along the walls, lay human skeletons in strange, frozen postures. Shackles still bound their hands and feet. The peasants stared in horror.

'Remove the shackles from these skeletons,' said Pan M., 'and bring them to me. These relics of antiquity, they deserve to be preserved. '

They took the shackles to their master. He showed them off to his neighbors, boasting of their ancient origins, though anyone with eyes could see they were not so different from those used today.

The peasants collected the bones and buried them together in a single grave at the nearest cemetery. A priest was summoned, prayers were said, and a great wooden cross erected over the mound.

They say that the Weeping Woman appeared once more that evening, wearing her usual mourning veil. She laid wildflowers on the grave, knelt before the cross, and wept. No one dared approach. From a distance, those who witnessed it whispered a prayer for the dead: '*Eternal rest grant unto them, O Lord...*'

For several more nights, the Weeping Woman returned, kneeling in silence and leaving flowers by the grave. But then she was seen no more.

She appeared again five *versts* from Polatsk, on the banks of the Palata River, where the water curves through forest and flows toward the wide plains near the Dzvina. She was seen at sunset, sitting on a stone beneath the birches. Peasants returning from the fields, travelers from the city – many bore witness.

The word spread quickly.

As before, opinions were divided, but most believed that treasure lay buried beneath her feet.

In Polatsk, people spoke of wars long past. Some said that an army, facing inevitable defeat, had buried its riches on that hill – silver, gold, church relics, even weapons – and marked the spot with a large stone in hopes that one of their number might return one day to retrieve it. But centuries had passed. The hill remained. The stone too. And beneath it, the untouched treasure.

Spurred by such talk, a group of young men from Polatsk made a pact. They would go there at night, uncover the hoard, and divide it among themselves. They took the necessary tools and slipped out of the city under the cover of darkness.

The night was clear and still. Stars shimmered in the heavens. A full moon hung above them. They kept to the shadows. They passed the Church of St. Francis Xavier, where the bones of Jesuit fathers and townsfolk rest. At

Spas, hearing the watchmen calling to one another in the stillness, they turned from the road and followed the curve of the river.

Soon they reached the hill.

There stood the stone, half-sunk in sand, covered in old moss. They cleared around it, pushed it aside, and began to dig. They drove a rapier deep into the soil, and the blade rang against metal. There could be no doubt – the treasure was right there. They started digging.

The deeper they dug, the more the sand filled the pit. The treasure was not deep, but seemed to sink just beyond reach, as though not wanting to be taken.

While they discussed what to do, black clouds moved in from the east, veiling the entire sky and hiding the moon. Darkness fell so thick they could barely see one another. It began to drizzle.

'It will be easier to dig when the sand is wet,' said one of them. 'So let's not waste time.'

Encouraging each other, they resumed their work and dug a long, wide pit, too large to fill again easily.

Their shovels scraped against iron.

'Iron! Iron and money!' they shouted with joy. But when they cleared around the object, hoping to lift it, they discovered it was heavy iron armor. It covered the chest of a skeleton. A sword lay beside the bones, and an iron helmet rested upon the skull. They stood silent, struck by how cruelly their hope had deceived them.

Then a braver one said:

'Let's leave the skeleton, but take the armor as a keepsake of this night.'

No sooner had they made this decision than a bolt of lightning split the sky, illuminating the hilltop, and there before them stood a giant clad in iron, holding a gleaming sword above their heads. Terror pierced their hearts.

Thunder shook the earth. The giant's voice roared:

'Wretched souls! You have sold yourselves for gold and silver. Thinking only of wealth, you have defiled the remains of a Hero who ended his life here in glory. The dawn of resurrection shall shine forth – and you shall be disgraced before the whole world!'

The thunder echoed in the heavens. The giant vanished.

Frozen with fear, they stood like phantoms in the night. Lightning flashed again, and in its pale light they saw the pit filled with sand, the ground untouched, as though no hand had disturbed it.

They forgot their rapier and shovels. They even forgot the road back to the city. They ran across fields and meadows, certain that the giant was chasing them, sword in hand.

At sunrise, they staggered back to the city, pale and gaunt, as though ill. Shaken, they told others what had happened, though not everyone believed them.

After this, the Weeping Woman was seen again, not just beyond the city, but in the cemetery near the stone Church of St. Xavier. There, arms raised, she wandered from grave to grave, and at times stood motionless, like a stone pillar carved in grief. Passersby who saw her at night fled in terror, as if from a vampire, and spread word of the marvels they had witnessed.

She was also seen at the Church of St. Casimir. She would sit at the threshold from dusk until dawn. Sometimes she wept in the field, seated upon a stone, or by the bank of the Dzvina. But her sobbing stirred few hearts. Few raised their eyes to heaven to pray for mercy. Some ignored her. Others only dreamed of treasure."

"In my opinion," said Zavalnia, "this is a warning for

people to change their ways. But it's a shame that today people are so learned they think they know everything. They believe in no miracles and seek only treasure, thinking that they might have what they desire without work. They would sell for gold what our fathers valued more than life itself."

"But isn't searching for treasure not evil in itself?" I asked. "A wealthy man can do much good."

"A wealthy man can indeed do good," my uncle agreed. "But first let him learn, so he might come to know and love what *is* good. Then God will make him a worthy steward of earthly riches – like that old man, when the wasp's nest became gold before his eyes. But most chase wealth not to do good, but to avoid work – or worse, to do harm. But what happened next?"

"When our learned and wealthy gentlemen travel in fine *phaetons*[32] or hunt in forests, hillsides, and wastelands, this Weeping Woman sometimes appears before them like an orphan girl in poor peasant dress, raising her tear-filled blue eyes as if begging for mercy. But none of them sees her. None pays her heed.

Not far from Lake Rablo, where my hut stands on an island – Pan Zavalnia must know the place – there is a hill called Pachanouskaya. It is the tallest in the region. Its slopes are cloaked in forest, but its crown is smooth and bare.

Many tales swirl around that hill. They say a monastery and church once stood there. No trace remains now, but on quiet nights, people say they've heard bells and distant singing echoing from underground.

Others say that on the very summit, at night, the Weeping Woman appears in her mourning dress, kneeling, eyes lifted to the stars, praying through tears. Then the sky opens, a shaft of golden light bursts forth, rousing birds and beasts from slumber, and her tears become crystal springs.

From that day on, any person who climbs Pachanouskaya Hill for the first time, unaware of the tale, will find a spring of clear water, and near it, a sorrowful orphan in peasant dress. If he drinks, and if he recognizes her, his eyes will be opened. From the top of that hill, he shall see all mysteries and all truths.

People went up that hill. Some saw the spring and the orphan girl. But they paid no attention. Later, when they heard the tale and returned, they could find neither the girl nor the spring."

"This Weeping Woman, who was seen near Polatsk and across Belarus and one who appears in the guise of an orphan, is she one and the same?"

"Surely it is the same woman," said the blind Francisak, "but people are full of pride, they only seek out what profits them. They do not recognize her. Although she appears across the land in same guise, they do not see her."

"You, Janka," said my uncle, "are a learned man. Do you understand who the Weeping Woman is?"

"Miracles," I said, "must be understood with the heart, not with books."

We spoke a while longer of the Weeping Woman. Then the rooster crowed.

"It's past midnight," said the blind Francisak. "Pan Zavalnia, allow the traveler to rest."

"Thank you," said my uncle. "It was a tale worth hearing."

He put out the light, and I went to my room. I thought about the Weeping Woman until the rooster crowed for a second time.

SON OF THE STORM

The sun rose through the misty air. Frost etched the windowpanes with fine ice. Birch firewood crackled in the stove. Zavalnia and the blind Francisak sat by the fire, speaking of neighbors, the rich and the poor, of beggars wandering the land, of the joys of life, of prophecies, and of the inexplicable.

"In winter," said Zavalnia, "folk come to visit me, and then I have a chance to hear what's stirring in the world. But in spring and summer, I live like a hermit. Only dark forests and water around me. Sometimes the sound of a hunter's horn or the whiz of an arrow tells me that guests are nearby. Young lords come out of the woods with their hounds and take their rest here. But you won't hear anything of substance from them. They speak only of dogs and horses."

"I've been a wanderer nearly all my life," said the blind man. "I've met people with all kinds of minds and souls. Being blind, I cannot see their faces or their form. In my imagination, they take the shapes of strange and fearsome spirits. Their words, whirling in my head, remind me of the many paths our God Almighty uses to lead us through life's storm to eternity, where we await rest, joy, and reward.

The tales of those who suffer linger in the heart, remembered for years. But how tiresome it is to hear the prattle of the gentry, who live their lives in leisure and amusement, hoping only to dazzle one another with wit!

Once, during my travels, I met a pilgrim. I do not know who he was or whence he came. He called himself the Son of the Storm. From what I gathered, he had tasted grief in full. It wasn't exile that tormented him – no, something else disturbed his soul, a different understanding of happiness."

"Did he speak to you of his life? What a strange man, calling himself the Son of the Storm."

"He spoke with me for many hours."

"It must have been an unusual conversation."

"I'll tell you what happened. A storm caught me on the road, a downpour, wild winds. My guide, seeing no village or tavern nearby, drove the horse into a thick forest, hoping to shelter us under the trees. The rain and hail roared through the branches. Thunder rolled above, and we grew anxious. Standing beneath the dark limbs of a fir tree, I pulled my cloak over my head and prayed.

'There's a man nearby,' said my guide. 'He's traveling on foot, cloaked, with a knapsack slung on a stick over his shoulder. He looks up at the sky – it seems the thunder and lightning amuse him more than they trouble him. His face is sunburned and pale, worn from long roads.'

'Perhaps he is a foreigner, passing through Belarus on his way north.'

'His cloak is soaked through, but he doesn't seem to mind. He's walking calmly toward us.'

'This is not his first storm,' I said. 'He must be no stranger to hardship.'

'It is not the first storm I've encountered,' said the stranger, having overheard. 'Indeed, I have grown used to hardship. And more than that, I love the sound of the wind, the ripples of black clouds, the fire of the lightning bolts.'

He came closer and asked:

'To the right of these woods, I saw a stone palace on a hill. Do you know whose it is?'

'I am not from these parts, and what's more, I am blind. All is hidden from me.'

'Blind! You dwell in the world without seeing it. What a sorrowful fate!'

'What can I do? God saw fit to lay this misfortune upon me. I must endure patiently.'

'Can you really endure patiently? Then you are blessed. I am not, though I walk the world freely, without need of a guide.'

'And what sent you on this long journey?'

'My fate. Ah! If you had eyes, the marks of sorrow on my face would tell you everything.'

'From what lands do you come? What is your name?'

'I come from far away. And my name is the Son of the Storm.'

'A strange name.'

'There is nothing strange in it. In a rich palace, surrounded by flatterers and servants, lives the Son of Fortune. He is cool and shining, like a gold coin, and he looks down on his subjects who, like bees, gather honey from the meadows for his pleasure. In a cottage beneath a thatched roof lives the Son of Patience. His soul clings to the soil that feeds and clothes him. But I... I am the child of parents who were hounded by Storm and Restlessness. My father lived for years in iron shackles that cut into his flesh. While I was yet in my mother's womb, she wept endlessly, and her sorrow shaped my nature. I was born with the mark of misfortune on my brow.'

'You remind me of the Weeping Woman,' I said. 'They say she appears in many places, throwing up her hands in grief, weeping bitterly.'

'You've heard of her, but you've never seen her, for you have no eyes.'

'Even those who saw her did not understand who she is or where she comes from.'

'They did not understand,' he said, 'because they did not think about her. Oh! That time, when all I knew were the groves and meadows near my parents' humble home – it passed so quickly. I loved to wander the hills and forests alone. Every tree and flower filled my head with dreams. And then, she came to me, the goddess clad in a rainbow dress, crowned with flowers. From the highest peaks, she showed me the wide world where eagles soar under the clouds. From that moment, my soul burned with longing to fly far and high, to see what lies beyond the horizon. She vanished, but I still wander at the mercy of the Storm!'

'And who was that goddess?'

'The very one you call the Weeping Woman.'

'Then you know her?'

'I traveled distant lands. Among foreign peoples, her voice echoed in my ears. I crossed seas, but even the waves could not drown out her sorrow. Wherever I went, her image remained before me. And now the wind has scattered the clouds. Farewell. By sunset, I will be far from here.'

He walked away. But his strange name and sorrowful story lingered in my thoughts. For many nights afterward, I pictured his face and could not sleep."

"And you've never met him again?"

"Never. Nor heard anyone speak of him."

"What a wretched soul! He will wander the world and suffer wherever he goes. Why doesn't he turn to God? Providence brings comfort. The Lord would grant peace to his sorrows."

THE STORM

My uncle and the blind Francisak continued speaking, recalling various stories from their lives. Evening was drawing near. In December, the days are short. Not much time had passed since noon, and already the room had begun to darken. Suddenly, a wind howled behind the walls.

"The weather is changing," said my uncle, peering out the window. "The whole sky is clouded, not a single star out there. The moon rises late these days – the night will be pitch black, and the wind is blowing from the north. The frost will not let up."

The storm grew stronger, lifting the snow into the air. A thick, impenetrable darkness descended over the land. Snowdrifts piled high against doors and windows.

"People must be returning from the Polatsk fair," said my uncle. "The path across the lake is likely buried in snow already."

Saying this, he placed a candle on the windowsill.

Just then, the dogs began barking in the yard. My uncle threw on his fur coat and stepped outside to listen for travelers' voices.

He returned quickly.

"We must act," he said. "The storm has raised so much snow that the light in the window is barely visible."

He lit a candle in a lantern and, with the servant's help, tied it firmly to a tall pole near the gate.

Upon returning inside, he turned to Francisak:

"My house is like a harbor on the edge of a stormy sea. I must do what I can to keep travelers from trouble."

As Zavalnia said this, Pani Malhreta, who had been in

the room all along, could no longer contain her long-harbored resentment at these guests who gather here for the night from God knows where.

"The whole market will end up here," she grumbled, complaining about the expenses of the late-night hassle. "There'll be no sleep for me. I've lost my health from it already."

"You speak so, madam, because you understand nothing," said my uncle. "What if Pan Maragowski is on the road with his children? Such a storm! God forbid any trouble should befall them."

"I heard it myself, Maragowski promised to come by *Kuttsia,*[33] Christmas Eve, and that's tomorrow. Surely, tonight he's staying near Polatsk."

"That, madam, is no concern of yours. I know better."

"Not my concern? And who must think of bread and food for this gathering of beggars, whose tales you love to listen to? Soon we'll have nothing to eat ourselves."

"You have neither faith nor love for your neighbor," said my uncle, now angry. "You begrudge bread to those in need, forgetting that all things come from God. It is through earthly charity that we earn peace of mind and a hope for the life to come. We take nothing with us to the grave, and cursed is the miser who has no faith in Divine Providence."

Pani Malhreta left the room in silence. My uncle turned to blind Francisak:

"Did you hear that, Pan Francisak? Some people love their crumbs more than life itself. They think they'll live forever and try to root themselves in this world for eternity. My parents never thought that way, may they rest in peace. I remember, when I was eighteen, my father bought cloth in Polatsk, an ell cost five zlotys back then.

He had a coat made for me, gave me a belt, and said:

'Go out into the world. Make your own fortune. Our fathers left us no estate, and we'll leave none to you. I give you my blessing – earn your bread and be an honest man. God's omnipotence will not abandon you. Love your neighbors and live in harmony. If misfortune strikes, endure it. If you serve, be loyal and diligent. Remember this saying: as you make your bed, so you will lie on it. If God grants you wealth and power – do not begrudge your neighbor. For the merciful shall obtain mercy, and inherit the kingdom of heaven.'

And to my mother, who had tears in her eyes, he said:

'Do not weep, dear wife. He will suffer a little in youth, but he'll be happy in time.'

With their blessing, a knapsack on my back and a walking stick in hand, I left home.

I went first to the commissioner of the Ahinsky[34] princes and asked for his protection. He took me into service, told me to practice writing and study the registries. Soon I understood the work well. I always strove to earn a good name through diligence. I listened with interest to all the talk about farming. And when I felt I had learned enough, I asked the commissioner to help me obtain the post of steward on one of the prince's estates.

'You are too young,' said the commissioner. 'Diligence alone is not enough to manage an estate. You must have experience and knowledge of the land, where to sow what. You must know the right time to sow peas, wheat, barley, or oats. And what's most difficult, you must be able to predict the weather change when haymaking time comes. Oh! A steward needs to use all his wisdom so that the hay doesn't rot in the meadow.'

'Benefactor,' I said, 'even the wisest steward once learned from others. If I lack experience, I'll ask for advice from those who have it.'

'Very well, Pan Zavalnia,' said the commissioner. 'I'll speak to the prince. Just don't disgrace my recommendation.'

'With God's help, I'll do everything to merit your trust,' I said.

And soon I became the steward of the Mahilna estate. I received thirty *talers* a year, and permission to keep a few of my own horses for travel through the villages. I took to the work with all my strength to justify the commissioner's trust, win the prince's favor, and make a name for myself.

The Lord blessed my labor and efforts. That summer was kind. The land yielded abundantly. The rye grew so tall and thick that you could walk a road through the field and not even see a man's hat. The wheat, barley, oats – all swayed in the wind like ripples on a lake.

One evening, I was in the meadow where peasants were raking hay. Thunderclouds gathered over the forest, and I wanted everything finished before the rain came. The prince, returning from a hunt, passed through the estate and was pleased to see the bounty in the fields. He rode up to the workers and called out to me:

'Pan Zavalnia! Pan Zavalnia! Come here!'

I ran to him at once.

'I'm very pleased with everything,' he said. 'You're a diligent steward. It's a joy to look at: in this estate, the harvest is much better than the others.'

'God's grace, Your Excellency,' I said. 'The weather's been good. I hope the yield won't disappoint – the rye has eared well.'

'It is true that the summer is good, but I also see your hard work. Thank you, thank you, Pan Zavalnia.'

He rode off, and I returned to the laborers.

A few days later, the commissioner sent his

congratulations, for the prince had ordered my pay raised by ten *talers*. At forty *talers* a year, I could live in comfort and help my parents as long as they lived.

The prince, may he rest in peace, was a man of the old ways. Pious and charitable. I pray for his soul. He was a father to his servants. He always comforted the poor and helped the unfortunate.

I served him fifteen years. Then I leased a small estate. I never begrudged bread to others. My door was open to neighbors and wanderers. I married and bought this land and house, where I live still."

As my uncle spoke, the dogs in the yard began barking. There was a knock at the gate, and a voice cried out:

"Sir! Open the gate! Let us in, we are frozen through. God have mercy, such a stormy night!"

The servant opened the gate. Creaking over the snow, several carts arrived.

"Who lives here?" they asked.

"Pan Zavalnia," answered the servant.

Several travelers entered the servants' room. My uncle sent me to call Pani Malhreta. When she came, he said:

"Do not be angry, madam, at these travelers. If we had been caught by a storm like this on the road, we too would be begging for shelter. No one wants to perish on the lake. Everyone values life, and will try to save themselves from misfortune the best way they can. God will judge harshly those who turn away the unfortunate. Please give them supper, and do not worry about the future, for God provides."

He went to the servants' room.

Half an hour later, he returned, speaking with a traveler dressed in an old frock coat that was sewn from quality green cloth. His hair was cropped short, thick sideburns and mustache framed his weary face. His manner betrayed that he was not a peasant, but a man who had served at court for a long time.

"What brings you on such a long journey?" asked my uncle. "It's no small thing, traveling through all of Livonia and Courland!"

"You know the saying," replied the traveler. "'*A foolish head gives no rest to the feet.*' And that is the cause of my journey. My master decided to build a textile factory, dreaming of mountains of gold.

Neighbors tried to dissuade him, saying:
'We Belarusians should begin not with factories, but with the land. Farming brings the greatest profit here. Raise livestock. Fertilize your fields. Expand your meadows. Teach your subjects virtue, so they love their homeland. Don't rob them of their property. Build fewer taverns and keep more grain in reserve.'

But he paid no heed. He mortgaged the estate, bought machines, spent vast sums, hired a foreign factory manager, sent some of his subjects to the capital to learn the craft, and others to earn money to support the factory. Meanwhile, the farm fell into ruin, and the peasants into misery. I myself heard them sing, out in the field:

'*We cannot live here,*
We will wander the world.
The summers are lean,
The lords are cruel.
Took the cows,
Drove them to the manor.
There is no bread, no salt,
No happiness, no good fortune.
The fields are empty,
There is nothing to sow.

We will not live.
We will wander the world.'

And so they did. Within a year, nearly a third of his subjects abandoned their homes and set off wandering the world.

My master saw his error. The factory, not yet fully built, was already falling into decline. There was no money for wool, or foreign dyes, or even the factory manager's salary. All hope had fled.

Then came word from traders in Riga – they had seen peasants from our estate there. So my master sent me to retrieve them with help from the local authorities."

THE ORGANIST FROM RASONY

Suddenly, the doors swung open, and in walked the organist from Rasony, his coat white with snow. As soon as he crossed the threshold, he exclaimed:

"*Laudetur Jesus Christus!*"[35] and laid a bundle of colorful Christmas wafers on the table.

"Ah! Thank you, many thanks indeed!" said my uncle. "I was expecting Pan Andrey, but I had begun to worry that this year he might have forgotten where Zavalnia lives."

"How could I forget Pan Zavalnia, especially on such a wild night? When I saw the bright lantern shining on the house of a kind and good man who looks after the lives of travelers, I knew where I must go."

"I only get visitors once Lake Nieszczarda freezes," my uncle said, "and so I live like a hermit, surrounded by forest and water, from spring to autumn."

The organist turned to blind Francisak:

"Oh, it's been ages! A true citizen of the world, and yet you've forgotten all about Rasony. People there still remember how you sang in the choir during the Jubilee. While others needed hymnals, Pan Francisak knew every song by heart. When will we see you again?"

"I live far away now."

"But you live wherever kind and truly loving friends are found, and you have many of those all over Belarus."

"Thanks to Pan B.'s kindness, I now have a house of my own on an island in the middle of Lake Rablo. I intend to end my wandering there, as long as the good Lord grants me many more years."

"I know Pan B. well, he is a good man. His estate in

Rabschyzna is right by Lake Rablo. I've visited it a few times. It must be at least sixty *versts* from here. But I'm trembling now, completely frozen. The wind and frost are unbearable."

"Then let's have a glass of *harelka*, Pan Andrey," said my uncle, "and soon there'll be a warm supper to go with it. That'll warm you up."

"*Harelka* would do nicely. As they say, it cools in summer and warms in winter."

After *harelka* and some snacks, the cheerful organist said:

"Pan Zavalnia has many guests tonight, and surely, new tales too."

"Everyone encounters something different in their life, and so everyone tells unique stories."

"And Janka – the philosopher from the Jesuit academy – I imagine he's told many by now. I heard he loved books even back in school."

"His stories are scholarly. He told me about some ancient pagan peoples who lived God knows when. Their names are so complicated, I forget them the next day."

"I also attended Jesuit schools," said the organist, "and I still remember Latin by heart, translating Cicero's speeches and *De arte poetica*. I still recall Horace's line: '*Omne tulit punctum qui miscuit utile dulci*'.[36] But once I realized it was all just *vanitas vanitatum* – vanity of vanities – I no longer wanted to dig deeper into such wisdom. Why philosophize when it is better to believe with the heart? So I turned to music, and now, thank God, I serve the Church and am content."

"Then it's your turn, Pan Andrey," said Zavalnia. "Tell us something new."

"Isn't it late already? What time is it?"

"I have no clock," said my uncle, "but I know it's still a

long while before midnight."

"I have a clock at home," said the organist, "a keepsake from the parish priest. When it chimes, a little cuckoo appears and calls out the hour. A traveler once stayed with me, and when he heard the cuckoo clock, he told me a story about a desperate young man and fiery spirits..."

Fiery Spirits

Everyone sat close to the organist. Silence reigned in the room, broken only by the murmur of the storm beyond the walls. He began his tale:

"A young man named Albert, well-mannered and handsome, inherited several thousand *talers* from his parents. Not realizing that money is easy to lose but hard to earn, he made no effort to save what he had. He indulged in games and entertainment, until he finally saw that his coffer was like a body bereft of its soul, and the many friends he once had, vanished.

Malvina, his beloved, was born and raised in the city. She knew the world and agreed with the common opinion among women, that the heart can be given to the one for whom the soul yearns, but the hand – only to one who guarantees a well-established livelihood with gold and honor.

Malvina loved Albert and enjoyed long conversations with him. Consumed by pleasant chatter, the evenings would fly by quickly, and the clock on the wall would chime the hours one after another, while the gray cuckoo let out its melancholy call from the little open hatch.

'The sad voice of the cuckoo sparks melancholy thoughts,' said Albert. 'It seems to tell the heart that even spring has its bitterness, that time flies quickly, youth will pass soon, and at the end of life, one will look upon everything with cold detachment. Malvina, let's enjoy this time while our youth still allows us to feel pleasure.'

'Spring, summer, and autumn in a human life each have their adornments,' said Malvina, 'but only when one does not know poverty and can satisfy all their desires.'

'Is wealth the greatest happiness?'

'Without it, even love grows cold.'

'So, money is what you love, then?' said Albert.

'Who doesn't love what is absolutely necessary?'

Upon hearing these words, Albert sat in silence for a while, then took his hat and rose to leave.

'Why are you in such a hurry to go home today?' asked Malvina.

'I am not a rich man. I need to think about how to live in this world.'

'You should have done that sooner.'

'No wonder the cuckoo's voice saddened me. It was a foreboding.'

He said this and left.

After returning home, Albert threw himself on his bed but couldn't sleep. The world that appeared in his dreams was not the one he had known. At last, he realized that true bond and true love are rare. Where are human hearts? People think only of outdoing one another, chasing after vanity, yearning for luxury, deceiving those close to them and themselves, babbling about faith and love for others.

These thoughts tormented him. He began to despise his acquaintances and former friends. He scorned love. Envy and anger filled his soul.

The next day, seized by dark thoughts, Albert wandered alone into the fields. At last, he entered a thick forest. As he walked through the shadows of tall fir trees, his sorrow deepened into despair.

'Oh! If there truly exists a wicked spirit who can make a man rich,' he said to himself, 'who could help me even for a short while – I would worship him now.'

No sooner had he said this than he noticed someone sitting on a rotting stump under a tree. The figure was enormous, with a long, sharp nose, a lean, ruddy face, a fiery beard, and flame-colored hair. His faded clothing still held a trace of red. Albert froze in silence, watching him anxiously.

'I saw your sorrow,' said the stranger, 'and I am ready to help you. What do you want?'

'A better life. I suffer from poverty, and friends have betrayed me.'

'Worship the darkness, and the spirit of fire will serve you. Your gold and friends will return. But you must be cunning and perceptive, or your weak nature will destroy you.'

'What must I do for the spirit to serve me?'

'Listen and obey. Prick your finger and give me a drop of blood.'

Albert did as he was told.

'Just one drop,' said the stranger, 'is enough to fill a viper with venom. Now go, with this blood. As you leave the forest, climb the nearest hill. There you will find a viper crawling. It once tried to bite a child, but the mother's cry frightened it, and it lost its venom. Now, banished by the other vipers, it wanders alone. You will recognize it by the yellow tail, a sign of weakened power.[37] Let it lick a drop of your blood – it will instantly regain its venom and its strength. Follow it – and it will grant you its wisdom and its wealth. You will see a spirit in every spark of fire. Nikitron[38] will be your servant. He will be born from flame whenever you call.'

Having said this, the stranger stood, walked into the forest, and disappeared.

Through the wilderness, Albert headed in the direction shown by the stranger. By noon, he emerged from the forest, climbed a sandy hill, and came upon a massive viper with a yellow tail. It lacked the strength to flee, and only raised its head and glared at him with fiery eyes. Using a birch leaf, Albert offered the creature a drop of his blood. The viper swallowed it, and the yellow tint along its tail began to fade. Within half an hour, it had fully recovered.

Revived, the viper slid from the hill, weaving through bushes and heather, deeper and deeper into the woods. Albert followed it with quickened steps.

As the sun set in the west and dusk began to fall, he saw a grand palace where flames glowed in every window. The viper coiled up the steps and entered a great hall. Albert followed. Inside, tables were laid with food and wine, enchanting music played. Gilded mirrors and paintings in ornate golden frames adorned the walls. Albert marveled at the luxury, wandering from one wonder to the next. A voice invited him to sit at the table, to eat and drink, for all this had been prepared for him.

After dinner, the viper returned holding a gold coin in its mouth. Lifting its head, it offered the coin to Albert. On one side of the coin blazed a flame, on the other – a crown with the image of a serpent.

As Albert studied the coin, the voice echoed once more: '*As long as you possess it, you will have as much gold as you desire.*'

The viper vanished, and he was left alone in the hall. Recalling the words of the red-bearded stranger in the woods, Albert turned to the candle burning near him and called out:

'Nikitron!'

The candle's flame flared high. A tall, lithe, and radiant figure emerged from the fire, leapt to the floor, and stood before Albert as a man in scarlet robes.

'What are your orders?' asked the spirit.

''Take me home. At once.'

Albert soared through the sky, over forests and hills, and within moments found himself back in his room.

From his pocket, Albert took out the golden coin he had received from the viper. He placed it in a small box and whispered to himself:

'Oh, if only this box was full of gold!'

In the blink of an eye, the box brimmed with golden ducats. Albert gasped, unable to believe his own eyes. He stood motionless, afraid to look away, fearing the treasure might vanish if he blinked.

Neighbors witnessed an astonishing transformation. Albert purchased the most lavish chandeliers and clocks. His home glittered with gold and silver, his horses and carriages gleamed, his footmen wore fine livery. It was as though he owned a thousand souls. He held grand balls and entertained guests endlessly. The supply of rare wines seemed inexhaustible.

Word of his newfound fortune spread far and wide. Like everyone else, Malvina wondered how he had acquired such wealth. For months, she hoped he might come to see her, but he never did. He had changed. She waited in vain. Pride alone now filled his heart.

Autumn arrived, and with it came long, brooding evenings. Tired of endless amusements and empty praise, Albert chose to remain home alone. Birch logs crackled in the hearth, the mantel clock played its gentle melody, and the autumn wind sighed outside the windows. He sat before the fire, eyes fixed on the flames, and daydreamed about his past, the ingratitude and betrayal of friends who had abandoned him in misfortune and despair.

His thoughts drifted to Malvina. Memory conjured the soft glow of her presence until late into the night, and that final evening when the cuckoo clock prompted the conversation that sent him spiraling into unbearable despair. Memory awakened the forgotten longing, and with it, the desire to see her.

He resolved to see her again, but hesitated: '*No. She loves wealth. Now that I am rich, I own her heart. I will not lower myself as I once did. I'll send her a gift, a lavish one, and she will come running.*'

He turned to the fire and called out:

'Nikitron!'

The birch log crackled like a pistol shot. A glowing coal sprang from the fire, rolled across the floor and expanded. It morphed into a towering figure of a giant.

'What are your orders?' the spirit said, looking at Albert with fiery eyes.

'I don't want to see you in such a terrifying form,' Albert said. 'Return to the fire. Bathe in white flame, and come back to me with a bright face, gentle eyes, and the fine appearance of a young man.'

Like a gust of smoke, the spirit vanished into the hearth. A few minutes later, a pale tongue of flame leapt forth and reformed into the shape of a graceful young man, awaiting Albert's command.

'While I write a letter to Malvina, bring me diamond earrings, diamond bracelets, and a head ornament with rubies and diamonds,' Albert commanded.

Like a bolt of lightning, the spirit darted through the window, and before Albert had even finished the letter, the jewels were already on the table. The spirit, now in the form of a young man, stood silently beside them.

Albert sealed the letter and ordered that it be delivered to Malvina along with the jewels. He sent his horses and carriage to bring her to him.

Left alone, he paced the room, imagining the joy with which she would receive the lavish gifts, and the emotion with which she would greet him after the long separation. He knew that a man radiant with fortune, dressed in fine attire and frequenting luxurious salons – is a man whom any woman would place above others. In that moment, he would be like a god in her eyes.

Meanwhile, Malvina was sitting in her room with a visiting neighbor, chatting about various peculiar things. Eventually, their conversation turned to Albert. Where had he gotten such wealth? Rumors were flying. Some claimed he had traveled abroad and won millions at cards. Others said he had unearthed a buried treasure. Still others whispered that he had mastered black magic and gained his fortune through a pact with an evil spirit. But all of it remained speculation.

Malvina shared how Albert used to visit her, always professing his love. She recalled the final evening they spent together, when she had coldly told him that love without money grows cold, and how he had left, angry, and never returned.

Just then, the sound of a carriage stopping at the porch interrupted their conversation. Both women stood. First, they saw the carriage through the window. Then the footman appeared. A young man entered, handed over a letter and a box of glittering gifts. Malvina met the messenger's gaze, and something stirred uneasily in her heart. She meant to say something, but he had already vanished.

Awestruck, she looked at the dazzling diamonds. She had never seen such splendor, not even in her dreams. With trembling fingers, she broke the seal of the letter and saw Albert's signature. She read it to the end, then stood up stunned, unsure what to do.

'Albert sent me these gifts,' she said at last. 'He's asking me to come to him at once, in this carriage. I don't know what to do.'

'Of course you must go immediately,' her friend replied without hesitation.

'But won't he lose respect for me if I do?'

'Clearly, he didn't worry about that when he sent his horses and asked you to come this very evening.'

'What a change in him!' Malvina exclaimed. 'Before, when he visited me, every conversation was tinged with uncertainty, and now he's so full of himself!'

'He sent such rich gifts, he has every right to be self-assured. And in the great wide world, it's not considered disgraceful to make good use of a rich man's favor.'

'Then I'll go.'

'And quickly. If impatience clouds his mood, he won't greet you with a kind eye.'

Malvina rushed to her dressing table and took out her finest gown, while her friend helped style her hair, making sure everything was just right. She adorned herself with the diamonds Albert had sent, stepped into the waiting carriage, and arrived at his residence a mere half an hour later.

Albert welcomed her in the foyer and led her into the

drawing room, where everything exuded taste and elegance, and wealth shimmered in every corner. Malvina was awestruck by such a dramatic transformation in his fortune. In her eyes, Albert was a completely different man. His features had taken on a strange allure, and his words, she noticed, were filled with extraordinary intelligence and wit.

Immediately, trays of exquisite fruits and preserves appeared on the table. He invited her to help herself, and began recounting how an unexpected longing to see her had taken hold of him that very day.

Every word from her lover felt like a decree.

'Did you ever think of me,' Albert asked, 'after the last time we saw each other?'

'How could I not, when everyone talks about your newfound happiness every day?'

'And what do they say?'

'All sorts of things, but nothing certain.'

'Let them keep guessing. I'll only say this: I came by my wealth without wronging anyone.'

'I haven't heard anyone say you did.'

They remained alone, talking and reminiscing about all that had passed between them. The clock on the wall played a soft melody and struck midnight.

'Would you like to see my home theater?' asked Albert.

'But who will perform in the theater when there are only two of us here?'

'I keep the actors locked in a box. They'll appear before you shortly.'

'Isn't this going to be something frightening? For heaven's sake, don't scare me. It's exactly midnight.'

'Do you think I'm so cruel as to mock your fears? There's nothing to fear. You'll see wonders beyond your comprehension.'

Saying this, he took out a piece of agate flint and a firestarter. Standing beside her, he began striking sparks. Malvina beheld a sight beyond imagination: the sparks that fell to the floor turned into flickering flames, and from those flames, children were born, flaming curls of hair crowning their heads like smoldering flax or cotton. Their eyes glowed red like embers. Shimmering butterfly wings flapped from their shoulders. Some flitted near the ceiling, performing impossible feats in the air, others cavorted on tables, sofas, and on the floor, darting near chandeliers and paintings, shifting shapes, becoming tiny animals, birds, and insects.

'Oh! That's enough – please, stop!' Malvina cried. 'I can't look at these horrors any longer. Something terrible is gripping me with fear.'

'Such a delicate soul! What's so frightening about them? These are merely cupids, the kind you've seen in paintings of the beautiful Venus.'

'Oh, Albert! But the fire on their heads and the terrible look in their eyes!... They make my blood run cold.'

Albert waved his hand, and the vision vanished at once, like a passing dream. Terrified, Malvina couldn't calm herself for a long time. He laughed at her trembling nature. When the fear passed and the mood lightened, they continued talking about this and that until the morning star rose in the sky.

After returning home, Malvina could not forget the strange wonders she had witnessed. In secret, she confided in her friend. As they discussed it together, they decided that the beings she had seen were evil spirits disguised as children. Albert, they concluded, must be a black magician, and that was the source of his wealth.

The story passed from friend to friend, and soon it became common knowledge in cities and villages alike.

Everyone spoke of it, fearfully.

The elders warned the young and naïve to stay away from Albert and avoid his friendship. They said that the indecent amusements in his house, the drunken revelry, and the immoral conversations corrupted the moral and physical strength of those who gathered to partake in shameful pleasures.

A year passed. Then another. Albert never restrained his spending. Everything was done according to his will. The entertainments never ceased. Though Malvina had no more doubt about his dealings with the evil spirit, she surrendered herself to his desires.

One evening, Albert and a group of idlers lounged about, playing cards and drinking wine until midnight. The host and his guests were in high spirits. Amid the merriment, one of them said:

'Tell us, Albert, is it true what they say? That you're a black magician? Summon a spirit for us, we've never seen one.'

'I know exactly who's been spreading those rumors,' Albert replied. 'But tonight, I won't hide anything. I'll show you everything there is to see.'

He turned to the candleflame and called out, 'Nikitron!'

Everyone froze, staring in awe at the spectacle that followed: the flame leapt toward the ceiling, and from it emerged a trembling, translucent figure. It drifted downward and took the shape of a young man, who stood silently, awaiting Albert's command.

'Fly to Malvina,' said Albert, 'and bring her at once.'

The spirit shot through the window like lightning. Less than half an hour later, Malvina entered the room, pale with fear, her voice trembling:

'Why did you summon me, Albert? Do you want me to

be humiliated in front of your guests?'

'You are not alone,' he said, and, glancing at the paintings of mythological nymphs on the walls, he added, 'Here are some friends for you.'

In an instant, life-sized naked nymphs stepped out from the canvases and descended from the walls.

Everyone in the room was paralyzed with fear. Malvina screamed and collapsed to the floor.

'Nikitron!' Albert called again. The spirit reappeared, and Albert ordered him to take Malvina home. She regained consciousness, lying on her bed, trembling as she recalled the terrifying scene.

Neighbors, friends, and acquaintances all understood the truth: Albert was a black magician. Parents, relatives, and elders warned the youth to steer clear of him. They tried to bring him back to a righteous life.

But it was all in vain.

Each day, Albert's grand house teemed with godless and dissolute youth. And he himself became more and more unrestrained in his desires and debauchery. He mocked the idea of neighborly love, seduced and dishonored women and girls of all social ranks. His gold never ran out, and nothing held value to him anymore. Flatterers and party goers praised and idolized him, while honorable men and parents cursed him bitterly.

Years passed. At last, Albert grew sick from his excesses. The luxury he had once relished now repulsed him. Everywhere he went, he encountered nothing but unbearable bitterness. A heavy gloom filled his rich salons.

One day, he heard the sound of church bells, and someone informed him they were tolling for a deceased man. At that, his face changed, and he began pacing the room restlessly, without saying a word to his guests.

He looked out the window and saw people in

mourning, carrying torches as they followed a coffin on a cart. He jumped back from the window.

He shuddered violently when he heard that someone who had been at his home just the night before was now deceased.

From that moment, melancholy and dread consumed his thoughts. The flatterers no longer entertained him. Women no longer charmed him. He discovered a thousand flaws in Malvina, grew cold, and wanted nothing more to do with her.

Lost in solitude and sorrow, Albert wandered through the fields until he entered a dark forest. There, seated on a tree stump, was a man with fiery red hair and a scarlet coat. Albert recognized him at once. It was the same man who had taught him how to summon gold and control the fiery spirit.

'Still not satisfied?' the red man asked.

'I find no joy in anything,' Albert said. 'A strange, gnawing anxiety clouds my mind.'

'Perhaps Malvina betrayed you?'

'Malvina loved wealth, and still does. I never needed her love.'

'But you have the coin, with its golden flame that conquers all.'

'Yes. But it cannot buy peace.'

'The fiery spirit still obeys your every command.'

'But he cannot bring peace either.'

'You never knew how to use happiness or fortune. I warned you to be cunning and wise, or your weak nature would ruin you. And now, neither the golden flame, nor the fiery spirit, nor your beloved's gaze can warm you.'

'I despise everything,' said Albert. 'I want to feel nothing, to be numb, indifferent as a corpse, cold as a block of ice.'

'Then heed my final advice. Gather all your friends and go to the cemetery before midnight. You'll see tiny tongues of cold fire dancing on the graves – invite them to your soirée.'

With those words, he took a few steps back and vanished.

Albert rushed home and, without delay, did exactly as the strange man in the forest had advised. He left his guests behind and made his way to the cemetery. The night was dark and silent. Scattered across the graves, wooden crosses and weathered stones were barely visible. Tiny blue flames flickered here and there like melting candles.

'Cold spirits!' Albert called out. 'Tonight, I invite you to my home. I need your help. I want to be like you and despise the world.'

No sooner had he spoken than pale phantoms appeared, giants in eerie, terrifying forms. They bowed to him and promised to fulfill his wish with zeal.

Meanwhile, Albert's house echoed with noise and cheer. The salons were brightly lit, and laughter filled every room. When the host returned, his face was pale and uneasy.

'What's wrong, Albert?' his guests asked, one after another. 'Why so somber? What could possibly trouble you? Even if you spent a hundred years scattering the treasures fate has bestowed on you, you'd never run out.'

'Will any of us live that long?' said Albert. 'No man can delay sunset to prolong the day. And joy cannot be summoned back once it flies away.'

'Why dwell on the bleak?' said one guest. 'Who knows what the future holds? Let's live for today. Drink with us, and your gloomy thoughts will go away.'

'*Vinum cor laetificat!*'[39] said another. 'Why worry now about what tomorrow brings?'

> *'Bring the wine quickly,*
> *Let the day pass in joy.*
> *By my soul, my friend,*
> *I must drink myself blind!'*

'I'm expecting special guests tonight,' Albert said. 'They'll be visiting my home for the first time.'

'What guests?' asked one. 'And from where?'

'You'll know when you see them.'

'Then be sure to greet them more warmly than you greeted us. A toast to the host!'

Glasses clinked and foamed with wine. Voices rang out: '*Long live Albert!*'

Drunk on strong spirits, they boasted to each other about who could drink more. Noise and chatter of merry guests echoed in every room. Caught up in the cheer, Albert drained well over a glass of strong wine. But it barely touched him, his fleeting escape into oblivion quickly gave way to sorrow, which crept back in to torment him once more.

Midnight. The clock on a distant tower struck twelve. The clock in the corner of the lounge had barely finished the melody, when all the candles suddenly went out. Only a single lamp remained, glowing dimly under a shroud of mist.

From the corners and the center of the salon emerged monstrous shapes – terrifying creatures dressed in white, their eyes ablaze, their faces mottled with gangrenous rot. Blackened skeletons leaned on chairs and tables with crumbling arms. The fumes of alcohol evaporated. Screaming, the guests fled in panic. Some fainted right where they stood.

Pale and unmoving, Albert watched in silence. A

shiver ran through him, and in that moment, a terrible chill entered his chest, freezing him from the inside.

The monsters vanished. The guests who had fainted came to. But Albert's warmth never returned. His body was as cold and lifeless as a lump of gold.

He lived a few more years, but nothing could warm him. In spring and summer alike, frost coursed through his veins. They say that anyone who sat near him for a conversation would soon flee, as the cold that emanated from his lips was impossible to endure even for a few minutes.

At night, he was haunted by the cemetery phantoms he had invited. Strange voices called his name: '*Albert! Albert!*' not only in darkness, but also in broad daylight. He would ask visitors if they too had heard the voices calling his name. But each time, they looked at him with surprise and said that they had not.

Doctors were summoned from distant lands. They examined him, consulted each other, prescribed a multitude of treatments, but their wisdom and care were in vain.

'God's punishment has finally caught up with the dark magician and tempter,' the elders said.

And across towns and villages, the common folk passed the story from mouth to mouth: Albert was tormented by seizures[40] and every affliction imaginable, punished for his godless life, not getting even a moment of peace.

He was usually alone. The balls and raucous soirées were gone for good. Visitors grew rare, and those who came soon hurried to leave, chilled by the cold in his voice. One by one, they all drifted away. Only a servant would appear at the master's call.

The day was bleak. The wind howled, clouds blotted

out the sun. Silence hung over Albert's house like a shroud. A large flock of crows circled overhead, their hoarse cawing carried by the wind. By twilight, the windows seemed draped in black mourning cloth. Candlelight flickered faintly in the panes, but not for long. They found him dead, seated in a chair, his hands and feet stiffened as though he had frozen in the heart of winter."

"And what happened to Malvina, his beloved?" asked Zavalnia.

"She had diamonds and money, and easily found herself another suitor. No mournful thoughts stirred when the cuckoo clock chimed. She moved to the capital and, lost in the noise of the big city, soon forgot all about the past and about Albert."

"Such a death always awaits those who seek happiness only in this world, but do not care about the next," said my uncle, "What a terrible death for poor Albert!"

The organist stood and glanced out the window.

"Several stars are already shining, and the wind has died down. Tomorrow's weather will be good. I have a few more visits to make before returning home. So, Pan Zavalnia, let the traveler get some rest. I'll need to rise early tomorrow."

The beds were ready, and the fire was put out after evening prayers. Thinking of poor Albert, I drifted off to sleep.

CHRISTMAS EVE

I awoke and, still lying in bed, recalled the tales of the blind Francisak and the organist – the Weeping Woman, the Son of the Storm, the Fiery Spirits. All those wonders rose in my thoughts as strange, solitary, and terrifying visions. At that moment, my uncle opened the door, looked at me, and said:

"Get up, Janka. Do not grow accustomed to idleness. Winter nights are long enough for rest. Travelers set out before dawn, only the gentry lie abed till daylight, while others must think and work for them. Remember, you are a poor man and must serve yourself – put an end to these habits."

Zavalnia donned his fur coat, stepped outside, and ordered the servants to clear the snowdrifts from the windows and walls of the storeroom.

I rose quickly. The house lay quiet and a little dim. Light, weak and pale, pressed through windows crusted with ice and snow. In the servants' room I found the blind Francisak seated on a bench, while Pani Malhreta was preparing *kuttsia* and speaking to him of her household: the various breeds of hens she raised; the great, long-legged rooster so clumsy that a small barnyard cock would defeat and often wound him; her geese, which she tended through summer yet could not always protect from foxes; and the time a hunter on the lake mistook her ducks for wild ones and killed several with a single shot. Since then she kept her ducks close, never letting them stray too far from the yard.

While they spoke, my uncle tapped on the window, calling:

"I see someone coming from across the lake. It is Pan

Maragowski, returning from Polatsk with his children. Mistress, see that the room is made ready – the floor is not yet swept."

The swift horses turned off the main path, skirted the lakeshore, and soon reached the gate. My uncle greeted the arrivals: in the carriage sat Pan Maragowski with three children beside him, bundled in bear-skin and scarves so that only their eyes were visible. Pani Malhreta hurried out to lead the children inside.

For breakfast, warmed beer was served. Feeling the heat, the schoolboys began to buzz like bees in a hive, each telling of his studies, his friends and teachers, and the incidents of school life. Blind Francisak joined them, and they secretly recited verses they had committed to memory, hoping to surprise and delight their father.

They proudly displayed their awards before me: Klauber engravings of various sizes, crosses, and copper medals taken from a small box. They recited lessons learned from the *Alwar* and translated the *Holy History* from Latin. Pan Maragowski told my uncle that Stas and Juzik had been praised for diligence and good conduct, rewarded by the prefect and their teachers. My uncle was delighted, promising to have them fitted with new coats and to give them money for their school needs.

They spoke about the Krasny Fair in Polatsk. Maragowski talked about the prices of rye, oats, and barley; of domestic birds brought from every quarter; of the price of flax and hemp; and of merchants who came from other towns with scarves, cloth, silk, cotton, and other goods for clothing. He also spoke of gentry acquaintances who travelled on business and to purchase household necessities.

The whole day passed in conversation. The sun sank behind the forest, and evening drew on. Several neighbors from the shores of Lake Nieszczarda, invited to *kuttsia* with their wives and children, arrived at my uncle's house.

The first star appeared. In the center of the room a long table was set, strewn with hay and covered in a white cloth. Upon it were laid the fasting dishes with honey and the finest fish. Zavalnia broke the wafer with Pan Maragowski, then with each guest in turn. He shared how Prince Ahinsky, a gracious and kindly lord, had once invited all his neighbors to his house for this holy evening, rich and poor alike, so long as they were gentrymen of decent standing; how he welcomed each with warmth, spoke openly with everyone, and entertained them with tales of the past.

Maragowski remembered how, in earlier days, unlike today, these customs were strictly observed in every household of the district. Some gentry, he said, had abandoned the old traditions, for which God would not reward them, and times are getting worse and worse.

As the talk went on, certain guests slipped their hands beneath the tablecloth, trying to draw the longest dry straw – for luck. They compared them, making wishes: that flax would grow tall in spring, or that young maidens might marry quickly. They searched for grains of rye, wheat, or other cereals under the hay, for to find one there was a sign of a bountiful harvest.

After supper, they stepped outside. Under the clear, star-studded sky, criss-crossed by fiery meteor paths, they spoke of hopes for a good spring and an autumn rich in fruits and grain.

Oh, sweet memories of the old customs and the joys of our homeland! Fleeting as dreams, gentle as ancestral faith, yet etched forever in memory. Dearest companions to a solitary heart, for the soul in exile yearns for them as though for a paradise lost.

END OF VOLUME TWO

VOLUME THREE

MUSINGS OF A SOLITARY MAN

I sat upon the shores of the Gulf of Finland, marveling at the magical scenes of May nights from sunset to sunrise. There were no stars, white light had flooded the whole celestial dome, filling the expanse of the sea. May nights in a foreign land! You have always borne witness to my sorrowful and solitary songs, when my thoughts turned to the hills and forests of my native country, even as I sat here upon the bay's shore.

The spires of the capital's temples burned with golden fire, and silence reigned. The clock in the tower struck, its deep sound carrying to the distant outskirts of the city. A boat glided over the calm waters, sailors' songs drifted across the surface. In the lush gardens, music played, and the revelries lasted late into the night. Beneath the canopies of park trees, pleasant *têtes-à-têtes* continued, undisturbed.

Oh, May nights of my homeland! I loved to watch the

sunset from the shores of Lake Nieszczarda, and even the most exquisite music could not match the tender, enchanting song of the nightingale or the lonely call of the cuckoo. Wild forests are dearer to the heart than splendid parks! The rustle of your branches would plunge me into contemplation, in the shade of your ancient trees I always sensed nature's hidden mysteries. In old folk tales I found both truth and feeling, I sensed their wisdom and recognized in them the prayers of the people. This was a hundred times more precious to me than the shallow amusements of luxurious city salons.

The sea! I have read many poems about you, I have compared your calm and stormy waves with the lakes of my homeland, lakes that sparkle like crystal among overgrown shores, or roar in a fierce storm. In my youth I adorned mankind with kindness and justice, the future with hope, and, as though in a safe harbor, I dreamed in peace of storm-tossed skies and the vast ocean waves.

The sea! I discovered another world in your depths, a happy and strange one, of which I heard in many tales of the common folk. There was once a maiden named Hanna, daughter of the great Ocean, queen of spirits, a marvel of beauty. All the invisible powers of earth and sea obeyed her command. A miracle of kindness, she cherished the noble character of a young man who descended to the depths of the sea and stood before the great Ocean to serve him in exchange for the release of his father. But he was weak and could not fulfill the commands of the Master of the Sea. Coming to the rescue of her beloved, Hanna commanded the spirits herself, and in a single night raised palaces of coral and precious pearl. The Ocean rewarded the youth's virtue and wisdom by giving him his daughter Hanna for a wife.

The sea! I no longer think of you as I once did. You are

like blind fortune – raising some to riches, casting others into the bottomless deep. Your winter breast cannot be softened when a sailor, driven far from home, is doomed to perish alone from hunger or grief upon a deserted island shore. Even in fair weather, voracious monsters do not slumber in your depths, but gaze with open jaws upon the sea-traveller. Oh, sea! You are the world itself, with its countless and uncertain paths.

The weather changes, the wind blows from the east, a swollen sail whitens over the water. Oh, people of the great wide world! Lift your eyes to the heavens from your tall and splendid mansions! Heavy clouds hang over the city, forming strange apparitions up above: an enormous castle in the air, surrounded by walls and ramparts, with towers rising high. Nearby, giant knights on horseback gather into ranks, and moments later, only ruins remain, while the entire army dissolves into smoke. Like a fiery serpent, lightning bolts through the heart of the cloud.

Oh, people of the great world! Look to the sky from your lofty dwellings, read the signs that God's own hand inscribes in the shifting outlines of the clouds that are always there, right before your eyes. They proclaim that nothing on this earth is lasting: your mansions will crumble into ruin, your power, riches, honor, and glory will scatter like smoke into the air.

Spring! Your smile is swift, your gentle breezes pass quickly, the colors of the garden fade too soon. Damp mists will creep across the earth, the birds will fly to warmer lands. The wind will whirl yellow leaves over the cemetery, scattering them at the foot of masterful monuments and silent statues that stand above the graves of famous men. Once, fortune had showered them with flowers. But today, the wind covers cold marble with sand, and their names would vanish into oblivion, had they not crowned themselves in life with the diadem of truth.

Truth! You are the messenger of heaven in this vale of sorrow. You are an angel, a guardian, a mentor in life. Enlighten us with your light when true faith – the most precious treasure of our ancestors, the purest beam of heavenly light – is dimmed by the mists of the tangled wisdom of the arrogant and deceitful philosophers.

When nature sleeps beneath the snow, when the north wind howls, the long dark nights pass while thousands of lights burn in the windows, the merry life of the capital does not cease. And I, in my solitude, love to lose myself in dreams. My thoughts fly to my homeland, I summon revered elders from their graves, and in my mind I see and hear them speak of happier times – of the golden age, when a man plowed his own field and built a house for himself and his children. Harvests were better then: the plowman sang a cheerful song as he worked in the field, elk and wild goats roamed the forests, the hunter easily found his prey, and the fisherman cast his net into the water with perfect trust.

But when men divided the fields and forests with iron chains, when each sought wealth, fine clothes, and costly carriages – then the world changed. The rich began to oppress the poor, angering God, who no longer blessed human toil. The harvests failed, and honeydew, descending before sunrise like a terrible poison upon the grass, wrought great harm upon the livestock.

Even now, the elders speak of the strange signs in the heavens when the Swedish forces met the great army of the Northern Caesar[41] upon the Baltic shore. Narva and other fortresses shuddered beneath the victors' weapons. The glare of terrible fires, floating in the clouds above the sea edge, often stained the midnight sky all over Belarus with blood. Trembling, people looked up toward where cavalry and infantry clashed in the smoky, crimson clouds, and the vision held until dawn.

Often they speak of the Year of the Goosefoot,[42] when plague and famine ravaged Belarus in the time of the Swedish war. The land lay bare of snow, the hills without grass, like barren steppes. The north wind, sweeping across the empty fields as over sand dunes, stripped away the dry earth and killed the tender shoots with its breath. The ground split from the frost, and fish perished in the lakes, shackled beneath thick ice.

Spring came, the trees and meadows awoke, but the farmer's heart was heavy: goosefoot covered the fields, rye ears grew far apart, the lakeshores were strewn with dead fish, and plague and hunger spread through the land.

At midnight, strange and terrifying wonders occurred outside the windows of village huts. The cry of an infant woke the sleepers, but when someone went out to bring the child in, there was no one in the yard, and the crying had ceased. Only the dogs barked near the neighboring huts. This happened often, driving everyone into despair.

"*God's punishment for grievous sins*," people said, weeping bitter tears each day before the icon of the Virgin.

And in their talk they remember you with gratitude. You, the noble souls who were benefactors to your subjects, neighbors, and poor compatriots. When the crops failed, you gave freely to poor peasants, to widows and orphans. You supported those crushed by hardship and injustice with wise counsel, revived hope in their hearts, and revealed God's mercy and omnipotence. None left your threshold without comfort, even a beggar praised heaven with joy upon leaving your doorstep. You sought no earthly reward for your generosity, no vain glory such as the weak crave the way children covet toys. Your reward and your glory are before the face of God.

O noble ashes of our fathers!
Your graves are unadorned,
No marble pillars stand above them;
Only birches cast mourning shadows
Over moss-grown stones and pine crosses.
Glorious ancestor! The angel of merciless truth
God will send to awaken your children;
Your charity will inspire the young,
And golden ages will shine over us…
On the day of Holy Judgment the world will tremble,
The trumpet will wake the dead.
Glorious ancestor! You will stand before God
In honor and glory forever.[43]

GUESTS AT ZAVALNIA'S HOUSE

Before the New Year, my uncle, the blind Francisak, and two neighboring landowners sat together, recalling the bygone days. They spoke of past harvests and of the misfortunes that had befallen the land when grain withered in the fields and livestock perished of pestilence. They discussed how best to improve the fields and meadows, how to raise a fine herd, the profits a diligent farmer might earn from such care, and how to graft the orchard trees. The talk went on without pause until noon, and resumed again after the midday meal.

At last, my uncle said to the guests:

"On the Second Day of Christmas, I visited Pan Maragowski. There were many guests there whom I had never met before, and I must say, their conversation held no interest for me. God knows what they didn't speak of, flitting from one topic to the next: dogs and horses, luck and losses at cards, gossip about their friends, praising some and condemning others. In time they turned to the Bible, and there their true ignorance showed. They spoke of matters they neither understood nor, I suspect, had ever read about. Pan Maragowski could not bear it and asked them not to poison the minds of the youth. As for me, I far prefer the company of good neighbors such as you, and nothing in our talk today could offend the Almighty."

"This is the golden youth of the new age," said Pan Sivoha. "Once the frost strikes the tender sprouts, they will come to their senses as soon as God's hand falls upon them in anger."

"I noticed," said my uncle, "that Janka sat silent through all of it, watching from a distance and refusing to take part in their disputes."

"Uncle, I remembered what I once heard from my teacher: people become skeptics not because they see contradictions in faith, but because, with minds feeble and senses dulled by a dissolute life, they cannot feel, nor love, nor understand the truth of religion. That is why I kept silent, for what use is there in arguing with those whose knowledge and feelings are so limited?"

"That is true. They do not understand what it is to be a good man. They think only of the honors and heraldry of their ancestors. Why not look instead to their virtues – they honored their faith, and God blessed their lives."

Interrupting the conversation, Stas said to his father:

"And who will tell stories today?"

"It's your turn," he said, smiling.

"I, father, will tell you about Twardowski."[44]

"Good, tell us, and we shall all listen."

"Oh! I've heard much of Twardowski," said Pan Latyshevich. "He was a great sorcerer, but perhaps Stas will tell us something new."

TWARDOWSKI AND HIS PUPIL

"The landlord with whom we live," said Stas, "told us that Twardowski attended the schools in Polatsk. He studied well, but did not obey his teachers, and secretly read forbidden books until he no longer feared mortal sin. In time, he learned sorcery and sold his soul to an evil spirit. Neither the professors nor the priest knew about this when they appointed him to supervise several primary school students.

In his free hours, Twardowski entertained the boys in his care, occasionally showing them strange marvels. One day, when the weather was clear and calm, the students were leaning out the window, blowing soap bubbles. Standing beside them, Twardowski said:

'Look! Tiny devils are flying in the air, riding on your soap bubbles.'

And sure enough, atop each bubble appeared tiny bright-eyed creatures, with wings like cupids and faces full of strange grimaces. They peered at everyone in turn. Frightened, one of the boys cried out, *'Jesus, Mary!'* – and at once, everything vanished. Neither the priest nor the professors learned a word of it.

Hugon, whom Twardowki liked more than any other pupil, was also among them. During walks outside the city, Twardowski spoke to him the most, and never refused him when Hugon wished to buy something and asked for money. Twardowski praised him often, as though he were the best student of them all.

Around nine o'clock in the evening when the boys went to bed, Twardowski would often leave the house and head over to his acquaintances in the city, returning at midnight. A separate room, where he sometime stayed, was always locked, and no one knew what books he kept there. Hugon too was never permitted to enter unsupervised.

One night, however, Twardowski left without locking the door. At ten o'clock everyone went to sleep, but Hugon kept his lamp lit and sat up alone. As the bell of the Jesuit church struck midnight, and Twardowski had not yet returned, Hugon noticed the key still in the lock. He entered the room.

Upon the table lay a huge book in an old vellum binding. He looked into it, amazed – for the first time in his life he saw white ink on black paper. No sooner had he read half a page than a grim little dwarf appeared before him, eyes burning with a white flame, face black as coal.

'Why did you summon me?' the evil spirit asked, glaring at Hugon, who sat frozen with terror.

The demon struck him dead on the spot, then vanished.

After midnight, Twardowski returned and found his friend's body lying beside the open book. Understanding what had happened, he summoned the demon.

'Why did you kill the poor lad?' the sorcerer demanded.

'So that he would not reveal your secret to those who should not know it,' replied the spirit.

'It should have been handled differently,' said Twardowski. 'Neither you nor I can bring him back to life, and I could be accused of murder and punished for it. We must hide this crime. Enter his body, and be his soul until the time comes for him to die.'

The demon instantly entered the corpse, and Hugon rose again, but was now somehow different. His eyes gleamed with a strange, sinister light. His face was unchanged, yet something in it repelled anyone who looked upon him.

Soon after, he returned to school. Professors and classmates noticed a change in him, but no one knew what it was.

At Mass, he behaved immodestly, making others laugh, and when the priest offered Holy Communion, he would flee the church, pressing a handkerchief to his nose as if to staunch a nosebleed.

No admonition or punishment had any effect, and he was expelled. From that day on, he became a sworn enemy of the Jesuits. He wrote slanderous verses, spoke against the holy faith, and set a corrupt example for all who spoke with him. At last, he left Polatsk and vanished, God knows where."

"Well done, Stas," said Pan Sivoha. "A short tale, but a good one. I am certain some of our young gentlemen still harbor the thoughts of that demon in their hearts."

"There is a lesson here, Stas," my uncle added, "that we must avoid evil men. It was Twardowski's friendship that doomed Hugon, giving the demon a vessel for his malice."

"Oh, and what if Pan Hugon," said Latyshevich, "had become a judge, or a secretary, or some other official? Imagine the harm he could have done then!"

At that moment, Pani Malhreta entered from the servants' room with a letter in hand.

"Jakush has arrived," she said. "Here is a letter from Pan Maragowski."

My uncle read it, then passed it to me.

"Pan Maragowski is very kind to you. He asks that you visit him. You may go tomorrow after Holy Mass and stay a few days. But call Jakush in here, he is a talkative fellow, and I enjoyed his story about the werewolf."

As soon as Jakush entered, my uncle ordered food and drink to be set before him, and they began speaking of the guests he had seen at Pan Maragowski's house. The strangest of them all, in my uncle's opinion, was the thin, long-haired, mustached Pan Chubkevich, who spoke endlessly of his ancestors' fame, his urgent need to marry, and – for his affairs were in a critical state – the need to find a wife with at least two hundred souls in her dowry.

At the mention of Chubkevich, Jakush scowled, shook his head, and said:

"That Chubkevich should first take a good look at himself, to see what his own soul is worth. He has sold young lads and girls to God knows whom, ignoring the pleas and tears of their poor mothers. He will answer before God for their torment. If he were to find himself a White Magpie, that would be a match fit for him indeed! I am surprised that our master, who cares for his subjects as a father cares for his own children, would invite such a man into his house."

"Tell me," asked my uncle, "who is this White Magpie you speak of?"

"It is better, sir, that I tell you of the White Magpie than speak another word about Chubkevich, may God punish him."

The White Magpie

"Gentlemen, you all know Lake Jazna, that dark forested place where three districts meet: Polatsk, Siebezh, and Nievel. Not far from its shores there once stood a large estate. In it lived a lord who, even now, is remembered as Skamaroha. He held subjects in all three districts.

So, Pan Skamaroha was of an extremely restless temperament, arrogant and greedy. He only visited his neighbors with complaints. He had money, but always sued and wronged the poor, widows, and orphans. His subjects' lives were hell on earth.

Few people came to his house. A huge black dog never left his side, and the servants entered only when he whistled for them.

One evening Skamaroha sat alone. As usual, he gazed in the mirror, twisted his mustache, and studied his round face, which, people said, looked like a full moon. Then he sat down, lit his pipe, and sank into thought, while his dog slept on the floor beside him.

As he mulled over schemes to enlarge his fortune, gray dusk descended upon the land. Suddenly, clouds gathered over his abode, the wind roared, and rain lashed the walls. Darkness filled the room, only a dim glimmer seeped through the windows.

Skamaroha had barely shaken himself from his thoughts when a flash of lightning lit the chamber, and he saw a strange, terrible figure in the corner by the door. He cried out in fear, calling for his servants, but thunder and wind drowned his cries. No one heard, no one came.

A tall, thin figure approached Skamaroha.

'Cease your cries,' it said. 'No one will hear you, and your black hound lies fast asleep.'

'Who are you, and how did you get here?'

'Be patient, you will soon find out,' the apparition replied, striking a spark and lighting the candle on the table before the mirror.

In the glow, Skamaroha saw a manlike creature: spindly legs, bulging round eyes, and a small sharp face that resembled a bird's.

With a trembling voice, he cried:

'What a dreadful face! Surely an evil spirit stands before me.'

'Quiet yourself. You and I are not so different, and I can bring you great profit.'

'Why did you come so silently that even my dog did not hear?'

'Do you not hear the storm? I hid here from the downpour and lightning. As for the dog, he sleeps a deep sleep and will not wake until I rouse him.

Sit down, be calm, and I will tell you everything. I rest during the day, but when the sun sets I wander the world: I learn what men think, what they speak, what they eat and drink. I know how to cast deep sleep on dogs and guards. I listen to the words of the commoners and to the secret thoughts of their masters. My eye is swift, my hearing so fine I catch a whisper through the thickest walls. Faces reveal a man's character to me. I stir men to talk, and I remember all of it. I enter through the narrowest crack, and doors do not creak when I open them.'

Skamaroha whistled for servants and kicked his dog.

'It is useless,' the stranger said. 'No one hears you. The wind howls, the rain pours, and the dog will not wake.'

'Why do you wander the world? Why gather such knowledge?'

'I am the messenger of the White Magpie. I know of your thoughts and plans.'

'And who is this White Magpie you speak of?'

'Oh! The White Magpie astonishes the world with her wisdom. Her face is a marvel of beauty, her figure tall and majestic. Her garments are wrought of diamonds and pearls. She dwells in a palace you have never dreamed of. Lords and sages bow before her. At her command, spirits draw treasures from earth and sea. She has tamed wild bears who serve her like obedient dogs. She surpasses all sorcerers. At times she clothes herself in the feathers of a white bird to visit those she favors, and she rewards them with riches and happiness.'

Looking at the messenger, Skamaroha said:

'You speak of strange, incomprehensible things.'

'Tomorrow, at this very hour, I shall return, and the White Magpie will come to rest beneath your roof. Receive her well, be mindful of your words. Let no servant enter at midnight, as her first visit must remain secret.'

He opened the window and looked out.

'The clouds are parting, only the wind still blows. Thunder will not strike me tonight. Half an hour from now I shall be speaking to the White Magpie about you.'

Saying this, he leapt out the window. Skamaroha saw only a black beast dash across the yard and vanish.

Skamaroha stood motionless in the center of the room. Anxiety gripped him, a shiver passed through his body. What was this apparition? A vision? Or some evil spirit bent on dragging him into misfortune? The clock struck. Midnight had come. He whistled: the dog awoke, bristling, eyes glowing with fire, circling the room and whining. Servants gathered outside the door awaiting orders.

'For half an hour or more I called you, and none came. What does this mean? You shield your eyes like men risen from graves. Was the night not long enough?'

First Servant: 'I do not know, sir, but a great heaviness came over us. We sat silent, unable to speak. Our eyes grew heavy, we could not look up, and we all fell asleep against our will.'

Skamaroha pondered, then asked:

'And did you dream?'

First Servant: 'I had a strange dream. I saw our late master, and I walked with him through a wilderness swarming with serpents that barred his path. He looked sorrowful and said not a word, only pressed further among the rocks. Then I saw a place unlike our land, and ruins. In the west, the sun set in black clouds, and a bare forest rustled. Beside the road, fierce beasts appeared. I cried: *'Sir, let us return, the night is near and the way is perilous!'* He wept: *'The night will be long and terrible. The morning bell will not greet the sun soon. These beasts I do not fear, but they may tear you apart – do not leave my side.'* Then the monsters attacked. I fainted from fear and awoke trembling.'

Second Servant: 'I walked by a murky river, its banks studded with stones that seemed like men in long filthy garments. A giant appeared, broad-shouldered, with terrible eyes. I tried to flee but my legs were as though shackled, I could not move. He struck me, flinging me near the center of the river. The water carried me away. I screamed for help, but only the stones answered with laughter, and their mocking echoed over the river banks. Then I saw my father in the distance. He was raising his hands to heaven, while my mother fainted, for they could not help me. Then suddenly, I stood over an abyss, and that frightening giant found me again. He pushed me into the abyss, and I woke up in terror.'

Third Servant: 'I dreamed of a storm. It tore roofs off houses, and the wind carried a demon and dropped it right in front of the porch...'

'Enough of this nonsense! Wind and damp brought drowsiness, hot blood made your brains feverish, and awakened fantastic dreams in your heads. Go back to your quarters and sleep.'

Left alone, Skamaroha paced the room. Strange thoughts swirled in his head, the dreadful figure stood before his eyes. He shuddered at its repulsive form. Yet he loved gold so much that he longed for it, and would accept even from a demon's hand. The beauty of the White Magpie enticed him. He yearned to see her soon and win her favor.

He paced the room, then stood like a pillar, lost in thought. He picked up a book, tossed it aside, stroked his dog. He hoped sleep would calm him, but he leapt again from bed, lit a candle, thinking on and on. Near dawn he dozed at last, but even then the messenger of the White

Magpie haunted him in his restless sleep.

Morning was quiet. The sun rose high, herds grazed, plowmen tilled the fields. Skamaroha lay pondering the strange events and his prophetic dreams. At last he whistled, and a servant ran in.

'Hurry and make all the rooms spotless. Wash the floors, dust the walls and ceilings of cobwebs. Polish the furniture and bronze. Mirrors must shine. Clean the icons and the windows until they are like new. Tell the steward to set the estate in order.'

'Is the master expecting an important guest?' asked the astonished servant.

'Your business is not to ask but to obey. Go and pass the orders to the others.'

Skamaroha wandered the park, lost in thought beneath the linden trees. He whistled for the dog and headed to the field. Wandering around everywhere, he impatiently awaited the evening.

The servants marveled at his sudden change and whispered of the dreams that had plagued them during the storm. Yet their work was swift, and by sunset the furniture, bronze and mirrors gleamed like new.

Night came. Skamaroha ordered the dog removed and forbade entry to his room. He smoked his pipe and paced back and forth. He opened the window - silence reigned, and a handful of stars already prickled the sky. He lit a candle, and in its glow he saw yesterday's guest standing in the corner. Thin legs, eyes like fiery sparks, a bewildering smile on his ugly face. Skamaroha recoiled.

'I cannot look at you without disgust, your face fills me with dread.'

'You have weak nerves. In time you will lose your fear, and as we get to know each other better, you'll start looking at everything without fear or disgust. And you'll be better off for it. You have prepared well. She will be here soon.'

As soon as he said this, a magpie flew through the window, larger and more graceful than others, her feathers white as snow, her eyes black and shining. She landed on the table, then fluttered to the floor, and in an instant became a lady of wondrous beauty: tall, rosy-faced, her eyes large and brilliant, her garments glittering with precious jewels. Skamaroha stood speechless. She broke the silence:

'Flying here, I saw beautiful mountains and forests of this land. There are so many lakes here. Tell me, do the people want for anything?'

'Yes, Mistress,' he whispered, bowing. 'Nature has given us all we need.'

'I have long wished to visit this land and its people. I hope to make new friends here.'

'Many will count it their greatest happiness to meet you, Mistress.'

'And the subjects?'

'They are content, the meadows and hills give ample grass for herds.'

The White Magpie sat in a chair, and Skamaroha beside her. He spoke long of the Drysa and Dzvina. He told her about the people in the area, his reputation among neighbors, the income from the farms. He described how they traded with Riga when the rivers flood in spring, and how that benefits the locals. The conversation continued uninterrupted until midnight.

'I will visit again, and you shall present me to your good neighbors. But now I must hasten home: it is midnight, and the journey is long.'

She bowed, turned into a white magpie once more, and flew into the night.

Astonished, Skamaroha stared after her. Returning to his chair he saw the messenger still in the room, holding a great sack of gold.

'The White Magpie sends this gift, so that you remain loyal and bring others into her devotion. She will come again when your neighbors are gathered.'

He sprang out the window and was gone.

Skamaroha paced the room alone. Strange visions swirled in his head. The rich attire and exquisite beauty of the White Magpie stood still before his eyes. He could not forget her even for a moment, and because of his thoughts, sleep eluded him. He did not sleep a wink.

At dawn, he whistled. The servant entered with the dog at his heels. Petting the dog, Skamaroha asked:

'Were you tormented by dreams again last night?'

'Oh, sir! Heaviness came over us again. Our sleep was short and restless. The night watchmen heard dogs howl, beasts roar, and saw a dragon flying northward, trailing sparks and flames, perhaps bearing gold for some soul that had sold itself to the devil. The steward says folk saw a woman weeping in the cemetery, and her voice filled everyone with sorrow.'

Skamaroha frowned and strode across the room.

'Don't say such nonsense. You talk of nothing but miracles and prophecies like those superstitious old women – every little thing unsettles you and robs you of peace. Tell them to ready the horses, I will visit Pan L. and Pan S., and others.'

From estate to estate he went, telling of the White Magpie's beauty, wealth, and wisdom. Everyone listened with great interest. Some warned of hidden treachery, afraid that a great misfortune might befall them. Others were delighted and begged Skamaroha to put in a good word to the White Magpie when she visits again. They eagerly awaited the day they meet her.

Guests soon gathered at his house, ardent supporters of the White Magpie though they had never seen her. They barred the servants so they would not hear the secret conversations of the masters. They filled the table with wine, and Skamaroha spoke again of her wisdom and beauty, swearing that no painting had ever revealed such perfection.

The clock struck midnight. The night was clear, calm, and the full moon shone through the open window. Raising his glass, Skamaroha said:

'To the health of the lady who has been our constant theme this evening.'

As he said this, the White Magpie bolted in like lightning and perched among the glasses. Everyone leapt in astonishment. The room went silent. She circled the table, inspected the guests, and landed on the floor, swift as the wind, – and everyone saw a woman of extraordinary beauty, adorned in diamonds and pearls.

'I hurried here, hoping for friendly faces, and I was not deceived. I see hearts full of goodwill. Tell me your desires, and I shall think on your happiness.'

'Yes, madam,' said Skamaroha. 'Your name has constantly been on our lips. These are your most devout admirers and most loyal servants – until the end.'

Then the White Magpie sat in a chair, and kindly spoke to each guest, asking after their estates and incomes, sharing her observations and counsel.

Time flew by quickly. Again Skamaroha raised his glass:

'To our Mistress!'

And all the guests raised full glasses and shouted together: '*Long live the White Magpie!*' and drained their cups.

She rose, thanked them, tasted her wine, and set down the glass. They drank and talked till dawn.

As the clouds turned pink before the sunrise, she thanked the host for his hospitality and the guests for their kind wishes, transformed back into a white magpie, and vanished into the sky.

People said she went thus from house to house, always at night, visiting those she had first met in Pan Skamaroha's house. Everywhere, wine flowed and glasses were raised to her health.

Soon, the premonitions of the common people – that a dreadful witch had secretly sent out pests everywhere to harm the peasants – began to come true. I will tell you, gentlemen, of an incident that happened not far from here, in the village of Klishkova. Everyone remembers it to this day.

Out of nowhere, all the milking cows began to wither, and their milk disappeared completely. It was sorcery, no doubt about it. Everyone lamented and complained, but no one could discover the source of the evil. By chance, a guard from Klishkova was returning home before sunrise. He saw a magpie white as snow fly out of the house of a woman for whom the master of that village had built a new dwelling with enormous windows. The guard told others. They began to suspect that a witch lived there, and started watching her to prove her guilt.

In the end, they learned the truth. On *Kupalle*[44] night the sorceress hid in the deep forest, gathering dew in her hands and summoning evil spirits to collect milk for her vessels. Meanwhile, a servant girl – hired only days earlier and unaware of her mistress's designs – washed all the clay jugs and wooden tubs, turned them upside down, and left them to dry. The evil spirits did not see this and all night long poured milk onto the ground. In the morning the entire village saw a river of milk flowing from beneath the witch's house. She would surely have met her death, had she not instantly turned into a bird and flown far away.

Soon there were breaks in the rye,[46] and with them, a multitude of nimble little creatures, too quick to be killed, who sheared the sheep in their pens. Meanwhile, bears attacked beehives everywhere, destroying the bees.

I will tell you something even stranger, gentlemen: packs of werewolves prowled the fields, so that it was too terrifying to venture out."

"Why call them werewolves?" asked my uncle. "Perhaps they were real wolves that had run in from other forests, fleeing wildfires? Bears and other beasts migrate in this way."

"I am certain," said Jakush, "that they were werewolves, for it is said that some bore necks of white, black, or other colors."

"And why is that?"

"Because they were people turned into beasts. Whatever color scarf they had worn over their shoulders, that color became the fur on their necks."

"You speak of strange things!"

"But it is true. It was a wretched time. People lamented their misery, and the howling of the werewolves tore at their hearts."

"So what became of Pan Skamaroha and the other followers of the White Magpie?"

"Hearing the curses of the people and learning from demons that hunters with loaded guns were searching for her, the White Magpie fled far away and never appeared in our land again. But the evil she had sown spread across the land. Those who once drank to her health now drink the tears of the poor. Pan Skamaroha left these parts, and some say he now guards the countless treasures of the White Magpie's palace in the form of a terrible bear."

Here Jakush ended his tale of the White Magpie and picked up his hat.

"Where are you hurrying?" asked my uncle. "Did your master order you home today?"

"My master gave me leave to go to the tavern for the festivities, to see my friends and take some pleasure. But I must be home before dawn, before anyone at the manor wakes up. The sun is already low, soon it will be dark."

"Give my regards to your master, and tell him that Janka will visit tomorrow after Holy Mass."

The Tormented Spirit

The blind Francisak remained silent during Zavalnia's conversation with the guests. He seemed lost in sorrowful thoughts while Jakush was telling the story of the White Magpie, yet his face betrayed that the tale had deeply touched his soul. To break the silence, my uncle said:

"Pan Francisak has been quiet for a long time. It seems something troubles him."

"My happiness ended in childhood, on the day the world went dark for me. In the midst of this never-ending night, I hear the wailing of the unfortunate. The suffering of others pierces the heart of one who has himself come to know sorrow."

"Oh, merciful God, all things pass in time. Janka, ask them to bring *harelka* and some snacks. It's time for refreshment. Life is short – let us drink."

When they had drunk and eaten, my uncle said to the guests:

"Thank God, the New Year is only minutes away. In His mercy He has allowed us to greet it in health. Before the rooster crows and the last hour of the year is up, let Pan Francisak share something he once heard in the world, for in his life he has met many people and remembers every conversation he's had with them. After that, it will be Pan Sivoha's turn."

"My stories are unlikely to please, for I remember only the sad ones."

"In our land, everyone is sad," said Sivoha. "My stories will not make anyone laugh either. Let Pan Francisak begin. Meanwhile I'll try to think of something."

"Well then, if it is the will of the host and the guests," said the blind man, and began:

"Many years ago, I was traveling from Polatsk to Nievel. After leaving the city, I soon found myself in the forest. The trees rustled above my head, the horse trudged slowly, as if pulling a heavy cart over sandy hills. I sat, daydreaming about this and that, while my companion walked beside me on foot. Interrupting my thoughts, he said:

'We have traveled twenty-five *versts*. The village of Babaviki and its tavern are near, and the horse needs to rest there. A few more *versts* and we'll reach the river with good pasture. After grazing the horse we'll go on through the night, for the heat of day torments both us and the animal.'

I agreed gladly.

We reached the village. My companion busied himself with the cart, while I sat in the tavern, listening to the peasants talk about a certain man. Their debate grew heated. One man claimed he was driven by fate and suffered innocently at the hands of everyone he met, condemned to wander the world. Another one called him a parasite and an evildoer, best avoided altogether. Their argument swelled to the point of blows.

'For several weeks now,' one said, 'he has appeared here

and there. It seems some know him, for he visits certain people, stays a while, then wanders again through the hills and forests. He is quiet and gentle. Some even say he has shared his last bread and last coin with the poor.'

'He must be mad, to give away his last bread and money without thought for tomorrow. A sensible man first takes care of himself. Life is no open field to cross. Without a den to shield you from rain and storm, what kind of life is that? He'll have no kind word from me.'

Then a third man turned to me:

'I see you're bound for Nievel. Be careful, lest you find trouble. In these forests, God alone knows what may befall you if you meet that man.'

'I do not fear,' I answered, 'for I carry no treasure.'

'Well then, safe journey to you!'

The peasants exited the tavern quarreling.

Soon my companion returned.

'I've harnessed the horse,' he said. 'Let's go on. It's better by the river, where there's plenty of grass and water. We'll rest more easily there.'

Saying this, he helped me to the cart.

We reached the riverbank. He led the horse to graze while I sat beneath a tree. Evening drew on. A cuckoo complained sorrowfully above, while a nightingale sang its tender song in the thicket nearby. Alone, I fell into quiet reverie.

'A beautiful evening,' said a voice beside me, breaking my thoughts.

'Yes, beautiful,' I replied. 'Quiet everywhere, and the nightingale sings like magic.'

'But you enjoy only half its pleasure, you hear the song, but cannot see the blue sky or the spring adornment of hills and forests.'

'I have wandered long in the world without seeing it.'

'It is unfortunate not to see the world, but just as unfortunate to see too much with clear eyes.'

'A man can see and hear no further than his nature allows.'

'Do you believe in wonders? I not only see and hear far, but also change form.'

'I cannot see how a man can change his form.'

'You cannot see me, and so you cannot see.'

'Who are you? A local, or a wanderer like me?'

'I am the Tormented Spirit. I hasten to eternity faster than most.'

'I sense restlessness in your soul.'

'Yes, restlessness. It is hard for a tormented soul to be calm. As a sick man turns in bed, seeking relief from pain, so I change my form, seeking the same. I will tell you of my terrible sin. When my hopes deceived me and my soul plunged into despair, I thought only in the cemetery might I find the magic flying herb that brings peace and happiness. Dreaming of it, I wandered all night among the graves like a werewolf, thinking of the spirits, envying their peace. I sinned, ah! Perhaps that sin poisoned my blood, set all my nerves on edge, and shook my very nature. Stricken with illness, my hearing grew sharp, my eyes became like those of a spirit. I see and hear far – a terrible affliction! Unable to endure it, I change my form, yet find no relief.'

'What did you see and hear in the world,' I asked, 'that so torments your soul?'

'I saw wild monsters tearing women and children. The mountains did not stir at the cries of the condemned, only echoes repeated their groans before falling silent. Seeing this, I became a monster myself, cursing the stars that looked indifferently from the heavens, and the clouds that did not strike the fiends with fiery thunderbolts.

And more: I saw giants who looked on all men as pitiful dwarfs. They dreamed of glory yet trembled at the slightest change of weather. They trod a wide road anxiously, afraid of thorns. I saw them, and sensed their small souls in vast bodies. My nature shuddered. I know not how, but I seemed to look down on those giants and despise their greatness.

At noon, weary, I sat to rest in the shade of a birch. A clever man walked the road. I sensed his poisoned blood from afar. He tried to deceive me, coming in the form of a snake, hiding in grass and shrubs. But he failed, for I too took the form of a snake. He met my eyes but could not endure my gaze. He darted into the woods and vanished.

It would take too long to recount all the forms I have unwillingly, painfully assumed in my wandering through villages and towns. When lights blazed in rich houses, music played and glasses clinked, a poor hungry peasant under a thatched roof raised his tearful eyes to the heavens. And I, in the form of a beast, sought shelter under a fir tree, listening to the wind howl in the deep forest.

Men, seeing the changes in me, could not understand what I had become. They called me restless and wild.

Quiet... do you hear? Voices shouting: '*Wolf! Wolf!*' They have seen me – as a wolf! They will shoot. Farewell! I must flee into the forest and leave this land forever.'

Branches crashed as he ran, and I, still sitting, pondered his words as if they were a strange dream. My companion returned.

'The sun is low,' he said. 'Time to harness the horse. Let us move on.'

'Did you see anyone near me?'

'No one here,' he replied. 'But far off I saw something running over the hill. I know not if it was man or beast.'"

"It must have been the same man," said Zavalnia, "about whom they argued in the tavern."

"Indeed, it must have been. Truly, a tormented spirit. All that night I could not put him from my mind. He appeared to me in many forms. I recalled the quarrel in the tavern, the curses and judgments spoken of him. Such is the talk of men: some praised to heaven, others reviled as worthless. But God alone is just judge. When the world ends, then it will be known who lived what life, and why they changed their form."

"Pan Francisak's tale is sad," said Latyshevich. "God forbid such a disposition. A sensitive man will never be calm or happy."

"All his stories are like that," said my uncle. "I remember he once told me of a man who called himself the Son of the Storm, who wandered the earth and found peace nowhere."

NEW YEAR'S EVE

Clouds covered the sky like a thick fog. Maples and birches stood silently beside my uncle's house. Snow-laden firs resembled white columns. Evening twilight dimmed the air, and in the room, a candle burned upon the table. My uncle, the blind Francisak, Pan Sivoha, and Pan Latyshevich had moved from storytelling to a discussion of the happy and unhappy lives of their neighbors and acquaintances.

"Thanks be to God, we have lived through another year," said Zavalnia. "I was born and raised in this land. I have not traveled far, yet I have seen much in life. I remember many changes! If any of our ancestors were to rise from the grave and behold today's customs, they would not recognize their homeland. To them it would seem as though they had awakened in a foreign land. And what will my children live to see? I spare no expense on their upbringing, I do what I can, but when they step into the world, beyond my sight and their teachers' reach, may God protect their souls from the wicked and the godless."

"Oh, Pan Zavalnia," said Sivoha, "we ourselves are to blame that the devils multiplied in our land. It is the folly of the gentry, the greed and discord among the nobles. I won't dwell on it, the tale is well known. To this day we have not forgotten the old verses:

> *'The Cat killed the Calf,*
> *The Beetle and Frog judged the Cat,*
> *But the case was bad,*
> *So they sent it to Viciebsk.'*

And what did they do in Viciebsk? The Cat was one of the nobles, greedy for wealth. Trusting in his friends' protection, he not only ceased no harm, but began doing more than before. The Calf perished for the truth, and is remembered always as a good soul."

"It is ever the same with us," said Pan Latyshevich. "We gathered once for a council beyond the Dzvina in Ushachi..."

"But enough of this. Such talk only brings sorrow. If we continue with these memories, we shall greet the New Year in tears."

Meanwhile, the rooster crowed in the servants' room.

"Bravo, bravo!" cried Zavalnia. "No need to weep – a change is coming. Evening has scarcely begun and already the rooster crows. It is a sign the wind will rise, and someone from the lake will visit us. May it be a good soul, so that we welcome the New Year in company of more friends."

As he always did, he lit a candle, set it on the windowsill, and added:

"It is the sign that the host is home – and all are welcome."

Sivoha glanced out the window.

"No doubt the weather will soon change. Not a single star in the sky. In summer, I have noticed that if a rooster crows at sunset, and then in the morning I send the mowers to the field – it will surely rain, and in rain, even a dull scythe cuts well."

"A wise farmer must watch all signs," said Latyshevich. "If at the end of December and beginning of January storms bring deep snow, then in summer the meadows will yield plenty of grass and the fields – a rich harvest. This winter should please the farmer: frost and north wind cannot harm rye or wheat beneath such snow."

"In summer," said Zavalnia, "Pani Malhreta foretells the weather by the herd returning from pasture. If the first cow to come back is black, there will be a storm. If it is white, the weather will be fair."

At that moment Pani Malhreta entered the room.

"What is this?" she asked, seeing the candle on the windowsill. "The night is quiet. No travelers will be wandering the lake."

"Your ladyship did not hear the rooster crow several times just now. The wind may soon drift the snow across the road, blinding the path so that one cannot see five steps ahead. Such misfortunes have befallen us before: men have frozen upon the lake, never to be revived."

"A strange man! He loves to pass time with peasants, and thinks his guests take pleasure in it too."

With these words she left, slamming the door.

"What a woman," said my uncle. "Who can tell what swarms in her head? Such they are – ever eager to flaunt their title. But to my mind, the truly noble is he who keeps God's commandments in life."

"I knew men of feeble will," said the blind man, "who boasted of their ancestors' fame, yet lived so basely that they were unworthy of being called human."

"We have strayed far in our talk. Pan Sivoha promised us a tale."

"I remember," said Pan Sivoha and began his story.

The Screaming Hair

"In Viciebsk, I once ran into a doctor from our area, Pan M. It so happened that we both came to the city on business. After we chatted about this and that, the doctor asked:

'Where will you have lunch?'

'Wherever God allows,' I replied. 'We have money, we won't go hungry in the city.'

'Let's go to Karlisan's tavern, they always serve well there.'

'Won't that be too expensive?'

'No more than anywhere else. And if we pay a little more, the meal will taste all the better. Let's not be stingy with ourselves.'

I agreed. We entered a large hall where several people were eating, smoking pipes, and laughing at the shortcomings and oddities of their friends and neighbors. They mocked everyone, sparing neither women nor old men.

At the table, I watched these frivolous fools with surprise: how they boasted of their wit, how they roared with laughter till the glasses clinked, how they admired themselves in the mirror, like vain young girls ready for marriage.

'It is good to visit a tavern from time to time,' said the doctor. 'Here, people shed their masks more readily, and it is easier to see who is who.'

As soon as he had spoken, a man entered. He was tall, with thick bristling hair, restless eyes, and a full pale face, a mixture of bile and water. Everyone stared at him. He sat on the sofa, clutched his head, and groaned:

'They have no peace.'

He called for a glass of rum, drank half, then sat quietly for a few minutes as if deep in thought. Rising, he examined himself in the mirror.

'Oh!' he said, putting his hand to his head. 'At least now they are still, quieted for a while.'

Everyone looked on in astonishment. My companion said:

'You seem unwell, sir. You suffer from an illness of the head, and I fear rum will not help you, it may even do harm.'

'Who asked for your counsel?'

'I am a doctor. It is my duty.'

'A doctor, and yet you know nothing of my suffering. Tell me instead, which death is easier? For I have no hope of recovery, and so must die.'

'I swore to prolong human life, not to point the way to

death. Death comes of itself.'

'That is true – but who does not know it?'

'Yes, everyone knows it – but not everyone thinks of it.'

'Some love life. But those who suffer as I do have nothing to live for in this world.'

'What illness afflicts you?'

'It was the hair – yes, the hair – that ruined my life!'

At this, laughter rose from the next table.

'Ah! Hair from a fair braid!'

'You should not have cut it, for without it, beauty fades like a plucked flower.'

'He tired of his hair, cut it off with scissors, and it came alive in the moonlight.'

'His hair sang sweetly, but he did not know how to cherish it.'

'Look, look how the sun strikes his head, the hair stirs as if alive!'

Hearing this mockery, the poor man glared at them, leapt up, and paced the room in silence.

The young men all picked up their hats, ready to leave. One of them called:

'Farewell, Pan Henryk! Drink more rum, and all will be well!'

'See what I have become,' Henryk said to the doctor. 'A laughingstock. They jeer at another's misfortune. Wherever I go, they remind me of my past, only to wound me further.'

'Your nerves are too delicate,' said the doctor, 'if you let such people anger you. Listening to their gossip just now, I understood what sort they are.'

'I was not always like this. Once I cared little for either laughter or groans. Nothing touched me – until the hair, my hair, destroyed my nature.'

He fell silent, listening, then suddenly pointed to his

head:

'There – one has begun to sing, and the rest are stirring. Soon they will all be screaming together. You cannot see what is happening on my head!'

He hastily seized the glass to drain the rum.

'Listen,' said the doctor. 'Ask for water and sugar, mix it with the rum and it will harm you less. But better still, give it up altogether.'

Henryk took the glass, stood before the mirror, touched his hair with his hand, and shrugged. He then turned to the doctor, looked at him anxiously, and said:

'I refuse to give it up – unless you find a better cure. But I accept your first advice.'

He asked for water, made a punch, and drank it.

'Tell me of your life. If I knew the cause of your torment, perhaps I could help.'

'Perhaps you know how to bring back the past?'

'The past teaches us to live in the present.'

'My affliction is new. Neither simple folk with their instincts, nor doctors with their sciences, can cure it. But since you sincerely wish me well, I will tell you what I have endured.

I was the only child of my parents. All my whims were their command. The servants obeyed my every word, and my home tutor taught French in such a way that, studying for only an hour, I experienced no annoyance and clouded none of the cheerful thoughts that seemed more valuable than literacy.

When I was fifteen, my father took me to Riga for a year, so that I could study German and French with the best teachers, and see and learn everything I would need from people renowned in social circles.

My father left me more money than I needed, and I picked the flowers of a happy, careless life. No one reminded me that all things pass, that human health is fragile, and that the joys of youth are no more than a dream.

When I returned home from the city, I spent my days hunting from morning till night. My father spared no expense: he kept marksmen and greyhounds, I was allowed as many servants as I wished, I had fine horses and ordered fashionable carriages.

A few years later, I was elected to the district council. I made many friends in the city. I often hosted cheerful soirées at my house, where guests stayed till dawn, seated at cards or over wine.

Four years passed. My parents left this world, and I returned home intending to run the estate. But it was drowned in debt. My father's creditors came, threatening me, reminding me of loans. The court demanded unpaid taxes going back years. For the first time in my life, I grew afraid, and I became fearful of the future.

'You need to marry,' a neighbor advised me. 'Panna Amelia, the daughter of the commissioner who now manages Pan G.'s estates, is a beautiful, well-educated girl, and I hear she has a dowry of more than ten thousand silver rubles. Her father has amassed a fortune as commissioner and trustee. As for her not being related to the local gentry, who do as they please in elections – pay it no mind. In your case, you need money, not family ties, which in truth would be of no use to you anyway.'

I saw my neighbor's advice came from the heart. I agreed to the proposal and asked for his help. Ten thousand silver rubles – even less – would suffice to free the estate from its burdens. Moreover, I had already heard much of the virtues of the commissioner's daughter. So together we went to visit her parents.

Seeing Amelia for the first time, I discerned her

wonderful qualities: a slender figure that an artist might immortalize in portrait, a face that testified to a gentle character, blue eyes filled with quiet melancholy and dreamlike enchantment. Speaking with her about the fickleness of fortune, I learned that she was raised to humbly believe in premonitions and the unexplained mysteries of nature.

My neighbor laid bare to her parents the debts of my estate. Both they and their daughter consented. After the wedding, I was the happiest of men. I brought my wife home and paid off every debt.

Ah! Why did I not trust my intuition? Doctor, do you not agree that a sensitive soul hears more clearly the warning voice of an angel than all the wisdom of science and experience?'

'I have noticed the same,' said the doctor, 'though not all possess such instinct.'

'Then why did I not heed Amelia's intuition?'

'In what matter? And what befell you?'

'For three years we were happy, though differences in our thoughts sometimes led to disputes. But every quarrel ended peacefully. Seeing my stubbornness, Amelia would change the subject rather than prolong disagreement.

One spring evening, in fair weather, we went walking in a nearby forest. Birds sang all around us. Yet Amelia fell silent, as if lost in melancholy thoughts.

'I see,' I said, 'your intuition whispers in your ear, that is why you fall silent and look so sad.'

'Indeed,' she answered softly. 'A sadness has come over me. I know not why.'

'The songs of nightingales and cuckoos trouble your nerves.'

'Perhaps so,' she replied in a quiet voice.

At that moment an old man in black approached along

a narrow path. His face was pale, his bright eyes glowed beneath thick brows, and a covered basket hung from his shoulders. Curious, I asked when we drew near:

'Who are you, old man, and where do you come from?'

Removing his crumpled hat and bowing, he answered:

'I live everywhere, seeking kind souls and fighting superstition.'

His reply intrigued me.

'And what made you take up such a struggle?'

'Because neither they nor I understood their true interest. I have traveled the world, I know human needs. I have learned nature's most hidden secrets. I wished to bring relief to the poor of this barren land. Instead of gratitude, I met with curses, and never found shelter anywhere.'

'What did you do here in our land?'

'I meant to do good, yet twice I was forced to flee. Twenty years have passed, and still I remember. Once I discovered how to extract gold, and sought to perfect my method and reveal it to the locals. Pan ***, a wealthy nobleman, had an estate near Polatsk. He gave me a small room for my studies and the improvement of my science. A terrible misfortune befell me there. I had left some white powders on my table. Pan ***'s wife entered, thinking them medicine. Suffering from a headache, she mixed one with water, drank it, and died instantly. I was guiltless, yet to escape trial I fled.

Later, I attempted to reveal my secret to another nobleman, but when at midnight in the cemetery we made trial, both he and his servant fainted in horror. Fearing persecution, I left them there, in the cemetery. I fled and never showed my face there again, resolving never to reveal my secrets.'"

Here Zavalnia interrupted Sivoha's tale:

"I remember a traveler told me of a sorcerer who taught Pan *** to make gold, and whose servant Karpa carried under his shirt an egg laid by a rooster, from which he raised a dragon. Surely it is the same sorcerer. Continue, we are listening."

"Henryk, noticing that the doctor and I listened intently, paid no heed to the tavern staff who laughed and chatted nearby. He continued:

'And what have you in the basket under your coat?' I asked.

'Rabbits,' he replied. 'If a kind soul grants me a hut, I will raise them, and they will soon multiply, giving me an income from this small enterprise.'

'Open it and show us your rabbits.'

He opened the basket, and Amelia recoiled with a scream.

'Ah! What terrible bats! Hide them! I cannot bear the sight of such creatures!'

I looked and saw only young black rabbits. The old man quickly said:

'Look closer, madam – merely small black rabbits.'

And taking one by the ears, he lifted it from the basket.

'Ah! A hideous bat! Have mercy and hide it, I cannot endure such filth!'

I was astonished. Supposing Amelia's fear a strange fancy and stubbornness, I told the old man to pass the night at the farmstead, and that in the morning he would be given a house. He bowed and went to the manor.

We returned home in silence. Amelia was pale and trembling, with tears in her eyes. I wondered why she disputed such an obvious truth. I clearly saw young rabbits with my own eyes.

At last I said:

'So, Amelia, will you insist the old man carried bats? What whim was this, to mock him and accuse him of lies?'

'I did not accuse him,' she said. 'But must I not believe my own eyes?'

'It grieves me you embarrassed the poor man. He struck me as educated and intelligent, though unlucky.'

'His gaze and face were terrifying. Why did you stop him at all? You should have just let him pass.'

'Your words surprise me. I did not merely stop him. I gave him, a poor man, shelter, and he may live on my estate as long as he pleases.'

Amelia said no more. Our argument was over, and we both returned home in silence.

Not far from the estate, near the river, stood a solitary hut in a spruce forest. In my late father's time, a peasant had lived there. Later, I gave him a house in the nearest village, annexing the field he once tilled to my own land. The next morning, I rose early and led the old man to this empty hut, so that he might have shelter in his old age. He thanked me, and at once released his rabbits into the middle of the house.

He lived alone. Sometimes he wandered through the fields or beneath the forest canopy. At night he did not sleep, but made sudden appearances here and there, dressed in his black clothes, like a dreadful ghost. When the peasants met him by moonlight, they fled as though from a werewolf. Strange rumors spread about him: that at midnight a flock of bats circled above his hut, and that owls and crows came flying at his summons.

Hearing these inventions of the common folk, I only laughed. I visited the old man in his lonely dwelling and often spent hours conversing with him. In autumn, I listened to the rustle of the ancient firs above his roof and gazed at his face, on which a cheerful smile seemed eternally imprinted. On the sandy hill among the pines, a great brood of black rabbits lived, darting in and out of their burrows. Watching them, I felt myself change: gloomy thoughts filled my soul.

Amelia refused to see him, and disliked even hearing his name. I, on the contrary, delighted in his company, and in a few months he had gained such influence over me that I believed his every word.

In late September, just before sunset, I stepped into the old man's hut. The autumn wind howled against the wall, and there he sat, leaning on his hands, gazing at the many rabbits that filled the house and yard. Seeing me, he said:

'It is strange. For all the time I have lived on your estate, visiting all the local woods, I have seen many kinds of trees. Yet I have found no oaks nearby. Only two ancient specimens, a hundred years old or more, stand a few miles from here, with a ring of saplings around them, grown, I suppose, from acorns scattered by the wind.'

'I never noticed this,' I said. 'We have enough other trees for household needs.'

'Elms and birches are useful, yes,' he replied, 'but what can rival the beauty of an oak grove? Mighty trees, kings among their kind! I advise you to have these saplings dug up this autumn and planted all across the hill behind the lake, where not a single tree now stands.'

'We should wait many years for them to grow large,' I said. 'And I shall not live to see tall, sprawling oaks upon that hill, for human life is all too short.'

He looked at me sternly, and a shiver passed through me as he repeated my words, mocking:

'Human life is short, indeed. But why dwell on it? You

are young and healthy, you will live a hundred years upon this earth, and enjoy your time surrounded by friends in the shade of those oaks. Stop doubting. You are a man – and everything must serve you.'

I heeded his counsel. The next day I commanded the gardener to meet the old man, who would show him the young oaks to be transplanted to the hill.

Hearing my command, the gardener turned pale with fear and spoke in a voice not his own:

'What good is it? The oak does not bloom, and its fruit is useless. If it is only for beauty, then lindens would serve better on that hill.'

'I did not ask your opinion,' I said coldly. 'Obey my order.'

'I have heard from the elders,' he whispered, 'that those who plant oaks or acorns will not live out the year.'[47]

'If I hear this nonsense again,' I shouted, 'you will have five hundred lashes. Now do as I command!'

Terrified and unwilling to defy me further, the gardener went away, but soon sought an opportunity to beg my wife to dissuade me from this plan.

That evening, while I was out, he crept into Amelia's room, fell to his knees before her with tears in his eyes, and told her everything.

When I returned, Amelia greeted me with a smile:

'Henryk, why have you decided to plant oaks? I see no need or beauty in them. The poor gardener came to me in great distress, saying that transplanting oaks brings misfortune, for this tree drains the strength and shortens the life of the one who grows it. I know such superstitions come from ignorance, yet do we have the right to treat people harshly for it? Should we not rather find a way to guide them from their foolish beliefs? We are all human, and it is a great sin to commit injustice against our neighbor.'

'As I see,' I answered angrily, 'you and the gardener are alike – eager to defend nonsense. But your intercession will be in vain.'

'That terrible old man must have given you this advice,' she cried. 'Then let him take the gardener's place, and do it all himself, for he does nothing all day but wander the fields and forests.'

'These are my people,' I retorted. 'They will do as I command.'

Tears streamed from Amelia's eyes, and she left the room.

When the gardener saw there was no hope, he fetched young oaks from the forest and planted them in the designated place. After this, he grew melancholy. All efforts to convince him that oaks cannot harm human health were in vain. He withered, and by spring, just as the saplings came into leaf, he was dead.

After his death, I told the old man of the gardener's fears, naivety and weakness of spirit. He only frowned with disdain and said:

'Very well. There is no need to grieve. Fools are countless, and you have lost but one.'

The second crime of the old man further shattered the peace between me and my wife. I was preparing to build a new wooden house, but lacked enough brick for the foundation. Searching for a place to set up a kiln, I walked through the fields. The old man met me there, pointed toward the cemetery and the chapel beside it, and said:

'What an unsuitable place for a graveyard! From your manor window you are always confronted with wooden crosses and the little chapel. What a dreary sight! When you host guests – many cheerful youths among them – these crosses and that chapel stand ever before their eyes, stirring melancholy. Better, I say, to move the peasants' cemetery far beyond the forest, where human eyes seldom fall upon it. Use the bricks of the chapel for your new foundation, and sow oats in its place, so that no sign remains to betray that bones once rotted beneath that earth.'

I praised the old man's sound advice, his understanding of human nature and of nature's secrets. At once I ordered the wooden crosses torn down, the gravestones gathered into a heap, and the chapel demolished, its bricks carried to the manor.

In vain did the peasants plead with me not to destroy their shrine, not to disturb the resting place of their ancestors. In vain did the priest warn me that I was taking a great sin upon my soul. In vain did the older neighbors rebuke me for going against the customs of our forefathers. At last, when Amelia saw that every plea was useless, she said:

'Henryk, your father and grandfather lived their lives with this chapel and cemetery at their side, and neither the graves nor the crosses troubled them. At sunrise and sunset, they prayed there for the souls of their departed peasants. This is the custom throughout our land: cemeteries stand in sight and near the road, so that when seeing the crosses and the graves, travelers might pray for the souls of the departed. Surely it is that terrible old man who gave you this godless advice. But remember, Henryk – God sees everything.'

'This does not concern you!' I shouted. 'I know what I am doing. The old man you call terrible laughs at your stupidity – you waste too much care on those who no longer even exist.'

And I stood my ground. Two days later there was no trace of the cemetery, and the chapel's bricks lay in the foundation of my new house, into which I moved a few months later.

After that, Amelia changed even more. Her eyes and face were always clouded with sadness. She said she saw ghosts in the new house, suffered terrible nightmares, and sometimes heard moans at midnight. Morning and evening she knelt long in prayer, and her face altered so much that acquaintances scarcely knew her, though little time had passed.

When I told the old man of my wife's suffering, he nodded and said:

'You, sir, know little of what a woman is! This is only anger and stubbornness – because she cannot rule her husband and have all things her way. I could reveal to you a secret, but better to let it remain the eternal mystery of my soul, for some already say it is I who sow discord in your house.'

'Have mercy and tell me. Who could be more concerned than her own husband?'

'I am grateful for your kindness,' he said. 'You gave shelter to an old man who has walked dreadful paths, endured many trials, and learned to keep a cold heart when looking into the secrets of human thought and deed. I will tell you what I have known for months, what I have told no one: your wife has living hair on her head.'

'I have never heard of such a thing, and cannot understand what it means.'

'Let me explain how I discovered it. I remember that day, it was clear and quiet. The guests gathered at your estate. After dinner, everyone went out walking in the fields to enjoy the fine weather. You, sir, walked with two elderly men, deep in conversation. Your wife went ahead, surrounded by the younger company, who glanced often at her braid. As they neared the grove, I hid behind a tree to see why they stared so intently. My eyes are sharp, and I noticed that in the sun her hair moved – her braid was alive upon her head. Remember this well: there are marvels in the world, strange magic. The youth could not turn their eyes away, not knowing what secret force had set their hearts aflame.'

'Is such a thing possible?' I exclaimed.

'Of course. And I will tell you how to prove it. Not only is her hair alive, but among it is one strand which, after sunset, when twilight covers the earth, begins to scream – and screams all night until dawn. That is why she cannot sleep long, why she wakes moaning and weeping. If she goes to a separate room to pray, get close and listen. Better yet, listen at midnight, when that hair shrieks the loudest.'

I was shaken and resolved to learn the truth. That evening, when Amelia went to her chamber with a candle to pray, I crept to the door and listened. I heard a faint buzzing, as though a mosquito hovered near my temple. I stood still for several minutes, then stole away without waiting for her to finish her prayers.

After midnight, I laid out cards in my chamber, pretending to read my fortune, to see if my desires and intentions would come to pass. When everyone fell asleep and the household fell silent, I extinguished the candle and entered the bedroom like a night terror. Amelia lay moaning in her sleep, the moonlight falling through the windowpane across her feet. And in my head I heard again the sound – the buzz of a fly caught in a spider web. A shiver passed through me.

'Now I know the truth!' I thought, and did not shut my eyes all night.

In the morning, I told the old man.

'Now you believe me! I spoke the truth,' said the old

man. 'But there is more. You must ensure that this living hair does not draw the eyes of the youth. Command your wife to cut off her braid, and bring it to me before the rooster crows. Then I will show you wonders once more.'

Amelia suspected nothing of my dark agreement or my dreadful intent. Greeting me, she said in a calm voice:

'What is wrong with you, Henryk? You seem worn with sleeplessness. Last night you stayed up playing cards alone, and by dawn you were no longer in the house.'

'I could not sleep,' I answered. 'And at first light I left, for your hair – that screaming hair upon your head – gave me no rest.'

'Is this a riddle? I do not understand you. I have never heard of screaming hair.'

'The way your hair moved delighted the guests...'

'Speak plainly, Henryk,' she said, 'for I am not skilled at riddles.'

'Then I will speak plainly. I want you to cut your hair. It is more fitting that a married woman cover her head.'

'A strange whim has lodged itself in your mind.'

'Strange, perhaps, but just,' I said. 'I do not want you to flaunt your braid, as it draws every gaze as if by enchantment. Be so kind, if you value my peace of mind, command that it be cut.'

'I understand now,' said Amelia. 'anything for your peace of mind.'

She called a maid, ordered her to cut the braid, and, bursting into tears, withdrew to another room.

Around midnight, I carried Amelia's braid to the old man's hut. A dim light glowed in his window. Entering, I found him seated at the table, leaning on one hand in deep contemplation. In the corner, black rabbits moved about, their eyes burning like rubies. He rose and asked:

'Did you do as I advised?'

'I did, here is my wife's hair.'

I placed the braid upon the table.

'Soon,' he said, 'you will see a miracle.'

He fetched a large wooden bowl, filled it with water, and cast part of the braid into it. Then he stood, staring intently. The flame on the table dwindled, the moon's pale crescent broke through black clouds, the wind rose, and the forest roared. I looked at the old man – his lips, white as those of a corpse, moved as if whispering a charm. A chill seized me, dread creeped through my veins. At last he said:

'Come closer and see what is happening.'

I leaned over the bowl – and wonder of wonders! The hair writhed and twisted in every direction, darting like leeches through the water. I stared in horrid fascination. At last, he took the soaked strands and the rest of the braid outside, flung them into the river, and, in the moonlight, I thought I saw them writhing still upon the surface.

When the old man returned, he said:

'Rest easy. That hair will no longer draw eyes with its secret power.'

Amelia wept in secret for a long time after what I had done. Her health withered by the day. She could no longer sleep, for each time her eyes closed she saw ghosts rising from their graves.

A terrible incident occurred before sunset. One evening, Amelia was sitting in the garden alone. As twilight fell and dew chilled the air, she returned from the garden to her chamber. She had scarcely crossed the threshold when she gave a silent cry and collapsed as if dead. Her face was bloodless. We laid her on the bed and barely revived her.

When she opened her eyes, she whispered that she had seen the old man before her, but in a monstrous form: his eyes glowed with bloody fire, and in his hands he brandished a great dagger, threatening to kill her.

Stricken with pity, I summoned a doctor at once. Messengers rode daily to the city for medical prescriptions. Everything possible was done to help her. Yet nothing availed, nothing brought relief. Amelia's suffering deepened, her weakness grew.

Hearing of their daughter's dangerous illness, Amelia's parents came to visit. The doctor urged that she be taken to their house, where her thoughts might calm, and the medicines take better effect.

I agreed. Amelia departed with her parents, promising to return when she regained her strength.

Three days later, I received a letter sealed in black:

'Amelia ended her lonely life yesterday at five in the afternoon.'

As soon as I read this, all the hair on my head bristled and shrieked in terror. A great fear seized me, and I finally understood the misfortune to which that terrible old man had led me. I seized a loaded pistol and ran, determined to kill him on the spot... but scarcely had I opened the door when a huge flock of bats burst from the empty hut. With a terrible squealing they whirled above the hut and the trees, and there was no trace left of the old man or his rabbits.

I abandoned my home. I dared not live there, dared not go into the fields or look upon the meadows, hills, and forests – for the dark, devilish figure of the old man rose before my eyes wherever I turned.

So, doctor, that's my life's confession.'

After a short silence, he laid his hand upon his head and, gazing into the mirror, said:

'Even now, the hair moves and screams. Tell me, do you know how to help me in my misfortune?'

To comfort him, the doctor invited him to his home, gave him his address, and we soon left the tavern, leaving Henryk behind. Two days later, I departed from Viciebsk and never saw him again."

"A terrible old man!" said Zavalnia. "Is it not the same demon whom Twardowski once commanded to revive Hugon's body? He wanders now from place to place across the world, bringing nothing but harm to mankind."

"What a dreadful tale Pan Sivoha has told us!" said Latyshevich. "My memory is nothing like his. I've heard many stories, but what I hear today, I forget tomorrow."

THE GYPSY NAMED BASIL

We went on talking and sharing our thoughts about the stories told that evening. As we did so, the wind began to rustle the trees surrounding the house. My uncle glanced at the candle burning on the windowsill and said:

"It was not for nothing that the rooster crowed right after sunset. The weather is turning: the wind has risen, and the main thing now is to keep the fire burning brightly in the window."

He got up, replaced the candle, and turned to me:

"Janka, call Pani Malhreta here. Such a strange woman! Many times, as today, when guests tell the most wondrous tales, I sit as if glued to my seat, while she shows no interest whatsoever, even grows angry, refusing to come into the room, saying it is sinful not only to speak of devils and witchcraft, but even to listen to such things."

When Pani Malhreta arrived, my uncle said:

"Mistress is always alone, she would not listen to the wondrous tale with which Pan Sivoha entertained us just now. In Viciebsk, he once met a man with hair that screamed on his head."

"Oh, I know your stories! Who could believe that hair could scream?"

"Let it be as you say. Madam does not wish to believe – but still, we have one request of you: order that some good *harelka* and honey be brought, and cranberries prepared. We shall bid farewell to the old year and welcome the new one with *palionka*,[48] which will be all the more pleasant because the northern wind only sharpens the frost."

The wind howled outside, while *harelka* flamed on the

table. Zavalnia carefully measured out the required spices to prepare a fine drink. Pan Latyshevich conversed with the blind Francisak. Standing by Pan Sivoha, Stas and Yuzik spoke of their school friends, of spring walks in the fields, and of the student theater. Gazing into the blue flame of the *palionka*, I recalled the tales I had heard in my uncle's house, and the story about fiery spirits swirled in my mind. It seemed that Nikitron might leap from that flame if summoned.

Suddenly the door swung open, and a man I had never seen before entered the room. Tall, dark-faced, black-haired, with eyes like two glowing embers. He was dressed like a Cossack, with a whip tucked into his belt on the left side.

"I bow at the feet of my kind host and benefactor!" he declared loudly.

"Ah! How are you, Basil! Where has God sent you from?"

"I have come far, benefactor! I wandered here and there, even to the estate of the Dominican priests near Harbacheu. I froze to the bone crossing the lake – the frost was cruel, the wind cut through me. Seeing the light in the window, I hurried here as the nearest place to find warmth."

"Or perhaps," said Sivoha, "because the horse could go no further?"

"Oh no! My horse could run another four miles yet."

"Well, you did right to come to me. We will greet the New Year together."

"Now is the very time for fortune-telling," said Sivoha. "Tell us, then, what fate awaits each of us in the coming year."

"Why tell fortunes? What is destined to be will be. For me, a gypsy, fate decrees to wander from place to place, to live in a tent in the fields, and for you, sir – to manage your estate."

"Did you trade away many old horses this year, exchanging them for young ones?"

"In this land, people know as much about horses as the gypsies do. They will not let themselves be cheated."

"Tell me, Basil," said my uncle, "why do you not settle down and make a home? Your life would be more peaceful that way."

"That is how my ancestors lived. They must have touched jabber-weed[49] to their temples and, seeing the future, scorned everything else, leaving us only these customs."

"What kind of herb is that?" I asked. "Does it grow in our land, or elsewhere?"

"He will tell us about the herb later," said my uncle. "Now let him warm himself. Sit down, Pan Basil – perhaps you have not even had dinner yet?"

"Benefactor, I have not thought of dinner, nor has my horse."

"Your horse will not go hungry: I have hay. And, thank God, I have bread to feed the traveler too."

And Zavalnia ordered that dinner be brought for the gypsy.

Seated at the table, Basil ate with a great appetite. When he was satisfied, he began to speak of the past, praising the kindness and generous hand of those acquaintances from whom he had once profitably bought fine horses. Then he lamented his own nature – too trusting, he said, and for that reason sustaining losses in trade, often losing heart and giving up important plans, unable to attend the horse fairs of Beshankovichi and Asveya.

He praised certain places in Belarus, especially the

banks of the Drysa and Dzvina, where, with rich summer pastures, he bred good horses and often remained until late autumn. He spoke, too, of his winters and those of other gypsies, and how, having mastery over fire, they build vast bonfires beneath thatched roofs, and yet the flames do not touch the straw.

Meanwhile, the *palionka* was ready. Zavalnia poured it into glasses, led the blind Francisak to the table, set a hot drink before him, and invited the others closer. Tasting it, each guest praised its flavor and color, which shone like dark ruby in the candlelight. This led to a discussion of the price and quality of local spirits and foreign wines.

"How unreasonable," said Pan Sivoha, "to import arrack and wine from Riga – when I hear the Germans add harmful spices to it – and to pay so much for it. Better to spend that money elsewhere. We have our own drinks with excellent taste, and without ill effect. This *palionka*, for instance! A sick man may drink a glass, and not only will it not harm him, it will help! It is the only remedy for cold and fever."

"True, benefactor," said Basil, holding a half-empty glass and staring into his bowl. "Such is our pitiful gypsy life! When we seek shelter in some empty building on a winter's night, there is no stove, no ceiling, only walls. The wind whistles through the cracks, my wife shivers by the fire, and the children whimper as they toss and turn, trying to draw closer to the heat... Oh, to give them but a glass of *palionka* then – they would forget the cold, and the nightingales would sing to them in the dead of winter, as if it were spring."

"That is true," said Pan Latyshevich. "And what of our March beer, or mead-*trainyak*! Last year before *Kalyady*, I went to the city for household needs. A fierce storm caught me on the way. I lodged in Polatsk in a cold room, and from that I took a chill. The next day came headache and fever. But with no time to waste, I went about the city, buying what I needed. I also visited the Jesuit monastery. There in the corridor Father Pope greeted me. He kept a cellar with excellent aged mead in huge barrels.

He looked at me once and said:

'Why has your face changed so, and why do you seem restless? Are you unwell?'

'Unwell,' I admitted. 'I traveled in bad weather and lodged in a cold room, so I caught a chill.'

'I shall cure you,' he said.

He led me to the cellar, poured a huge mug of *trainyak*. As I drank, warmth spread through my body, sweat broke upon me, and the illness passed."

"Pleasant medicine!" said Zavalnia. "But Basil spoke of a strange jabber-weed, touched to the temples. That is something worth hearing about. Do us this favor, tell us more. We shall listen with great attention. For everyone knows of mead and beer already."

"Oh! Jabber-weed is truly wondrous, its marvels are many and mysterious. Even fire loses its force before it, while the human eye perceives the world differently and sees the future."

Saying this, the gypsy began his tale.

Jabber-Weed

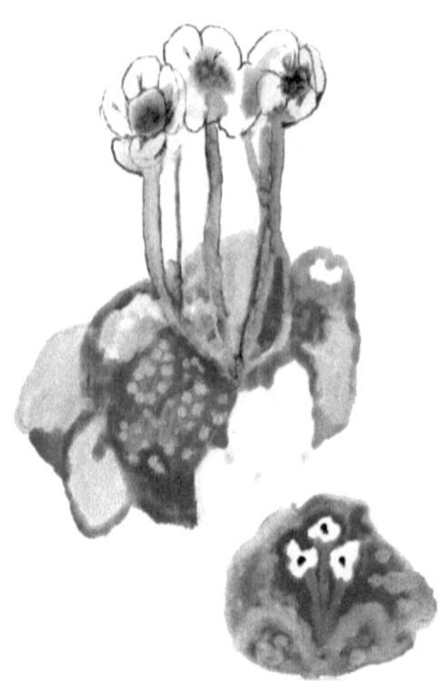

"Once upon a time, a wise gypsy named Shylka lived in this land. He knew the powers of spirits that influenced human health, healed the sick, studied the secrets of destiny, and foretold the future. He never erred in his divinations, and so people, both young and old, came to him from every direction in search of advice.

In the evenings, when his scattered family gathered in the tent, he laid out all manner of dried herbs that brought healing to man and beast alike. Immersed in his work, he was suddenly interrupted by a young man named Adolf, who quietly approached and broke the silence:

'How are you, Shylka! I came to learn what fate awaits me, what future lies before Alma, and what she thinks of me.'

Shylka took Adolf's hand, frowned, and, after gazing silently at his palm for several minutes, nodded his head and shrugged. At last, he looked into his eyes and said:

'Do not ask, sir, about Alma's fate, nor about your own.'

'Why not? I long to know, to tear the veil from my eyes as soon as possible.'

'Then touch jabber-weed to your temples. At so young an age, the bright veil that hides your future will fall away from your eyes.'

'I want that herb.'

'You have plenty of curiosity – but have you as much courage?' asked Shylka.

'Tell me where it grows. I will go at midnight, even among wild beasts if I must.'

'Walk until you see see two sandy hills on the left, and below them, in the marsh, grow small birches and willows. The lakeshore is overgrown with thick reeds, and at the spot where the meadow begins you will see a pole sticking out of the water like a mast. Fishermen placed this mark to warn others not to cast their nets there, for whenever they do, the nets are cut clean through as if by a knife.

There, sharp stones jut from the depths, and among them, bright as a star, the underwater jabber-weed shines. The spirit Pharon[50] made his dwelling there, for he loved these herbs. When the weather is calm and the midday sun blazes in the sky, he sits alone in the depths, leaning with his right hand upon a large stone, gazing at the radiant jabber-weed, and drifts into slumber amid enchanting visions of the future.

But when the sun sets, Pharon covers the jabber-weed with a dense tangle of plants, twined around the stones like hops, concealing it from fish and waves alike, so that neither creatures nor waters may disturb its leaves. He himself rises from the lake, floating on the vapors into the fields to wander meadows and forest edges.

Tomorrow, if the clouds do not hide the sun and the lake lies calm as glass, go at the hottest hour – and mark that moment carefully. Enter the lake, walk beneath the water until you reach Pharon's dwelling: he will be asleep, leaning against the stone, while the jabber-weed gleams in the light. Pluck a leaf, but do not return the way you came. You must cross the entire lake. On the far shore, apply the jabber-weed to your temple, and you will see great marvels and learn your future.'

'Am I a fish,' said Adolf, 'to cross a whole lake beneath the water?'

'Keep this in your mouth, and no harm will come to you.'

Saying this, Shylka gave him a piece of bark.

At noon, Adolf waded deeper and deeper until he vanished beneath the surface. Passing through the realm of mute, cold beings, he encountered strange translucent creatures with a hundred heads and a hundred legs, who stirred from numbness, lifted their shoulders, and sank once more into slumber on the lakebed. At last he reached the place, and there he saw the jabber-weed. Like crystal in the sun, its leaves flashed with brilliant light, while the spirit Pharon, hidden among the greenery and leaning against a stone, lay resting, resembling a vast clump of seaweed. Above him and the jabber-weed, thousands of water-beings swarmed. Adolf plucked a leaf and, without waking the spirit, walked on.

Emerging from the water, he drew a long breath, came ashore on a green meadow, and rested. He touched the cold leaf of the jabber-weed to his temple, and at once he felt himself transformed. Entirely new landscapes unfolded before his eyes.

Where on a hill among birches once stood a stone church, there was now crumbling ruin, without doors or roof, only stumps of walls protruding from the ground. Where once a village had been, there was now emptiness, only two old pear trees remained, the very ones he had seen days ago in the orchard. The field near him, once rich with grain, now lay overrun with wild grass, as though no plow had touched it in years.

Anguish seized his heart. He turned from the lake and walked on, across the very places he had trodden days before with a rifle on his back, and everywhere he looked, he saw change.

He went far, forgetting the way back, and the sun was

already low. Walking quickly, he searched for a human dwelling where he might rest, spend the night, and ask the way home.

When the day had faded and thick twilight lay across the meadows, Adolf came to a village entirely unfamiliar to him. Near one of the houses, music played – a violinist and a bagpiper performed a cheerful tune, while several youths danced in the open air.

Standing nearby, Adolf watched the dancers. He overheard several elderly strangers speaking among themselves:

'Isn't it shameful to dance?' said the first. 'Such hard times now! There are shortages everywhere.'

'Do you think they have a soul?' said the second. 'Their words are fine, but their deeds are not. They do not fear God's punishment.'

This encounter left such a painful impression on Adolf that he could not find a word to say. He withdrew hastily, circled the houses, and spent the night in an inn near the village.

At sunrise, he prepared for the road, told the innkeeper where he lived, and asked which way he should go to return home.

'I have never heard of such a land,' the innkeeper replied. 'It seems you live far from us.'

Astonished, Adolf asked other villagers, but all repeated the same thing as the innkeeper. So he readied himself for a long journey: he bought provisions for several days, slung a bag over his shoulder, and set out southward.

Meanwhile, the weather changed. Thunder rolled across the skies, and Adolf saw black clouds sweeping in. The wind rose. Finding no human dwellings near the road, he hurried into the depths of the forest to seek shelter beneath the pines from the coming downpour.

There he saw an old man sitting on a rotten stump. The pines rustled overhead, and the wind tossed his white hair. Adolf came nearer and, looking closely, recognized the gypsy Shylka. The old man rose and, bowing, said:

'Good day, Pan Adolf!'

'Ah! It is you, Shylka! I hardly recognized you. How quickly you have aged! When I saw you only a few days ago, you had no gray hair on your head, and now it is white as milk.'

'No, Pan Adolf, it was not a few days ago. It has been more than ten years since you saw me. Tell me, young man, where are you bound?'

'I do not know where my home is, or where I am now, or where this road will lead me. The sky is hidden by clouds, and a storm is overhead.'

'The weather such as it was when I told you of the jabber-weed and the spirit Pharon – it will not return soon. Your home lies far away, your friends and acquaintances seldom recall your name, thinking you long departed from this world.'

'Tell me, Shylka, which way shall I take to get home?'

'Walking through this wild forest, you will come to three roads. To the left and to the right, the roads will be broad. But between them lies a narrow grassy path, winding through rocky fields and dark forests. Do not fear to take that narrow path. Pay no heed to the broad roads on left or right. I will tell you what befalls those who choose them, seeking comfort.

To the left, enchanting landscapes delight the eye. Hills are lush with greenery, sweet fruits ripen on the trees, meadows abound in fragrant flowers, lakes are calm and clear as mirrors, reflecting clouds and the trees that grow on their shores. Springs murmur, pure as crystal, and leaves in fair groves whisper in the breeze.

But in those meadows and groves the *rusalki* play, with beautiful wreaths of cornflowers upon their heads, lips coral-red, eyes bright, long hair streaming on their shoulders. They greet travelers softly. Some are frivolous, ever merry. They sing and dance, beguile and amuse with playful talk, luring the wanderer into the darkness of the forest. Once lost there, the unfortunate never finds his way back. Other *rusalki* are pensive, melancholy in their eyes, their words stirring the soul, their tender songs piercing the heart like an arrow, drawing thought into deep sorrow. Having driven the listener into despair with their charms, they vanish.

To the right, mountains rise high, and on their summits stand splendid castles glittering with gold and silver. The lords of this glory despise poverty and suffering, yet they suffer themselves, for every midnight skeletons dance in their halls, tormenting with dreadful terror and extinguishing their brilliance.

So farewell, Pan Adolf, I cannot go with you, for I must walk another road.'

With that, Shylka slung his bag over his shoulder and went slowly on his way.

Adolf entered the forest. The day was overcast, the wind stirred the thick branches. The young man pensively recalled the past, which seemed but yesterday to him. He drew out the jabber-weed leaf, wrapped in paper, marveled at its mysterious power, and regretted his venture into the underwater realm of Pharon, realizing now what his desire to know the future had cost him. He put away the leaf, sighed, and walked on.

He came to the place Shylka had spoken of, and without even glancing at the two wide roads to left and right, he went along the narrow path through rocky fields and dark forests.

He walked alone, with no one to speak a word to. Rarely did a soul dare pass there. Adolf saw only frightened wild beasts darting into the thicket. He heard nothing but the hammer of woodpeckers on dry pines and the cries of jays.

Evening came. Worn from the day's journey, Adolf lay down on a hill and fell asleep, resting his head on a stone. He slept soundly, but not for long. As dusk deepened in the sky, he rose in haste to find a human dwelling where he might pass the night under a roof.

As he walked, he climbed a hill, but from the summit he saw no people, only smoke, thick as fog, rising not far beyond a birch grove. Scarcely had he approached when a woman stepped from the grove – tall, clad in white, her face streaming with tears, a sword in her hand. She stopped by the road.[51]

****

The rooster crowed.

"This is no longer a sign of changing weather," said my uncle. "It is midnight – the New Year has come. Let us greet the guest, though what tidings it brings, who can say?"

He spoke, poured *palionka* into the glasses, and they all drank to one another, wishing happiness in the home, good health, and a bountiful harvest in the coming summer.

Having drained his glass, Pan Latyshevich set it on the table and said:

"We do not know what is to come, only this one certainty: with every passing year there are fewer and fewer of us old folk. May God protect the younger generation, that they may endure in virtue and not forget the customs and ways of their forefathers!"

"Oh, come now, Pan Latyshevich, with such talk of death you spoil our cheer. That is not right," said Basil. "A wave of sadness came over me, as though I had not drunk a drop. Why speak of such things now? I am a gypsy, I have nothing but my horse, and yet I have no wish to ride off to the next world."

Saying this, he poured himself another glass, drank it, and wished everyone health and good spirits.

"Basil is tender-hearted," said Sivoha. "Everything moves him. But we must remember, he has not yet finished his story."

"Yes, I have not finished my story – perhaps one day I will."

My uncle refilled the glasses and, handing one to blind Francisak, said:

"Pan Francisak has been silent and downcast all evening. Drink with us! I wish you and your children nothing but happiness. May heaven bless all good people, the harvests of the past year, and happy years to come!"

BRIGHTNESS IN THE SKY

A flash of bright light struck the window and flooded the room. Everyone fell silent in fright, then rushed outside, thinking a neighbor's house was on fire. But in the sky they beheld a brilliance so clear it was hard to gaze upon. It spread wide, like an immense river of fire. The fields, forests, and snow-covered mountains glowed in its radiance with an otherworldly beauty. Clouds, ablaze with red flames, lay still on the horizon, as though splendid palaces and soaring spires were being consumed by the fire. We stood in silence, long observing this strange and terrible vision of the heavens. At last, the fiery river began to fade, dissolving into the air. The clouds dimmed, and once again darkness veiled the sky and the earth.

"God grant," said my uncle, after returning indoors, "that this is a good sign. Three times in my life have I witnessed such a marvel, and each time, the year that followed brought unexpected events."

"I once knew an old man who remembered the Year of the Goosefoot," said Pan Latyshevich. "He often told how castles seemed to burn suspended in the air, and armies clashed in the flames. It was a dreadful time. People survived only on goosefoot and grass. But a year later, God showed mercy, and the granaries everywhere filled again with rye."

"Hunger is no stranger in our land," said Sivoha. "When spring comes, it is rare that a peasant has both a crust of bread on the table and seed for the field. This endless misfortune has so etched itself into memory that every unexplained wonder is taken as a bad omen. Let us be frugal and diligent. Those who labor and pray to God live in prosperity and give aid to others."

The blind Francisak sighed:

"We greet and bid farewell to each year with the same song. The world is a pilgrimage, and the heavens – a warning. In summer, when thunder shakes the earth, I think of the Almighty and His mercy. Let His will be done. Our future lies in His hands."

"I once heard a tale," said Sivoha. "One summer evening, after sunset, before Sunday, the night was clear and still. The workers had led the horses to pasture for the night. After a long day, some peasants spoke of their households, others sang on their way back from *corvée*. Suddenly they saw a wondrous sight above: the sky opened wide, and it seemed angels stood there, clothed in light, their garments whiter than snow, halos brighter than the sun around their heads. Everyone fell to the ground, and those who prayed with true sincerity received God's grace and lived the rest of their days without want."

"I have heard that story as well," said Zavalnia. "And I too believe the heavens hear a sincere and heartfelt prayer. But where is Basil? He has not finished his tale."

Everyone looked around, but Basil was no longer in the room.

"He must have gone to sleep," said Sivoha. "I noticed he could scarcely sit upright and was already nodding off. But, sir, it is time for us to rest also. Tomorrow we must not oversleep the Holy Mass."

"But the story of the jabber-weed remains unfinished."

With that, my uncle stepped out and ordered the beds to be prepared for the guests.

The fire was extinguished. Everyone slept soundly.

END OF VOLUME THREE

VOLUME FOUR

COMPANION ON THE JOURNEY

Everywhere, nature is wondrous, beautiful, and varied; storms and springtime weather follow in turn. An astonished pilgrim gazes at the gloomy, cheerful, and wild views of hills and forests, and encounters people who, understanding his thoughts and feelings, are willing to share with him the burden of deep longing. Everywhere, there is happiness and misery: an inexplicable destiny leads us along the many paths of life. So why does one always yearn for one's native land as a child yearns for his mother?

These thoughts enveloped me as I traveled alone through many fields and dark forests, far from my homeland. It was already around noon – the sky was clear, the day was quiet and scorching hot. Exhausted by the journey and the sun, I sat on the side of the road under the leafy curtain of a few birches. A water stream murmured nearby, a gentle breeze blew from the field and caressed me. Surrendering to my dreams, I recalled the adventures of past years and did not notice someone approaching – tall, with a knapsack on his back, a face tanned by the sun and wind, thin, worn out by a difficult journey. He began:

"Isn't it wonderful to rest here in the shade of the birches by the spring?"

"It's difficult to keep walking in this heat," I replied. "And it might be a long way to a village or an inn."

"It's best to walk once the sun sets and the nightingales begin to sing in the forests. But right now, it's silent everywhere: even the birds are wearied by the heat."

"Where are you going?" I asked the stranger.

"That way, far away," he pointed with his hand.

"So be my companion then, for I am also going in that direction."

"Very well! But it seems I've seen you somewhere before. Perhaps on the banks of the Dzvina? Are we fellow countrymen?"

"Maybe. The happiest days of my life passed there."

"I am Seviaryn," said the traveler. "Time and sorrow have changed my face, and cheerful thoughts have forever parted from me. Today, I am no longer the same as I once was. Such is my path."

"I remember now: you once led the way in revelries."

"I did, until I looked around myself. And after I saw and understood everything, I wander the world and find no peace."

"Life's journey," I said. "It is like a nightmare."

"And it is no easy task to endure until the dawn that awakens you from these terrifying dreams."

"How long has it been," I asked, "since you last saw the native hills and forests of your homeland?"

"I visited that land not long ago," he replied. "I saw the hills still in their place, and the forests have grown even larger than before. Many, many changes! Gloomy times, years with no harvest. Peasants no longer cheer or celebrate, and you won't hear the song of the plowman or the shepherd in the field. Only at the cemetery does the Weeping Woman touch the souls of passersby with her lament."

"Once, there were better times. What a joy it was to see the holiday attire and festivities of the people on celebrations and weddings."

"Do you remember?" asked Seviaryn. "That village on the banks of the Obal River, do you remember it? Once, a wealthy farmer named Lukash married off his daughter there. At the time, both of us were keenly interested in folk observances and wedding songs. There was plenty for the guests to do: food and drink were abundant. Do you remember this song:

> *'Guests arrived,*
> *Full yard, full yard.*
> *Choose, Marynka,*
> *Which is yours, which is yours.*
> *The one in blue,*
> *On a gray horse –*
> *That's my matchmaker.*
> *And the one in satin,*
> *With a yellow belt –*
> *That's my brother-in-law.*
> *Sumptuously dressed,*
> *On a bay horse –*
> *That's my father-in-law.*
> *On a black horse,*
> *The young one –*
> *That's my sweetheart.'*

The words of this song recalled the prosperity of old times: people once had silk scarves, clothes of fine textiles, beautiful belts, horses tall and well-fed; they had everything they could wish for. They were happy. And now, just one glance – and the heart is filled with sadness! Lukash's house stands empty, without windows or doors. The cherry trees have gone wild, the apple trees he once grafted have withered. Without his care, the garden has grown over with wild grass. The Obal River has not changed its course, it hurries to the Dzvina in its same banks. But it has been long since people's lips were last touched by a smile; sad thoughts are now reflected on their pale, joyless faces. I asked: where are those elders who were known for their kindness and hospitality? Their doors were always open to neighbors and pilgrims, they hosted many gatherings in their homes. They never turned away the poor, widows, or orphans. The elders are gone. Only memories of them remain."

"Our land," I said. "It has experienced many changes of fortune and misfortune. God willing, the black clouds and dark storms will dissipate, spring will bloom, and prosperity will rain on our fields and meadows."

"There is much truth in folk tales," said Seviaryn. "I remember, in the Polatsk district, I heard the peasants talk about treasures hidden in the ground. I once heard a story that fits well with this conversation.

In the Sitnianskie forests, near the Stradan River, there are hills, allegedly created by people themselves. They say there once was a city there, destroyed by enemies. Then, several centuries later, an estate stood in its place. A nobleman lived there, his name, Dominik, is still remembered even now. One day, the ground collapsed on the hill near the estate. The servants immediately reported it to the master. He ordered the depth of the sinkhole measured, but the longest pole could not reach the bottom. *'There must be treasure there,'* he decided. *'I want to send someone down with a lantern to inspect that dark vault.'* But when, overcome with fear, no one volunteered to go, he forced one of his men, threatening to punish disobedience with death.

The man had no choice. When he reached the bottom with a lantern in hand, he found an open door, a vault on pillars, and sepulchral silence everywhere. Fearfully, he walked through the empty space and finally entered a huge room. There, illuminated by the lantern, a myriad of weapons and ornaments gleamed with silver and gold. A woman slept in a chair near the table, her head resting on her right hand. Long hair fell disheveled over her shoulders, traces of tears marked her pale face, black attire a sign of deep mourning. Huge, terrifying bears slept at her feet. Countless treasures lay in open iron chests

As the man looked around in fear, the woman awoke and said:

'Are you seeking treasures in this underground palace? I can find no peace because of your greed.'

At her words, the fierce beasts stirred, their eyes aflame, fur standing on their backs.

'Forgive me, lady,' pleaded the condemned man. 'I do not seek treasures. I was sent here by the mad command of my master. I had to obey or perish for disobedience.'

The woman calmed the beasts. Her eyes filled with tears, and she said:

'Oh, the unfortunate! You people have not yet cast pride and cruelty from your heart. Had you come of your own will, you would have perished here. I forgive you. Go, and tell the cruel people: *Treasures will bring you no happiness until mercy softens your hearts. Earthly gifts enrich only those who treat another as neighbor and friend.*'"

And so, resting in the tree shade, we talked for a long time about the fickleness of fate. How once, when God had blessed the work of our ancestors, the harvests in the fields were generous, and vast herds grazed upon the hills. And how later, poverty and hunger spread through the land. We spoke of the current harvests and human suffering, of the elders who have passed into eternity, and those who seek happiness in distant lands.

The sun was setting. Prepared to go, Seviaryn rose and said:

"Let's keep walking. I'll accompany you until the sun

sets. And when we reach the fork in the road, it will separate us."

Walking through forests and fields, Seviaryn told me of the eastern and southern lands, of the beautiful landscapes he encountered there, of the large herds grazing in the steppes and mountains, of the land that demands little labor and rewards with rich harvests every year, and of the comforts of the local inhabitants.

Time passed quickly in our conversation. Soon I saw before me a cemetery, a chapel, wooden crosses, and two roads: one leading into a dense forest, the other stretching on through fields and hills.

"Here is the end of our journey and our conversation," said Seviaryn, sitting on a gravestone. He looked into the sky, surrendered to melancholy thoughts, while I was seized by sadness. In that moment, both of us resembled those mournful tombstones.

The sun hid behind a ruby cloud in the west. The sky was clear, the river gleamed from afar like a mirror. The air was so quiet one could hear ducks crossing a distant lake to spend the night. An orchestra of forest birds erupted, and a nightingale sang in a nearby bush.

"How sincerely nature rejoices in spring weather," said Seviaryn. "But true joy is not given to man. When the sun sets, the rich grieve that their whole life will pass like a single day, gone forever, and death will take their merriment away. The poor grieve when the sun rises – for it awakens them to suffering and toil. And he who has peered into the secrets of human life, weighed and measured his desires and feelings, burdened his mind, dulled his vision – he wanders the world without seeing the star of hope. Everywhere, his path is strewn with thorns, and even beneath the morning sun he looks upon the graves with indifference.

The day ended, fog descended into the valleys, and twilight covered the earth. This is the end of our short journey together, the end of our conversation. Today is not like before – we part by the grave, so we shall meet again after death."

Saying this, he shook my hand and quickly went on his way, soon disappearing into the forest, which swallowed the horizon like a black cloud.

Still and silent as a monument, I stood over the grave for a while, then continued on alone, carrying a heavy sorrow in my soul.

Sorrow

Star clusters above either fade or gleam,

Midnight clouds veil heavenly crypt.

All sinks into silence, into dream –

Yet shadows of past days deny me sleep.

O friends! Once we lived in brighter hours;

Now life bristles with thorns and bitter flowers.

So many search for peace upon this earth,

Yet carry only grief, and bleed from birth.

Unfortunate is he – such is his fate –

Who reads in hearts both noble and base traits;

Who keeps his memory and longing fast,

Coiled in his breast like a serpent's grasp.

The world to him's a barren wilderness,

Nothing to soothe the eye, the soul distressed;

His heart weighs heavy, thought beats on,

Through sleepless nights and weary dawns.

Hope

The black curtain of cloud parts away,
The sky grows pale along the eastern line;
And, like a lantern through the drifting gray,
One star breaks forth with brighter light to shine.

The sailor, weary of the storming sea,
Still steers beneath that faithful star of hope;
Caravans cross the sands of Araby,
Their eyes uplifted as the deserts slope.

O star! To you the wanderer lifts his gaze,
A stone of sorrow pressing on his heart;
When grief's dark cloud obscures his thought's faint rays,
You calm the storm, though only for a part.

In vain cold reason hunts for fleeting cheer,
In vain it counts its legions bound in clay;
But he who walks in honesty sees clear –
His foresight lights the stars, the sun, the day.

God

Morning lights the field and drowsy wood,
Clouds flare like rubies in the eastern sky;
Above the lake the cranes cry where they stood,
While nightingales in tangled branches vie.

O Lord! All nature lifts its thanks to You:
At Your command, the spring breaks forth in bloom;
At Your command, the autumn rains ensue,
And migrant wings foretell the tempest's gloom.

All Your creation feels Your tenderness:
Where deserts smolder under endless flame,
Where frozen seas lie locked in iciness,
The smallest creature shelters in Your name.

Though life's long path is set with thorns that tear,
Rest, lonely wanderer, in God's embrace:
His watchful eye beholds the viper's lair,
His angel walks beside you every place.

COUNSEL

In mid-March, the day was gloomy, and wet snow fell across the yard. Inside the house, my uncle was speaking with the fisherman Rodzka about luck in fishing, the household, and the troubles of impoverished peasants who, once the fields were free of snow, would have nothing to sow this year.

As they conversed, I sat thinking about travel, daydreaming of foreign lands – a world vastly different from ours, where landscapes are more beautiful, meadows bloom more brightly, harvests are richer, and people seem a hundred times happier. My uncle interrupted my thoughts, saying:

"Janka has been staying with Pan Maragowski for a long time. He has visited other neighbors, enjoyed their hospitality, and befriended the youth, as if bidding them farewell forever. He is always melancholy, always pensive, and now plans to leave us this spring, imagining that somewhere far away riches flow like a river."

"I do not seek wealth," I replied, "but I wish to know the minds and lives of people in distant lands. In youth, one must learn, one must see the world."

"You shall see, and experience, and come to understand," my uncle answered, "that even there – where the land generously rewards the peasant, where forests bloom like an earthly paradise – people are still the same. Happiness is only found where one lives as God commanded: works diligently and without greed, does not forget his neighbor, and hopes for the best.

In our land, the winter is long and fickle, sometimes wet, sometimes frosty and stormy. Water pools in the valleys, while the north wind on the hilltops destroys wheat and rye. Yet diligence and hard work can overcome anything. When I first acquired this estate, the land resembled a wild wasteland, but I did not give in to despair. I strove to improve what I could. I dug ditches, drained the lowlands, and raised beautiful birch groves in their place. I made good meadows, raised livestock, and now, praise God, the fields bear fruit.

The gentry who hold serfs waste their wealth on carriages, clothing, and cards. Come spring, they often run out of money and come to Pan Zavalnia. But he who works hard and trusts in God can be happy and content here, too."

"I know that well, dear uncle," I said, "but living here, I neither hear nor see what happens elsewhere in the world, as though my eyes were veiled. Such a life is sad."

"That is what education does!" he said. "You are restless, yearning to know more, and your thoughts drift somewhere far away. You want to see the great world, you feel cramped here with us, wanting to break free like a bird from a cage."

Rodzka had been silent, listening intently to this exchange. At last he spoke:

"Our ancestors did not envy the rich who lived far away. They had food and clothing from their own labor. But today greed has brought evil – to extract money from the underground – and so have come the gloomy years and the gloomy life."

"Rodzka," I said, "you talk of evil spirits, but you have never seen them yourself."

"Shouldn't I believe what people say?" answered the fisherman. "Perhaps, you have not heard what happened at Sitna Lake. Many tales are told of it."

"I do not know. What happened there?"

"Then I shall tell you. Near that lake lies the village of Sitna, with the road from Polatsk to Nievel on one side, and on the other – a dense, dark spruce forest. One summer's eve, the weather was calm, the sun had set, and stars filled the sky. The peasants, having returned from the fields, were busy about their homes, when suddenly they heard singing from across the lake, near the shore behind the black forest thicket.

The voice was so loud and eerie that frightened flocks of ducks rose into the air, beasts fled from the woods across the fields and hills, and dogs whimpered as if sensing something dreadful. The villagers trembled as they made out the words clearly enough:

> *Sitna is mine,*
> *And Hlubokae is mine,*
> *And Skobria is mine,*
> *And Shevina is mine,*
> *And Jazna is mine,*
> *And Nieszczarda is mine,*
> *And Niavedra is mine,*
> *And Nievelskae is mine.*
> *If it's mine, then it's mine, it's all mine.*

Thus someone sang, over and over, from evening until midnight, naming not only the lakes but all the rivers as well. None dared approach to see who sang so dreadfully. At last the bravest fisherman summoned his courage. He took an oak stick and several stones, and when the singing rose again, he crept closer. From behind a tree he spied a figure, dressed and shaped exactly like an *ostash*:[52] broad beard, round face, leather apron. The stranger sat on a rotten stump, bellowing his song at the top of his lungs.

Convinced it was an *ostash* performing some ritual, the

fisherman called out:

'Do not claim our lakes and rivers!' and hurled a stone with all his might, striking him in the side.

'Ah, ah! You've broken my ribs!' the demon howled, leaping into the water. The whole lake churned, waves lashing against the shore. The fisherman turned pale and trembled with fear. But from that moment, the demon sang no more, nor claimed our waters as his own."

"Oh! If only all evil spirits could be punished in such a way," my uncle exclaimed.

"That demon was frightened by a stone," Rodzka replied, "but there are beings in the sky far more terrible. So, sir, do not leave our land. Better times will come, and you will fare better among your own."

"Times change, and people change," said my uncle. "In the past, our youth neither knew nor cared to know what happened in faraway places. Everyone lived peacefully and happily. But now even the educated are seized by melancholy. As soon as they finish their studies, they are filled with longing, and they abandon their native fields, setting out on distant journeys, hoping foreign winds will scatter their restless thoughts.

I have sons, and surely this house will be too small for them. The fields I have cultivated, these groves I planted. They will not satisfy their longing. Yet I will not stand in their way, so long as God strengthens their hearts with love for their fathers' customs."

"No one ever dreamt of those *ostashes* before," said Rodzka, "and now they will soon take away our land and water, forcing us to flee far away."

Rodzka sighed, picked up his hat and the sack in which he had brought the fish.

"Are you already in a hurry to get home? It isn't late

yet," said my uncle.

"The sun has set, the sky is gloomy, and the night will be dark. I must hurry."

"It's Lent now," said my uncle. "If you catch anything – don't forget about me."

TRAVELERS

When it grew dark, a strong wind arose and howled against the walls; wet snow swept down in thick sheets.

"Unfortunate is the traveler," said my uncle, "who finds himself in the middle of the lake on such a stormy night. The path is treacherous, and it is all too easy to lose one's way in such darkness."

As he spoke, he placed a lit candle on the windowsill. But when he saw how the wet snow clung to the glass, plastering it white as though bricked over, he called for a servant and ordered:

"Light a candle in the lantern, fasten it securely at the very gate so the wind will not tear it loose. Step outside often, and if you hear any travelers' voices, inform me at once. The night is dark and stormy – misfortune lurks nearby."

The servant set about securing the lantern, while Zavalnia threw on his fur coat and went out to make sure everything was done quickly and properly.

An hour later, the dogs began to whine in the yard. Despite the howling wind and the rustling of dense trees around the house, the voices of travelers carried across from the lakeshore. Their cries came from the same spot, as though something held them there. My uncle immediately sent the servants to their aid. The swampy shore had been washed out, and the first horse, pulling a heavy cart, had stumbled into the water. Only after a long struggle, and with much joint effort, did they succeed in hauling it back onto solid ground.

At last, several snow-covered carts pulled into the yard. The horses were unhitched, and the travelers ushered inside. To warm them and lift their spirits, my uncle poured each a generous shot of *harelka* and ordered supper to be served, on the condition that every guest would repay the hospitality with a tale or some episode from his life.

When the meal was finished, my uncle settled back onto the bed, I took a seat beside him, and the servants sat along the bench. One of the travelers – an elderly man with a pale face, yet whose strong, well-formed build spoke of both physical and moral strength – began his story.

The Centenarian and the Dark Guest

"In my youth, I knew an old man who lived next door to us. His name was Haraska, and he was truly a man of the old ways. Such people no longer walk our land. Twenty years have passed since his death, yet his life and his passing were so strange, so unforgettable, that it seems as if I had witnessed it all only yesterday.

His wife and family had long since passed on to the other world. Only his grandson remained with him, helping in the fields, while a hired woman prepared his meals and tended the one cow. The hut stood solitary on a hill, a *verst* away from our village, surrounded by enough pasture to feed the animal.

Haraska remembered his youth with astonishing clarity. On holidays or in the evenings, when the plowmen and mowers came home from the fields, he would visit us, sit on the sill, and recount how our ancestors once lived –

simply, without vanity or craving for finery. Their flocks and fields fulfilled all their desires. They did not envy the inhabitants of distant lands, nor flee there in pursuit of wealth, for they had no need of it. They were happy and content.

At eighty, Haraska was not yet worn down by toil. With plow in hand in the field, or scythe in the meadow, he outpaced the young. His strength was inhuman. When the nets yielded no good catch, he would fold them in the boat, hoist them on his shoulders along with all his gear, and stride to another lake. He was so strong and healthy that, like an ancient green oak, he greeted his hundredth year still upright and unbent.

Then came a gloomy autumn. In the long evenings, we sat around the torch, each to his task: my father weaving nets, the women spinning yarn, I bending barrel hoops. Our talk turned, as it often did, to old Haraska.

'Why has he not come to visit of late?' said my father. 'He is a good man, and time flies quickly in his company. I'd be glad of his presence – this dark autumn evening would pass more lightly.'

No sooner had he spoken than the door opened. Haraska stood in the middle of the house. We looked upon him with dread. He was silent, motionless, his face sorrowful and strange, his figure tall and faint, as if grown larger than before. With every passing moment he grew lighter, more transparent, until at last he dissolved into the air. A shiver passed through us all, our hands fell to our sides. We stared at one another, not knowing what it meant. At last, my father broke the silence:

'Tomorrow we must learn what is happening at Haraska's house. Is he well? This vision forebodes misfortune.'

Even as he spoke, a neighbor entered with his own tale.

That evening he had guests in his home. They sat on benches, chatting idly, when the talk turned to Haraska and his recollections of his youth and of the old lords. Suddenly the door opened, as if by a mighty gust of wind. The neighbor's son ran to close it – but Haraska himself entered. He greeted no one, but, silent like a shadow, he passed silently by the table, and into the darkened mudroom. Startled, they took up a torch, but found no soul there. Women and children were stricken with fear and dared not step outside.

Soon others came to my father, each with his own account of having seen Haraska in a similar fashion – sometimes even in daylight, on a porch or by a gate, always pensive and alone. And when they drew near, he vanished.

'Tomorrow is Sunday, a day off,' said the neighbor. 'After Holy Mass we will all go to Haraska and learn the truth. The centenarian may seem strong, but at his age the end may come swiftly.'

The next day, just before noon, my father, I, and several others from our village set out. But before we reached his door, Haraska's grandson came to greet us:

'Grandfather sends me to ask you to visit him today.'

'How is he? Is he well?' asked my father. 'We miss his stories, and we've begun to worry for him.'

'He is well, though he speaks less now, is more thoughtful, and works ceaselessly.'

'What kind of work?' asked a neighbor. 'And for whom?'

'For himself.'

'What work is that?'

'You shall see when you come.'

'Well, then let's go without delay,' said my father. 'We'll satisfy our curiosity once we get there.'

We followed him to the hut without delay.

There, in the middle of the room, stood an oak coffin set upon two stools. The house was swept and scrubbed, the benches clean. Dressed in new white linen, and looking like a swan, Haraska greeted us at the threshold:

'Welcome, dear friends, to my abode. I have called you to see the house of eternity, which I have built with my own hands. Soon, I shall move into it.'

'Oh! But you are still strong,' said my father. 'You may even bury some of us first.'

'The young *may*, but the old *must* die. Yet let us not speak of that now. Sit, dear guests. Let us pass the time in good company.'

He invited all of us to sit at the table. His grandson brought *harelka*, the maid set out dishes, and Haraska urged us to eat and drink. But he himself touched neither food nor drink.

'How could it have happened, grandfather,' asked one guest after a glass of *harelka*, 'that you did not leave the house yesterday, but people saw you everywhere?'

'You were in my house too,' said my father. 'My wife, children and I all saw clearly: your figure appeared in the middle of the room and vanished in an instant.'

'You visited me as well. You greeted neither the guests nor the host, then quickly went out to the mudroom and hid in the dark corner of the house, where we couldn't find you even with a light.'

Haraska looked at the guests with unease. His face darkened. After thinking for a moment, the old man said:

'As I built my last dwelling, I thought of you, and my soul visited you. My thoughts carried me back to the places of my youth, where I was born, grew up, walked the paths of life, knew joy and sorrow, bright days and dark. All has passed swiftly, like a dream.'

'But surely the old people never dreamed of what we

see now,' said my father, 'the gentry managed their estates well, and everything was better than it is today.'

'I looked into the eyes of many lords,' said the old man. 'I guessed their thoughts, followed their orders, satisfied all their whims. Thank God, for my service they trusted me. Our villages were sold and changed hands many times. There were many owners, and each one ruled in his own way. But back then we lived well. But when Pan Z. took over the Kazulin estate after the death of his parents, we came to know the meaning of grief.

He yearned to impress his neighbors with his wealth. He brought expensive flowers and orchard trees from faraway lands, rode in fancy carriages, kept many lackeys, but there was no order in the house. Guests gathered to drink expensive wine, and every year expenses exceeded the income from the estate. So the troubles began.

'This won't end well,' knowledgeable people told Pan Z. But he heeded no advice, preferring instead the counsel of unscrupulous men who took advantage of his ignorance.

Around that time a stranger appeared at our estate, and no one knew whence he came. I forgot his name, but I still see his face before me: thin, always pale, with a huge nose, thick eyebrows, and a madman's gaze. His clothes were black, long, and strange. In all my life I had never seen anyone dressed like that. This stranger was always near Pan Z., like an inseparable shadow, praising his actions, saying that he entertained and enjoyed himself like a true gentleman, heir of famous ancestors, should. He promised to show him marvels and reveal a source of never-ending wealth. He told tales of wonders that happened far away, at the very edge of the world. He mocked the customs and traditions inherited from our forefathers. Some gentry approved of his ideas, but servants and peasants alike cursed him, mockingly calling him "the guest in black."

A year passed, then another, and things kept getting worse. Pan Z.'s peasants grew impoverished; they left their homes and wandered the world in search of sustenance. Misery reigned at the manor house. Passing by, neighbors and acquaintances avoided our estate. The guest in black visited only occasionally, advising the master to sell his people and raise money that way. The master followed his advice, sending many youths off to faraway places. But this did not make him rich, and the guest in black disappeared for good soon after.

Creditors pursued the nobleman in court, and the authorities demanded years' worth of unpaid taxes. The court confiscated the estate and handed it to a trustee, leaving Pan Z. only a few lackeys for his service. I was one of them. We lived in a remote farmstead; my master was a bachelor. After a few months I began noticing odd changes in him. He would sit in silence for hours, as if in despair, clutching his head, muttering to himself, pacing the room, awake from sunset until sunrise.

One night, near midnight, I heard the master's voice and saw a light in the window. I thought he must have called for someone, so I entered the room. He was speaking loudly, as if arguing, yet he was alone. Perplexed, I stood watching him, but he did not notice me. Finally, I said:

'I heard your voice, sir, and thought you had called, but you are alone and speaking to yourself.'

He shot me a troubled look, pointed at the wall, and said:

'Alone? Then who is this?'

I looked closer: there was a shadow the size of a man, with a long nose and bristling hair. I recognized the guest in black. Gripped by fear, I stood frozen, shivers running through me. The shadow moved along the wall and vanished.

'He is gone for now, but he will not leave me be,' said the master. 'And you – go. This is no place for you.'

I left, overcome with fear. It seemed that the terrible shadow stood before me, and I could not sleep all night. Whenever I told others about the apparition, no one believed me; they mocked me, saying I had been frightened by my own shadow. But I thought otherwise and could not put it from my mind.

Several weeks passed. Pan Z. was always alone and always restless. One evening he said to me: 'I feel unwell today. Come after supper and sleep here, for if anything happens, you would not hear me from your own room.'

I made my bed on the floor and extinguished the light. The night was clear and quiet, the moon was full. My master could not sleep: he sighed, rose, sat up, lay down again. I heard his every movement for a while, and as soon as I fell asleep a loud voice woke me. I leapt up and saw my master sitting on the bed, talking loudly, as if to himself, though I could not understand his words. The pale moonlight filled the room, illuminating everything. Suddenly, I noticed a frightening shadow the size of a man on the wall opposite the bed. Turning to face the window, it moved as though alive. A long nose, bristling hair – I recognized the guest in black. Gripped by terror, I shouted:

'Sir, command that the fire be lit!'

'Why light the fire?' said the master. 'It is only midnight.'

'This terrible shadow frightens me,' I replied.

'It is not you, but me whom he will not leave.'

He rose from the bed, walked around the room, and ordered me not to move from my place. The rooster crowed. The shadow made its way along the wall to the door and vanished. My master sat motionless like stone. I lay watching him, shivering, sleepless until dawn.

Once, that shadow appeared at noon, in bright sunlight. I saw a sudden change in my master's face: he turned pale as a corpse and paced briskly, muttering incomprehensible words.

Barely able to speak, I said:

'Sir, command that a priest be called, to pray and sprinkle holy water on the walls. This house must have stood empty for a long time, and a demon settled here. Or some sorcerer summoned him to torment us by day as well as by night.'

My master looked at me with a mocking smile.

'This house must have been sprinkled with holy water many times already. This matter is not for your mind to solve.'

Another time, at sunset, my master returned from a walk, upset. He entered the room and sat clutching his head.

'The good sir must be suffering from a migraine?' I asked.

'There is such a noise in my head, I can find no relief,' he replied.

'I could recommend a cure, if you would hear me.'

'I'll listen – if your advice is a good one.'

'People say that if there is noise in the head, it helps to stand by the church bells as they call believers to Mass. Then enter the holy place, kneel before the altar, pray earnestly, and listen to the liturgy. Many were cured that way. It might help you also.'

He looked at me with the same mocking smile stretched across his sickly face.

'Perhaps that could help someone like you, but the

music of the bells will not cure me.'

I have seen many misfortunes and strange things in my life, but this was the most terrifying one. My master could not endure it, and died of unending torment,' said the old man.

He lowered his head before the icon of the Mother of God in silent prayer, and everyone watched quietly.

It was already evening. The sun had disappeared behind the forest. When he finished his prayer, Haraska looked out the window: a single evening star shone in the sky. He gazed at it for a long while, and a tear rolled down his cheek. Turning to his guests, he said:

'Time flies quickly in the company of good friends – so too does life itself. In my youth I loved to watch this evening star, seeking hope and comfort in sorrow.'

He lit a wax candle, placed it by the coffin, and continued:

'I built myself a home without windows or doors. Here I shall rest in peace; no sadness, worry, or trouble will disturb my sleep. My hope is with God.'

With that, the old man placed the coffin on the floor and went to lie in it.

'What are you doing!' cried one of the guests, seizing his hand. 'Why would you, still healthy and strong, lie in the coffin? When the time comes, we will lay you there ourselves. For now, live and enjoy the sun!'

'You will not grow any taller,' said my father. 'And I see that the coffin fits you exactly. Do not remind us that we must lose you someday. Instead, let us reminisce about the past.'

'I want to rest after my labors. It is night already, the stars are shining,' said Haraska, and lay in the coffin.

We stood around watching him. His face turned

ghostly white, his eyes closed.

'Enough, enough of this rehearsal. Get up,' said my father, taking him by the hand.

'Get up, Haraska!' shouted the guests.

They tried to lift him from the coffin, but when they saw he was already dead they grew pale and stood dumbstruck for a long time."

"What a strange old man," said Zavalnia. "He knew he was living his last hours, and, bidding farewell to this world, he invited his friends to witness him depart for his eternal home. He thought of death all his life. And to reward him, the merciful God revealed to him the hour of judgment and mercy. As for the guest in black, who gave his master no peace – this is already his third appearance in our tales. The evil spirit does not rest, it is always seeking to do harm and befriends those who turn their backs on their neighbors. This is God's punishment. Now let us hear what your companion has to say."

The Nature's Sorcerer and Vargin the Cat

"Strange wonders occurred in days past," said the second traveler. "I also heard from the elders about extraordinary people. The stories of one of them remain etched in my memory most vividly.

There once lived in our land a simple peasant named Tamash. It was said that he was born with all his teeth. As he grew up, though he had never studied magic, he knew all the secrets of the sorcerers. No demon could hide from him – Tamash recognized them in every guise, every transformation, wherever they appeared. He was kind to everyone, and he possessed knowledge of secret words that helped overcome evil spirits, eased suffering, and aided the unfortunate. Afflicted with illness and finding no relief from learned doctors and expensive medicines, noblemen sent for Tamash, and he restored their health and peace of mind with mysterious words. I will tell you of a few such cases.

One day, Pan N. returned from the city and brought home a cat. I do not know where or how he acquired it, but it was no ordinary cat. When he placed it on the floor, everyone in the household stepped back, circling around, watching in amazement as it majestically walked about the house, purring as it examined each person. It behaved as though it had always belonged there.

Pan N. said to his wife:

'Look, Antosia, what a marvelous cat – large, with shiny fur, black as coal, and eyes that burn like embers. Truly, this is Vargin, the king of all cats. I barely managed to acquire this rarity.'

The cat leapt onto the table. The lady stroked it as it squinted its eyes, arched its black back, and walked across the table, purring. She lifted it into her arms – the beautiful, affectionate creature instantly won her over.

The cat enjoyed every privilege: it drank the richest milk, slept on a soft bed, and came running whenever the lady called, '*Vargin!*' He brought her joy, and everyone adored him.

A month passed, then another. The cat was the favorite of the household, living like a true feline king. But after several months, people began to notice a change in the lady of the house. She grew capricious. No one could guess what she wanted. She became irritable, restless, quarrelsome, started punishing maids and servants without cause, scolding neighbors, shouting at her husband. In the entire estate, only the cat was content and happy.

'What is this?' Pan N. wondered. 'Such an unexpected change in Antosia.'

He consulted elders and wise men. They agreed that the lady was ill, for she often wept, complained, clutched her head, and collapsed on her bed as if in great pain. No one could ease her suffering, save for the cat, who purred beside her.

'She surely has spasms,' said Pan N. 'We need to call the doctor.'

The doctor came and prescribed medicine. The costs

were enormous, yet nothing helped. The doctor was baffled. More doctors were summoned. They consulted, changed remedies – all in vain. None knew the nature of the illness.

When learned physicians failed, and the lady grew weaker and more restless, friends and neighbors urged Pan N. to call Tamash.

'Tamash,' they said, 'was born with teeth. Nature endowed him with the healing power of words. One must believe in mysteries and miracles, even if human reason cannot grasp them.'

Pan N. listened, then summoned the sorcerer.

The lady lay on her bed. The lieutenant's wife, who had come to visit, sat beside her. The maids crowded at the door, awaiting orders. The cat purred nearby.

Pan N. entered with Tamash. At once, the cat turned its fiery eyes upon him, bristled, hissed, and darted under the bed.

Tamash muttered secret words as he approached. Seeing him, the lady sprang up in rage. She opened her mouth to speak – but, instead, a swarm of wasps poured out, scattering through the room, stinging everyone, tangling themselves in hair. The cat leapt wildly from table to table, flung itself against windows and walls, then hid behind the stove, giving out a piercing cry. Terror seized everyone present; the lady collapsed on her bed. Tamash opened the door, and the swarm of stinging insects dispersed outside.

'Let the patient rest,' said Tamash. 'In a few hours she will be well.'

'Tell me, Tamash,' begged Pan N., 'what caused this affliction? How could venomous insects nest in her head, when even doctors couldn't discern her illness?'

'There is nothing strange here,' replied Tamash. 'The

lady played too often with the cat. Its unclean purring bred poisonous wasps in her head, as in a nest.'

'The cat?! Vargin?!' exclaimed Pan N. 'How can that be? Such a beautiful, gentle creature – everyone loved it, it had everything!'

'Be cautious. Cats, especially black ones, carry poison within.'

With that, he took his hat and left.

'Hang the cat!" roared Pan N., his rage frightening everyone. 'Pull it out from behind the stove! Hang it!'

'What a shame,' said the lieutenant's wife, 'to trust a sorcerer's deceit. How could poisonous wasps come from a cat? Do not commit such cruelty. I will take the cat myself. This is a rare cat, it will do no harm in my house.'

'Hang it at once!' cried Pan N.

A servant entered the room, searched for the cat behind the stove, but did not find it there. The master and the servant looked in every corner – under the tables and beds, behind the furniture – but could not find Vargin anywhere. The doors and windows were shut. How, then, had it escaped? They stood bewildered, for the cat seemed to have vanished into thin air.

The lady became calm and healthy again. Everyone in the area marveled at what had happened. The doctors mocked the gullibility of the common folk, but the people believed in the power of Tamash's words and continued to seek his advice, which brought relief to their suffering. The lieutenant's wife wished she could have taken Vargin home with her, and regretted not knowing where the poor creature was hiding from the unjust wrath of the master.

Once, while entertaining neighbors in her home, she shared her thoughts about Vargin the Cat:

'I have never seen anything more beautiful than that extraordinary creature: black as coal, its fur shiny, smooth, and soft like velvet, its tail bushy as a sable's, its eyes full of fire, burning like candles. A huge cat! Oh! If I could only have a cat like that – I would pay a great sum for such a rarity.'

As they talked, Zosia, the eldest daughter of the lieutenant's wife, ran in shouting:

'Oh, Mama! What a huge cat is sitting in the living room!'

They opened the door and saw a black cat in the dark corner, its eyes glowing like candles. The hostess immediately recognized Vargin, and barely had she said '*Vargin!*' that he approached her, purring. The lady lifted him in her arms, carried him into the room, and placed him on the floor. Vargin walked about majestically, while the children and guests crowded around, mesmerized and singing praises to the extraordinary creature.

'Zosia, you must make sure that Vargin is always fed and cared for,' said the lieutenant's wife. 'I am so pleased that he has appeared in my home. The misfortune he endured at Pan N.'s house will not befall him here. How could a cat so beautiful carry poison or harm anyone with his purring?'

For several weeks, Vargin was the happiest of cats. He had the best milk, everyone loved him, especially the children. They tossed him a ball, which he skillfully caught with his paws. He ran about the room with the children, pranced on chairs, tables, and sofas, played in the garden with the younger ones, and entertained them by climbing trees. After play and walks, he lay with the children on the grass in the shade of great linden trees; and when he returned to the house, Zosia would greet him, lift him into her arms, caress him with her lovely hand, and Vargin would fall asleep on her lap, purring.

But soon enough, everyone began to notice a change.

The children, who had been calm before, now climbed onto tables and dressers, grimacing or squinting like owls, afraid of the light. They twisted their bodies into monstrous shapes, hurled themselves at windows, and rushed toward water, shouting at everyone. Zosia too was completely transformed. At times, she grew very angry or sat in sadness, complaining about everyone and everything. At other times, she was overly joyful, dancing alone, spinning about the room, talking nonsense. She became frivolous, capricious, and no one could please her.

One day, the lieutenant's wife was entertaining guests, while the children played on the floor. Zosia turned around several times, then sat in the corner, lonely and sad, while Vargin settled into an armchair, purring, his eyes narrowed.

'I see strange changes in your house,' said a friend of the lieutenant's wife. 'The children, especially your eldest daughter, are not themselves. I have heard that black cats can be very harmful. Could Vargin have infected them? People say doctors are helpless in such cases. You must send for Tamash. He alone can heal.'

As she spoke, Vargin squealed in a voice that was not feline, leapt through the open window, and vanished.

The lieutenant's wife turned pale, and everyone was filled with fear. She now saw the truth, realized her mistake and its dire consequences. She sent a carriage at once to summon Tamash, pleading with him to hurry and save her from the misfortune.

Tamash arrived. She told him of the trouble that had befallen her home. The sorcerer looked at the young lady and the children, shrugged his shoulders, and said:

'Be calm, madam. Although the children are already afflicted, it is not too late. The creatures bred by the cat's purring can be driven from their heads.'

He commanded all the children to line up in the middle of the room, then approached them and whispered secret words.

Everyone watched anxiously. Tiny, eerie creatures poured out of the children: frogs and mice fell and crawled about the room, seeking refuge in the cracks, their high-pitched squeaks piercing the ear. From Zosia's head, moths of various colors and sizes burst out, fluttering under the ceiling. The mother watched, trembling with fear. Seeing her anguish, Tamash waved his hand, and the moths and monsters vanished at once.

To calm the distressed woman, Tamash assured her that the children would not suffer such an affliction again, provided she remembered the experience and remained vigilant, keeping her children safe from unclean play.

After the exorcism, when the children had gone to their room and Tamash had taken up his hat to leave, Judge Dademukha arrived. He was a wealthy man, and reputedly wise, for neighbors and acquaintances often sought his counsel in legal matters. The judge entered, greeted the hostess, glanced at Tamash, and said:

'What is this sorcerer doing here?'

The lieutenant's wife told him of the misfortune brought on by the black cat. Dademukha laughed heartily at the story and, addressing Tamash, said:

'You are a clever trickster. I've heard much of your magic, but beware lest it bring you trouble.'

'I have never harmed anyone,' replied Tamash.

'You deceive people.'

The guests and the hostess defended Tamash, insisting that there was no deception in the miracles they had themselves witnessed.

'But where is Vargin now?' asked the judge. 'I want to see him. What an unusual beast! Perhaps the lady of the house, not wishing to keep a cat that brought her such grief, will allow me to take him? I love such rarities. I have heard tales of cats that told stories and legends in blooming orchards, and of princes and lords traveling far to behold such wonders. And having this cat, whose purring can spawn butterflies, gnats, and other creatures, would be no less of a marvel. People would come from afar to see him.'

'I would gladly give him to the judge, but he escaped through the window.'

'Oh! What a pity,' said Dademukha. Then, turning to Tamash: 'Can you not catch him with your magic and deliver him to me?'

'You may take him now if you like.'

No sooner had Tamash spoken than Vargin the Cat suddenly appeared. Everyone stared in silence. The cat stood by the stove, arching his back, his bushy tail coiled on the floor like a viper, his eyes burning like two glowing embers.

'I am afraid to approach him,' said the judge. 'He must have been severely punished to be so angry. But what a huge cat!'

'Take him now, but beware later.'

Judge Dademukha ordered a servant to carry the cat to the carriage, and, after a brief delay, bade farewell to the lieutenant's wife. Tamash also departed.

Not long after, strange rumours began to spread about Judge Dademukha. What was happening to him? He became unbearable, suspecting everyone of malice, of ill intent, of plotting betrayal. He inspected his weapons each evening, loaded pistols and muskets, and did not sleep at night, as though fearing an attack. His wrath was dreadful. He punished servants harshly, often and without cause. No soul in his household felt safe or at peace. Only Vargin the

Cat remained at his side, eyes aglow, purring endlessly to amuse the judge.

Most troubling to Judge Dademukha was the thought that all the estates in the Polatsk and Nievel districts had once belonged to his family. He wearied the residents, summoning them to court, boasting of his lineage, and telling everyone how his ancestors had lived grandly, eating and drinking richly, and enjoying life as true lords.

One day, several officials arrived at the judge's house on business. They say he was in a good mood, and received them warmly. Amidst jokes and conversation, one of them noticed Vargin on an armchair.

'Oh! This is the very cat that was once at Pan N.'s and then at the lieutenant's wife's house, where his purring spawned poisonous wasps, moths, and other creatures in people's heads. Learned doctors could not help, but Tamash whispered his words and cured everyone.'

'Haha! Can such nonsense be believed?!' The judge nearly rolled with laughter. 'This cat has been with me for months, and I am perfectly well – no parasite troubles me.'

'Yet, Your Honor,' joked another, 'was it not the cat who suggested you start the case against Captain C.? I doubt it will succeed, I see no merit in your claims.'

'This cat has not studied law,' said the judge. 'I know what I am doing.'

'I have never met this 'Tamash,' said another guest. 'Can we not call him here? If he lives nearby, let him come and whisper his magic words. Perhaps, we too shall witness a miracle.'

'Surely, you want to discover,' laughed the judge, 'whether I have gnats in my head! To satisfy your curiosity, I will send for him at once. Let him come and treat me. We shall see whether he can deceive us with his whispering.'

As the judge ordered his servant to fetch Tamash, the

cat hissed, leapt from the chair, and, crouching under the table, voiced his fury in wild, restless purring. His eyes blazed, his fur bristled on back and tail – as if he faced an enemy.

'Vargin fears Tamash,' said one of the guests. 'The very mention of his name unsettles him.'

The judge lifted the cat in his arms, set Vargin beside him, stroking to calm him, but the creature's eyes still flamed, its fur bristled.

Clouds veiled the sky. Twilight dimmed the earth. Candles flickered in the judge's house, as voices disputed various court cases. The host vehemently defended the legality of his claims, declaring that he must triumph, that he would spare no expense to seize the estates of his rivals and force them into ruin.

Then, from nowhere, a shocking sight: the cat grew to the size of a dog and howled with a ferocious, canine voice. The host and his guests were petrified, unable to utter a word.

The door swung open. Tamash entered. The cat sprang, darted through the window with a force that pushed out the frame, sending the glass shattering as it vanished into the night.

Tamash approached the host, who stared at him in a trance, and whispered his magic words. A yet more terrifying sight followed: bubbles – like soap bubbles – streamed from every opening in the judge's head, and, bursting against the ceiling, morphed into dreadful shapes – winged vipers, dragons, and abominations like rotting skeletons. They floated above, dropping bones and skulls to the floor. Pale like corpses risen from graves, everyone looked on in terror. Finally, Tamash waved his hand, and the snakes, dragons, and skeletons vanished. He himself departed, leaving the host and his guests speechless with fear.

The wind touched the candle flames through the broken window. A rooster crowed in the distance. The clock struck midnight. After a long silence, everyone regained their senses. The miracle they had witnessed with their own eyes sent shivers down their spines, and now they believed in the power of Tamash's words, which even spirits obey. With tears in his eyes, Judge Dademukha confessed that all his claims had been unjust. He swore to live in harmony and friendship with everyone, and never again to force unreasonable burdens upon his neighbors.

Tamash helped many unfortunate peasants, too many to remember. It is a pity he left our land and went to a far-off place."

"Why," Zavalnia asked, "did he leave his friends and homeland?"

"Opinions differ. Some say that gentry and learned doctors insisted that words are like wind, incapable of helping or harming, that all illnesses were already well understood, and that apothecaries carried every necessary cure. They claimed such malicious cats never existed, and that Tamash deceived everyone with tricks, exploiting people's credulity. At last, they persecuted him, so he fled and hid from his ill-wishers.

Others say that even his friends grew skeptical, insisting: '*We need no magic words! Show us the herbs, and we shall cure ourselves.*' Tamash knew the power of every plant. To please them, he wandered meadows, swamps, riverbanks, and lakes, teaching them which herbs were poisonous, which were healing, where each grew, and how it should be used. Thus, he cared for his friends.

One May evening, when all of nature rejoices and birds sing in the fields and groves, Tamash wandered, lost in thought, through his native land, gathering herbs and flowers. At sunset, in a valley, amidst light and transparent mist, he saw a *rusalka* of extraordinary beauty. A wreath of flowers crowned her head, dew sparkled on her hair, and her dress, white as snow, was sprinkled with blossoms. Singing in an enchanting voice, she bewitched Tamash, and he followed her, never to return."

"Has Vargin the Cat appeared anywhere else?" asked my uncle.

"He appears even now, from time to time. Recently, in our estate, when the owner's son and his men came to the lodge at midnight, they saw a huge black cat in the first room. The doors and windows were shut, yet there he was. When they tried to catch him, he made no sound – instead he swept over tables, cabinets, and sofas like a light breeze, not lingering anywhere. At last, he sat in a corner, and when they surrounded him, he vanished, sending chills down their spines.

At times, on stormy nights when the wind howls against the walls, one hears his dreadful purring, and a heavy sadness seizes the soul. From time to time, at midnight, people see his fiery eyes burning like two candles. A distressing sight. But not everyone takes this seriously – only simple folk pray, begging God to deliver them from that demon."

"The storm is raging outside," said my uncle. "The wind howls against the wall, snow drifts over the roads. You will not leave early tomorrow, nor is there any need to hurry: I have bread and hay, thank God. Let us talk a while longer, until the rooster crows. What tale will your third companion tell us?"

The Strange Staff

The third traveler was still young, with a short mustache and a soft beard. His face was alive with health and keen memory. He began his tale:

"In my life, I have yet to encounter anything worth special attention, but I have heard many stories told during the long winter evenings. I'll share one of them – the story of a strange staff.

Once, a wealthy man employed a young, hardworking, and honest servant named Aleshka. He was diligent, obedient, and always eager to please his master. For three years he served without trouble. But in the fourth, he received only three *talers* for all his labor, and so he left in search of better fortune.

'It is so hard to be poor in this world,' he thought as he walked. 'If only I had money, I would do much good. There are those crippled or worn down by age who cannot earn bread no matter how they toil. If I could, I would provide for them, so that they might live in peace the rest of their days.'

As soon as he thought this, he came upon a beggar. The man was missing an arm and looked exhausted from travel and hunger. Aleshka took out a *taler*, gave it to him, and walked on.

Not much farther, he met a blind man, guided by a boy of ten. The blind man was a beggar, and Aleshka gave him his second *taler*.

Then he saw a third old man, bent low, his beard and

hair as white as snow. Leaning on a staff, he begged in a trembling voice. Aleshka gave him his last *taler* and said:

'Take it – my last coin. I do not need it today, though I know not what tomorrow may bring.'

'Do not worry about tomorrow,' said the beggar. 'I give you this staff, which supported me in my old age. If ever you are in need, raise its end – the one touching the earth – toward the sky, and whatever you wish will come true.'

With that, he handed the staff to Aleshka and vanished.

Aleshka stood for a long time, pondering the being who had appeared as a beggar, and the mysterious power of the staff he now held. Lost in thought, he walked on.

Soon he came to a forest veiled in smoke like thick fog. A terrible fire raged there. Driven by the wind, the flames devoured the pines, while elk and wild goats fled into the lake, swimming across to escape the flames. Villagers fought desperately to halt the fire, but it had nearly reached the fields and threatened to engulf the crops.

Aleshka remembered the beggar's words and lifted the staff. At once, the flames sank as though doused with water, leaving only black smoke coiling up into the sky. The people watched in amazement, while Aleshka walked on.

Then the sky darkened, a storm cloud rose from behind the mountains, overtaking half the heavens. Lightning flashed without pause, thunder cracked, the wind roared, and beasts fled the pastures as fear seized the villagers.

Aleshka raised the staff again, and the wind scattered the clouds in all directions. The storm passed without harm.

Later, when the fields and meadows, which burned under a merciless sun, withered, he summoned rainclouds with his staff. A generous downpour revived the earth.

He helped many poor and destitute people, and they thanked fate.

At last, he journeyed to a faraway land beyond forests, waters, and mountains. It was a vast country, laid waste by a sorcerer who had sent forth evil spirits. For days and weeks Aleshka walked, passing deserted villages and ruined towns, until he reached a dark forest where an overgrown path was hidden. There he met a giant. The tallest birches barely reached his shoulders. With one hand he uprooted ancient oaks and planted them elsewhere.

When he saw the traveler, he roared:

'Why have you come here, to these dark forests? You will perish like a worthless worm!'

'I am not as fearful as you think,' replied Aleshka, and raised the staff to the sky.

The forest roared, trees toppled as if torn by a storm, and the giant himself fell like a great oak. He begged for mercy.

'Who are you, and what are you doing in this desolate wilderness?' asked Aleshka.

'Not far from here lies the border of the kingdom of the Great Sorcerer,' said the giant. 'I am Dubina,[53] his servant. I guard these dark forests, but now I wish to serve you.'

'Then rise and guard the forests,' said Aleshka, 'but do not harm travelers – help them instead.'

With that, Aleshka walked on.

He passed through endless pine woods, seeing only the trees before him and the strip of the sky above. He met no one but wild beasts, and only now and then, from far off, came the cry of an owl. After he crossed these dark wastelands, a vast valley opened before him, with a wide river flowing through its middle. Dense reeds crowded the banks, and countless streams emptied into it.

On a high bank sat a giant that resembled a massive rock. The hair on his head was so coarse the wind could not stir it. An enormous mustache jutted from beneath his nose, which he cast into the river to haul up great fish for food.

Seeing Aleshka, the giant shouted:

'Why have you come here? Neither a fishing boat nor a wild beast has ever crossed this river. Only birds may pass. You will perish here for your foolish bravery!'

'I am not afraid of your threats,' replied Aleshka, and he raised the staff to the sky.

The water swirled. The river, as if tumbling from high mountains, began to tear away its banks with a furious current. The giant toppled like a rock loosened by a torrent. He bowed down and begged forgiveness.

'Who are you? Why do you live here alone and forbid others to pass?' asked Aleshka.

'Not far from here lies the border of the kingdom of the Great Sorcerer. I am Prud, his servant. I guard this river so that no one may cross. But now I wish to serve you.'

'Then rise,' said Aleshka. 'You may continue to fish these waters, but do not attack travelers, nor forbid their passage. Aid the unfortunate in need. Now show me where to cross.'

At these words, the river calmed, and Prud cast his mustache across to the other bank. Aleshka crossed upon it like on a floating bridge, climbed the high shore, and walked on.

Before long, he saw the peaks of vast mountains rising above the earth like clouds on a rowan night. As he drew near, he beheld a giant more fearsome and powerful than Dubina or Prud. The monster was gathering mountains in one place, stacking them one atop another, building a wall already higher than the clouds.

When the giant saw the wanderer, he roared in a voice that shook the earth like thunder:

'Where are you going, wretch? Neither eagle nor falcon flies beyond this place, and the clouds themselves halt here. You will perish like a worthless worm!'

'I am not afraid of your threats,' Aleshka replied, raising the staff toward the sky.

The mountains came crashing down, the earth trembled, and the giant collapsed in terror, begging forgiveness.

'Who are you?' asked Aleshka. 'Whom do you serve, carrying mountains on your shoulders? And who needs a wall higher than the clouds?'

'I am Harynia, servant of the Great Sorcerer,' the giant confessed. 'Here lies the border of his kingdom. He hates birds, clouds, and wind. He would extinguish the sun and stars, leaving only darkness. But Heaven itself favors you – you are stronger than my master. I wish to abandon this toil and serve you instead, going wherever you command.'

'Then lead me to the kingdom of the Great Sorcerer, show me the way.'

So Aleshka came into a land of gloom, where all nature lay silent. Neither man nor beast stirred. The ruins of old castles crowned the hills, while in the valleys stood figures that looked like beggars in sorrowful contemplation, turned to stone. Here and there bent birches rose through the fog, and lonesome willows drooped over stagnant waters. The forests stood black and mute, without a bird's song – only crows wheeled everywhere.

From the forests rose flocks of black birds, hovering like a stormcloud. Dark fogs drifted outward, forming strange and dreadful shapes – phantom armies on horseback, riding through the air before dissolving into smoke.

'What are these phantoms?' asked Aleshka.

'These are the forces of the Great Sorcerer, weakened by the wind that roams the world.'

'And these stone figures, which from afar look like people turned to rock?'

'They are the inhabitants of this land. The bent birches and willows by the waters are their wives, mothers, and sisters. Only your staff can break the spell.'

Then Aleshka raised the staff toward the sky. A gentle breeze stirred, the mists scattered, and spring light spread over the land. The forests rustled, the trees turned green again. Birdsong filled the air. The stone-like people lifted their hands and eyes to heaven. The birches and willows by the riverbanks became beautiful women, walking across flowered meadows. Springs murmured, rivers and lakes shone like mirrors, villages and castles filled with people, and soon enough, the whole land blossomed anew.

Aleshka remained there and married a beautiful and wealthy princess. A grand wedding was held in the palace, which glittered with silver and gold. Princes, counts, and other noble guests gathered, and music played for many days and nights. I too was there, drinking mead and wine, and having a good time."

"A fine tale," said Zavalnia. "For three *taler*s given away to beggars, he freed an entire land from its curse and found happiness. But it is not yet midnight. Perhaps your fourth companion will also tell us a story?"

HOUSEHOLD MATTERS

"I would gladly tell you stories and tales until sunrise, if only my heart were calm. It is not the past, but the future that weighs upon me, filling all my thoughts. It is difficult to speak of anything else."

"You must be expecting trouble, if you are so anxious," said my uncle.

"It is already March. Spring draws near, and, around here, this season does not bring much joy to anyone. For some, it is so grievous they cannot find rest at night."

"In spring, many peasants worry whether they have enough seed for sowing. Perhaps your concern is the same?"

"Where I come from, trouble never walks alone. Misfortunes come from all directions, until everything falls from one's hands, and little hope remains for respite after hard labor. My son spent the winter in the city and earned ten silver rubles. With that money, I bought seed in Polatsk. Praise God, I now have something to sow. But who will plow the field? Who will go to *corvée*? In my household there are only three men fit for work, and each year I must overexert myself, for my sons are sent far away to earn money that brings no benefit to our home. I do not know whether I can manage the work alone this year. My health is poor, my strength wanes, and I have no means to hire help."

"I do not know where this greed has come from," said my uncle. "In striving to gain much, they lose even more. I always say: the land – the land alone – can satisfy all our needs. It is on this that we should fix our attention, this we should strive to improve. Then we would live like the good lords: their barns and fields an unending source of treasure, living well and able to help others. In the old days it was not customary to send people to faraway lands to earn money, for every lord had *ducats* in his treasury, and every peasant had *talers* in his purse, paid his dues, had all he needed, and lived in peace."

"Our old master often said the same, God rest his soul – the whole district remembers him still. He knew every farmer on his estate, how each worked, how each tended the land. He cared for his peasants, always thinking how to improve their lives. In springtime, everyone had as much seed as he required."

At that moment the dogs barked in the courtyard, and someone knocked loudly at the gate. My uncle sent a servant to open it.

ANDREY THE ORGANIST

The door opened, and Andrey stepped inside, covered in wet snow. Shaking the flakes from his hat and coat, he said:

"Praise be to Jesus Christ! Peace to this house."

"Forever and ever. Amen. Peace to you as well. But it seems, Andrey, there is little peace outside," replied my uncle.

"God forbid! So much is happening out there – rain, snow, wind, a blizzard. Passing through the forest was trouble enough, but when I reached the open field I lost my way, and would surely have perished had I not seen the lantern burning above Pan Zavalnia's gate. At that sight I gave thanks to God, for I knew I had found safe harbor from the storm."

"I am grateful you do not forget me," said my uncle. "The winter road is vanishing, and soon I shall live here like a hermit: few will come to visit me."

While they spoke, the travelers and servants made their way to the common quarters.

"I fear I have interrupted your pleasant evening," Andrey said. "No doubt your guests were sharing many fine tales with Pan Zavalnia."

"Let them rest now," answered my uncle. "The wind howls in the yard – it is hard to hear even the rooster's crow. Perhaps it is already midnight."

"Were they crossing the lake? I believe the ice is still strong. Tomorrow, when I return home, I too shall cross Nieszczarda."

"It is better to take another road. Longer, yes – but safer. Already it is hard to reach the shore. Their horse fell into the water. Only with great effort did we pull it out. But a traveler must first warm himself and eat. Janka, ask Pani Malhreta to prepare supper for our guest. I have excellent fish – fisherman Rodzka brought it today. He is a good man, he never forgets me."

"I heard people say Rodzka is a sorcerer. There is even a tale told about him.

Not far from Haradzec Hill, where the river meets the lake, Rodzka often cast his nets at sunset and always returned with a boat full of fish. A fisherman who lived nearby grew envious, saying Rodzka fished in another man's waters, and forbade him those shores. Rodzka warned him – he would see such horrors that not only would he profit nothing, but he would never forget the punishment. And so it was. One evening, in calm and clear weather, the envious fisherman rowed out and cast his net. As he hauled it in, thinking he had caught a fine haul of bream, he saw monstrous creatures entangled there – huge heads with fiery eyes, their leathery wings beating the water amid shrieks and cries. Some rose into the air and circled above his head. Terror seized him, his hair stood on end, he screamed like a madman, and nearly toppled into the lake. He would have drowned, had his neighbors not heard his cries and come to his rescue."

"Believe no such gossip, Andrey," my uncle said. "That is a slanderous lie. Rodzka is a good and pious man, and I can prove it. He never begins fishing with a new net until the priest has blessed it with holy water. On holy days he attends church, both in Harbachova and Rasony. He was exemplary at the Jubilee services, and he goes faithfully to confession. Besides, everyone knows how he despises the *ostashes*, godless sorcerers that fraternize with the evil spirit."

My uncle then spoke at length about the *ostashes'*

dealings with dark powers, recounting all he had heard from Rodzka. By the time the tale was done, the table was set.

After supper, Andrey said:

"To thank our host for his hospitality, it would be fitting to share an entertaining tale before sleep – but none comes to mind. So instead I will gift you something more useful than any story: the Vilnia calendar for 1817, this very year. Within, you will find much that is clever, useful and curious: advice on farming, secrets that may be new even to Pan Zavalnia – how to guard cabbages from caterpillars, whiten linen, raise poultry, brew vinegar, and improve all kinds of orchard trees. There are riddles, anecdotes, and stories as well."

"Many thanks," said my uncle. "A farmer has great need of such a book. It even speaks of the weather, though not always accurately. Still, its advice on haymaking and harvest is helpful. But tell me, Andrey, what do these figures mean: bull, lion, crab, maiden, scales, twins? I always see them in calendars, yet do not know their purpose."

"They are signs of the heavens, under which men are born and which shape their lives. But I do not know this well, for I never finished all my schooling nor traveled in the skies. Janka would know better."

"There will be a solar eclipse this year," said my uncle, leafing through the calendar.

"Men may predict eclipses of the sun," Andrey replied, "but not the eclipse that can plunge a man's heart into sorrow."

"Do you have some ill news?" my uncle asked.

"I heard a grievous word from our parish priest. Sad indeed, but I will share it with Pan Zavalnia. God grant it may not come to pass."

He leaned close and whispered in secret.

I saw the shadow fall on my uncle's face. He grew silent and sat long in thought. At last he said:

"It is time to sleep. Perhaps my dreams will bring better things. Surely it must be past midnight already."

A bed was brought into the room. Andrey, weary from the road, soon fell into deep slumber. My uncle lingered, whispering his prayers longer than usual. Only after the rooster crowed a second time did he extinguish the light.

DEPARTURE

Spring. A warm breeze drifted through the air, the sun grew stronger with each passing day, and the ice on Nieszczarda darkened and began to break apart. The lake lay deserted. Only white terns soared overhead, streams ran down from the hills, flooding the plain, while the river spilled into meadows and forests. Tall birches and willow thickets rose from the submerged earth, their silhouettes etched against the crystal surface of the water. Larks sang above the fields, and the cries of cranes echoed from afar.

By the end of April, the earth had clothed itself in green. The shepherd was driving the herd to pasture, and the plowman worked the fields until dusk. On clear days, the beauty of the hills and forests delighted the eye. Evening brought the chorus of birds and the enchanting songs of nightingales from the groves. By night, fishermen lit bonfires along the shores of Nieszczarda, while ducks and water hens called from the dense reeds.

Amid the joy of nature, in such fair weather, my heart was heavy with longing, my thoughts clouded with sorrow. I wandered fields and forests, bidding farewell to the spring of my native land. The future loomed before me like a distant, barren wilderness, filled with abysses, wild beasts, and serpents.

One evening, as the sun inclined toward the west and my uncle returned from the fields, he called me and asked:

"Why are you so pensive and gloomy?"

"I am thinking of the journey."

"When do you intend to leave our land?"

"I wish to leave tomorrow. My decision is made, and the sooner the better. Besides, spring weather such as this is the best for travelers."

"If you are resolved, I will not hold you back. Tomorrow you shall have a horse and provisions for the road. But before you depart for good, go and visit Pan Maragowski, Pan Sivoha, and the blind Francisak. Your path already lies in their direction, and it will not take you far out of the way. They have come to love you and sincerely wish you happiness."

In the morning, when everything was ready, Pan Zavalnia said:

"Janka, let me leave you with the counsel that I once received from my own father:

'Go out into the world, seek your own fortune. Love God, your neighbor, and the truth. Providence will not forsake you. Be diligent and faithful in your duties. If sorrow meets you on the road of life, bear it with patience; and if misfortune strikes, do not despair. Remember: nothing on this earth endures – only the same stars, the same sun shine above us as on the day the world was created.

Should you encounter people happier than we are – people whose villages and towns are ever filled with song, music, and festivity, whose land is like a splendid garden, rewarding the farmer each year with abundance – do not forget the suffering of your countrymen. Let your prayer rise with theirs to God. And perhaps, one day, our forests and fields too shall resound with joy, God willing.

Many years from now, you may return to this land. By then you will no longer find the old companions with whom you shared so many evenings in my home. And I too shall be gone from this world; perhaps someone will show you my grave. Farewell, and remember these words of mine.'"

An hour later, the tall forests surrounding my uncle's estate vanished from sight, as did the clear mirror of Lake Nieszczarda and its green shores.

THE END

The Wooden Old Man and the Insect Woman

The sun had already set in the west. The sky was clear, the air still, and the forest filled with melodious and savage cries of birds. Night was approaching, and I quickened my pace, eager to leave the woods before darkness fell. Stepping out into the fields, I saw a charming gentry home on a hilltop. Golden ears of wheat ripened in the fertile fields, and a great herd of cows was returning from pasture. Trusting in the warm hospitality of the Belarusian folk, I made my way toward the house, hoping to find rest after a day's journey.

I soon met a man returning from the fields. He was elderly, with a tanned face, gray hair, and a bearing that was both calm and alert. He wore a homespun coat of gray. Judging him to be the master of the estate, I greeted him and asked kindly for permission to stay until morning.

"Please, come," he replied with sincerity. "The days are long now, and one may travel far without haste. The Lord God must have guided you this way toward Polatsk, but it is still forty *versts* through wastelands and sandy forests. It would be dreary and unsafe to walk through the dark night alone."

As we neared the house, two large dogs greeted us in the yard and eyed me cautiously.

"Do not be afraid," the merchant said. "They will not harm a man, but they will never let a wild beast near, and they are the best guards for our livestock. Dogs such as these are a necessity here, for wolves and bears have more than once attacked our neighbors' pens."

He led me into a room furnished with a table, chairs, and other pieces all made of birch – simple, but sturdy and well-crafted. On the walls hung icons of the Savior and the Mother of God in wicker frames, with inscriptions beneath that read *"Klauber sculpsit"*. There were also portraits of St. Ignatius Loyola, Andrey Bobola, Francis Xavier, and others, engraved long ago in a Polatsk printing house. On a shelf in the corner, I noticed a wooden bust, bald and broad-nosed, resembling the head of Socrates. Its face was pitted, battered, and scorched in places.

The hostess entered from the garden, surrounded by children. The eldest daughter, Anelya, had raven-black hair, a slender form, and bright, lively eyes. Nature had so richly endowed her that no silk or precious ornament could add to her beauty. I looked at this happy family with great delight.

"Are you from our county, or from far-off lands?" the hostess asked.

"I have known the vicinity of Polatsk since childhood," I replied, "but in pursuit of my fortune I lived far away for many years, and now I have returned for a visit. So much has changed – only the hills and forests remain as before."

"And how long ago did you leave your land?"

"It has already been eighteen years."

The merchant studied me closely. "I believe I have seen you here before, but I cannot recall your name."

I told him, and at once he grasped my hand with joy.

"I am Z... We were schoolmates once."

A long conversation followed about the happy past. We spoke of the friends of our youth and teachers from the schools of Polatsk, of old acquaintances – who lived, where, and how; who had left the homeland, and when; and of the elders who had already departed to our eternal home.

Afterward, Pan Z... took a wooden bust from the shelf.

"Do you remember this Old Man? He once looked

finer, when he peered from behind a narrow window, dispensing warnings and advice. You can see on his face how much he has suffered before ending up here with me. He is a dear keepsake. When I look at him, I recall his wise counsel, and I pass it on to my own children. My young son already knows well what the Wooden Old Man permits and forbids."

"Oh! This Old Man must have wandered far and endured much after bidding farewell to the cloister. The world greeted him cruelly: a hole bored in his head, his eyes gouged, his lips scorched. People do not love the truth. Perhaps he chose to remain mute on his journey, never offending anyone with his warnings."

"People are difficult to please. Perhaps he suffered for his silence. Let me tell you of his wanderings and of other strange events I have heard from neighbors. But first, let the traveler take some refreshment."

The table was set with *harelka* and various dishes. Anelya brought ripe raspberries she had gathered in the garden, along with fine apples. Pan Z... praised his fruit trees, which he himself had planted and grafted. While the gracious host urged me to eat, the door opened and an old man entered, leaning on a cane. His head and mustache were white. Once he had been mighty and strong, but age had bent his tall frame.

"Ah, Pan Rotmistr," Pan Z... greeted him warmly, "you have come at the right time. Allow me to present a dear guest, once my schoolmate, who wandered far and now returns to his homeland after many years. We shall spend the evening in pleasant conversation, with much to recall after such a long absence."

Soon the *samovar* was brought in, and tea poured. The old Pan Rotmistr, seated at the table, turned to the hostess and said:

"My lady, once upon a time tea was used as a remedy for headaches, but now people cannot live without it – the world has changed so."

Pan Z... set his glass down on the table.

"Now listen," he said to me. "I will tell you the strange story of the Wooden Old Man."

The children, though they had likely heard the tale more than once, gathered eagerly about their father, their faces full of curiosity.

WHAT HAPPENED TO THE WOODEN OLD MAN

"In Polatsk, when the Jesuit walls were being rebuilt by decree, all that was deemed useless or unnecessary was cast out with the rubble. The poor Wooden Old Man met the same fate. Covered with lime and broken bricks, he lay forgotten near the wall, his face and hair already discolored by sun, rain, and time. Laborers hired to clear the ruins dug him out from the debris and, thinking their master might find some use for him, took him to a merchant.

The merchant studied the figure carefully, suspecting it might be the likeness of some great man. He summoned his factor, a Jew named Zalman, and asked what he thought of it. Could this be the bust of a prince, or some ancient philosopher?

'I know very well,' Zalman replied with a sly smile, 'that it is neither prince nor sage. But when this head peered from behind the wall, it spoke – and people said it spoke wisely. I saw it with my own eyes.'

'It spoke? How could that be? It is only wood! Surely there was some magic in it?'

'Perhaps so,' Zalman shrugged. 'But why would you want it? Give it to me, I'll pay you for it.'

'You think to cheat me,' the merchant snapped. 'Nonsense – a wooden head that speaks! That cannot be.'

As they argued, a stranger approached, a man fashionably dressed, perhaps an official or a teacher. Gazing at the head, he declared:

'This is the likeness of the Greek philosopher Socrates. I have read of him and seen his portrait, and the resemblance is striking. He endured much suffering from his wife Xanthippe, and paid dearly for the truth he spoke to the world.'

The merchant, delighted to have found such a treasure – the bust of the great Socrates, of whose wisdom he had heard – drove the Jew away from the Old Man and decided to keep it in his village house. He intended to speak of the suffering of Socrates, so it might serve as a warning for his wife Efima, who, in his eyes, was much like Xanthippe.

A few days later, the Wooden Old Man and the merchant moved to the village, several dozen *versts* from Polatsk. The master brought it into the house, proudly showed it to his wife, and explained that it was the bust of a famous Greek philosopher.

Efima glanced askance at the Old Man.

'This wooden monstrosity, with its beard and nose, looks a great deal like you – was it worth hauling it around?'

In vain did the husband try to convince her that it was a great rarity; the unfortunate Old Man was on the verge of being thrown out of the house and left to spend the night under the open sky. Fortunately, a neighbor and friend arrived. He calmed Efima and persuaded her that the face bore nothing repulsive, and could well be the likeness of a hermit or monk who had once lived piously, and therefore deserved a measure of respect.

At last, Efima agreed to keep the Old Man in the house, though she often spat at it, called it a monstrosity, and gave it an angry side eye. The merchant explained to his friends that this was the bust of the famous philosopher Socrates, and placed it on the wall between two windows.

In the middle of the night, when everyone slept and the rooster had not yet crowed, Efima awoke with a scream and roused her husband to light the fire quickly, for the

Wooden Old Man had terrified her, and she trembled with fear. Surprised, the husband rose and lit a lamp.

'This wooden old man,' said Efima, 'haunted my dreams all night in dreadful forms. I fled through wild forests and swamps while he pursued me with a torch, wishing to cast me into a fiery abyss. When I awoke, trembling with fear, I saw him in the moonlight upon the wall. His eyes shone, and he looked at me with anger. Oh! Have mercy, take this monstrosity away.'

Remembering what the Jew had once told him, the husband thought that perhaps there really was some magic in it – but he said nothing of this to his wife. Instead, he took the Old Man down from the wall, carried it into the bakery, and set it upon the stove, telling Efima that the dream and the Old Man's terrifying eyes were but a figment of her troubled mind. Nevertheless, the light was left burning for the rest of the night, and Efima only managed to sleep just before dawn.

Abandoned on the stove in the bakery, the Old Man grew blackened from the smoke that hung daily beneath the ceiling like a stormcloud. After some time, the merchant's maids and a few village girls took him down to frighten the servants who were to sleep on the hay in the dark after supper.

The girls hurried to the barn ahead of them. They wrapped a bundle of straw in a sheet, leaving the Old Man's head protruding at the top. They meant to set it up like a scarecrow against the wall, but suddenly an unusual sound arose about them, and the Old Man's eyes glowed with fire. The girls scattered, screaming; some fainted in the road, while others ran into the house pale as though lifeless. Family members rushed to help. The bundle of straw and the Old Man were later found by the wall. Efima declared that the devil was in it, while her husband and other men argued that it was only the girls' frightened imagination. Yet the Old Man did not return to the house: he was flung into the barn, where he lay upon the damp earth.

News of the apparition spread swiftly. Usvoisky, an innkeeper five *versts* away, scoffed at such tales. Having served fifteen years as a lackey in Pan N.'s estate, he had read several French novels in translation and had, as he boasted, a sound understanding of unusual events. He dismissed miracles and magic as nonsense. Yet, curious to see the Wooden Old Man for himself, he came to the merchant. In the barn, they found the head lying in a dark corner, already moldy from the damp. The merchant told him it was the head of Socrates, who had spoken truth to the world, and that his wife detested it. Usvoisky believed him, for he too had heard of the famous philosopher. He begged the merchant to give him the Old Man, promising repayment with *harelka* or in some other way. The merchant agreed, knowing his wife would never reconcile herself to the presence of the philosopher's head.

Usvoisky took it to his inn, placed it on the bench behind the long table, and proudly showed it to any guest who came to drink. He insisted that the face resembled Socrates, the ancient philosopher who had suffered and died for the truth.

Weeks later, on a holy day, many peasants and servants from Pan N.'s estate gathered at the tavern. After sunset, at dusk, a few drunken servants decided to prank Usvoisky. When he stepped out for a moment, they seized the Old Man, bored two holes in the top of the head, poured in water, and pierced the eyes with an awl. Like tears, the drops trickled down its face. They set the weeping Old Man back on the bench.

When Usvoisky returned, they cried:

'Look, your Socrates is weeping – surely because you've wronged him, or won't give him *harelka*!'

As the innkeeper looked in astonishment, the dogs in the yard lifted their heads and howled, the cattle bellowed in the barn, the hens darted about in terror, shrieking. Wind roared around the tavern, filling everyone with dread. The company sobered at once and prayed until calm was restored. Later, I heard that when the pranksters returned to the manor, their master, enraged for no clear reason, ordered them flogged for tarrying so long at the tavern.

Usvoisky examined the Old Man and begged that it never be mocked again. Months passed, and the event was forgotten. One evening, entertaining neighbors, he himself grew careless. Taking a cigar from his pocket, he said to the Old Man:

'Since you don't drink *harelka* with us, at least smoke a cigar. A gentleman gave me a few, I'll spare one for you.'

He set the lit cigar in the Old Man's mouth. At that very moment, the neighbors burst in crying that the inn's roof was aflame. The innkeeper sobered instantly; the guests fled, people gathered, and the roof was dismantled, the building barely saved.

Secretly, Usvoisky pondered how to rid himself of the Old Man, yet was afraid of treating him with disrespect, by fire or water, lest punishment befall him again. He waited for a chance to pass him on, meanwhile keeping him not on the bench, but locked in a cupboard.

Not far away, east of the forest, lived Pan Khapatsky, wealthy in serfs, once an assessor, then a judge, educated to the point of believing in nothing and mocking everything. One day, riding in a light carriage, he visited Usvoisky, with whom he traded horses. Eager to be rid of the Old Man, Usvoisky brought him out of the cupboard, set him on the table, and said:

'Look, Your Honor, what a rarity. Can you tell whose face this is?'

Khapatsky laughed.

'Some bald, bearded peasant.'

'No, Your Honor, this is none other than Socrates, the great philosopher. Great secrets lie within this head. I esteem you highly and wish to offer it to you as a token of my friendship.' He told him all that had happened at the merchant's and in his own inn.

Khapatsky laughed until tears ran down, mocking people's folly. Then he drew a snuffbox from his pocket.

'Well, Old Man,' he said, 'you were angered by the cigar, so now I'll treat you to good tobacco.'

Saying this, he filled the Old Man's nose with a pinch of tobacco.

'What are you doing, Your Honor? By God, let nothing bad come of this!'

'Don't worry, he won't get angry about this. After all, as you say, this is the head of the great philosopher Socrates, and wise heads love tobacco because it helps them think.'

Usvoisky crossed himself and prayed silently, fearing something bad might happen in his inn.

'Don't be afraid, the Old Man won't misbehave with me, for I myself possess at least as much knowledge as Socrates. Well then, say farewell to it, Pan Usvoisky.'

He sat in the carriage, placed the Old Man on his knees, whipped the horse, and vanished around the bend, while the innkeeper stood there for a long time, watching him leave.

It was about an hour and a half past noon. Pan Khapatsky's estate was behind the forest, no more than four *versts* from the inn, but – a strange thing! – the horse ran and ran, passing hills and forests. Khapatsky saw only unfamiliar landscapes, passed through villages, estates, and fields, but nowhere could he see his own home. He met travelers, wanted to ask them where he was, but the horse ran so fast that he couldn't exchange a word with anyone.

The sun set behind the mountains, and it was already evening. Gray twilight enveloped the road. Foaming all over, the horse now moved at a slow pace. Khapatsky thought about finding a village to spend the night and ask for directions. Suddenly, a black stormcloud covered the sky, and the night became so dark that you couldn't see a step ahead. It began to pour. The unlucky traveler didn't know what to do, but in the flash of lightning, he noticed a small structure by the road. It was a cemetery, and in it stood an old wooden chapel from long ago. Khapatsky turned off the road to shelter from the storm. He left the horse in a quiet spot behind the wall and entered the chapel himself, waiting in the corner for the storm to pass. Then he took the snuffbox from his pocket, and no sooner had he opened it than, in the flash of lightning, he saw a huge dried-out hand stretch over the snuffbox, ready to take a pinch of tobacco.

Frightened, Khapatsky dropped the snuffbox, ran outside, and, despite the rain and wind, rushed into the field, not knowing where he was going. Fortunately, the clouds soon dispersed, and he saw the morning star in the east and a village on a hill nearby. He hurried there and saw peasants going to mow the meadow. From them, he learned he was near Viciebsk, several dozen *versts* away from his home. Accompanied by the group of mowers, he returned to the cemetery, found the horse and carriage where he had left them, and found the snuffbox on the chapel floor – but the Old Man was gone. Khapatsky had no recollection of how or where he had lost it. A few days later, Pan Khapatsky returned home, and from then on remembered all too well that although he knew no less than Socrates, there were still things incomprehensible even to him.

For almost a year, strange rumors circulated about the Old Man. Some said that a pilgrim, carrying him in his hands, appeared in several villages, teaching people how to be virtuous, reminding them to honor the ancient customs and traditions of their ancestors, and not to stray from the true faith. He blessed the obedient and pious, and fled from the non-believers and the depraved.

Others said that one evening, before sunset, shepherds and plowmen witnessed a strange apparition. A beautiful woman dressed in white, like an angel, was seen adorning the Old Man's head with wreaths of flowers out in the meadow. When curious folk tried to approach, the woman, like a spirit, moved away – neither ditches nor thick brush hindered her. She walked onto the lake and, like a white cloud, rose above the clear water and vanished. Many wondrous stories were told.

Now, let me tell you how, after a long and strange journey, this Wooden Old Man finally found its way to me. You know our Belarus well. During a crop failure, only flax provides and meets our needs, if God blesses our fields. Two years ago, I had a lot of it. Traders buy it from us and then, gathering it from all over Belarus, transport it on ships along the Dzvina all the way to Riga. Wanting to sell my goods, I visited a merchant. I found his house in great disorder, while his wife Efima was in a wild frenzy, almost tearing the house apart, lamenting at her husband: he had brought an enchanted monstrosity that gave her no peace. The merchant, who had returned home just an hour earlier, swore to her that he was not to blame. I barely managed to contain this outburst. Later, I asked the merchant what caused so much distress in his wife. He informed me that the head of the philosopher Socrates had somehow appeared to her by the window, and now lay behind the wall. He took me out of the house to show me the Old Man and pleaded with me to take it away. I put it in the carriage, talked to the merchant about the flax, and returned home.

Some time later, I heard the neighbors talking:

'Always quarreling with her husband, Efima fell out of love with him and wanted to leave him for good. She may have had a special friend who encouraged her to do so. So when her husband was away, she packed everything she could take with her to leave him an empty house. Then suddenly, she looked out the window and saw the wooden head of that Old Man. No one knows whence it came or how it appeared at the window. Efima screamed in fear and fainted. The family members heard this from the other room, ran in to help. They brought her back to her senses, and tossed the Old Man out the window so she wouldn't see it again. At that moment, the merchant arrived, and a terrible storm broke out, but thankfully, she wasn't able to leave her husband an empty house.'

I've had this Old Man for two years now, and thank God, everything is going well. I treasure it as the most precious keepsake."

When Pan Z... finished telling his story, Pan Rotmistr spoke up:

"And I, an old man, will tell you an old story about the Insect Woman and this Old Man, because people said that some woman adorned him with flowers. It is true, and she has already atoned for her sins. I'll tell you what I've heard from others, but whether it really happened or not is not my concern."

THE INSECT WOMAN

"A long time ago, there lived a wealthy lady in our land. I no longer recall her name, but that is not what matters here. The lady tormented her serfs and servants, neglected her faith and Christian duties, and came to believe that people were her property just like any other object, and that she had the right to do with them whatever she pleased.

She plundered the impoverished peasants, squandering the fruits of their hard labor on luxuries, while the people starved to death. She adorned herself in fine silk and diamonds, while her serfs had nothing to protect themselves from the cold and wind. If anyone was accused of anything, the punishment was merciless. She often punished harshly even when one was not guilty. The lady became enraged whenever a local girl wished to marry a free and wealthy man, and she would chain the poor girl as though she had committed a grave crime.

Living this way, the spiteful woman eventually realized that she had grown old, and her conscience began to whisper that her cruel reign would one day come to an end. Her health began to fail. Seeing her imminent death, she sought to change her ways. She became devout and merciful, gave alms to beggars, and left money to the monasteries in Polatsk so that people would pray for her health and long life. Bells rang in all the churches, people gathered, announcements were made from the pulpits, and the prayers of the pious ascended to the heavens together with the news of her devoted donations. Soothed by the prayers of the faithful, God showed mercy to the sinner, granting her a long life on this earth to await her repentance.

She lived for a hundred years, but not only did she fail to change for the better, anger and cruelty grew even stronger in her heart. Most of her serfs abandoned her home and wandered the world in search of sustenance, while her lackeys fled, cursing their mistress. Neighbors hated her. No one wanted to visit, meet, or even approach her estate. Anger consumed her body, destroying it, and she wasted away with each passing day.

Living this way for a long time, forgotten by others, she withered away. First, she shrank into a sickly little dwarf, then diminished further until she was the size of an infant, becoming thinner and thinner. At last, she transformed into a strange insect, with long transparent wings growing from either side. But the same malice continued to burn in her heart.

Many years passed. The sinful woman lived on, as though cursed, in the form of a winged creature. Anyone who approached her home saw her buzz out with a terrifying scream, scaring off the passersby and circling above their heads.

A new successor, Pan A., arrived from afar and took over the estate. When the neighbors told him about the attacks of the terrifying insect, he ordered all windows to be opened and the rooms to be fumigated. In vain she charged into their faces, attempting to frighten them with shrieks and screams. She was driven out by the smoke and forced to hide among the trees in the garden. Malice boiled in her heart, and she sought to drive the new master from the house by any means.

Pan A.'s lackeys recounted the strange noises and squeaks they heard under the floorboards and in the corners at midnight. At times, eerie phantoms and strange creatures resembling frogs and beetles with black, cat-like heads and eyes glowing like embers appeared out of nowhere. When approached, they vanished at once, falling through holes or cracks in the wall. The servants insisted these were evil spirits and advised the master to summon a priest to consecrate the house. The master laughed, attributing these marvels to superstition, as he himself had seen nothing of the sort.

Several days later, at noon, the sky was clear. Pan A. opened the windows and sat alone in the room, deep in thought. Suddenly, the Insect Woman flew in, buzzing around the room, her squeaky voice full of curses. She landed on the table before him – he perceived that she bore a feminine form, with dry limbs thin and jointed like a bee's legs, and a slender body. Then she took off from the table, circled Pan A.'s head, and attempted to get into his hair. Defending himself as one would from a bee, he covered his head with a scarf and fled the house in fright, instructing the servants to drive out the dreadful creature with smoke and close the windows.

Several days passed. When Pan A. was reading a novel under a linden tree in the garden, the Insect Woman reappeared. She spat a drop of poison that burned through the pages of the book as well as his clothes. Buzzing around his head, she cursed and swore at him in a squeaky human voice. Trembling with fear, Pan A. ran into his room and pondered long on how to rid himself of the dreadful creature.

The Insect Woman avenged herself whenever possible. Once, when Pan A. was out inspecting his fields, she buzzed beside him and frightened his horse with a piercing scream, causing it to gallop through ditches and hills until it threw its master. He lay bloodied and breathless until the ploughmen came running. They carried him home, and the doctor barely saved his life.

The entire district gossiped about the wicked woman

who had transformed into a terrifying insect. Everyone pitied Pan A., but no one visited the sick man, for they were afraid to approach his estate.

When Pan A. recovered and pondered how to rid himself of the cursed Insect Woman and the evil spirits she had likely befriended, he recalled the counsel of his servants and resolved to invite a priest to consecrate the house. After sunset, when the Insect Woman slept hidden in the grass, he ordered the horses harnessed and rode out to Polatsk by night.

In the morning, after Holy Mass, acquaintances met him, inquiring curiously about the strange Insect Woman and the unlucky accident with the horse, for word had already spread through the city.

He arrived at the monastery and recounted what had happened to him, amazing everyone. The priest, a man of pious life, said:

'This must be evil spirits, and a sorceress who has utterly renounced God. We must help Pan A., care for his peace, and care also for her soul.'

That very morning, Pan A. and the priest set off for home, unafraid of the Insect Woman.

They arrived at the estate. After reciting prayers, the priest sprinkled the rooms with holy water. What happened then is terrifying even to recall. With horrid squeals and hissing, eerie creatures poured from every corner: moths with fiery tongues instead of wings, fat worms that breathed smoke rising upwards like bubbles, noisy crickets, and winged reptiles circling over the floor.

'These are the sins of the sorceress,' said the priest. He ordered the windows opened. The horrifying creatures squealed and hissed as they flew out and vanished into the air.

Once the house was cleansed with holy water, Pan A.

led the priest to the garden, whence the harmful insect came. As the priest recited his prayers, a squeaky voice rang out from the depths of a gooseberry bush, first with curses and blasphemy, then with lamentations, moans, and weeping. The entire household gathered to witness these marvels. The priest sprinkled the bushes with holy water and commanded her to fly out and sit upon a linden branch. Swift as an arrow, she darted forth and perched on a linden leaf. Everyone marveled at her: one could clearly discern a female form within the insect. The priest took her from the leaf, placed her in a glass jar, and carried her into the room.

Without fear, everyone now gawked at the tiny creature: long hairs fell from her head, which was no bigger than a pea; her tiny earrings sparkled, and a necklace glowed on her neck like a string of corals. She wore a yellow silk dress, fastened with a belt of the same color. Her face was pale, and it was plain she was writhing in anger.

The following day, the Insect Woman and the priest arrived in Polatsk. Everyone in the monastery beheld the marvel, and the townsfolk came in crowds to witness the unheard-of wonder. They threw food into the glass jar, but the Insect Woman sat in silence without touching anything. She remained quiet, full of anxiety and rage.

'We must now think about her soul,' said the priest, and carried her in the jar to a quiet corner of the monastery where there was a long corridor: the Architecture Hall on one side, and a museum on the other. Near the hall, a wooden bust of the philosopher Socrates peered from a niche in the wall, as though from a window. The priest placed the Insect Woman into the hollow of the Socrates' bust before many onlookers who recited prayers, and spoke to her on spiritual matters. But what was happening to the head of Socrates! It is too terrifying to recall! It looked like an ignited bomb, thrashing in all directions. Everyone nearby turned pale, afraid it might burst and injure them. The priest continued praying without pause, preaching of the Lord's mercy and love of one's neighbor.

These rituals for the Insect Woman continued every evening as she stared out from the unfortunate head of Socrates. Fear gripped anyone who dared to walk that corridor. The wooden bust, from which they had once heard so much wise and godly advice, now cursed and swore at every passerby. Students were too afraid to approach the Wooden Old Man, for he was no longer a kind mentor to them, but a cruel adversary.

The teachings and prayers continued for several months. At last, a spark of faith and mercy reached the Insect Woman's heart, and the wooden bust grew calmer. Words full of divine fear and love of others fell from her lips. Once, she appeared before the priest in a beautiful form, like that of an angel, a radiant beam encircling her face, adorned in a dress whiter than snow. She thanked him for the prayers, teachings, and care bestowed upon her, and in an instant, she was gone. The priest knelt before the altar, thanking heaven for the return and salvation of this soul."

When Pan Rotmistr finished his story, Panna Anelya and the younger children of Pan Z. bid their parents goodnight and went to another room to say their evening prayers.

"What an interesting story," said the host. "The incident with the Old Man, where the philosopher's head became the abode of an unfortunate sinner – I have never heard of such a thing before. That is a new tale to add to the life of the Wooden Old Man."

We talked until late into the night, reminiscing about the past, about schoolmates and acquaintances – both living, and those already resting in their graves. Our conversation was interwoven with both sadness and hope. At last, Pan Rotmistr picked up his cane and top hat, intending to leave for home, but the host insisted he stay the night. They extinguished the fire, and I, completely exhausted from my foot-journey, fell into a deep sleep.

A WALK IN THE FIELD

My rest was short but pleasant. I woke at dawn. Pan Rotmistr was still asleep, and I, not wishing to disturb his peaceful slumber, lay pondering the adventures of the Wooden Old Man and the Insect Woman. It seemed to me that the head was gazing at me, reminding me of the trials and suffering that await a person on the path of life, while the sinful woman appeared in my thoughts both as a dreadful wasp and as a radiant angel, whispering to my soul that only faith, love of God, and love of one's neighbor are the true guides to happiness.

As I was lost in thought, a ray of the rising sun shone through the window. I heard the host's voice – he had risen before everyone else and was already giving orders to the workers for the day.

The shepherd's song carried from the pasture. Pan Rotmistr awoke. As we dressed – he thinking of his home, and I of the journey that still lay ahead – Pan Ziamelski entered, greeted us, and addressed me:

"Why do you rise so early? Making such a journey on foot is hard work, you need a good rest. Do you think I will allow you to say goodbye today? No – you will stay with me a few more days, for once you go far to the north, God only knows when we shall meet again – perhaps not until the next world! I am asking Pan Rotmistr to remain with us as well, for there are others to manage his household in his absence."

I yielded to the host, and so did Pan Rotmistr.

From the other room came the voices of the children, already awake. A guitar sounded, and with it, a sweet, melodious voice – Anelya's. Every morning, like an angel greeting the new day, she praised the Almighty and sang to the guitar:

'When the morning dawns arise,
To You, O Earth, to You, O Sea,
To You all beings raise their cries –
Be praised, great God, eternally!'

Joined with that harmony, my own thoughts soared to the heavens, and that morning I said my prayers with a tear in my eye.

Soon the whole family gathered. After breakfast we went out into the fields. Pan Ziamelski led us into a dense grove, where every tree testified to the diligence of its master, and the whole forest resembled a beautiful orchard. He told us that once it had been wasteland, but through his care and labor a grove flourished here within only a few years. Amid the brush, the meadows now yielded lush tall grasses and countless fragrant flowers.

Recalling the tale of the Insect Woman, the eldest son showed Pan Rotmistr a captured dragonfly, asking if it was anything like her. The younger children gathered flowers and brought them to Anelya, who crowned their heads with wreaths.

Leisurely we strolled, sometimes resting in the shade of thick birches, passing the time in pleasant conversation. After lunch, we inspected the farm until the sun slanted westward, the dew fell on the grass, and the workers with scythes and rakes returned from the hayfield.

That evening, when the family was once more assembled, the host asked Pan Rotmistr whether he remembered any old tales, or perhaps had heard another story of the Wooden Old Man.

"When I was still a student in Polatsk," said Pan

Rotmistr, "I loved listening to stories. My landlord had long served at the Jesuit monastery and often told of unusual things he had heard from others – prophecies of the Wooden Old Man given to certain students. Some of these stories I remember to this day."

THE STUDENT LUCIFUGA

"Once, there was an extremely lazy student in Polatsk. He often ran away from the collegium, wandering from place to place, and after enduring hunger and cold, he would return to his parental home. Though he knew he would be punished for such actions and sent back under a teacher's supervision, he fled whenever he had the chance. His father was not a wealthy man, but he wished to enrich his child – if not with estates, then at least with knowledge. He often escorted him from home to the city, and when words of admonition did not help, he paid those who agreed to act as his son's unrelenting guardians, never leaving him in work or leisure. Under such strict supervision, Lucifuga was forced to study, though he still idled. Nature had endowed him with talent and ability, and he might have been the best of students, but he was first only in disobedience and mischief.

Late July marked the beginning of summer holidays at the Polatsk schools. After examinations and before departing for home, the students would gather to speak with the Wooden Old Man. Each asked about his own concerns. Some wished to know what their teachers thought of their diligence and conduct; others – whether they would advance to the next grade after the summer, or be rewarded with a book or icons for their perseverance and success.

The lazy one was among these students.

'Tell me, Old Man,' he asked, 'how did the teachers judge my diligence and behavior, and will I advance to the next grade?'

The Old Man answered in a sorrowful voice, like

thunder rolling from a distant storm cloud:

'Oh, Lucifuga! Lucifuga! You are like a vile cockroach that hides from daylight beneath the floorboards or in a dark crack. You torment your parents and teachers without the least thought of changing your ways. The light of learning and virtue is the lantern that guides one through the voyage of life. Without such a light, you will drift in darkness and never reach the harbor of peace, of soul and of happiness.'

All the students who heard him laughed loudly, repeating: *'Lucifuga! Lucifuga!'* From then on he bore no other name than the one the Wooden Old Man had given him.

Angry, he left his friends and ran through the dark monastery corridor, muttering:

'That hollow wooden head babbles nonsense, handing out foolish nicknames for a laugh. Oh! If only I had a stone in my pocket, that bald head would learn sorrow!'

He continued to carouse with his friends as before, and whenever he was reminded of the Old Man's prophecy and called Lucifuga, he replied:

'Knowledge does not bring happiness – Fortune does. Many have not struggled over books, yet live in luxury. I mean to live as I please, refusing myself nothing.'

Four years passed. His parents died, and Lucifuga flew out into the world, chasing pleasures and amusements like a moth chases light. He flitted from flower to flower, gathering nothing but poison. He met many other lucifugas like himself and joyfully befriended them. Heavenly daylight began to weary him, so he shut his eyes and slept through the day, while at night he played cards with his companions, who deftly emptied his pockets, leaving him often with nothing.

At last, he went farther afield, to a great city. There he

quickly found acquaintances and gained entrance to homes where noisy parties drew youth from every direction. It was there he met a lady named Aurelia – thin, pale, hollow, and airy. She cared only for lightness, grace, and slenderness, flitting about the salons like the wind. She spent long sleepless nights at balls and soirées, waltzing effortlessly, gliding tirelessly over the floor, always encircled by admirers. She rose from bed only when the sun was setting.

Lucifuga met her at a ball and was captivated. He also learned that Panna Aurelia owned an estate and possessed great wealth – things he always needed.

One morning, returning home at dawn, he closed the shutters but could not sleep: Aurelia's image stood before his eyes. He recalled how gracefully she danced, how slender and lively she was, ethereal and, it seemed, of similar nature to himself. Oh! If only he could have a wife like her, he would be the happiest of men. Eternal love and harmony would reign between them – together with an estate and money. And so he resolved: come what may, he would declare his love and ask for her hand in marriage.

Lucifuga achieved what he wanted and married Aurelia. Love and harmony lasted through autumn and winter. Time flew happily in theaters and concerts; they attended balls and received guests. He played cards until dawn, while she charmed the youth with her dancing, lively spirit, and cheerful conversation.

In spring, they went to the country estate, strolling beneath the clear evening sky, resting in the linden shade, listening to nightingales and larks. But, alas! That spring brought Lucifuga only suffering and shattered all his hopes.

One evening, at sunset, they went for a walk in the field. The sky was clear, the air calm. Walking near the forest, they spoke of their acquaintances. Aurelia eagerly praised a young admirer who was exceptionally skilled in dancing, while Lucifuga extolled a friend who never lost at cards. An argument broke out between them, and as Aurelia, proving her point, grew increasingly angry, the forest rustled and the wind whistled over the field. The light airy creature she was, Aurelia was lifted up like a feather and, before anyone could react, ascended higher and higher. Soon she was flying over the birch grove, while her husband watched helplessly, waving his arms, not knowing what to do.

Aurelia was carried by the wind like a moth. Lucifuga ran across fields, forests, and hills, hoping she might be caught on a hilltop or in a tall tree. Passing nearby, people of every rank looked on in astonishment. Some laughed, others pitied Lucifuga, but no one could help.

He ran for as long as he could see her from afar, but when night fell, Aurelia disappeared from sight. Poor Lucifuga stopped in the middle of the dark forest, hearing only owls around him, at a loss for where to go. He wandered all night, and the forest seemed endless. Exhausted, he sat beneath a tree, looked up at the starry sky, and recalled the prophecy of the Wooden Old Man. A heavy sorrow pressed upon his heart:

'Where is Aurelia? Is she alive? Will she ever return to me?' he sighed, tears flowing from his eyes.

Thus he roamed the forest without sleep. Dawn broke in the east, the clouds turned pink. Seeing the daylight, Lucifuga calmed a little, and headed east. When the sun was already high, he heard the sound of church bells, which led him out of the forest to a village.

This village was unfamiliar – he had wandered far from home. Entering a peasant's hut, pale and worn from the night's wandering, he told the host of his misfortune. The man listened for a long time, marveling that a woman could be so light as to be carried away by the wind. Glancing with satisfaction at his own wife, who was busy with household chores, he pitied the guest, invited him to rest, and promised to help him home.

Lucifuga returned to his wife's village. It was empty – no sign of Aurelia. He sent people to search for her everywhere. They returned without news. Soon the rumor spread throughout the region, and even the city knew that Lucifuga's wife had been carried away by the wind. Some pitied him; others laughed themselves to tears at such a tale.

Pondering what to do, he rarely left the house. One evening, he sat alone in a dim, silent room when a servant rushed in announcing a messenger with a letter. With indescribable joy he recognized Aurelia's familiar hand.

But reading it, he froze as if turned to stone. Aurelia was alive, but her love for him was gone. She wrote that her flight had ended fifty *versts* from home, and she was now living at the estate of an old friend. She had no intention of returning to a husband whose character and views differed so greatly from her own. She was arranging a divorce, sparing no expense.

Lucifuga soon lost his wife, his estate, and all his hopes. Friends and acquaintances who once feasted at his table now mocked his misfortune. Unable to bear the humiliation, he withdrew from everyone.

Years passed. No one heard from Lucifuga. They only remembered his wedding and divorce. Later, rumors spread that he lived aimlessly, hating all things under the sun, cursing the present day, with no faith in the future.

In time, everyone passing through the corridor by the Architectural Hall of the Jesuit collegium in Polatsk heard the Wooden Old Man's voice calling:

'Oh! Lucifuga! Lucifuga!'

Hearing this, students and teachers laughed, remarking that the Wooden Old Man had remembered Lucifuga at last.

Midnight came. Many in the Jesuit monastery were still awake. Hearing an unusual commotion in the corridor, they stepped out of their rooms. In the faint moonlight by the wall stood a monstrosity with many legs. Terrified, they scattered and told the others. Then, gathering with lit candles, they returned, but, blinded by the light, the creature had already vanished, though the clatter of its legs still echoed in the dark. Shaken, they remained in their rooms until dawn.

In the morning, the monks compared accounts of the night's horrors. A Jesuit gatekeeper said he had heard clattering in the corridor, then groans from below. When he stepped out, he saw a hideous creature moving like a boat on water, its many legs rising and falling like oars.

Terrified, he cried, '*Let every spirit praise the Lord!*'

At this, the monster vanished, and he spent the night in prayer.

Some students witnessed a strange sight late at night as they sat in their rooms without lighting a candle. Feeling fearful and restless, many turned around to see a monster that would instantly vanish. The students gathered together, and no one spent the night alone.

There was an eerie incident during the daytime too. A musician who served at the Jesuit church, and who had once been friends with the student Lucifuga, was alone in a room at noon, practicing pieces by famous composers on his flute. Then he set the sheet music aside, turned his back to the window, and played from memory variations that came to mind. He spotted a cockroach emerging from under the floorboard in the dark corner, crawling to the middle of the room, stopping, then beginning to swell and grow larger. From under the black shell then peeked out a human head that stared at the musician with frightening eyes. He recognized Lucifuga's face. Terrified, he dropped the flute, leapt away from the window, and at that very moment a sunbeam shot through the glass directly onto the creature. In an instant, it was gone. The musician ran out of the room and down the corridor, shouting, '*Lucifuga! Lucifuga!*'

Everyone stared at him in shock, asking what had happened, but he, pale as a corpse, remained silent and looked around in bewilderment. It took a long time before he regained his senses and recounted the horror of what had happened.

These horrors repeated for several more nights. Finally, the rector ordered for Candlemas candles to be lit in various parts of the monastery so that their light would spread through the corridors. Peace returned, and Lucifuga appeared no more."

As Rotmistr told his story, the children stood near their father, and one of them began to cry. The father asked the child why he was crying.

"I'm afraid of Lucifuga," the son replied.

Then Pan Ziamelski ordered everyone to their rooms, to pray and go to sleep.

The younger children, with their mother and Panna Anelya, bid their father and guests goodnight, and left.

"We'll stay a bit longer," said the host, "Rotmistr knows many interesting stories about the Wooden Old Man, let him tell us more."

"You already know what the Wooden Old Man prophesied to the student Lucifuga," Rotmistr said. "Now I'll tell you what he prophesied to a proud philosopher."

THE PROUD PHILOSOPHER

"There was once a student in Polatsk, who had no other name among his peers than "the Philosopher" because of his great affinity for the subject. The school-taught authors were not enough for him. He strove to acquire and read forbidden and anti-religious books by French philosophers. He usually read at night, when everyone was asleep, and during the day and evening he would recount what he had read to his peers, then engage them in debates, in which he triumphantly prevailed.

Upon learning of this, the professors and the prefect-priest would pay unannounced visits to his room, admonish him, seize his books, throw them into the fire before his very eyes, and impose penances. But this only made him more cautious. He hid the forbidden books well and, after reading them, told no one.

When he completed his studies and was about to return home to astonish the world with his erudition, he bade farewell to his teachers and, together with his friends, paid a visit to the Wooden Old Man.

'Tell me, oh head of wise Socrates,' he asked, 'I have already read many works of philosophy – what do you say to that?'

'Many, many,' the Old Man replied, 'and more still shall you read – but at life's end, you shall be the greatest fool, and die as one.'

Everyone present laughed. The student only spat in anger.

'The hollow wooden head talks nonsense,' he said and left.

Settling in the village, he spared no expense in creating

his library. He bought all kinds of philosophical works in many languages. The youth who often gathered at his place to hear about intellectual matters were regaled with tales of wonders and explanations of nature's mysteries, which he himself did not understand. He became known as a learned man, a true philosopher.

He found himself an assistant – a foreigner, also a philosopher – paid him well, and provided every comfort. The assistant praised him, calling him a genius in philosophy and, exploiting his gullibility, slipped blasphemies into his already foolish convictions.

Soon enough, the young Philosopher became proud, believing himself to be a person of distinction, looking down on everyone as one might look down on ants from a mountain top.

One Sunday, the Philosopher asked his companion, smiling:

'Shall we go to church today?'

'What is there to do at church, unless you need to meet someone there?'

'I wanted to see the neighbors and invite them over.'

'Well then. That won't take much time.'

They arrived for Mass. The church was full of worshippers. The Philosopher jumped out of the carriage and entered the church. But as he stood in the midst of the crowd – a miracle! – what happened to his broad shoulders and towering height? In an instant, he became as small as a wooden doll. Those standing close recognized him and looked on either with fear or a mocking smile. Everyone stepped away from him. Terrified and not understanding what was happening, he quickly fled the Lord's sanctuary, ran to the carriage where he found his companion, and recounted the strange event. His friend laughed to tears, insisting it was all due to the nerves or some other illness.

The Philosopher returned home troubled, and, following this incident, did not return to the church again.

Throughout the Polatsk district, the common folk passed the story to one another, saying that the Philosopher had gravely offended the Lord God.

A few days later, the invited neighbors gathered at the Philosopher's house. Among these guests were the youths who greatly admired the host's conjectures. In their eyes, every word attributed to an ancient author was the highest wisdom. They marveled at the depth of his knowledge. Whatever the Philosopher spoke about – his wise remarks captivated everyone. The host was triumphant in his ability to give an explanation for any mystery.

It was a fine day, the sky was blue, and all the guests went for a walk in the field, with the host joining them. The air was clear, the scenery was pleasing to the eye, numerous flocks grazed on the hills, ducks and white geese swam on the calm lake, birdsong echoed through the groves, and hard-working bees buzzed around the meadows and the linden blossoms. The clear day and beautiful landscapes delighted everyone. The Philosopher discoursed on various phenomena of life. Finally, he declared that man was a part of God himself, that his soul, delving into learning, understands all wonders and sees all mysteries. To him, good deeds were angels, while sin belonged to the evil spirit or Satan.

As he reflected, his head suddenly vanished under his hood, everything went dark before his eyes, and the scenic landscapes disappeared from view. The Philosopher pulled back his hood, revealing a dreadful sight to the guests: he had no head – only a tiny knob, like a poppyhead, rose from the base of his neck. Everyone stood aghast, faces pale as ash, struck speechless by the uncanny sight.

The guests remained silent for a long time. Fidgeting

in one spot, the Philosopher muttered unintelligible words in a squeaky voice. Breath barely escaped his chest. But as soon as he raised his hands to the sky, everyone saw a regular human head once more upon his shoulders.

The guests looked at one another, not knowing what to make of it, while the assistant laughed to tears, insisting that the vision was due to the heat of the midday sun, and advising everyone to return to the house, as a walk in scorching heat was not good for health.

They all convinced themselves that what they had witnessed was a natural occurrence, and persuaded their host that it was caused by a rush of blood. Soon enough, everything was forgotten. The Philosopher remained steadfast in his views, and his triumphs continued.

Not only did he carry on deceiving, but he even dared to publish his reflections in a magazine, going against religion and common sense. Old neighbors, to whom he read these writings, warned him:

'Abandon your errors. Believe as your parents did. They lived happily and in peace. Their simple faith earned them a reward. What truth could be higher than the truth of faith? God himself revealed it in the Gospel, and this wisdom, like the heavenly sun, illuminates the whole wide world and reveals mysteries. Let human reason rest, for this is beyond understanding. Mistaken convictions lead people to disaster, while faith leads to salvation.'

But he heeded no advice. All warnings were in vain.

At dusk, the Philosopher was returning from a walk and passed a hill where, in the shade of several birch trees, stood an old wooden chapel in a cemetery, with towering stones and tilted crosses. There he saw several peasants kneeling, praying for the souls of the departed. The Philosopher marveled at their simplicity. *'Poor people,'* he thought to himself, *'they believe that the inhabitants of the other world hear them, or need their prayers.'*

No sooner had he thought this than he was seized by a strange unease, and as he hurried home, he noticed a huge skeleton walking next to him. This frightened him so much that, upon returning home, he remained in a daze for a long time. It was in vain that his friend tried to convince him that this had an ordinary explanation. Several times in the evening, the skeleton came into his room and stood by the table. With a piercing scream, the Philosopher would summon everyone in the house. When he shut his eyes to sleep, it seemed that a terrible vampire, leaning on a decayed hand, loomed over his face, staring him straight in the eye. *'Corpse! Corpse!'* – with a piercing cry, the Philosopher would leap from his bed. Haunted by these visions for a long time, he changed: his face turned pale, he became weak, tormented by restless thoughts without end. Weary of the changes, his assistant left him and departed for distant lands.

Before, the Philosopher had been strong in his resolve and believed in nothing. Now, superstitions tormented his soul and drove him to despair. In the middle of the night, whenever he heard the groans of a nightbird or the mournful cries of an owl, he became extremely anxious in anticipation of a disaster at home. If a dog howled in the yard, he would run to see which way the dog's muzzle was facing, believing that was the direction in which a terrible fire would destroy the village or burn the forest. He grew even more disturbed when the dog howled without lifting its nose, as though sniffing something buried beneath the earth. Despair engulfed him, for this foretold the death of someone in the household. Unable to shake off the terrible prophecy, he would order the horses to be harnessed and flee to the city, or to an acquaintance or neighbor.

Trembling with fear, he would recount what had

happened at home, and they would try in vain to convince him that his angst was groundless.

The moon had a strange influence on the Philosopher. It filled him with anxiety, and he could not remain in a room flooded with pale moonlight.

In the heat of summer, he sat alone by the window, looking out over the field. As if on a lake, the wind raised waves on the near-ripe rye. He was pleased with the good harvest and hoped for great income from the estate that year. Suddenly, a sharp crack, like a pistol shot, jolted his nerves. The Philosopher jumped back from the window and saw that the portrait of his late grandfather had split in two within its shattered frame. This incident frightened him so much that he died a few days later."

The host spoke to me:

"When we went to school, do you remember how many youths of different characters and abilities there were? Now they have all scattered around the world. I think there are many lucifugas and proud philosophers among them. We will suffer should one of them take up a post in spiritual or public leadership."

"It is the Iron Age now," I said. "People are only becoming worse."

"Indeed, it is the Iron Age," said Rotmistr. "The peaceful and joyful life is disappearing. It seems people fear one another. One hears complaints and groans all too often. Oh, how well the Wooden Old Man prophesied to one of my colleagues, who had an extraordinary disposition and far overstepped in his cheerfulness – for whenever he became like that, every detail in his dreams appeared in the form of a strange giant. His name was Seviaryn. For this, I called him the Dreamer. Let me tell you about the games of his imagination."

SEVIARYN THE DREAMER

"He was one of the best students. Beloved by his teachers, he received many awards. He had a great desire to learn foreign languages and already spoke several quite well. Most of all, he loved poetry: the idylls of Theocritus Gessner, and Shymanovich captivated him. In all the world, he saw Arcadia. To him, every man bore the simplicity and sincerity of a shepherd. When he went walking outside the city, he saw naiads in the streams, nymphs dancing in the meadows, and dryads smiling at him from beneath the green canopy of the trees. In other words, everywhere he went, he encountered the ancient Golden Age of the Greeks. He was unaware that misfortune even existed in the world, and always remained cheerful, making others cheerful too.

One day, when teachers and students visited the museum with its many marvels and paintings by famous artists, they stopped in front of the Wooden Old Man and spoke to him. Having caught a handful of flies, Seviaryn ran up and asked the Old Man:

'Take a guess, what do I have in my hand?'

The Old Man shook his head and replied:

'Oh, unfortunate one! You shall be cast out from the Eden of your dreams, and shall walk a thorny path. Worthless insects, in the form of monsters, will pursue you.'

Seviaryn released the flies, laughed, and ran off.

After completing his studies, the Dreamer left the city and flew out into the world like a bird freed from a cage, at the very moment when spring adorned the trees and meadows with fragrant blossoms. And he, poor soul, believed that his spring would bloom forever. But how quickly the gloomy autumn arrived!

At first, it was only in his imagination that he saw beautiful goddesses in groves and meadows. But soon he met them in reality as well. One of them was Panna Adelya, mistress of an estate, beautiful and well-mannered. Seviaryn gave his heart to her, and Adelya became his only dream. He loved her for four years. I will not describe the happy and unhappy moments of that time. Such stories are always the same, though different writers describe them differently. I will neither praise nor blame women either, for all daughters of Eve are as nature has created them. I will only say that the serpent of gold and pride led Adelya astray: she betrayed Seviaryn and married another.

First love, especially an unhappy one, is the best lesson, after which a person begins to read the book of the world, to discern the mysteries of the heart, and to watch the relations of friends and kin with closer attention. From there, the paths of human life take their direction towards successes and failures. Time and again, one encounters mocking eyes and fickle friendships. Seviaryn realized that the world is no paradise, and people are no angels.

He became a loner after this. His dreams turned dreadful, he fled from others. Solitude became dear to him, the only sight that pleased him was the sky – and even that only when thunder rolled through black clouds, when the wind howled, the forests roared, and waves crashed upon the shore. In worthless insects he recognized the silhouettes of ill-meaning people. Lost in his fantasies, he spoke of wonders, and all who knew him mocked him, calling him mad.

When I traveled through the land where he lived, I visited him as a friend from my childhood. I entered his room and saw him sitting alone, lost in thought, pale, his clothes and hair disheveled.

'How are you, Seviaryn?'

Awakened from his dreams, he stood up and looked at me for a long time, not recognizing me. I introduced myself.

'Ah! I have been waiting for you a long time!' he said, shook my hand, and sat me down beside him, while he himself returned to his dreams and sat mute.

'How many years have passed,' I broke the silence, 'since we parted from our young friends and teachers. Those were happy times! Do you ever think back to those amusements, conversations, May walks, pleasant dreams and jokes, in which you always led the way?'

'My dreams and jokes are gone forever. I see things differently now: a man could only be happy if turned into stone, covered by sand, so that he sees and hears nothing of what happens in the world.'

'How you have changed!' I was astonished. 'Has everything under the sun grown wearisome to you?'

'Everything. I could tell you much, but I am afraid. Do you see? The flies are everywhere. Nasty creatures, flying in and out through the open window. They will spread the word around the world – about all we do, how we live, what we say, how we pray. Do you see the tears in my eyes? You never saw them before. Such is the change in me. But listen, I will tell you something. Have you ever noticed how terrifying these flies are? I sit alone here in my quiet room, and they swarm around me. I look at them with fear because I see them transform into strange monsters. Their dull grey wings resemble tailcoats worn by grotesque little men, their faces take on different shapes – some round and wide with bloody blotches, others dried out, with a sharp goatee and long hair. And all these monsters gawk at me:

some mocking, others threatening.'

'There has been a great change in your dreams,' I said. 'You once delighted in Greek poetry and the purest forms of love from the times past. But now your fantasies are full of mourning.'

'But listen, I will tell you something more,' he said. 'About these vile flies. Once, I loved reading poetry, and writing it too. I thought to express in verse my feelings for my family and for Adelya, whom I loved sincerely. I sent her my songs, as proof of my affection. She read them and put them on the table. But even there, the flies – having nothing else to do – swarmed about, mocking my feelings, buzzing around Adelya's ear until she forgot me and my poems altogether. Even now they give me no peace. Whenever I write something, they mock and smear everything, these dreadful flies.'

'But these flies you complain of... they have always been, and always will be...'

Here he interrupted me, seizing my hand:

'Have you ever seen locusts?'

'There are no locusts in our land,' I replied. 'They are in the east. There they attack meadows and fields.'

'You have not seen this fat, monstrous insect,' he said. 'Its back is etched with strange hieroglyphs. And he who can read them will find the words: *Divine Punishment*. But is God's punishment only there, in the far east, and not here with us? Come, let us go into the field, I will show you locusts.'

He led me to the bank of a swift river, where foaming waves roared among the stones. Passing through meadows, it hid itself in dense brush. We sat upon a high bank in the shade of an alder. Seviaryn gazed thoughtfully at the water. A breeze drifted from the fields, the trees rustled; he stirred from his thoughts and said to me:

'I often come to these places. I like to sit here in solitude and think back to the past. I recall all the conversations I once had with Adelya, though she has long forgotten me, as if I were already buried.'

Suddenly he pointed to the water:

'Look, look! There flies a locust! Do you see it? With double grey wings – it flies everywhere, devouring everything, in the air and on the ground. I will tell you more: it does not die. Like Satan, it appears in different forms. When the grass and leaves on the trees turn yellow, and the cold autumn winds blow, it falls upon the water, sheds its wings, and turns into a water monster that devours everything it encounters. When spring returns, it grows new wings. With gaping maw, like a flying wyrm, it slays all it meets. This monstrosity has conquered land and water alike, forever hungry for prey. Is it not exactly this that has contaminated human hearts, causing people to oppress one another?'

'Some dark melancholy,' I said, 'clouds your thoughts. You see everything in dreadful light. Poor man, you will never find peace with thoughts like these.'

'You have not guessed!' he cried. 'I have a great idea: I will go on a journey. To faraway lands, where eternal spring reigns, I will dwell peacefully in the mountains, beside a waterfall or in a wild forest. I will forget Adelya, for an eternity will lie between us. Eternity!...'

'And will you forget your native land too?'

'Oh no!' he replied. 'If I never return to my Homeland, and die alone upon some mountain peak in a foreign land, then the ravens will carry my bones – for better to lie with birds than with worms.'

I spent the entire day with him. We wandered over hilltops and through forests, and he spoke of his dreams without ceasing. He kept me overnight. Once back at the house, we talked long into the evening. At night, he often stirred, rose from the bed, and paced the room. I slept little, my rest disturbed every hour.

When we awoke the next day, the sun was already high. He greeted me with a somewhat more cheerful face, asked about my acquaintances and neighbors, and about myself – whether I often returned home after we parted ways at school, what countries I had visited, and how I had lived my life. He thanked me warmly for visiting, and when I ordered the horses to be harnessed to depart, he earnestly begged me to stay for lunch. I could not refuse his heartfelt plea.

After lunch, Seviaryn brought out the finest wine that he had kept for a long time.

'Let us drink,' he said. 'This is our last farewell; we shall meet again, perhaps, but only in the next world.'

Then he ordered the horses harnessed, walked with me a long way, and bade me farewell with tears in his eyes.

And indeed, that was the last time we ever saw one another. Soon after, I learned that Seviaryn had abandoned the small hut where his parents once lived, departed forever, and no one knows where he went – whether he is still alive, or whether he has already died in a foreign land, among a foreign people."

GHOSTS

Pan Ziamelski spoke to me:

"In the same way, my old friend once left his homeland, and for eighteen years we knew nothing of where in the world he wandered. At times we imagine that somewhere far away there must be a better land, better people. God knows, our parents lived in peace here, but for us a different fate was destined. For myself, I thank God that I spent my youth where I was born. God willing, my bones will rest here as well."

"As for me," said the old Rotmistr, "I have traveled much. If I wished to tell you the story of my life, I would have to recall the whole history of Napoleon's glorious wars. It was not dreams that drove me to wander the world with weapons in hand, nor the pursuit of vain glory, but rather the hope that one day I might cherish the memory of my past deeds and die in peace among my countrymen. Yet God willed otherwise. My son now wanders somewhere in a foreign land, and I, with but little time left to live, will likely never see him again..."

The old Rotmistr fell silent, and tears streamed down his face. My heart and thoughts grew heavy with sorrow.

"God is great and almighty," I said softly, "and we must place our trust in Him."

Our conversation was broken by silence. At last, Rotmistr wiped his tears with a handkerchief and said:

"It is true, those who believe – encounter miracles."

At that very moment, a strange apparition rose before our eyes: a tall woman, clad in a garment white as snow, her face beautiful as an angel's, a wreath of fresh roses upon her brow, with the Wooden Old Man cradled in her hands. We froze in awe. In an instant, she vanished.

A heavy silence fell. We looked at one another, unable to utter a word.

So we sat for some time, until suddenly the door opened and the mistress of the household entered.

"What is this?" she wondered. "You have been talking all night long, and do you not hear? The second rooster has already crowed – it will soon be dawn."

"Pan Rotmistr," said Ziamelski, "has so captivated us with his stories that we forgot all about sleep. Besides, we have all just seen a strange vision: a woman with flowers upon her head, holding in her hands a Wooden Old Man just like ours."

"In my dream," she replied, "I too beheld marvels such as I had never imagined while awake. I dreamed of a beautiful morning, so still that even the hairs upon my head did not stir. There was not a cloud in the sky. The sun was rising, yet it did not dazzle – the light spread about like pure gold. A great many people had gathered, all silent, as if awaiting someone, all gazing eastward. Then an angel descended, stood in the east, struck the sun with his hand, and it rang across the whole earth, as though someone had struck a great bell. That sound pierced the hearts of men. Everyone knelt, and I too prayed. An old man, the very likeness of our Wooden Old Man, approached me and said: '*Pray!*'

Afterwards, it seemed to me that I wandered alone across a field. I saw rare clouds drifting in the sky, white as snow. One cloud descended before me; I lifted it up and saw that something was written upon it, yet I could not read the words. Once more the Old Man appeared and said: 'I will read it to you – listen well and remember. It is written here: *God will give glory to the righteous before the world.*'

At that, I awoke and could not fall asleep again. Hearing that you were still talking, I came to tell you my dream."

Having said this, she left.

Rotmistr sighed and exclaimed:

"God have mercy!" Then, pacing the room, he began to pray.

The conversation was over. Our beds were prepared in that very room.

"Do not be in haste to rise early tomorrow," said our host. "The morning star is already shining in the east, and since the night has been sleepless, let the day make it up to you."

Bidding us good night, he left the room.

FAREWELL

I awoke and looked out the window: through a crack in the shutters a bright sunbeam streamed into the room. Rotmistr, pacing from corner to corner and whispering prayers, turned to me and said:

"It is nearly noon. We have slept well, I too only awoke recently, but now it is already time to depart for home."

He stepped out, summoned the servant, and ordered the windows opened. I hastened to dress, for in all my travels I had never once risen so late.

The house lay quiet. The servant told me that the master and mistress had gone to the field with the workers, and had taken the children as well, so as not to disturb our rest.

Rotmistr and I soon followed to the field, and returned with our host and his family.

After breakfast, Pan Rotmistr took leave of the household. Pressing my hand, he said:

"I dwell far from your native land. Remember me now and then – our nightly conversations, our dreams and visions. We shall not meet again, for I am already near the grave."

Pan Ziamelski, his wife, children, and I accompanied Rotmistr to the boundary with the neighbors. The mistress and children turned homeward, while Ziamelski and I went on to walk the groves and sown fields.

As we wandered, he spoke much of his land – what grain should be sown where, how new methods might be introduced into peasant farming, though such experiments had not fared well with his neighbors.

"Farming," he said, "requires little invention, but

diligence and experience. God helps the one who works. We labor to breed livestock and to enrich the land. Our ancestors prospered here in peace. May he who praises God always have enough. It is He whom we must ask how to improve the fields and tend the herds."

By the lakeshore, where the early buckwheat was ripening, Ziamelski clapped his hands. A vast flock of wild ducks rose from the field like a cloud.

"They bring nothing but harm," he said. "Here we have countless lakes and rivers, and so the ducks have multiplied. To guard every field near water would require a shooter at each. The farmer is beset not only by ill-minded men, but by wild birds and beasts as well. Last year, I had a splendid crop of oats near that dark forest, but in a few nights a bear ruined everything – nothing remained but trampled straw. Such a beast preys not only on livestock and bees, but ravages the fields as well. I keep good dogs – they guard the herds from wolves and bears – but no one can defend the crops from such ruin."

Thus we talked as we walked. A wind sprang up, and thunder rumbled far beyond the forest. We looked up: a great black cloud was rising from the east. Like a serpent, lightning writhed through the sky. We hurried to the field, where the workers were raking hay. Scarcely had they finished and returned home when the sun hid behind the stormcloud, darkness fell, and the wind rose. The livestock fled to their barns. Stretching their necks, the geese flapped their wings like sails and ran from the fields, shrieking.

A sudden bout of rain with hail lashed against the windows. We threw holy herbs on the coals, and the entire family knelt, pleading with God for mercy. The noise of the trees, the downpour, and the thunderbolts instilled fear. But soon enough a strong wind dispersed the clouds.

The storm ended, revealing the blue sky and the sun from behind them.

The host went out into the field and soon returned cheerful.

"Thank God, the storm did no harm. A light rain is falling; let it be, the workers can rest in the house."

The day was drawing to a close. I told my compatriots about the adventures that had happened in my life after I left Belarus. Everyone listened with interest to the wonders of the northern capital – the theaters, concerts, and the ways of its inhabitants. But most of all, they were fascinated by tales of dangerous sea voyages, storms, mountains, and shores of distant foreign lands.

"I never had the desire or interest to visit foreign countries," said the host. "I was always captivated by the memorable verses that a boy once sang in the Jesuit theater in Polatsk, playing the *kobza*:

> *'Happy is he who is far from disputes,*
> *As in those past years,*
> *Does not lounge, but works diligently,*
> *So he is always lucky in everything.'*

Indeed, happy is he who lives in the village and from the work of his own hands. Anelya, take the guitar and sing the song I composed when I remembered how we used to write verses back in school."

Anelya tuned the guitar and sang like a spring bird, with a voice both pleasant and melodious:

> *'Trees are famed for their beauty*
> *In our woods and groves.*
> *In our groves, the trees grow wide,*
> *Springtime birdsong fills the night.*

In the lush meadow,
Herds of livestock graze.
Buckwheat fields bloom behind the house,
And bees are abuzz with honey.
As the master in the field,
With a back that's bent,
God is the adviser and the witness –
The rye stands like a wall.
The thick of the forest
Is blessed by our diligent hunter.
There are fish in streams and rivers wide,
And the fisher casts with pride.'

After this song, Pan Ziamelski spoke much more about his farmstead – about the sale of hay, rye, oats, and other gifts of the land. The hostess praised the breeds of livestock, especially the sheep, which had long and soft wool. She spoke of the profits from the sale of milk and poultry. Panna Anelya took from the chest a white linen, thin as percale. She said that for her happiness, her father annually sows one field with flax, from which linen is woven under her supervision. She sells some of it in the city each year and buys muslin and silk for dresses at the shop.

I spent several days in pleasant conversation in the house of Pan Ziamelski, feeling the hospitality and sincerity of heart of his whole family throughout. I was unspeakably happy. That time passed like the most pleasant dream.

The sun rose on a calm, bright morning – it was time for the road. After breakfast, I said goodbye to everyone with tears in my eyes, and the memory of them remained in my soul forever.

A Soul
Not in
Its Own
Body

The vast expanse of Volhynia is mostly covered by forests, but to the west, steppes and entirely different landscapes reveal themselves to the eye. The Teteriv River flows through the town and outskirts of Cudnau. Steep cliffs tower over its western and eastern banks like ruins of time immemorial, as if nature itself had erected these walls to cut off Palesse from the rich and fertile land. From Cudnau to the borders of Padolle stretch fields that in summertime are sown with rich wheat. Here, with little effort from the plowman, the land yields a bountiful harvest. And though the inhabitants of these lands have everything they need for comfort, still tears, anxiety, and suffering are found among them, as everywhere else. There is no true happiness, no paradise on this earth.

Cholera, a severe Asiatic disease, swept across Eastern Europe in 1847, moving from place to place, striving north and west. This divine punishment was preceded by profound fear. It arrived in Volhynia in early June 1848, at the height of the summer heat, dreadful and terrifying in some areas. In the town of Cudnau and its surroundings, this calamity left behind many widows and orphans.

In autumn, when the danger of the terrible epidemic had passed, neighbors gathered in the house of Pan N., whom Pan Zyanon had come to know during his travels. A conversation began about cholera, about the deceased and those who had recovered. The guests, like sailors cast ashore after a terrible sea storm, recalled friends and acquaintances who had perished in the whirlpools, and those whom God had allowed to reach the shore and continue their life's pilgrimage.

"It's a pity about Samatnitsky," said one of the guests. "He was a good man! How he tried to help those who suffered from this disease, yet he himself died without care, for he lived alone on a homestead, where only the trees rustle above the roof."

"Where did you hear this, Maciej? Samatnitsky still lives on that homestead. I saw him recently with my own eyes."

"I know someone lives there, but it's not him, for I knew him well. He was a tall man, fair-haired, quite handsome. This one is someone entirely different, much shorter, thin, dark-haired, and even older."

"That is Samatnitsky. It's true, he is shorter and changed in the face, for he completely changed his body, and only I know how this came to pass."

"You speak of strange things, Pan Mikola," said the host. "We would all like to know how a person might change their appearance."

"It is impossible, incomprehensible, extraordinary, unheard of... and yet it happened."

"So explain this mystery to us!" shouted the guests. "For none of us can guess how that could have happened."

"I did not fully understand the secret myself," said Mikola, "so I will only share with you what I saw, and what he himself told me.

As you know, during the fierce cholera, Samatnitsky was braver than the doctors themselves. He rushed to any call, risking everything just to help others. He rubbed the sick with some mysterious ointments and gave them potions to drink, and with such good results that of those he tended – not a single one died.

One of my acquaintances, a townsman of Cudnau, told me of a strange incident. His wife suddenly felt severe pain in her midsection, and all the signs of that terrible disease appeared at once. So he hurried to our wondrous healer for help. When he arrived at the homestead, he froze, horrified by an incomprehensible sight: Samatnitsky was in the yard near the gate. He looked like a corpse, unable to control his hands or feet, his eyes wide open, his face pale. His lifeless body floated slightly above the ground, shifting in all directions as though turned by an invisible force. The townsman was about to run away, when he heard a voice:

'Wait a moment – first you must rub my body with medicine and save it from the plague, and then I will be ready to go with you.'

After a few minutes, the body stood on its feet. The healthy Samatnitsky adjusted his clothes and said:

'Well, now let us go, I know why you came – your wife will recover.'

And indeed, with the help of his mysterious medicine,

he saved her in a matter of hours.

But how did this strange doctor, who protected himself and saved others, fall into misfortune? One day, when he was about to go tend to the sick and was rubbing ointment on his body to protect it from the plague, someone whom he loved dearly fell gravely ill with cholera in a distant land. Samatnitsky knew this because, as they say, a soul unburdened by the body can see and hear far. He was so distressed that he forgot his body might meet misfortune if it were not kept safe in some secluded corner. Leaving his body by the farm gate, he flew off in haste to deliver the mysterious cure. Having rescued his beloved and returned home, he could not find his body – people had discovered and buried it, thinking he had died of the plague.

Without his body, poor Samatnitsky was invisible, unable to speak to anyone, for whenever someone heard his voice, they crossed themselves in fear, thinking a ghost was speaking. Unable to recover his body, he wandered invisibly for a long time, until at last he found a corpse lying by the roadside – its soul had only just departed. With his mysterious medicine, he made the blood circulate, then entered the body, returned to his homestead, and now lives there alone. No one recognized him; everyone believed him dead."

"He would have been better off," said the host, "had he departed for the other world for good, than remained wandering the earth in someone else's body."

"Whether he wills it or not," said Mikola, "he must suffer on earth until God's appointed hour."

As they spoke, the door swung open, and a stranger entered. His face was dark, gloomy, completely bloodless, expressionless, with a thin nose covered in dry skin, lips colorless, and eyes dull, as though shrouded in fog. A frock coat hung from his shoulders, covering his frail body.

"Yes, Pan Mikola," he began in a drawn-out, monotonous voice, "I am the same Samatnitsky you were just now speaking of. This alien body is a burden to me in this world, not worth my care. But the eyes of the soul see far, and the ears hear far. I know what you spoke of. Thank you for remembering me. A man in my condition makes no friends or acquaintances."

Everyone stared at the sad, unfamiliar figure in silence. Mikola broke it:

"Saving others from perishing, you yourself fell into a misfortune greater than death."

"None are to blame for my suffering."

"I once knew a Samatnitsky in Vilnia," said Zyanon. "Perhaps you have a cousin there?"

"That was me – but not as I once was."

"How long have you been living in this area?"

"For several years now. I did not return to where I had been before. No one would recognize me there now. And she would not recognize me either. She would not believe it is me, would not pity me, and would laugh as though I were a madman."

"Have you faced many trials in your life?"

"A seeker pursues mysteries, and trouble pursues the seeker. Zyanon, if you believe I am the same man you once knew in Vilnia, then come to my hut tomorrow. I have things to tell and questions to ask. Farewell for now. Think of me if you wish."

After he departed, the guests looked at one another, uncertain, not knowing what to think – he spoke like Samatnitsky, but looked entirely different.

"See?" said Mikola. "What do you make of our guest? Everything I told you is true: the face, lips, nose, eyes, hair, and everything else this body has – it is not his own. But still, this is the same Samatnitsky, for he said so himself and confirmed what I told you."

"But it seems," said Maciej, "that he was not accepted in the other world, so he had to return to earth again, for he is like a dead man. There is no life in him."

"What a strange guest," said the host. "I did not hold him up because, frankly, his arrival, like a visit from the other world, stirred an inexplicable feeling in me."

For the rest of the evening, the neighbors talked about Samatnitsky.

* * *

The day was autumnal. The sky hung overcast, trees rustled above the darkened roof of the farm, and the wind lifted yellow leaves into the air. Samatnitsky sat motionless by the window, like a wooden effigy. Zyanon entered the house, stopped, and stared at the host for a long time. Finally, in order to rouse him, the guest asked loudly:

"How are you, Pan Samatnitsky?"

Suddenly, as if driving away a dream, he jumped up and said:

"Thank you for visiting me. I did not greet such a wonderful guest because, at the time, I was far away from here."

"You must have been somewhere in the distant past? It is pleasant to visit those lands in one's thoughts every now and then."

"It's true, it is worse here. But there, where I was, the past and the present are always the same: with a calm face and a sweet smile, Adelya is enjoying the company of cheerful guests – one tells her of what he has heard, another of what he has read, about what new book has come out in print, about famous writers, about literary fame; about the Wheel of Fortune that turns this way or that, about what is happening in the wide world. And no one there mentioned me. Even Adelya, speaking with this one or that one – not a word about me."

"This is all too common: time erases inscriptions even on hard marble, while human memory is scattered by the lightest breeze, overshadowed by the smallest of clouds."

"I wished it so, thinking that in distant lands, in brand new places, among picturesque landscapes and new challenges, my thoughts and desires might change: I visited the steppes, witnessed many wonders, gazed into the mysteries of nature, but the clouds and steppe winds did not disperse, did not overshadow my memories."

"Your feelings did not change, but you probably took advantage of various discoveries in this land, which you did not know before. I would love to learn more about these discoveries."

"What did I gain by being here? Do you see what I am now? When I came to this land, I liked the mild climate, the expanse of fertile fields, the richness of blossoming orchards, the hospitality and kindness of the inhabitants. But several months later, I yearned to know more: first and foremost, I longed to visit Uman, to see the beautiful Sofia Park, glorified in Trambetsky's poetry – in my imagination that place appeared like an earthly paradise. I usually travel without much expense, and by the end of May I saw the vast steppes of Ukraine. Discovering the streets of Uman, I recalled the terrible atrocities that had taken place there during the Haidamak attacks.

Looking for the orchard, I learned the way from the locals and entered through the tall, beautifully architected gate. I saw a pond, enclosed by hills and forest brush on both sides, sparkling silently like a mirror. After admiring the statues of white marble that stood by the water, I proceeded further along the right side of the pond, delighting in ever-new landscapes. It is pleasant to look upon blooming nature in spring, and even more so when it is brought to perfection through art, effort, and expense. Then everything captivates the human eye. I saw grottos carved into wild cliffs overgrown with forests. I saw crystal waters flowing over mossy stones. I saw a huge granite boulder barely holding to the edge of a cliff, frightening passersby. In clear water springs, I saw fish glittering with gold and silver. Where hills and meadows were covered with the most beautiful flowers, and nightingale songs rang from the bushes, I saw the magical palace of Psyche and the beautiful island of the goddess Calypso. There one encounters everything a poet's imagination can conjure.

Alone, I wandered through the secluded corners of the orchard. The day was clear, everything bloomed as if in paradise, but my thoughts were gripped by sorrow. Like two black storm clouds, the future and the past hung before me and behind me, while a mournful foreboding wound itself into my dreams. All I longed to see were thorns, convinced that the whole reason nature created them was so that I might rest my gaze upon them throughout my life's journey."

Saying this, Samatnitsky fell silent, and it seemed he froze again: his figure motionless, his face as though carved from wood, betraying no sign of movement. Not seeing any signs of life, Zyanon looked at him anxiously. The silence lasted for a while, until finally, as if waking from a lethargic sleep, Samatnitsky spoke again:

"I travelled far, but there, too, I found thorns next to

flowers. But let me return to my story. While sitting and leaning my hand against a cliff, I surrendered to my sorrowful thoughts, when suddenly a Jew with a dry, gloomy, exhausted face, thin, wearing long clothes, approached me and said:

'I am a musician, playing the oboe without an instrument. I have traveled through many countries, and everywhere my playing was received with great enthusiasm. Perhaps the good sir will allow me to play something for him?'

'Play what you like,' I replied.

He twisted his lips, pressed his right hand to his straining chest, convulsive tremors ran across his face – and he played a mournful march. Listening to this sad music, observing the convulsions of his face and his chest, I could not remain indifferent. I thanked him as best I could and asked him not to play more, lest he strain his health. He took the payment, but looked at me as though offended.

'You know this orchard better than I do,' I said. 'Are there any thorn bushes here?'

'Why look for thorns?' he replied. 'Just look up – there is a huge tree growing over your head.'

I raised my eyes and saw a tall acacia with large sharp thorns. I wanted to say something to him, but the musician was already gone.

I wandered through the orchard a while longer. I entered dark grottos, gazed at streams of water, wild granite, and marble statues. Suddenly it began to grow dark, and the wind rustled in the oak groves. I saw storm clouds move in and hurried back to the city.

Zyanon, people follow many different paths to Eternity. But everything they saw and experienced on this earth – all their amusements, longings, their happy and unhappy dreams that appeared to them during their life's journey – they tell it all to the next generations.

The founder of the Sofia Park possessed vast estates, counted his treasures in millions, knew nothing of the sufferings of poverty, and thought of nothing but entertainment. He wanted this park – with its crystal waters and flowery valleys – to become the abode of Greek goddesses. And this he built among the vast steppes of Ukraine, where once the eye could find no rest.

***

There is another orchard several miles from Uman and a few *versts* from the town of Teplyk, it's called Haynerovka by the local inhabitants. After settling in the Ukrainian steppes, Pan Haynar – the founder of the orchard – saw the world differently. Traversing the gloomy desert of life, he neither dreamt of a golden age, nor of paradise on earth. He did not intend to charm anyone with wondrous landscapes, nor did he care about fame. He had different thoughts and different goals.

While I journeyed there, I heard many jokes, various opinions, and strange stories about that orchard, so I decided to see everything with my own eyes, meet the host, and understand his thinking.

In the steppe by the water, there were tall trees of a lone farmstead. I approached but did not see any kind of fence, did not meet a single person, not even a dog barked near the solitary hut. Silence reigned everywhere in the shade of the orchard trees, and only occasionally the branches rustled when touched by the wind. By the entrance, I noticed several beehives in the cherry orchard. A man was resting in the tree shade next to them, and a boy was sitting on the grass nearby. Noticing me, he immediately woke up his master. The man was elderly, dressed in white linen clothes, thin, his face lean, of a dark complexion; from under thick eyebrows, he peered at me with penetrating eyes. I approached and asked permission to look around the orchard and become familiar with the surroundings.

'My orchard,' he said, 'resembles a wild forest thicket; here no view will attract the eye.'

'Imitating nature,' I replied, 'is a worthier occupation than any refined decoration.'

'I did not think about that at all. I have other intentions.'

'Anywhere where higher thought and higher striving manifest themselves is more beneficial than any kind of imitation. Visiting this land for the first time, I want to remember that which cannot be found elsewhere.'

'Elsewhere, people have different needs. So let me be the interpreter of my thoughts because, not understanding them, people think and guess all kinds of things. The trails are very narrow and steep here, so let me go first; I will be your guide.'

I followed him in the shade of aspens. As though in a labyrinth, a narrow path meandered before us, with deep ditches and pits on both sides, their edges overgrown with thick willow bushes and tall grass. Here and there, I saw green, scum-covered water, and elsewhere in the shade of dense branches, giant leeches darted back and forth. A haze hung over the wild and gloomy expanse. The air was extremely humid, as if after an unexpected rain, although the day was hot.

'What is it – work or nature,' I asked, 'that gave these places such a gloomy and wild appearance? And what gain can come from this?'

'Take a look at the vast steppes of Ukraine and the

wide sown fields – the land is fertile and generous here, but the climate often causes crop failure. Winds and unusual heat prevail here, the sun scorches not only crops but also grasses in low-lying valleys, so much so that no pasture remains, and livestock goes without feed and water in the summer. I toiled for many years, digging these pits and ditches, planting trees and bushes to retain moisture. I have already done so much – the water from my orchard, flowing further, provides for the needs of the surrounding area and the town of Teplyk. A person who keeps taking steps toward his goal can change not only the land, but the atmosphere also. This humid haze that you are seeing in my gloomy orchard gathers rain clouds from the east and west, and waters the thirsty steppes. Look, even now, dark rain clouds have gathered above our heads and they aren't moving – you can see the clear sun in the distance, but here, we are in the shade.'

Thus, telling me about his thoughts and intentions, he led me further and further along the narrow paths of the wild labyrinth. At a point where a wide ditch separated these places from the steppe, I noticed some kind of cellar that led underground, its entrance was covered with thick brush.

'Why do you need this dark underground?' I asked.

'Here,' Haynar replied, 'is a cellar and an underground passage from one place to another. They serve not only for cooling the air and collecting moisture but also for other purposes. But let that never come to pass. Surely, you read about the terrible atrocities of Gonta and Zaliznyak, you know about the raids of his haidamaks, who spilled blood throughout all of Ukraine. In case of such raids, the labyrinth and its secret cellars in my orchard can serve as a refuge for the unfortunate locals. But that is only in case of emergency. Let's keep walking, I will show you more of what I have done.'

We stepped out onto a more open area in another part of the orchard, stopping near a square pond, about ten fathoms in width and length, its transparent water dark yellow, like smoky topaz. Here I saw bushes of plants with very dark greenery.

'Mineral waters are formed here,' continued the host. 'Although they are dark yellow in color, they are as clear as the purest crystal, and they do not contain the dreadful living things that can be seen through a magnifying glass in every drop of ordinary water. The inhabitants of Ukraine often visit Odessa: some to sell wheat, others – for sea baths. Selling products, they benefit, but seeking health on the shores of the Black Sea, they only increase unnecessary expenditures, as the journey is long and the salty water has little value for the sick. This spring will cure any ailment. I know this area well.'

'And I,' I said, 'intend to visit Odessa this year, but only out of curiosity.'

'Are you going to Odessa? I am very glad to hear, because I want to send something there. Please, will you take a small package with you?'

'With great pleasure, if it does not take up much space.'

'Small things take up little space.'

Saying this, Haynar called the boy, ordered him to bring four small bottles and a paper box. Then he led me deeper into the ravine. We walked among bushes and tall grass. In the shade of the thicket, two clear springs flowed from under the hill like two ribbons of pure silver, and after a few steps, hid under the ground again. First, he filled two bottles from one spring, added some powders, and the water suddenly turned sapphire blue. Then he filled the remaining two bottles from the other spring, and when he added another powder, the water acquired a beautiful carmine color. Then he carefully corked all four bottles and handed them to me, saying:

'When you are in Odessa, you will meet Pan Ryliec there. He is a very learned man, he has devoted his life to studying the mysteries of nature. I am sending him two bottles of this colored liquid, and the other two you keep for yourself. They are very beneficial and contain a great mystery, about which you can learn more, but from Pan Ryliec, not from me.'

We walked for a long time along the banks of another pond that was full of small islands planted with trees. Pan Haynar told me about various types of grasses that grew in his garden and about their magical properties. And when the sun sank beyond the horizon, I said my farewell to the orchard, thanked its host for his kind reception, and promised to deliver the entrusted liquids to Pan Ryliec.

Leaving the Ukrainian steppes, I visited Padolle, the region that has everything necessary for life. Here and there – wonderful nature, beautiful landscapes: oak groves and dense hornbeam forests turn the mountains green, groves look like orchards with fruit trees. Across wide and fertile fields, wheat ears sway like waves on the sea. The valleys bloom, overgrown with lush grasses. Ponds of clear water, with nearby villages and lush estates, shine like light. Cliffs rise like walls and pyramids along riverbanks, as though ruins of giant castles of old.

Zyanon, you must visit that land, you must see the high and rocky banks of the Buh and the Dniester, where nature has constructed humongous edifices from enormous stone boulders, under which caves and cellars darken – eternal abodes of darkness, eternal shelters of spirits of the night. You must see those rocky, wild, and mysterious ruins, whose peaks and slopes are covered with the gloomy shadows of dense shrubs. There, wonderful landscapes open to the eyes wherever you look. Thoughts come easily on the banks of these rivers, visitors carry on conversations about historical events, about people's fantasies, about all kinds of scientific discoveries from the time of the Great Flood to our days.

When I first visited there, I was unknown to anyone and had no acquaintances. Alone, I wandered along the banks of the Bug and the Dniester, and, lonesome, frequently exhausted by travel and the day's heat, before sunset, I would lean on a rock and gaze at the enchanting and mysterious landscapes. A longing would fill my chest, my eye wandered aimlessly, and my thoughts soared far, far away, to meet the eyes of Adelya that reflected her pure soul, which had more charm and beauty than all the wonders of nature."

After saying this, Samatnitsky again sat motionless for a while, as if no spark of life remained in him. Zyanon watched him for several minutes, and then, wishing to rouse him from this lethargic state, asked:

"Could you not find peace in that early paradise?"

He stirred and replied:

"And in suffering, I will not find it either."

"I would like to see that beautiful land."

"One who carries peace in his soul will find that even the darkest wilderness greets him with a gentle smile."

"Did you stay long in Padolle?"

"At the beginning of September, I moved onward, crossing wild and empty steppes. Having endured many setbacks and much sorrow, I reached the Black Sea. I reached Odessa.

* * *

Odessa is a city built in the new style: wide streets, sidewalks convenient for pedestrians, houses and churches of graceful architecture. When I visited the ports, markets, and the various traders in all quarters of the city, I sought Pan Ryliec, yet no one could tell me where he lived. Even a Jewish factor, whom I compensated generously, made inquiries but could not help. I began to despair, fearing I would never find him, nor learn the secret of the colored waters which I had so carefully preserved during the long and difficult journey.

Near my lodging on Greek Street there was a tavern, where daily and at every hour townsfolk gathered to discuss their commercial affairs. I too frequented it, and, as though in a theater, delighted in observing the representatives of different peoples. At each table, in each group, a different tongue was spoken; conversations rang out in German, Greek, and Italian.

Reading newspapers over my tea, I listened to merchants, commissioners, and foreigners recount countless stories. Then a man entered. He had a pensive face, was of medium height, stocky, heavy-browed; though he looked over fifty, he appeared strong and vigorous. The stranger ordered tea. He spread out papers covered with strange sketches, leaned his head upon his hand, and, gazing intently at them, fell into thought. Some patrons approached, peered curiously at the drawings and at the man, and withdrew – some with astonishment, others with a smile. After pondering for a while, he rubbed his forehead and said:

'More experience, more suffering. In the past, there were marvels of one kind, and in the future, there will be others.'

Saying this, he folded the papers and began to pour his tea.

Sitting nearby, and having heard Polish words from his lips, I wished to learn who he was, and addressed him:

'Are you a visitor or a resident?'

'I am a resident-traveler, like all men, and for ten years I have been conversing with this land.'

'I cannot,' I said, 'find the residence of Pan Ryliec. No one here knows him.'

'It is more peaceful for a man when no one knows him. Why do you seek him?' he asked, fixing me with a searching gaze, as though to probe my purpose.

'I was in Ukraine, in Haynar's orchard, and have brought some colored waters from him for Pan Ryliec.'

'I am Ryliec,' he said at last, his face brightening. 'You were in Ukraine? You met Haynar? You saw his orchard? Tell me everything you can! And those colored waters – they are of great importance to me. Come, let us go to my house. I long to hear the whole tale in detail.'

Having spoken thus, he hastily finished his tea, and we departed the tavern. At my apartment, he took the two bottles of colored water, and we got into a carriage. Just before the Kherson Gate, we turned toward the seashore.

Pan Ryliec's house stood alone, about half a mile from the city, sheltered by a grove of acacias from the north and east winds. We entered a room furnished with several old chairs, two ancient oak cabinets, and two heavy oak tables. Upon one lay heaps of sand of various colors, pieces of limestone with fossilized shells, fish, and reptiles, bones and skeletons of animals and birds, drawings of monstrous forms, bizarre and unseen creatures. The other table was piled with books, in bindings both ancient and new.

Pan Ryliec began to speak:

'This is my solitary dwelling. In the window – an image of the stormy sea. I sometimes delight in listening to the roar of the waves, watching the black, foaming swells and the flocks of white terns rising into the air. I love to read the poetry of our Ukrainian prophets. I have a book by Bohdan Zaleski – no one approaches the ease and beauty of his verse. I have Malczewski's touching tale *Maria*. Here are poetic works by Goszczyński, and the folk songs of Padura. Here also are the poems of Konstantyn Pietrowski – his story *Julia Potocka*, where the Cossack wars are depicted in frightful but truthful images. His verses are full of feeling, and his translations of Shakespeare's sonnets into Polish preserve the charm of the original, overcoming the difficulties of that form with great talent.

But I read poetry only to dispel melancholy thoughts. My usual labor is the study of the nature of the past. Lumps of earth in various colors, bones, skeletons, skulls, and all manner of fossils serve me in this. The colored liquids you have brought are of great value. The sapphire one is the water of cold: it gathers and compresses all things. The red liquid is the water of fire: it restores life to what is inert. Tomorrow I will begin the experiments. If you wish to witness wonders, come, and you will learn the secret of the waters and their marvelous power.'

Then Pan Ryliec and I spoke long about Ukraine, about Haynar and his orchard, and about my travels in Padolle. He recalled old acquaintances of his in those lands, recounted events of his own life, how he came to Odessa, and what fate befell him here. We talked until late into the evening.

The next day, at the appointed hour, I came to Pan Ryliec. He was busy with colored sands and fossils, grinding, sorting, removing particles, and laying them out upon the table. He asked me to assist him. I sifted the sands, washed small bits of lime, and poured them into glass jars. Our work lasted until sunset. When evening came, we sat by the window to rest. The autumn wind rustled through the thick acacias, the sea was restless, and Pan Ryliec, gazing at the black waves breaking on the shore, began to speak:

'When they began to rage, these salty waves overflowed the high shores and covered the vastness of the earth, leaving the creatures of the water as nothing more than eternal memory, etched into the depths of the soil, into limestone rocks, and into lofty mountains. Encountering these marvels, scholars discern traces of former life and delve into the mysterious past. Each strives to interpret these hieroglyphs according to his knowledge. They measure time by millennia; they plunge into remote antiquity, seeking to grasp with their minds the conditions of existence in this world. Yet their efforts are in vain: the depths of the earth, the mountains, and the rocks are corpses of bygone centuries – cold and silent, they will not tell of the beginning, the course of ages, the changes of life, nor of its end. To behold the vanished world, it must be resurrected, revived, so that its secrets may be studied and the beginning and the end of all things discovered.

In every age, nature is an unread book. Happy is the one who has glimpsed a fragment of the present and revived a fragment of the past. There are not enough words in human speech to describe every wonder.'

For half an hour we conversed about creatures of the land, the sea, and the air – how they had changed, why some species disappeared, leaving their remains only in the depths of the earth, in amber, and in limestone rock.

Then Pan Ryliec rose from his chair, lit two candles, and drew from a cabinet glass vessels of various shapes and sizes. He placed powders upon the table – some with metallic sheen, some crystalline, others gray, black, and red – and said:

'Now we shall study the mystery and power of the

colored liquids you have brought me from Pan Haynar. You shall witness their strength; you shall see the miracle of reviving creatures that have lain untouched in rocky graves for thousands of years. You shall also behold beings invisible to the human eye, whose motion and form even the microscope scarcely detects.'

Saying this, he left the room and quickly returned with a boy of about fifteen years: pale-faced, flat-nosed, with thick lips and coarse, bristly hair.

'This is my servant, deaf and mute,' said Pan Ryliec. 'In truth, he is precisely what I require: he does not hear my speech, and will reveal nothing to those who have no right to know. I count myself fortunate to have found such a helper.'

He ordered the boy to fill the prepared vessels with water, and then began the experiments. First, he set upon the table a bowl of salt sea-water and two lighted candles. I drew closer, eager to see what would be done. The scholar poured a handful of crushed limestone – composed of fossilized shells and other marine creatures – into the bowl. For a time, he silently watched the water mingling with the lime, then added several drops of the sapphire liquid. The bowl suddenly began to stir and seethe. After a few minutes, he added a drop of the red liquid and said:

'Look now.'

I saw living oysters and snails – they opened and closed their shells. Strange water-spiders, fish, small crayfish, and beetles of many colors moved swiftly back and forth.

'Much has changed in the sea,' he explained. 'Fish, oysters, snails, and other creatures are not as they once were.'

Then he signaled to the boy to replace the bowl with a copper basin, in which a little water stood. He poured gray and green liquids into it, added fat and a thick, tar-like oil.

Then he sprinkled in two handfuls of earth and two of crushed limestone, mixed all together, and into this blend added a few drops of the sapphire water.

The copper basin boiled; bubbles rose and burst in the air. An acrid gas, almost unbearable, spread through the room. He added a few more drops of the red water – and flame burst out. With a hiss and roar it burned, then died down. And when the flame was gone, I saw the basin full of monstrous creatures. Their eyes glowed with a bloody light.

Gazing at these horrifying beings, Pan Ryliec said:

'These are the monsters of the past; life has awakened in them, along with deadly poison. Woe to anyone who touches them: some will leave incurable wounds, others will kill outright. Good and evil have existed since the beginning of the world, yet both the physical and the moral realms have changed. It is necessary to revive these monsters of the past in order to better understand both the new world and the old.'

Saying this, he placed a sheet of white paper on the table, scattered a multicolored powder as fine as dust, and sprayed it with sapphire and red water. At once, a rainbow appeared on the paper, as though in a cloud. Suddenly, brilliant butterflies rose up. They swarmed through the room, then settled on the walls and windows, shining like the most beautiful flowers.

'This is the adornment of a world still young,' said Pan Ryliec. 'Butterflies delight and captivate the eye. Pearls, rubies, and diamonds sparkle on their wings. Yet once they bore no such colors. The physical world has changed – and in the moral world, so too have desires and dreams.'

With the help of those colored waters, Pan Ryliec revived more and more creatures until nearly midnight. Among them I saw centipedes, millipedes, beings with a hundred heads, horrifying, bizarre. It is impossible to describe their dreadful movements and fantastical forms.

'I have resurrected the nature of prehistoric times,' the scholar continued. 'You saw marine creatures, venomous monsters, and butterflies of radiant beauty. Look now at what they have become: instead of shells, monsters, and terrible creatures – only dirt and limestone. And where are the golden butterflies that sparkled with precious stones? Only dust remains. Nothing can endure in life once its time has passed. Time alone is undefeated; it reigns over this world.

Only the Solimandra[54] is immortal, it is pure fire, its flame burns forever. Yet the one who studies nature must revive it, if only for a moment. In my solitary life, this science is my greatest consolation. Thus I hide from the crowds, for among the locals the talk is only of commerce and treasure, while the maidens here are like flutes and clarinets – pleasant when they play or sing, but with nothing worth speaking of. Still, I have friends with whom I share my thoughts. Next Sunday I will invite them. Come as well, we shall have a pleasant evening in good company.'

We spoke until midnight. Returning home late, I could not sleep for a long time – creatures, living monsters, and butterflies still danced before my eyes.

The next day I rose early, placed two bottles of Haynar's waters on my table, and contemplated their vivid, beautiful colors, reflecting on the power I had seen them unleash. I daydreamed about the mysteries and wonders such a treasure might reveal. Sweet visions carried me along the streets of the city and down to the seashore. But alas! I did not foresee that human wisdom, which reveals the secrets of the world, may also bring ruin and suffering."

Samatnitsky paused for a few minutes as though

turned to stone. Then suddenly he stirred and began again:

"I saw Adelya. She does not change – oh, happy women! They do not follow the movement of the planets across the sky, nor seek out the mysteries of nature. They are swayed by beautiful adornments, merry entertainments, new friendships...

Sunday came, and, with it, the appointed hour. I hurried to Pan Ryliec's house on foot. It was seven o'clock. Here and there, dim lamps lit the dark streets. The sky was clear, though a cold wind blew from the sea. Approaching his hut, I heard thunder and saw candlelight flickering in the window.

Inside, the mute servant admitted me, and a strange sight met my eyes: five tall, elderly guests, with Pan Ryliec the sixth, stood around a table holding goblets of a drink that burned with fire. As they raised their cups they cried out: '*Hail the Solimandra!*' They drank, and it seemed to me they swallowed flame itself. Seeing me, the host exclaimed:

'You are late, and did not drink the flame in honor of the Solimandra, whose handful of ashes is a chainlink, whose resurrection and life are an endless chain.'

He poured me a goblet, set it alight, and I too, exclaiming '*Hail the Solimandra!*' drank, eager to please my host, and unwilling to stand apart from the rest.

Pan Ryliec then brought out Haynar's colored waters, ordering the boy to fill a copper basin and another vessel with water. In the presence of his guests he began again to resurrect shells, creatures, butterflies, and other beings from dirt and limestone. When the assembly marveled at the living remnants of a prehistoric age, he changed the water and called for leaves and grasses.

'Now let us look at the present,' he said. 'This red liquid will reveal to us creatures invisible even to the finest microscope.'

He dropped a single measure into seawater, and before our eyes strange, menacing creatures appeared, visibly growing in size. He drew some out and placed them on the table – fish, lizards, crocodilian forms. He did the same with spring water – other monsters emerged. Laying tree leaves and grasses on the table, he sprinkled them as well, and suddenly an otherwise unseen world appeared – winged dragons, sphinxes, centaurs, and hydras whirled around us. Unease seized the hearts of all who watched.

The experiments continued until midnight, followed by a discussion on the progress of science and the works of German and contemporary Polish philosophers. They debated at length about Trantowski, Bykhavets, Bochvits, and others. Yet it was Pan Ryliec's words that remained with me:

'I read the ancient Greek philosophers with the greatest delight. They sought truth sincerely, and at times succeeded in glimpsing a distant ray of the eternal light. But now, when the sun of the Gospel shines over the whole world, men wander in darkness, not knowing what they seek. They deemed the human soul a part of God – yet it is a creation of God, like all souls.'

These conversations lasted far into the night. When the clock struck two, the literary amusements ended and we all departed together. I returned home alone through dark and silent streets, my mind full of everything I had seen and heard.

During my stay in Odessa I visited Pan Ryliec's house several more times, drawn by his company and his learned discourse. When, before leaving the city, I came to bid him farewell and thank him for his kindness, he gave me two bottles of an alcohol tincture, two of oils, and several powders, warning:

'You now possess Haynar's waters and all you need for

the study of nature. Resurrect the past, recall creatures from their graves. Study the secrets of ages long gone and of the present world, and everywhere you will behold wonders others have never dreamed of. You will see the hand of the Creator. But do not cross the boundary – do not attempt to penetrate the spirit. For that, a higher power is required: revelation. Do not forget – you are but a man. Do not separate yourself from your body against the will of Him who joined you to it, and do not gaze with the eye of your soul into the soul of another, which is created as yours.'

Zyanon! I did not heed his warning – I ignored it. I did the opposite. The treasure I possess, the power of the colored waters, I used for something else. I forgot about the past and the future. I wanted paradise here, now, in this life. I longed to behold the Great Spirit in the form of an angel on this earth. I gazed onto Adelya, and to my soul she became that god, that ideal I had sought in this world. Wandering the steppes and the wild cliffs along the Teteriv, I thought only of her, I dreamed only of her. My soul cannot be at peace without her. I separated from my body, forgetting it and earthly life, and in doing so, I destroyed myself.

Zyanon, if any of my old, faraway acquaintances should ask about me, tell them that I live – but that my life is torment. And soon enough, I shall depart from here, leaving this foreign body behind, somewhere in a foreign land."

Samatnitsky fell silent. Zyanon looked at him with sorrow in his heart. He could not offer hope, for his hope had perished forever. He only promised to do as asked, and then set out once more on his journey.

ENDNOTES

1. *Kniazha*, literally "prince" (sometimes "king"), a hereditary ruler in medieval Eastern Europe. In the Belarusian context, the term referred to local princes who governed principalities and held both political and military power.

2. *Rusalka,* usually translated as "mermaid," but in Slavic folklore it is not a benign sea-maiden. A *rusalka* is a spirit of a young woman, often one who died untimely or violently, associated with rivers, lakes, or forests. In Belarusian tradition, *rusalki* are both alluring and dangerous: they can sing, dance, or entice men, but also bring illness or death.

3. *Corvée*, a system of compulsory, unpaid labor that peasants owed to their landlord, usually several days a week. In Belarusian lands of the 18th–19th centuries it was one of the main forms of serfdom, binding peasants to the estate and restricting their freedom of movement.

4. Northern capital refers to St. Petersburg, located at the eastern end of the Gulf of Finland.

5. Randar, likely a reference to the "arendar" figure – a Jewish leaseholder of land or taverns.

6. *Liasun*, a forest spirit in Belarusian folklore, guardian of the woods who could lead wanderers astray or punish those who disrespected the forest. He is often depicted as a tall man covered in hair, blending with trees and shadows, embodying both the protective and

dangerous aspects of the wilderness.

7. *Verst*, a traditional Russian measure of distance, widely used in Belarus and the Russian Empire until the early 20th century. One verst equals 500 *sazhen*, or approximately 1.067 kilometers (0.662 miles).

8. Dew herbs that grow on tussocks and are said to protect against witchcraft.

9. *Dzesiacina*, a traditional land measure used in the Polish-Lithuanian Commonwealth and the Russian Empire. Its size varied over time and region, but it was roughly equal to about one hectare (2.7 acres).

10. Among Belarusians, especially in the northern districts, there lives a belief that at midnight the forests always stir with rustling, and the waters of the lakes grow restless at the very moment the rooster crows.

11. *Volat*, a giant or mighty warrior in Belarusian folklore, often depicted as a guardian of the land, embodying extraordinary strength and stature.

12. Krasnapol, a township located 26 *versts* from Polatsk, place of a famous battle against the French, in which General Kulniev was killed.

13. *Asilak*, literally "a strongman" or "mighty one." In Belarusian folklore the term often describes a hero of great physical strength, sometimes with semi-mythical qualities.

14. *Vadzianik*, a malevolent water spirit in Belarusian folklore, believed to dwell in lakes and rivers and pose danger to humans.

15. *Chliaunik*, a barn spirit in Belarusian folklore, believed to torment livestock at night.

16. *Damavik*, household spirit in Belarusian folklore, believed to dwell in the home and sometimes torment cattle.

17. *Liasun*, see note 6.

18. Spas, short for the Spasa-Eufrasinneuski Monastery in Polatsk, one of the most important religious and cultural centers of medieval Belarus.

19. *Piarun*, the Slavic god of storms, thunder, and lightning, regarded as the supreme deity in the Slavic pantheon.

20. A nursery rhyme still exists about Baba Yaga:
Baba-Yaha,
Kościanaja naha,
Na stupie jedzieć,
Toukaczom pohaniajeć,
Miatłoj ślady zamiatajeć. (Polish)

Баба Яга,
Косьцяная нага,
На ступе едзець,
Тоўкачом поганяець,
Мятлой сьляды замятаець. (Belarusian)

Baba Yaga,
With a bony leg,
Rides in a mortar,

Drives it with a pestle,
Sweeps away her tracks with a broom. (English)

21. Barys and Hleb, sons of Prince Vladimir of Kyiv, the first Christian ruler of Rus'. Martyred in 1015 and canonized as saints, they are venerated across the Slavic lands, including Belarus. Their cult was especially strong in Polatsk and other Belarusian regions, where churches and monasteries were dedicated to them.

22. *Fugit irreparabile tempus,* latin, meaning "irretrievable time flees."

23. St. Ignatius of Loyola, or Ignatius Loyola (1491–1556), clergyman, theologian, priest, and founder of the Jesuit Order.

24. The Polatsk Academy, or the University of Polatsk, which existed from 1812 to 1820, established through the transformation of the Jesuit College.

25. "Competitions" is meant more broadly, referring to emulative scholarly rivalry, a classic Jesuit practice.

26. Latin:
"Disciple of the Lord, from what shall we begin?"
"From the sign of the Holy Cross."
"What is the sign of the Holy Cross?"
"It is the protection of body and soul."
"Let us make the sign of the Holy Cross."
"Let us make it."

27. A note added by Jan Barszczewski himself.

28. *Kuma*, literally "godmother" in Belarusian (paired with *kum*, "godfather"). In traditional East Slavic custom, *kuma* referred first of all to the woman who took on the role of spiritual kinship at a child's baptism. Over time, the term broadened into a common form of address in villages, used respectfully or familiarly for a married woman, even outside the godparent relationship. Thus in literature it can mean both a literal godmother and, more generally, a close, family-like female figure.

29. In folk belief, feeding a cursed or demonic child may invoke famine or ill fortune.

30. Plaksun, literally means "he who cries" or "weeper"

31. *Pahonia*, the historic coat of arms of the Grand Duchy of Lithuania (and present-day national coat of arms of Belarus), depicting a mounted knight with a raised sword. In the context of this *Nobleman Zavalnia*, it is a political allusion to coins from the time of the Polish–Lithuanian Commonwealth. The Commonwealth itself was partitioned and partially annexed by the Russian Empire in 1795 — roughly two decades before the events described in *Zavalnia*.

32. *Phaeton*, a light, four-wheeled, open carriage, popular in the 18th and 19th centuries. It was usually drawn by one or two horses and associated with the gentry or wealthy townsfolk. The name comes from Phaethon, the son of the sun god Helios in Greek mythology, who attempted to drive his father's chariot of the sun.

33. *Kuttsia* (also spelled *Kućcja* or *Kutia*), a traditional ritual dish made of boiled wheat or other grains, sweetened with honey, sometimes mixed with poppy

seeds, nuts, or dried fruit. It is especially associated with Christmas Eve and other important holidays in Belarusian, Ukrainian, and broader Eastern Slavic tradition. The dish symbolizes remembrance of ancestors and is often the central element of the sacred holiday meal.

34. Ahinsky (also Ogińscy), princely magnate family of Ruthenian origin in the Polish–Lithuanian Commonwealth, bearing the Oginiec coat of arms; they traced their lineage to the princes of Kozelsk and held vast estates in the Grand Duchy of Lithuania.

35. *Laudetur Jesus Christus,* latin, meaning "Praised be Jesus Christ."

36. *Omne tulit punctum qui miscuit utile dulci,* latin, meaning "The one who blends the useful with the sweet wins universal approval."

37. There is a belief that vipers that have lost their venom have yellow tails, which sets them apart from other vipers, as the latter no longer recognize it as one of their own.

38. *Nikitron,* one of eight evil spirits, whose names are *Jaron, Iron, Kitron, Nokitron, Faron, Farazon, Lidon, Stalidon.* They bring sickness, so Belarusians write their names with crosses on bread, and offer this bread to sick people in order to banish the evil spirit from the body. It is speculated that these beliefs came from gypsies, whom Belarusians traditionally considered to have ties to sorcery.

39. *Vinum cor laetificat!* latin meaning "Wine gladdens the heart of man."

40. *Trasca*, or seizures, or febral fever. Belarusians traditionally consider these ailments as possessions by evil spirits or beings that call one by name (usually, in spring). Whoever responds to the call will fall ill. Sometimes they are seen in the guise of a woman and have nine sisters.

41. Refers to the Great Northern War (1700–1721) between Russia and Sweden.

42. Year of the Goosefoot, a year marked by an abundant growth of goosefoot (*Chenopodium album*), a common cereal weed. Goosefoot was consumed during times of famine and hardship.

43. Poem by Jan Barszczewski

44. Twardowski, a legendary Polish and Belarusian-Lithuanian sorcerer, often compared to Faust, who according to folklore made a pact with the devil in exchange for magical powers. His tales were especially popular in the 16th–19th centuries, and he is sometimes tied to noble courts or to Kraków.

45. *Kupalle*, the traditional midsummer solstice festival celebrated across Belarus, Lithuania, Poland, and Ukraine. Rooted in pre-Christian rites, it combines fire and water rituals symbolizing purification, fertility, and renewal. Bonfires are lit, wreaths of herbs and flowers are floated on rivers to divine fate, and couples leap over flames to test their bond. With the Christianization of the region, Kupalle was merged with the Feast of St. John (Ivan Kupala), but it preserved its deeply pagan character as a celebration of nature's magic and life's abundance.

46. *Zalomy u žycie*, literally "breaks in the rye." A folk

belief tied to mysterious flattened patches in grain fields, thought to be the work of supernatural forces, witches, or spirits. While visually resembling what today might be called "crop circles," in Belarusian tradition they were considered omens or signs, often associated with misfortune or enchantment.

47. In some areas of Belarus there is a belief among the common folk that those who plant acorns or oak saplings will shorten their own lifespan, as their strength and vitality passes to the trees they planted.

48. *Palionka*, also known as *palionaya harelka*, is a traditional Belarusian alcoholic beverage made by infusing *harelka* or strong spirit with honey, sugar, and spices, then igniting the mixture to caramelize the ingredients and enhance the flavor. The controlled flaming process not only adds warmth and aroma but also slightly reduces the alcohol content, resulting in a smoother drink. *Palionka* is typically served warm in small glasses, often enjoyed during festive occasions or in cold weather.

49. According to Romani legends, jabber-weed grows in the water, protects one from fire, and helps see the future.

50. One of the eight spirits that can interact with humans.

51. Ending of the story is missing.

52. Ostash is a personal name turned into a folkloric shorthand for a magical or demonic figure.

53. Dubina (a "baton"), Prud (a "pond"), Harynia

(derived from "mountain") are *volats*, or giants, from pagan times. They remain in folk memory and are mentioned in fairy tales, along with Baba Yaga, Kupala, Czur and other deities.

54. *Solimandra* refers to a species of amphibian, the fire salamander (*Salamandra salamandra*). It was once believed that the salamander is born in and lives within fire.